CHILDREN IN THE CITY OF CZARS: A NOVEL

CHILDREN IN THE CITY OF CZARS: A NOVEL

BY IRMGARDE BROWN

Also by Irmgarde Brown
Sister Jane
Sister Jane's Lenten Journal

Co-authored with Benedict & Kathleen Schwartz
Evidence Now Seen:
How God Used One Couple to Touch the Lives of
Orphaned and Vulnerable Children in Zambia

Published in the United States by
Serey/Jones Publishers, Inc.
www.sereyjones.com

ISBN: 9781881276296 (paperback)

DEDICATION

For my daughter, Liliana Victoria Brown,

born in St. Petersburg, Russia, 1990, and adopted in 2006.

FOREWORD

St. Petersburg in the 1990s was a time of great upheaval and ambiguity. The USSR was in tatters and early in those years, Boris Yeltsin came into power. Suddenly, there were journalistic freedoms that had never been available before; and even more surprising, the rise of a market economy seemingly overnight. From the West, this all seemed like good news.

But the reality, for everyday people, was chaos. For years, their entire lives had been controlled by the State. They had been protected by mandated jobs and medical care. Their difficult lives were placated by easy access to the arts and sports which flourished under state support. No more. Even though food and clothing had been scarce in the Soviet Union, at least everyone was in it together. On the day that black shoes were available, everyone got black shoes. On the day the potatoes were on the shelves, everyone got potatoes. Now, daily life was eclipsed by those who managed to successfully take advantage of the new "system" over those who could not. Grocery stores had extravagant displays of foodstuffs, but few could afford to buy anything. The rich were no longer hiding behind the closed doors of the "Party," but gobbling up everything they could afford to acquire.

The rich became very rich, while the poor became not just poorer, but starving or addicted to drugs and alcohol. It has been estimated that in that first decade from 1991—2001, five million people died as a direct result of the new "economy." And along with these intense times came organized crime, petty crimes, and trafficking of everything from drugs to goods to people. The black market thrived. In the year 2000, the Russian ruble was only worth $.36. These circumstances and an ongoing debate between the two groups of reformers, particularly in St. Petersburg, ended with Yeltsin's victory along with his then deputy, Vladimir Putin, who would be elected president in March 2000.

As is often the case in times of political turmoil, it was the children who suffered the most. As parents died, orphaned children hit the streets, mostly into gangs or prostitution. Childcare, once a promised benefit from the State, became limited to overcrowded orphanages. Oftentimes, it wasn't just orphans who were dropped into these institutions, but any children whose parents were deemed socially incompetent to raise children (be it due to domestic violence, alcoholism, pornography, or poverty). The children, particularly in the '90s, were still promised support from the State such as a stipend for sundries and a monetary nest egg after "graduation" from the orphanage schools. Unfortunately, corruption in government was no different in orphanages, and large portions of the monies were embezzled; the children received next to nothing. In addition, a kind of Catch-22 arose from the fact that orphanages received government funds based on the number of children they housed. It behooved the directors to keep as many children as possible on the rolls, whether the institution could take care of them or not. Twelve years later, in response to the Magnitsky Act passed in the United States, which would allow the government to place sanctions on foreign monies in the United States, Putin banned all adoptions of Russian children by Americans. Putin's mandate is still in place to this day.

With the turn of the millennium, Putin cemented his power by responding to the "Chechen" problem and declaring war. As with many countries, war can energize an economy and drive nationalism, something much needed at the time.

It is in this context that "Children in the City of Czars" is set.

AUTHOR'S NOTE

The Russian language is a complex one that I do not speak. Instead, I have depended on my adopted daughter who grew up in St. Petersburg and is still fluent in Russian. I have included some Russian words to flavor the story. In most cases, the words are intelligible from the context if not actually translated within the text.

One very Russian convention I have kept, as best I could, was the use of formal names which is a standard way in which Russians speak to one another. Until a person is given permission to use a diminutive (nickname) or they are part of a family, people use both the first full name as well as the patronymic in conversation.

When we adopted our daughter, she asked that we give her an American name, and together we agreed upon Liliana Victoria. We did not realize at the time that she thought people would call her by those dual names. She was quite taken aback to discover that not only did Americans rarely include a middle name, but they also tended to shorten the first name as soon as possible. Therefore, Liliana became Lily right away and even Lil, which she squashed as best she could.

A patronymic is formed by grammatically adapting the father's first name for both males and females. For instance, if the father's name is Ivan (pronounced ee-von), then boys have the patronymic of Ivanovich and girls have Ivanovna. Therefore, our young Lebedev heroes are Fyodor Ivanovich, Elena Ivanovna, and Irina Vladimorovna (who had a different father, Vladimir).

Most diminutives in Russia keep some form of the formal name, but not always. Fyodor becomes Fedya, Elena becomes Lenushka, and Irina becomes Irishka. In truth, first names can have a myriad of diminutives attributed to them, but generally, I have limited each person to one. To help the reader make the transition to this Russian style, I have included here a list of characters.

LIST OF CHARACTERS

The Orphans Lebedev and their Extended Family		
Fyodor Ivanovich Lebedev	Fedya, Fedkins	12-year-old orphan, brother to Elena & Irina
Elena Ivanovna Margarita Lebedev	Lena, Lenushka	9-year-old orphan, sister to Fedya & Irina, at Children's House #24
Irina Vladimirovna Lebedev	Irishka	4-year-old orphan, sister to Elena & Fedya
Elizaveta Adreevna Ozola Lebedev		Mother to Fyodor, Elena & Irina; late husband Ivan; partner Vladimir
Uldis Ozols	Uldi	Maternal uncle to the Lebedev children, in Latvia, late wife Lauma
Vasiliy Chasikov-ich Nesterov	Vasya	Like an uncle to Lebedev children, friend of the family; an opera singer

The Orphanage Girls, Caregivers, and Social Workers		
Aniya		Friend to Elena, quiet one
Baiba		Latvian, 13 years old
Celestina Yama-dayevna		Roschino Winter Camp caregiver
Galina		Friend to Larissa and Tatiana
Klara		Caregiver at Irina's Children's House #8
Konstantin An-dreivich		Adult son to Celestina Yamadayevna, DJ at Roschino Winter Camp
Larissa		Mean girl, gypsy heritage
Lezunchik		Invisible cat friend to Irina at Children's House #8
Lubya		Caretaker in Elena's Children's House #24
Ludmilla Demo-chevna Putina		Director, Irina's Children's House #8
Lukina		Older girl, 13 years old, used as a messenger
Oksana		Prima Donna, orphanage girl
Olga Petrovna Abramovich		Lead social worker, fifties
Pyotr Konstantin Kotolvsky	Petya	Actor, boyfriend to Valentina, lover to Nataliya
Raisa		Orphanage girl, loud and rude

Svetlanas (2)		One called fat, the other not very bright
Tatiana		Mean girl, self-styled beauty
Valentina Alexandrovna Kovaleskaya	Valya	Social worker, late twenties, friend to Elena
Yevgeniya Kalmakovna		Director at Elena's Children's House #24
Yuliya		Fearful one, friend to Elena
Street Gang, Mafia, and their Women		
Aleksander Iakolev	Sasha	Director of pornographic movies
Alexis Alexandrovich Stepanov	Alyosha	Oligarch, Russian mafia, friend to Uncle Vasiliy
Borya	Bo-Bo	Dimitri's gang member
Nataliya (Natasha Vladimirovna)		Stage name, pornographic movie star, friend to Zoya
Yegor	Gogo	Stepanov's henchman; friend to Zoya
Zoya		A prostitute, entangled with both Dimitri and Yegor; friend to Nataliya

PART ONE: OCTOBER – NOVEMBER 2000

1
FEDYA

ST. PETERSBURG, RUSSIA

Too late. The *politsiya* were already in the building. He hid across the street behind the old green van with its jacked-up body and missing wheels. Moments later, he saw an old Lada brand car pull up beside the patrol car. Two women got out. They were the agency women, dressed in black coats with satchels over their shoulders, warm boots, and fur hats. He pulled back as one woman scanned the street. How long would it take for them to get inside the locked apartment? Would his sister let them in, or would she wait silently like he told her to do if strangers came to the door?

"If I'm not here, don't let anybody in. You understand?" he had said that morning.

"I know, Fedya, but why do you have to leave again? It's still early."

"I have business."

"What business? You're not old enough. You're not even thirteen yet."

"Older than you."

Little Irina yanked on his jacket three times. "Pick me up. Pick me up."

He swooped her up and sat her down on one of their two straight back chairs. He bent down, held her hands, and said, "Irishka, you must do as

2

Elena says. When I am gone, Elena is the boss." He turned to Elena. "It's getting cold. Don't we have anything warmer? Feel her hands."

"I told you. We need to leave this flat," Elena said. "We need a place with fewer broken windows."

A siren wailed as a car drove down the street. Fedya leaped up to look out the window. "Remember, don't open the door. Make them work for it."

"Who?"

He ignored her.

"Who, Fedya?"

"Moo," Irishka giggled. "Moo says the cow; *gaf-gaf* says the dog; *myau* says the cat; *kukareku* says the rooster." She giggled again. Fedya kissed Irishka on the forehead. He loved his baby sister's laugh. But she wasn't such a baby anymore, almost four. She should be in nursery school. And what of Elena? She had loved school. The whole setup was pointless.

He heard the church bells call the faithful to morning mass. If he wanted to catch up with Dima before the gang left the hideout for the day, he had to get going.

"I've got to go." He pulled a knit cap from his pocket and zipped up his jacket.

"Fedya, I don't like it, the way you're leaving so early today," Elena said.

"You think I do? I've got to go."

"But there's no food. I don't know what to give Irishka."

"You think I'm not hungry? I'm doing my best. I'm not a miracle worker."

"But you promised to—"

"Shut up!" Fedya had raised his hand to whack her, and she ducked. Irishka cried. He slapped the door instead, yanked it open, and slammed it behind him. He waited on the other side for her to bolt the door as shame washed over him. What an ass, he thought; just like Vladimir, his mother's last boyfriend and Irishka's father. No time to cry now. He had to make the call to the agency.

3

He reached the old hotel just in time. Most of the boys had left already to pickpocket the train or bus stations. Dima, being the leader, had slept in. As promised, Dima used his mobile to call the agency for Fedya.

"You should have told me the truth, Fedkins, about your sisters. You think we don't have sisters and brothers too? You're not the only one."

"I'm sorry."

"Trust, Fedkins. It all comes back to trust. So, give me the phone number."

Dima's voice sounded more like a man's, unlike his own squawks. Besides, Fedya didn't own a mobile. He owned nothing except his backpack and the few clothes he had slipped out of the flat and stashed in the gang hideout. Now that the police and social workers had arrived, he'd better catch up with the comrades or he'd get no share of the take. Dima had told him not to stick around once the enforcers arrived. If the authorities saw him, they'd grab him, too.

Fedya was about to walk away when he heard Irishka's cries. He turned and saw Elena walk out with their sister, holding her close, but all the while scanning the street. Did she see him? Would she guess he'd turned them in? Would she give him away? He ducked behind the van again. He heard the women talk about the miserable flat as they barked at the girls to get into the back seat of the car. Fedya chanced another look. Only the very top of Irishka's blond head was visible through the rear window, but Elena had turned full around and found his eyes. Or had she? He shivered. The car drove away. He had to believe they would be better off.

2
ELENA

Two weeks? Maybe three already. Elena tucked her feet up inside her nightgown and pulled the sweater tighter as she sat in the window seat and gazed at the snow through icy feathers growing on the glass. Behind her, covers rustled as the other girls stirred in their beds. One rocked in her sleep. Another snored. Someone else mumbled. Down the hall, voices argued. Lubya, the helper, probably wanted the leftover pork bones, or the housekeeper wanted the American magazine she'd found under a chair in the hall. Every night it was something. Every night, it was the same.

Elena's heart pounded. Was it a boy crossing the street? She put her hand to the glass. Stupid. Her brother would never come here; it was too dangerous. She put her hand back inside the sleeve of her sweater. Poor Fedya. He had tried so hard to protect them, but he had failed all the same.

When the agency women had come and pounded on their door that day, she and Irishka had been singing their family song about the swans in the lake. Irishka loved that song. *Stop thinking about Irishka.*

The *politsiya* had kept knocking and calling out. Elena had pulled Irishka into a corner.

5

"We must be quiet. Very quiet, Irishka."

"Why?"

"It's the agency people. Shh! Remember what Fedya told us?"

The little girl's eyes had gone wide with fear.

"Say nothing." Elena had put her finger to her lips again. "Nothing."

She had thought they would go away. Instead, the *politsiya* had forced open the door. Inside, the two girls had huddled under a blanket in a corner, afraid but silent, until the adults had found them.

Back then, she worried that Fedya would get caught, too. She mistrusted what she saw: was it really Fedya at the van across the street who watched them climb into the back seat of the black car? Would Fedya let them drive away like that? She would never know for sure.

Then she worried they would catch him later. Oh God, please don't let the agency people ever catch him. Don't let them put him in a room like this one with other sleepy, weepy children who don't remember their mamas or papas or what it was like to sled down the hill behind the opera house. No, don't be silly. They couldn't catch Fedya. Besides, even if they did, he would run away. Wouldn't he? He had grown strange the last few weeks in their flat. Quiet and secretive.

"What's wrong? Why are you so grumpy?" she had asked. "What happened to your eye? Where's the little wallet Mama gave you?"

"Quit asking me so many damn questions," he said. And for the first time, he struck her. She cried, but then he pulled her into his arms. Irishka cried too, and he pulled her in as well. They stood in a little huddle for a long time.

Now she was here, Children's House Number 24. Maybe she should run away. She hated it here, like a prison. But where could she go alone? Where could she go without Fedya and Irishka?

Headlights arced across the room, and she saw herself in the window like a flash photograph. Nothing much had changed except that Lubya had chopped her stringy dark brown hair very short. Elena felt tired and worn out, like an old *babushka*.

Before and after classes, every day, she sat like this in the dayroom window. She heard the other girls gossiping about her. They thought she couldn't hear or talk. They mocked her as if she waited for rescue.

At first, it was true; she had waited. But now, the waiting was over. Her brother would not come. Her little sister was gone. Elena was alone.

There was so little to break up the sameness of each day. Sometimes foreign visitors came. She stared at them without expression, to make them uncomfortable. They gave her fake smiles or made cooing sounds like little birds. Mostly, they shook their heads and turned away. She wasn't sure why they did that, but she didn't like it. They made her feel like an animal in the zoo. Oh yes, they were so sorry for her and for all the rest of them. So what? At first, she thought they might bring money or gifts. But they didn't. There was little hope for anything like that at Children's House Number 24.

One thing she liked about the foreigners, especially the Americans and Canadians: they looked and smelled clean. They squeaked like hair washed, crackled like frozen laundry, and smelled better than anyone else around.

As another car drove by outside, a light beam hovered as it caught her squarely in the face. She opened her mouth as though she could swallow the light. That wasn't it. She wasn't swallowing; she was screaming without sound. Elena knew better than to make noise and wake the other children or call attention to herself. She had learned that lesson too well.

They punished the girls in the oddest ways. When Vladimir lived with them before Irina was born, his punishments had been swift and harsh; but here, the suffering was a drawn-out, shameful affair. She didn't like being shamed. Once, after standing a long time in a corner, Elena devised a simple revenge against the caretaker. When no one was looking, Elena stuck a finger down her throat and threw up her dinner all over the woman. Oh, how she screeched as she ran for the kitchen.

Elena chuckled now at the memory. Maybe she should become an actress. *Da,* she would become rich and famous. She would walk down the street and everyone's head would turn. They would call out her name: Look, it's Elena Ivanovna. And the paparazzi would snap a million pictures and she would appear on the covers of those movie magazines they sold in the underpasses.

After ten more headlights, Elena slipped one arm out from under her sweater where she had kept it to stay warm and put her index finger on the window's ice. The glass was cold. She left her finger there all the same. She wanted to push a hole right through the glass. Slowly, the heat of her finger won the battle, and it left an oval spot on the glass. She made another spot and then another. And dot by dot, his name emerged: Fedya.

She stood. The icy coldness from the floor crept up through her stockinged feet. She hurried over to her bed where she kept her shoes and dug inside until she found the coin a tall woman with blue eyes and a red hat had given her that afternoon. It was a small silver coin, ever so thin, with a torch on one side and a man's face on the other. Elena carried it back to the window and scratched at the ice. No one must know about Fedya. She should not have conjured him up in this way. What if he heard her or saw her in his dreams? *Nyet*, she must let him go. He could not save her now. It was too late. He must be her secret. If they knew Fedya was her brother, they might look for him. And if they looked for him, they might find him. And if they found him, they would arrest him. He would never forgive her for that.

He didn't want to forgive her that other time. That time she had let it slip to the grocer's cousin, visiting from Kyiv, that they lived near Rukcikaya. The grocer's cousin. What was her name? She was nice, and she gave Elena three fat apples that day. But Fedya punished her when she got home. He shook her hard, and she cried. But then Irishka cried too, and he yelled at her for making Irishka cry. It wasn't fair. Sometimes Fedya acted like Vladimir, Irishka's father. What was her mother thinking when she brought that drunk into their lives? *Da,* when Fedya became angry, he acted just like Vladimir.

"You are so stupid!" Fedya had said, "You're almost ten! How long have we been on the street, and still you don't know the rules? Maybe I should drop you both off at the police station and be done with you."

"But Fedya, what did I do? I didn't tell her the address or anything. I said—"

"I know what you said, and you're going to ruin everything."

He had picked up Irina and rocked her and patted her and walked her around the cold room. He was always kind to their little sister, since she was only three; she would be four soon. October was upon them, and the rundown flat was getting colder with each passing week. Elena could smell winter coming. He worried about winter, too. That was the real reason he had screamed at her. She knew it. She could tell, but neither of them knew what to do.

8

Elena remembered a better day in early spring when they first moved into the flat. Everything had smelled of hope. The sun had filled the tall windows all day long. And when summer came, they had laid out their blankets and clothes right there by the open windows to hear the city sounds and look out at the sky. It was hard to sleep during the white nights. And sometimes, on their blankets in front of the windows, she and Fedya would tickle Irishka to hear her laugh.

Oh, Irishka. Elena couldn't bear to think about her sister and tried to close her mind to the sounds of her laughter, but it didn't work. Elena could hear her little voice calling, "Lenushka, Lenushka! I see you!" Only five years between them, yet Elena was like a mama to the baby girl and Fedya was, well, Fedya was the boss because Mama had said he was the head of the house. Sometimes he acted more like the ass. But they were family; they had each other.

Elena had tried to do her part by taking care of Irina when Fedya went out, but when the agency people came, they snatched the girl away from her all the same. She had tried to hold on, but the big woman with the cigarette breath had peeled their hands apart. Hadn't anyone heard their screams? Maybe it was like tonight; no genuine sound came out. Maybe she and Irishka had only imagined they were screaming. How could anyone endure it otherwise? How could anyone stand by and listen to Irina Vladimirovna and Elena Ivanovna scream for each other, scream for help? *Da,* that would explain it. There wasn't any sound coming out when they screamed; they were in an old-fashioned movie.

A touch to her shoulder interrupted her memories. She didn't stir or even jump. Fedya had taught her well.

"No matter how scared you are," he had said, "when they touch you, don't move and don't talk."

And so, she didn't say a word, not for days, weeks, or however long she had been here.

"Elena, you are trying to freeze to death, and I won't have it, not on my shift," Lubya said. "Now, come back to bed. Do you hear me? Are you listening? I know you can hear me, so don't act like you can't because I know you can. I've watched you; you can play-act dumb all you want. But I know you can hear, and I think you can speak. If you wanted to, you could speak. I know you can."

9

On and on she droned as she led Elena back to the little narrow bed, four beds down from the window. They were all the same, the beds, so you had to count. Her world: four beds down from the window.

All the way to the bed, Elena held the coin in her fist. It would be a secret, a small secret treasure. Little treasures gave her hope. The coin would be her first treasure in a new place, that's all. She would find a box and a place to hide it. *Da,* she would build a new treasure box where all her secrets could hide forever. She knew how to collect treasures. She had been collecting them as long as she could remember. Elena almost cried as she thought of their treasure box in the wall of the flat. Those memories would have to go. Everything from before had to go. Instead, she would collect new treasures to get ready for the day when she would be free again, and maybe she would find her sister and her brother, and they would all sled down the hill behind the opera house again.

3
FEDYA

St. Petersburg, Russia

It was for the best. He had done the right thing. That's what he thought as he stood in a doorway across the street from their old flat. The green van was still there. No change. Even though a few weeks had passed, and the authorities had probably taken everything out of the flat, Fedya needed to check, just in case. It was cold for November and too cold for standing around. He had watched the flat for over an hour to make sure no one had staked out to catch him. That's what Dima had told him to do after Fedya confessed he had to return to the flat. If Elena told the agency people about him, they might set a trap to detain him. That's how they caught Grisha, who was too sentimental, and went home to say goodbye to his grandmother.

The girls were better off, Fedya thought again. But he missed them. He missed having a family. Dima and the boys were all right, but they were rough. He still had bruises from the last fight over a warm coat he'd found. Now all he had was his brown jacket. And look at the weather. He had to keep moving. And he would keep moving as soon as he was sure none of the family stuff or money box were still in the old flat. He had to look for the box and maybe grab some clothes they had rolled up under the eaves. He needed a coat. Thank God Elena couldn't tell anyone about the box—that was the main reason he had kept it a secret from her. But now he wondered, had he hid it well enough? What about squatters?

He had to get going. Where were the aunties? Fedya leaned out and looked once more up the street. Finally, there they were: the two downstairs *babushka*s trudging home from Saturday night vigil. He smiled. You could almost set a clock by them; they would reach the gate soon. And the baker's brother was right behind them, rushing home to his family. Nothing much had changed after all. Fedya saw the aunties buzz themselves in at the front gate. He loped across the street and held the gate for them. "*Zdrasti*," thanks, he murmured. The women glared at him and blocked his way inside but said nothing. He nodded and pushed the gate shut for them, but not before he slipped a matchbook between the latch and the frame (another trick he'd learned from Dima). Then he ambled up the street toward Kazanskaya—Kazan Street.

At the corner, he turned back and ran straight for the gate, since he had to be the next person through it. In the summer, getting in and out of the courtyard had been no problem. Back then, the aunties had recognized both Fedya and the girls and assumed they lived with a family. But, in these few weeks, he had already become a stranger to them. He retrieved the matchbook and slipped through the gate easily. At the edge of the courtyard, he paused. Covered with snow, the old car parts, barrels, and rusty benches looked like statues in the Snow Maiden's garden. Fedya skirted the edges of the courtyard and worked his way back to the corner where the building's basement door had rotted through a long time ago and trash spilled out like apples on display at the market.

He climbed the old stairs two at a time. When he reached the top floor, the sixth, he gently pushed on the door of their old hideaway flat. It wouldn't move. *Dermo*! Blocked, locked, or bolted, that was not a good sign. He checked the other three doors on the landing and, luckily, found one ajar. The ruined interior of the neighboring apartment was dark, cold, and even breezy. A mirror of their old place, Fedya maneuvered the space well and quickly reached the broken front windows. Last summer, he had wiggled across this same ledge a few times. He hoped the snow and ice wouldn't be a danger now. When he looked out, most of the ledge was clear. He considered leaving his backpack to retrieve later but cast that thought aside. The pack was all he had. He pulled himself out onto the ledge and faced the wall for a better grip on the uneven stones. In moments, he was around the corner and through the kitchen window of their old flat.

He stepped to the doorway of the main room, waited for his eyes to adjust, then scanned the room. The tall windows gave him just enough light to make out a lump on the floor. *Dermo!* There were three or four other pallets and mattresses flung about. Thank God, all but one was empty. The whole place smelled of stale smoke and garbage. These squatters were pigs. A fury welled up inside him. He wanted to walk over to the lump and kick him as hard as he could. Elena's bottle collection still sat on the windowsill; a dead flower drooped to one side. And there, underneath the ledge, was the cardboard train he had made for Irishka, but it was on its side and didn't look much like a train anymore. His rage simmered, but then the lump on the floor moved and Fedya pulled back from the doorway. Fool! If the squatter woke up, it would be three times harder to get the box.

Fedya peeked around the doorjamb; the lump quieted and snored. He surveyed the rest of the room. Someone had broken the old wardrobe into pieces, probably for firewood. His heart sank. Damn, damn, damn! The squatters must have found the box that was behind it. But he had to be sure, so he crept around the back edge of the room to where the wardrobe used to stand. He felt for the grooves he had left in the floor molding. Not yet, not yet, there! He was a little encouraged. The tiny trap door appeared undisturbed. He took out his knife and slid it between the wall and the molding. It was loose, almost too loose. Before he could stop it, the entire piece fell forward and clattered onto the floor.

"What is that? Who's there?" a man's voice came through the darkened room.

The lump rolled to his knees. It was an older man, a drunk; a pungent smell of alcohol wafted across the room. The man tossed off his cover and Fedya recognized it as Elena's old blanket. The adrenaline pumped through his body as he considered this new atrocity. How did such a scumbag get hold of it? How dare those filthy hands touch his sister's blanket?

"Anton? What are you doing? Where have you been?" the old man asked as he stood shakily and stared at the gloomy spot in the corner where Fedya squatted.

Fedya stood up to face the man squarely, to prevent him from seeing the hole in the wall.

"Stay away. I don't want to hurt you, old man, but I will."

"Oh, you will, will you?"

The man lunged for him, but Fedya was quicker. He jumped aside, slashed out with his little knife, and nicked the man across his face.

"You little piece of shit. I'll kill you!" The fellow advanced more steadily now.

Fedya took a run and a leap and slammed both feet into the man's groin. Fedya crashed to the floor as well, but jumped up while the other lay collapsed in pain. Then Fedya rushed to the window, grabbed one of the old bottles and smashed it as hard as he could on the man's head. The man groaned, so Fedya grabbed another bottle and hit him again. There was glass everywhere. Then it was quiet. Fedya feared he had killed him, but had no desire to find out. He rushed to the hole in the molding and pulled out the cigar box. As he pulled it out, he found something else with it, a lumpy thing wrapped in material; there was no time to investigate.

He heard footsteps on the stairs. Fedya grabbed up his pack along with the box, the lumpy package, and his sister's blanket. He rushed through the kitchen and out through the window and around the ledge to the side. Instead of shuffling his way back to the first flat, he leaped to the roof of the next building. He ran as fast as he could, slid in the snow, and then leaped from one building roof to the next. Finally, at the fourth building, he found the hole in the roof he and Elena had used in the old days for fun and jumped down through it. Thankfully, the mattress padding they had put there in the summer was still in place.

Out on the street, Fedya kept running. After several minutes, and eight or nine blocks, he stopped, his breathing ragged. His body shook as though he was cold, but he was sweating. He needed a place to rest and wait out the night. He looked around to get his bearings. If he crossed Malookskaya—Malook Street, there would be a small park to the left. Behind the park, he remembered a building with a broken-down basement shop they had considered at one time for shelter. There, he could get a little protection from the cold, build a small fire, and maybe have enough light to check the box. He headed for the park. It was awkward walking with the backpack, the bundle, the box, and the blanket, but he made it.

He stopped at the steps that headed down into the shop and looked around. The street was quiet, with only a few lost souls in the park who didn't notice him. He eased down and hugged the wall of the building to avoid leaving footprints in the snow. At the bottom, he pushed on the little window next to the door and it swung open. He tossed in his stuff and crawled through. Fedya didn't know what kind of shop it used to be, maybe a barbershop or something like that. He didn't care. He was glad to be out of the wind.

Others had been there before him. Burned spots on the floor suggested someone else had built a small fire on the cement. He had hoped to do the same, but he saw no wood or old furniture and was too tired to forage in the park. Without a fire, it was too dark to see what he had in the box. It was best to wait until morning. Fedya hugged the box and the fabric-wrapped parcel to his chest, pulled up the edges of the blanket, and stepped to one corner to settle down, but found the stench too strong. He moved to the opposite corner, sat with his back against the wall, and wrapped himself up in the blanket he had taken back from the old uncle. He smiled. Someone would be cold tonight, if he wasn't dead.

Tomorrow, Fedya would head back to Dima's place and pick up his sleeping pack. Despite everything, he had successfully retrieved the box, and could finally allow himself a little hope that his plan was working. If the box was intact, it would mean he was one step closer to leaving the city to make his way to Rīga. He couldn't wait any longer. The girls would be fine. He had to believe that. And he had to search for his uncle, for without him, he and his sisters would never be reunited.

He laid his head on the old cigar box and fingered the lumpy package in the dark. Somehow familiar, he couldn't resist, and unwrapped the parcel by touch. He realized the unrolled fabric wasn't just any piece of material; it was Irishka's worn and torn baby blanket. It smelled like her, and his hands trembled as he remembered her blond hair and green eyes. But when he touched the object inside the blanket, he sucked in a loud breath. The tears came unbidden. He hadn't cried when the social workers and police picked up the girls. He hadn't cried when his mother died. But now, with Elena's precious American rag doll in his hands, her only doll, with its long blond braids, blue jumper, and red and white striped socks, he couldn't be strong anymore. He sobbed into the doll's soft belly. He held it close to his mouth, to muffle the sound. Eventually, he fell asleep.

It was not until the next morning that he wondered how Elena had managed to put the doll and baby blanket into the secret hole. How had she known? Apparently, he hadn't fooled her at all. He grinned. *Da,* she was clever, that one. Of course, she was clever; the blood of their family name, the *Lebedevs*—the Swans, bound them to each other.

With the light, Fedya sat up and brought the box to his lap. What had fortune left of his family treasures?

4

IRINA

CHILDREN'S HOUSE NUMBER EIGHT
ST. PETERSBURG, RUSSIA

Russian Nursery Rhyme

Little Kitty, smart and sly,

Went to market, bought a pie.

Then he went out for a stroll

And he bought himself a roll

Shall I eat them all up? Maybe.

But then what can I bring to Baby?

I know, I'll have myself a bite.

And save the rest for you, all right?

Irishka liked the nursery rhyme about the little kitty that Masha sang as she accompanied herself on her big guitar. When Masha finished, Irishka tugged at the singer's dress, demanding to hear the song again. "*Snova, snova!*"

"One more time," Masha said, and held up her finger for silence.

17

Music made Irishka feel better for a little while. But then, she would look around for brother Fedya and sister Lenushka, and they wouldn't be there. That made her want to cry or hit something.

After singing time, helpers Alya and Klara herded all of them into a line and began the rituals of potty sitting, body rinsing, teeth cleaning, nighttime diapers for the youngest ones, and night clothes. The children sat quietly and waited for a turn.

She always sat at the end of the line. Before, Klara had called her a bad girl because she wouldn't sit with the other children in line. Now she was a good girl. She didn't like to wait for her turn, but she didn't want to be a bad girl either.

She loved singing with Masha best of all. It made her think about her other life. If she closed her eyes and listened hard, she could pretend that she was listening to her sister singing or telling stories about Mama. Did her sister look like Masha, the singer?

"Hello, Irishka."

She twisted around to see who had spoken to her. Nothing. There was no one close by. That's funny, she thought. She turned back around; she didn't want to get in trouble.

"Irina Vladimirovna, where are your manners?"

Again, she whipped her head around but saw nothing. Except, wait; there was a faint outline of something in the shadows under the big radio table. She could see some movement, too. She turned back to look at the line of children and moved up. She looked back at the "something" and glanced around to see who else saw what she saw, but no one seemed to notice the voice.

"Who are you?" she whispered to the form in the shadows. She wondered who could hide under a table without making Alya or Klara angry?

First one paw and then another stretched out from under the table, and then a noble head with pointy ears, whiskers, and sparkling eyes followed.

"Oh!"

"Irishka, what is it?" Klara walked up to her.

She looked at Klara and then pointed to the huge cat, who stared at them. He smiled.

"What? What are you pointing at?"

Irishka stared back at Klara and almost said "Cat," but then she thought better of it. Instead, she shrugged her shoulders.

"Irishka, for heaven's sake, move along. I don't have time for this tonight," Klara muttered as she rushed up to blond-haired Katya, who was making poo-poo on the floor. "Stop, stop! Katya! *Nyet!* Bad girl!"

Irishka peered at the huge cat again, who continued to stare at her and smile.

"Irishka," the cat purred, "I don't think Klara can see me, do you?"

She shook her head in slow motion. She should be afraid of this giant cat, but she was not. And then, right before her eyes, the cat licked himself, and everywhere he licked, he changed color. With his tongue, he painted himself all over in light blue. She clapped her hands and giggled. She glanced up and saw Alya look at her in a funny way, her forehead all wrinkled, and her eyes squeezed like slits.

Irishka shrugged and laughed.

When Irishka turned back to look at the light blue cat, he sat right beside her. He was quick. She stared at him. She wasn't sure how she knew it was a boy cat, but she did.

"Are you a boy cat?"

Klara called out, "Irishka! Wake up! It's your turn," and the helper grabbed her by her bad, crooked arm and pulled her up from the floor.

"Ai!"

"Oh," Klara let go of the arm and dropped her hard onto her bottom.

"Ai, oooh."

"Come on now, Irishka, stop it. Let's go, here we go. You'll be all right. Give me your other arm." Irishka watched Klara glance around, to be sure no one had seen the drop or yank.

Irishka wanted to cry, but then she heard the big blue cat say, "Well, well, well, that wasn't nice. I think you need a friend here."

She got quiet, turned around, and nodded. But before she could thank the big blue cat, Klara dragged her into the bathing room. He was too much of a proper cat to come into a girl's bathing room where she had to take off her clothes. *Da,* he was a proper cat. And somewhere deep in her heart, she knew he would wait for her until she finished. He would not leave her. He would be her friend forever. She decided he needed a happy name. She called him Lezunchik, Happy One.

5

FEDYA

ST. PETERSBURG, RUSSIA

When he opened the old cigar box, instead of the money he expected, Fedya found a collection of objects. This was Elena's work: an envelope with a few family pictures from long ago, an oval frame with his mother and father's picture, a wedding ring, a baby's silver brush, a pressed leaf glued to a card, an empty bottle of perfume, and his mother's round silver pendant with two flying swans.

He remembered the day she had given him the pendant, the day she couldn't get out of bed anymore. He, in turn, had given it to Elena that same night. He recalled how Mama spoke to him as she took it off her neck and dropped it into his hand.

"Your father gave it to me, in the good times, for luck, before Yeltsin, before the fighting in the streets, before the conflict with the blacks in Chechnya. Those were better days." She had grown silent and looked out the window. "But then, the army took Ivan to fight. Before Chechnya, our family had such things as luck and even a little happiness, but he never came back. And our luck dried up like a burned twig."

Fedya leaned against the icy wall of the old shop now and dangled the circlet from his hand like a hypnotist. Maybe it was time to call the old luck back; why not? He could use it. So, he put the chain over his neck and dropped the pendant inside his shirt. It was cool to the skin and foreign, but it felt right.

Toward the bottom of the box, he found an object he had saved but forgotten about: the old American sports card his father had traded their last day together, when they had walked down the boulevard.

"Look at this, Fedya. This is incredibly old. In America, it's worth lots of money. You keep it, and someday, you'll see."

"This? Why? What is it, Papa? What is the man doing?"

"It's baseball, an American game they play in the summer. They play it with a stick and a ball. But that's not as important as the card itself. Someday, maybe we'll go to America, eh? We'll collect lots and lots of money."

Fedya didn't understand how such a card could be valuable. He didn't understand it then, and he didn't understand it now. All the same, he didn't want to throw it away, the only thing he had left from his father, Ivan Konstantinov.

Under the card, he found his mother's crucifix and their money stacked up underneath it. He had told Elena to throw that cross away.

He avoided touching the cross and reached for the money to count it: only 2,204 rubles. Not much left. He had tried to use the money sparingly. And yet, despite his efforts, he had less than half of what his mother had given him on the night she died.

"Fedya, this is all I have," she had said. "I wish it were more. I hid it from Irishka's father because of the drink. I'm glad he's gone. You forget about him. He was a…a…well, it doesn't matter anymore. Next week, Vasiliy comes back from his tour. He will come. And everything will be all right."

She pressed the money into his hand. She looked so pale in the dim light from the bedside lamp, but he could still make out the little wrinkle lines next to her eyes and the tiny notch in her cheek that hid itself until she smiled. She had smiled so seldom by then; there was no happy curve to her lips.

"You're going to get better, Mama."

She had shaken her head. Her hair was all plastered around her face with sweat and he could see a hairpin mangled into a knot of hair above her right ear. Then she started coughing again. He tried to hold her head and shoulders while she coughed.

"Let me call Auntie Sasha from her flat," he pleaded. "She'll know what to do."

"And I don't know what to do?" She chuckled and laid back her head. "Get me some water, please. But wait, before you do, you must listen to me."

Fedya sat back down beside her, his one hand still wrapped around the roll of money and its fat rubber band. He watched his mother rub the crucifix with her left thumb. Then she grabbed his wrist anew.

"If I die before Vasiliy comes, do not call anyone, Fedya. Wait for him."

"But Mama—"

She held up her hand, gesturing for him to stop. "Listen to me. You think you are so smart, but you don't listen. If you call anyone, there will be talk and people, maybe even the *politsiya* or the agency people will come and they will take you away; they'll take you to one children's house, Elena to another, and Irishka to another. You must wait, or run away." She paused, laboring to catch her breath.

"Stay together, Fedya. You must do everything you can to stay together. Wait for Vasiliy Chasikovich. He is my old friend. Remember how he came and sang to us? He has been away, singing, but he will come back. He will help you. Or go to Rīga. Find my brother, Uldis. You remember Uncle Uldi?" She coughed again and Fedya saw the blood spray onto the blanket. "Water, Fedya. Please, water."

He stuffed the money into the pocket of his pants and ran down the hall to the little kitchen they shared with Auntie Sasha and three other families. It was late and dark in the back room; no one was awake. He had banged his toe on a bucket and the noise frightened him, but no one came out. When he returned to their flat with a small glass of water, his mother was quiet.

"Mama, here is the water." He took her hand to help her drink, but it was limp. He looked at her face and then he saw her eyes were quite open. Her mouth was pursed into a small "oh" shape, as though caught by surprise. He stood there and gaped at her for a long time. He watched her skin lose its color. In those minutes, she became a corpse.

23

A terrible smell stirred him to action. When he moved, the glass he had set on the bed tipped over and spilled water all over the sheets and onto her clothes.

"I'm sorry, Mama. I'm sorry. You know how clumsy I am."

He tried to mop up the water with the edge of her blanket. The crucifix fell out of her hand and Fedya watched it tumble to the floor in slow motion.

Then he understood. Mama couldn't feel the cold water on her skin. She couldn't feel anything anymore. He had wanted to touch her face, but what was the point? He picked up the cross instead and looked at the miniature Christ his mother adored, hung by tiny nails, draped in a cloth, and topped with a crown of thorns. Despite all the pain and all the prayers and all the visits to the church, nothing was enough to save her. When he turned it over, he found an inscription: "For Elizaveta: Give me an undivided heart. Ps. 86:11." Meaningless. He dropped the crucifix into the empty water glass and set them aside.

His stomach roiled, but he knew he couldn't stand there any longer. He had to do something. First, he would wake up his sisters and get them dressed; they had to leave the apartment. What was his mother thinking? Wait for Uncle Vasiliy? How? Sit by and watch her body rot? But where could they go? Mama talked about Vasiliy Chasikovich so confidently. But where was he? Oh, why hadn't Fedya paid attention? Why hadn't he asked her more questions? He thought he had more time, that's why. And then, what about Uncle Uldi? He tried to remember how far Rīga was from St. Petersburg, but he couldn't think clearly. Could they get to Rīga? How? So many questions he couldn't answer.

He needed a plan for right then. They would need food. He could probably steal all the food from the kitchen that he could carry, but only food that did not need cooking. They wouldn't need coats, because it wasn't cold outside, but how long would it stay warm? Should they carry coats? Where are the coats? *Nyet*, that was stupid. Elena would have to hold on to Irishka. How much could she carry? All right, one bag for Elena and a small bag for Irishka, and two bags for Fedya, maybe three. But then, who would carry the food? It was more than he could figure out alone.

"Elena! Lenushka, wake up. You must wake up now."

"Why? It's still night, isn't it?"

24

"Elena Ivanovna, wake up. It's Mama. You must say goodbye to Mama because she is dead." He had shaken her a little more roughly than necessary. "Lenushka, listen to me. Wake up. Mama died."

"What? That's not funny, Fedya."

"I'm not trying to be funny. Get up. Mama died while you were asleep, and she warned me. She said we must run away and hide, or the agency people will come and take us away."

"Stop it. I don't want to say goodbye. I don't want to run away."

"Shut up. Shut up!" And then he had yanked her up. Oh God, why did he have to be so rough? He knew it wasn't fair, but he couldn't help it. "Just shut up and do what I say."

In the end, Elena was the one who suggested they hide on the top floor of their own building. Men sometimes came to work on the apartments, fixing them up, but no one had started on the top floors yet.

From the front window on the sixth floor, he and Elena watched people coming and going into their building during the day. At night, he sneaked back to their old floor and took more stuff from the flat and food from the kitchen. By the third day, the smell had brought Auntie Sasha to their mother's door. What a busybody. Everyone in the building had heard her scream when she found their dead mama.

Later, Fedya had watched the hospital men come and carry Mama outside in a big black bag and put her in an official car. Of course, the sisters hadn't known it was Mama, but Fedya knew right away. That afternoon, other official-looking people had come in and out as well as the *politsiya*. The next day, two city workers had come and carried the rest of their clothing and old furniture from the flat and left it on the street. He and Elena watched as neighbors carried away their pitiful family belongings, one piece after the other. Even old Auntie Sasha had pawed through Mama's clothes. Elena almost yelled down at her, but he had pulled her away from the window.

"Don't be stupid, Lenushka. You'll give us away."

"But those are Mama's clothes. They have no right."

"Mama? Mama? I want Mama," Irishka said.

"See what you've done?" he said. "Don't say her name again."

Then he whooshed Irishka up into the air and twirled her around. She giggled like always and when he set her down, she was quiet again and said, "Fedya, where is Mama?"

He stared at her but couldn't answer the question.

Elena kneeled beside Irishka and held both of her hands. "Irishka, Mama went on a long trip to be with Baby Jesus and Mother Mary."

"Why?" Irishka asked.

"It was her turn, Irishka. It was Mama's turn."

Fedya walked away from them and looked out the window.

"My turn," Irishka said, "I want a turn."

"*Nyet*, Irishka, not yet," Elena said. "When it's your turn, Mama will come and get you. So, you must watch and wait. See, Fedya's watching too."

A honk outside the shop snapped Fedya back to the present. Those days seemed long ago now, weeks ago, when his mother had given him thousands of rubles and commanded him to take care of his sisters. But he couldn't do it. Not then, anyway. He didn't know who to trust, or how to get to Rīga, or how to feed two little girls, or keep them warm, much less keep all three of them hidden from the *politsiya*. He had failed his mother. He had failed his sisters. The best choice had been to turn them in to the agency people, run away, and find a gang until he figured things out.

It was not so bad, the gang, except that he was the new boy. He had tried to pretend that he knew the street, but they figured he was green. They kept picking on him, so Dima taught him how to fight, and how to survive. Soon, Dima even let him deliver packages.

"You never told me, Fedkins, where are your parents?" They had been sitting on the roof of the old Black Willow Hotel where the gang hid out on the third floor.

"Dead," he had said.

"Both?" Fedya nodded. "Who did the agency people pick up?"

He went quiet. Sending the girls to an orphanage was his great shame.

"Just my little sisters. They're better off without me."

"*Nyet*. Together is better. You have no other relatives?"

26

"I think I have an uncle in Rīga, but that is far away."

"Not so far. A train ride, car ride, or a boat ride. Many Russians live there."

"Really?"

"Sure, I have some friends. With enough money, they might even drive you there."

"Why would they do that? Why would you help me like that?"

Dima laid back and looked up into the sky. "I had a brother like you once." He said no more.

That was the day Fedya had made a new plan: to go back to the flat, find the treasure box, and use the last of the money to find his uncle in Rīga.

6

ELENA

CHILDREN'S HOUSE TWENTY-FOUR
ST. PETERSBURG, RUSSIA

Elena felt ridiculous. They lined up the girls along their beds like soldiers waiting for inspection. Lubya, in a foul mood all morning, barked out orders to clean this and clean that and finally, to stand by their beds and wait. Elena looked at the girls again. They were different, *da*, and yet all the same: orphans, street girls, and castoffs from broken families. She didn't want to know them, but through observation alone, they left impressions anyway.

Larissa, the tomcat, slouched in front of bed number one closest to the window; she gnawed at her fingernails. She returned Elena's gaze with narrow eyes. Everyone made Larissa angry. Fedya had warned her about kids like that, those who waited for an excuse to start a fight.

Across from Larissa was a dark-headed girl who always laughed. Elena thought it strange how this girl thought everything was funny. Maybe she was crazy. No name came to mind.

There were two Svetlanas, but Elena could only remember the one who slept next to Larissa because she was so fat. Elena wondered how the girl could eat so much when the food was terrible.

The next girl was Oksana, bed number three. Of course, everyone knew her because she was such a butt-kisser. That's what Fedya would have called her. Today was no different. Oksana stood like a ballerina beside her bed. While only a few of the girls liked her, the adults gushed over her. She turned on the charm whenever the foreigners came through. Once, Elena overheard whispers that Oksana wanted to be adopted. Elena couldn't imagine living the rest of her life with strangers.

The newest girl, even newer than herself, stood across from Oksana and next to Elena. Her name was Yuliya, and she was afraid of everybody. Elena felt sorry for the girl, but she would not break her own vow of silence. If Elena could adapt, so could Yuliya.

Another girl Elena liked a little was Aniya, who slept on her other side. Although this girl always spoke in a whisper, Elena believed she had her own brand of toughness mixed with kindness. Whenever they made eye contact, unlike so many of the other girls who would say something mean, Aniya smiled at her.

Kiska was the one who always rocked to fall asleep. The girl had come from the farm and was happy to have a roof over her head and regular meals. But Kiska was a family girl, and she talked about her sisters and brothers constantly. How did she end up in a city orphanage? A mystery to be sure, but not Elena's problem.

Closer to the door was Tatiana, who Elena called the beauty queen. Even now, she draped over her bed like a minx. After Tatiana, Elena wasn't too sure. One girl was always loud and rude. Then there was the sick girl, almost bald. Even now, she sat on the edge of her bed because she was too weak to stand.

At the end of the line, on either side of the door, were the two oldest girls who had seniority: Lukina, who ran errands but was so stupid she had to whisper the instructions to herself repeatedly so she wouldn't forget; and Baiba, who was really a Latvian girl, or at least that's what the others said. At thirteen, she claimed the top position and would soon go to the upper school for teenaged girls. The teens could go out in the evenings to meet boys.

Elena heard voices down the hall and noticed everyone straighten a little as two women, a man, and the director, Yevgeniya Kalmakovna, came into the room. Helper Lubya followed behind the group like a little dog.

"Very nice, Lubya," Director Kalmakovna said, and then turned to the girls, "Good afternoon, *devochki*—girls," she greeted them.

"Good afternoon, Yevgeniya Kalmakovna," they all intoned, and then several of the girls curtsied and promptly looked down at their feet. Elena did not look down. She was too curious. While these visitors huddled in a private conversation and appeared to compare notes, Director Kalmakovna snapped her fingers at Lubya to take the sick girl out. Lubya scurried over to the girl, whispered in her ear, and they walked out together.

"*Devochki*," Director Kalmakovna bellowed as though everyone was deaf, "these are Olga Petrovna Abramovich, Valentina Alexandrovna Kovaleskaya, and Pyotr Konstantin Kotolvsky. They are social workers from the Pravit Bureau. They are looking for candidates to send on a six-week summer program to a foreign country. Please answer their questions as you would for me."

Of the two female guests, the oldest one had gray hair that peeked out from a fine fur hat. She wore a black wool dress and black, fur-lined boots. She had four ribbons pinned across her left breast that looked like medals. As she worked her way down the aisle, she talked to each girl. The director walked beside her and snapped her fingers for the girls to look up, while Olga Petrovna studied them, like pigs for the butcher.

The younger social worker held back and whispered a funny remark or a kind word. She made the girls smile.

When the older woman and the director reached Elena, they walked right past her without a look or a word. Elena fumed and threw up her middle finger at their backs. Kiska gasped, and Elena turned in time to see the younger social worker had caught her defiance. Instead of a rebuke, Valentina Alexandrovna turned to the man sulking at the door and asked, "Petya, do you want to help me interview any of the girls?"

He shrugged. "They are all the same to me, Valentina. It makes more work for you."

"Oh, Petya, stop it. I know you don't mean that." She stepped to Elena.

This Valentina was almost pretty, but a little too thin, with white-blond hair pulled away from her face in a French style. She wore a dark blue dress and around her neck a beautiful silky scarf in shades of purple and blue together. She wore black boots, but they were not very sensible, because they had high thin heels and pointed toes.

The social worker stood in front of Elena for several moments. Then she smoothed Elena's dark hair back from her face.

"Don't hide your face, it's pretty," she said.

"She doesn't talk," Larissa said from the window. "We think she's too stupid."

Several of the girls nearby giggled and Elena reddened.

"Is that so?" Valentina said as she lifted Elena's chin to peer into her eyes, "Well, I like mysteries."

"Valentina, come over here and talk to this one," Olga Petrovna called.

"*Da,* right away." Valentina looked again at Elena and said, "Don't go anywhere. We will have a pleasant conversation sometime soon."

Don't go anywhere? That was quite the joke. Elena followed the young social worker with her eyes as the woman headed straight for Oksana, of course. Oksana could make anyone think she was the chosen one.

Elena turned back to examine the man. He was quite handsome, but bored. He leaned against the doorframe and tried to ignore the Latvian girl who flirted with him.

"Are you a social worker, too? You don't look like one of those agency people." She blushed. "I mean...you know what I mean. You seem too young to be a government man."

He turned his head and looked straight at the girl. And then he barked like a dog. Everyone jumped. He laughed.

"Petya," Valentina said. "Stop scaring the girls, or you'll eat dinner on your own at the fish market."

Petya said, "My apologies, ladies, but that cruel woman abducted me. Oh, she may look kind and wonderful, the way she smiles and lights up a room, but she is a wicked witch right out of a fairy tale. We met on a cold, dark night. I came out of the stage door—"

"Oh my God, he's an actor!" one girl said.

"Tatiana, I will dismiss you to the day room if you are not quiet!" the director hissed as she came back down the aisle toward them.

31

"I'm sorry, Director Kalmakovna." Tatiana curtsied and pleaded for leniency with her eyes.

"It's my fault, Director," Petya said. "I wanted to tell them a tale of the unfortunate demise of an innocent young man beguiled by the Enchantress of Decembrist Square."

"Oh? And who might that be?" the director asked.

"The enchantress or the innocent man?" Petya feigned ignorance.

The director smiled a little. "Your fiancée told me you are incorrigible, but that she had to ask you along if she wanted to dine out today."

"Director Kalmakovna, you are a genius," Valentina called out from the other end of the room. "But I confess, he is an actor!"

"Oh?" Kalmakovna said as she surveyed Petya from head to toe.

"What about this one?" Valentina asked her colleague as she slowed past Elena on their way back to the door. Olga Petrovna turned to Elena.

"What is your name, child?" the older social worker asked.

"She doesn't talk, but we all know she's a fake," Larissa chirped from her bed again.

"Some trauma, Director?" Olga Petrovna asked.

"We're not sure. She's only been here a few weeks, but it's true, she hasn't said a word. This happens. It's best to wait them out," the director said.

"Maybe there isn't anything to say," Petya said from the door.

"Petya, please," Valentina said. He held up his hands in surrender. "What is her name, Director Kalmakovna, if we may know?"

"Name? Elena something. She has a sister in number eight," the director answered.

Elena's head snapped up as she heard this small piece of information about her sister, Irina.

"Well, there's nothing wrong with her hearing," Valentina added, and smiled.

"That may be, but we don't have time to work with girls like that," the older social worker said. She looked over her documents and added, "Director Kalmakovna, let's set the day after tomorrow as interview day.

Will that be all right? We'll talk again with," she looked down at her list, "Galina Vladislava, Larissa Evgenia, Oksana Antonovna, Yuliya Alexandrovna, and Tatiana Ivanovna."

"Very well, we'll have them ready on Tuesday," the director answered, and they started out.

Valentina looked at Elena with soft, warm eyes. "Elena is a beautiful name. I would like to know you better. Perhaps we can talk the next time I come to visit, but without the mischievous Pyotr Konstantin."

"Valentina, you malign me!" Petya said in mock outrage as they walked out the door.

Elena made a sudden and rash decision. "I can talk," she called after them.

All the girls in the room quieted; Valentina stopped and turned to look at her.

"Excuse me?" she asked.

"I can talk," Elena repeated.

"*Da,* of course you can. Thank you," Valentina said.

"I am Elena Ivanovna Margarita Lebedev, and I am ten years old, almost eleven," Elena said.

Valentina walked over to her and shook her hand. "I am happy to meet you, Elena Ivanovna Margarita Lebedev."

"Valentina, we're leaving, dear," Olga Petrovna called from the hallway.

"Coming!" she answered, but to Elena she said, "I will see you again." And then she was out the door.

The girls said nothing for a few moments, just long enough for Elena to hear Petya say, "Valentina, my beautiful sensitive Valentina, how many foundlings will you gather under your wings?"

And then the girls' noisy chatter drowned out the rest as they rushed over to her, all talking at once. Who knew her voice would give her momentary celebrity status?

7

FEDYA

ST. PETERSBURG, RUSSIA

Fedya pounded on the door.

"Oho, Dima, wake up you horse's *zadnica*. Open this door! Dima! Open up!"

Where were they? Fedya couldn't imagine the gang up and out so early, especially after yesterday's haul and subsequent carousing. Dima liked his vodka.

Fedya had walked from the little basement shop to the Black Willow building through the falling snow. He had wrapped the cigar box and doll in Elena's blanket, cinched his belt around the bundle, and attached it to his backpack. His mind was on the plan: pick up his sleeping gear at the Willow, and head to the train station to buy a ticket to Rīga. Despite what Dima had said about hiring a car, Fedya didn't trust a driver, even if he was supposed to be Dima's buddy.

Besides, things were different now. Everything felt more dangerous. Yesterday, Dima had shown him how to hold and shoot a gun since they had chosen him to be a lookout. Their raid on Stepanov's warehouse had been huge, and Dima celebrated like he was King of the Hill. How Dima had discovered that the warehouse belonged to one of the most powerful bosses in St. Petersburg, Fedya didn't know. But messing with Stepanov felt risky. Even now, Fedya had a bad feeling.

When no one came to the door, Fedya walked to the window at the end of the hall to check for any sign of the gang out back near the container. From the third floor, he could see a long way, since city workers had leveled the entire block, and yet, the Black Willow still stood. He flashed back to Dima's story about the old mansion turned hotel on his first night with the gang.

"Maybe a year ago," Dima had said, "the government came into the district to demolish several blocks to make way for new housing. But as often happens in our wonderful motherland, things didn't work out as they expected. In fact, when they tried to bulldoze the Willow, the machines stopped working, or a worker got hurt, or a water main broke, or it rained, or snowed. Then, they ran out of money."

"You were lucky," Fedya had said.

"Ah, but there's more to it than luck, my young friend. I know the secret: The Willow is cursed."

Fedya laughed. "You've been watching too many old American TV shows, Dimitri."

"You think so? I tell you, it all started before the revolution. This old place used to be the Sakharov mansion, full of rich nobles and tasty ladies. But then, the fighting came along; the rich ran away, and the poor came to stay. Ah, the poetry of it."

"Many years later," he said, "maybe the Petrograd years, an old *vedma*—witch, bought the property and ran it as a hotel." He laughed. "The government thought it was a hotel, but the Black Willow was born to be a bordello and the *vedma* became a powerful madam."

"What's that?" Fedya asked.

All the boys chortled.

"He needs to visit Zoya, Dima!" Kostya said.

"He's a virgin, all right," Borya said and stood up. "Maybe we should take care of that little bother ourselves."

"What?" Fedya whipped around to face Borya. "I'm not stupid, if that's what you mean."

Dima stepped in and shoved Borya back into his seat. "Relax, Bo-Bo, he's a kid. You were a kid once and didn't know your ass from anything else."

"What? Who said?" Borya had tried to get back up, but Dima pulled his knife and used the hilt to push him back, then pressed a sharp edge to his neck.

"I say," he replied, with all seriousness now. No one laughed. "I'm telling a story, Borya, and you're interrupting."

Borya had stared back at the young leader. There was no fear between them. In the end, Borya gave him the finger, which made Dima laugh and back away.

Dima had turned to Fedya and said, "A bordello is a cathouse, a whorehouse, a brothel. You understand me? Now, the story. The *vedma* was Antonina Dmitriyevna Chubais. She lived through it all: Petrograd, Leningrad, the Bolsheviks, and the Red Guard. And finally, when she was ancient, Antonina Dmitriyevna walked around the Black Willow seven times, placed hexed root, at the four corners of the building, and then drew seven circles and seven stars. She stood in the middle of a kub, a magic circle, and spoke the words that would safeguard the Black Willow for a hundred more years."

"How do you know all this?" Fedya asked.

"I was there. She needed a little boy to hold her up while she walked around the Black Willow. I was there with my great grandmother and so, you see, the Black Willow is really mine."

Blinking lights interrupted Fedya's thoughts. Trouble. Two police cars headed toward the Willow. Fedya ran back to the apartment to warn Dima. He pounded again. He tried the doorknob and found it unlocked. He barreled in and stopped short. There were bodies all over the place, and lots of blood. The smell was so strong it made him want to throw up. In the far corner, he saw his sleeping pack. He had to have it, so he hopped over bodies and grabbed it; he pushed down the bile that rose in his throat.

He had a minute more, maybe less; he held his breath. After a quick scan of the bodies, he didn't see Dima, but saw Borya, his clothing soaked in blood. Fedya couldn't delay any longer. Which way? He looked in the kitchen and remembered there was an old dumb waiter there. He slid open the doors. He almost pissed himself when he found someone inside with a gun. It was Dima, either dead or passed out, but with a gun pointed out and ready to shoot.

No time! No time! Fedya pushed the gun aside and squeezed into the small elevator. He released the rope, and it flew through the open lock and pulleys. Fast, they headed down too fast, and Fedya burned his hands as he tried to slow their descent. He got his foot on the rope and pressed as hard as he could. They slowed and stopped in between floors. Fedya wrapped the loose rope around Dima's boot to hold them in place. Dima groaned. Fedya slipped a hand across the boy's mouth.

"Shh. You must be quiet now," he said to the unconscious boy.

Voices and heavy footsteps echoed through the shaft from above. He wasn't sure if the *politsiya* would even try to open or dislodge the dumb waiter. He could only pray they wouldn't bother. For the moment, he and Dima were safe. There was nothing to do now but wait. It was hard to breathe with the packs and both boys together in an old box, but they were alive.

8

IRINA

CHILDREN'S HOUSE NUMBER 8
ST. PETERSBURG, RUSSIA

The Drum

Who made a hole in the drum, in the drum?

Who made a hole in the old drum?

On the drum our drummer drummed.

He drummed a mysterious march on the drum.

Drummer Adrian drummed on the drum.

He drummed and drummed,

He threw down the drum.

There came a ram, the ram ran up,

He butted a hole in the drum, the drum was done for.

Iurii Vladimirov

Russian Poetry for Children by Elena Sokol,
Univ of Tennessee Press, 1984.

Irishka sat with her back against the wall; her head leaned toward Lezunchik as she pounded a little drum made from an empty can of beans with two wooden spoons.

"Is it really necessary for you to pound so loudly? You are giving me a headache."

"*Da*. Loud is good," she said in time with the beat.

"Why?"

She stopped and looked at him. "I don't know. I want to hit something. Anything." And then she pounded the drum some more.

Lezunchik slowly stretched and nonchalantly pushed the can out of her reach.

"Bad cat!" she yelled.

"Irishka, stop pounding! Put the toy away and get into the story circle," Klara said as she struggled with Nina, who had put two legs into one pant leg.

"Uhrrrrr," Lezunchik purred, "story time is my favorite time."

"I want music. *Muzyku! Muzyku!*" she chanted and pounded.

Lezunchik stood. He was a very noble cat and could not be ignored when he wanted to be obeyed. And so, when he turned and stepped with both paws on her stomach and put his snout right into her face and sternly said, "Quiet!" she stopped her noise immediately.

"We are going to the story circle now. Come." He turned and walked gracefully toward the painted circle on the floor. "Leave the spoons and the drum," he said over his shoulder.

She stared at him. How did he know she had picked up the spoons and drum to take with her? He didn't look back. She narrowed her eyes at him. He walked on and ignored her. He was real magic. Sometimes his magic made her a little afraid of him. When he made his go-away magic, he would fade or go see-through. That scared her. She wanted to keep banging, but she didn't want to be alone.

"Wait, I'm coming. I'm coming," she said.

The other children were even slower to come to the circle. Both helpers ran like sheepdogs to round up the children.

Sometimes, Irishka forgot no one could see Lezunchik.

"I will tell you a story while we are waiting," Lezunchik said. "Would you like that?"

She nodded and laid her heavy head on the floor next to his huge, soft paws. She closed her eyes and listened, only to his voice, and not to the crying, yelling children and their shepherding workers.

"Once upon a time, there was a little mouse who lived in a very big house."

She opened one eye to look at him.

"I'm a poet," he smiled.

She squeezed her lips together in that "I don't think so" look, but then shut her eyes again to listen.

"The mouse lived all by herself and was very lonely. Sometimes, she would hear a noise and think someone was coming to visit her. So, she would run out of her little mouse-hole, down the hall, down the stairs, and into the kitchen. There, she would wait. But it would turn out the noise was the wind as it blew under the door, or a limb as it brushed up against the window. She was always so disappointed, and she climbed back up the stairs, walked back down the hall, and slipped back into her little mouse-hole home. It was a very nice little mouse-hole. And the little mouse was an excellent housekeeper. She always made up the matchbox bed and swept clean the floor with a pigeon feather. The mouse sat in her little rocking chair, pulled out her knitting from her mother's old thimble bucket, and clickity-clack, her needles flew as she whiled away the night. One day, however, there was an actual noise. She just knew it. She raced out of her mouse-hole, down the hall and down the steps, but before she could even get to the kitchen, she saw the most incredible sight by the kitchen door: a big white cat. For a full ten seconds, they stared at each other, but then the little mouse broke, turned, and ran as fast as she could. Run, run, run little mouse. Up the stairs, down the hall, and into her little mouse-hole; she was totally out of breath. The cat was right behind her. The little mouse flattened her body against the back wall of her mouse-hole home, but she could still see one big green eye look through the hole in the wall. And it was in that moment the little mouse learned an important lesson."

Irishka didn't move. They were both still and quiet.

"What?" she whispered. "What did she learn?"

"Sometimes a bad situation you know about now is better than a worse situation that might come next."

"Will it always be bad?" she asked with a brief tremor.

"*Nyet*, not always. But maybe for a little while more." Lezunchik licked her face before the tears could make a trail down her cheeks.

Later that day, Lezunchik meowed loudly and awoke Irishka.

"Let's play."

"I don't want to play," she said.

"Come on, bet you can't find me if I hide?"

"No fair, Lezunchik, you can get see-through."

"All right, you go hide and I'll come find you," he said.

She looked at him for a long time. She was tired today. Her head hurt. Her eyes itched, and she felt like coughing all the time. She was hot and grumpy.

"You know how I feel. Why are you making me play?"

"Oooh, oooh. I know. I know. I have the very best idea. Let's both hide and let Klara find us."

She laughed a little. "You are trying to get me in trouble again."

Lezunchik rubbed up against her. His fur felt cool to her face and hands. She wanted to lie down right there and go to sleep again.

"Just one game, Irina Vladimirovna, and we'll both lie down and take a catnap. Ho ho! Cat nap. Funny, *da*? Cat! Nap!"

"I'm not stupid. That's a very old joke. Everybody knows that one."

She stood up and looked around the room. Sure enough, the door to the hallway was ajar. On the other side of the room, Klara read a story to the stupid boy who ran around in circles every day screaming: "The soldiers are coming! The soldiers are coming!" Alya changing diapers—or at least, that's what it sounded like from the bathing room.

"Let's go then!" she said.

And off they went. She was in front and Lezunchik brought up the rear, out the door and down the hall, down the steps, and then to the right. There, they stopped to listen.

"That's the kitchen down that way; I think we should go the other way, don't you?" Lezunchik said.

"I know."

They heard voices in the kitchen and the sounds of dishes and utensils banging as the cook prepared the meal. They turned back and tip-toed past the stairway and through a large, heavy door that was partially open. Before them was another hallway, but this one had a rug in the middle and photographs on the walls of old women and little children in white hats. On both sides of the big outside door, there were pictures of men in uniforms. She looked through the little windows beside the door. It was very white outside except for the steps because someone had scraped them with a shovel.

She pointed across the street, "Look!" she said. "A park."

"That's not a park, you silly goose. That's where they put dead people."

"Oh," she said. "I know about that, I think."

"Let's look for a place to hide."

At the end of the hall was another big door, but she found it locked. They turned back and tested each one of the three doors opposite the outside door. The last door closest to her stairway opened when she turned the knob. It was a playroom with big chairs, a big toy box, and several toys on the floor.

"Oh, look!" she said as she made her way straight for a beautiful doll that sat in a little rocking chair on the floor.

"Hello," she said to the doll. "My name is Irishka. What is yours?" She set the doll to rocking, but the doll wouldn't speak. "Tell her to talk, Lezunchik."

"*Ya ne ponimayu pa russki*—I don't speak Russian," a woman's voice said from the other side of the room.

Irishka whirled about and stared, open-mouthed. There, by the window, stood a woman who looked like a movie star. She wore a black dress with gray fur around the wrists and a fancy hat with a pink and gray feather. The woman had very red lips and smiled at her.

"*Zdrastvuyte*—hello," the woman tried again, but her Russian was terrible.

Irishka giggled. She looked at Lezunchik to see what he thought, but he was playing his invisible game. She turned back to the woman.

"Blah, blah, blah, Anya," the lady said. The only word Irishka understood was Anya. She looked around to see if there was another little girl in the room. The doll must be Anya, so Irishka picked up the doll and carried it to the lady.

"The doll won't talk to me, but maybe it will talk to you," she said, and handed over the doll.

"*Spaciba*," the woman said.

The lady took Irishka's hand, and they sat on a couch that faced the window. She could tell the pretty lady had been crying. She patted the lady on the arm. This was what she always did for Elena when her papa would yell at them and make them cry. But this time, it didn't work, and the woman cried all over again. Irishka scooted away from her. When the lady talked again, the sounds were strange. The lady talked fast and soft; she pulled a little hanky out of her purse and blotted her eyes and made a big sound when she blew her nose. Irishka giggled, then the lady did too.

The lady got quiet and pointed to herself and said, "Mama?"

What a silly thing to say. Elena had told her their mama went with Jesus. And granted, Irishka couldn't remember what her first mama looked like, not exactly. But she wasn't stupid. She knew her real mama would talk to her in Russian, and certainly, would never, ever wear a hat with a feather! Irishka shook her head and said, "*Nyet*."

The woman's tears stopped, and more words spilled out, even faster than before. When she finally quieted, the lady put her hand on Irishka's face and forehead. She frowned. Sometimes Lezunchik got that look.

Irishka took a big breath, but it made her cough. The lady handed the Anya doll back to her. When the door opened, the lady stood up. Irishka knew she would be in trouble if Klara found her here, so she ducked down below the back of the settee.

Lezunchik, who must have been under the settee the whole time, said, "We're in for it now!"

The woman who came in wasn't Klara. This new woman seemed a little familiar, but Irishka couldn't remember. Her head felt very fuzzy.

Lezunchik said, "It's the visiting lady, you silly goose!" *Da*, it was the visiting lady who came into their rooms sometimes and watched the children play. Irishka didn't like it when the lady came because she was a stranger, so she and Lezunchik would sit in a corner and watch the visiting lady from far away.

Right now, visiting lady and feathered hat lady were talking loudly. Irishka decided she couldn't keep her eyes open another minute.

"Lezunchik, wake me up when they stop talking."

9
FEDYA

ST. PETERSBURG, RUSSIA

It could have been an hour, or it could have been two, Fedya didn't know. But he knew one thing for sure—he had to pee. He feared Dima wasn't doing well either; he hadn't heard a groan, a moan, or anything else in a long time. What would he do if Dima died right there in the dumbwaiter with him? He didn't want to think about it.

And so, despite the occasional noise or voices he could hear above, he decided to lower the dumb waiter the rest of the way. First, he pulled his jacket sleeves down around his hands, and gradually, he uncoiled the rope from around Dima's foot and released the ropes that held the dumbwaiter. The weight of both boys, along with the weight of the car, was almost more than Fedya could bear. He braced himself with both legs as best he could; he wasn't sure how much longer he could hold the rope. He could only hope the car wouldn't bang or crash when it reached the basement floor.

When it stopped, Fedya cautiously opened the doors. The cold basement air was dusty, but it was better than what he had been breathing. There was a little light from the high, small basement windows, but not much. He wondered if Dima had soiled himself. He knew dead people did that, so he crawled out right away, just in case.

He secured the ropes, yanked out his two packs, undid the wrapped cigar box and doll and put them inside the sleep pack, along with his blanket. He set them all down in a smaller room off the hallway. Then he searched out a corner where he could relieve himself. What a blessed release.

He headed back around to the dumbwaiter and reviewed his situation. How would he get them away from the building without being seen? Why was he the one who protected other people: first his mother, then his sisters, and now Dima? He was the worst one for this. Fedya stared at the older boy folded up in the dumbwaiter and took the gun away first. He stuffed it into his pants, thought better of it, and put it on the floor. The last thing he needed was to blow off his own leg. He grabbed Dima's feet and pulled him out of the elevator. Fedya cursed when the boy crashed to the floor. He dragged the body across the dirty floor and into the little room with his packs.

Dima wasn't a huge boy, thank God, but he was still bigger than Fedya. Right now, he seemed almost six feet tall. Dima was lean like a swimmer or gymnast and hadn't shaved yet that day, so his face was rough. His lips were pursed tight together like he was trying to hold his breath. His black hair looked greasy, and his face and hands were dirty. Fedya wasn't even sure how old Dima was, maybe eighteen.

Once Fedya got the body into the little room, he put his fingers under the boy's chin to look for a pulse but couldn't find one. Of course, he wasn't even sure where to put pressure on a neck to feel a beat. He put his ear against Dima's chest and heard unsteady heartbeats and felt a slow up and down movement as the boy breathed. Dima was alive, but barely. Fedya checked over the rest of his body and found the bloody towel wadded up under the boy's shirt along his side.

"Oh, God, Dima, did they shoot you, or what?" he asked out loud. But his own voice echoed and scared him even more.

They needed a doctor, or at least someone who knew about injuries and blood. Zoya. *Da,* if he could get Dima over to Zoya's place, she would know what to do. What could he use as a wagon or something? He searched through the old hotel kitchen and storage areas. There was nothing helpful, just old sinks, piles of crates, doors off hinges, broken glass, stacks of newspapers, a row of bins filled with metal pipes, pieces of lumber, tires, and other worthless garbage.

He heard moaning and dashed back to his friend.

"Dima? Dima? It's Fedya," he held up Dima's head.

The boy groaned a little more and tried to pull himself into a sitting position, but his arms flailed, and he cried out as he felt the pain in his side.

"Wait, Dima, you're hurt, I tell you. Dima, can you hear me? It's Fedya."

Dima laid back his head into Fedya's lap and tried to breathe more deeply. He opened his eyes to slits.

"So it is, my little man," he rasped. "I could use a drink, Fedkins. Could you get me a drink?"

"Not really, Dima. I mean, I could look for some water."

"Water? I mean vodka, if you have it," he said.

"Dima, you're hurt. Did someone shoot you? Most of the other comrades, they're dead, Dima. I mean, I saw Borya. See, I came by to get my other pack and I knocked, and no one answered, and I didn't know the door was open at first, but then, the *politsiya* came and I didn't know what to do and I tried the door again because I knew you needed to wake up if the police were here and—"

"Shut up, Fedya. I need to think. I'm pretty tired. Maybe I should take a nap."

"*Nyet. Nyet.* I don't think so. I don't think you should sleep, Dima. I think you're supposed to stay awake now." But Dima closed his eyes and sank back into silence.

"Dima. Please. I need to get you to Zoya's. Dima. Help me. I don't know how to get you to Zoya's."

Dima shook his head a little and tried to focus on Fedya's face. "What? Zoya? *Da,* a good idea. Take a bike; they're in the back container or maybe in room 408. No, don't go there, room 408. Don't go there."

"The big container? A bike?"

"Listen here, take this," he grappled around his neck and pulled out a chain with a small oblong black plastic case. "Take this key. Keep it safe for me. Alright? Guard it with your life."

"Sure, sure. But Dima—" It was too late. Dima passed out again.

He took the chain off Dima and put it around his neck. Now he wore two chains: one from his mother and one from Dima. His only choice was to find Zoya and bring her here. He took some of the stacked newspapers and wrapped them around and under Dima as best he could. He even wadded one up like a little pillow. What if Dima died? Should he take the boy's identification? And what about his money? If the *politsiya* found the money, they'd keep it. Besides, Dima wouldn't need money then.

His hands fumbled and shook, but he bent down to the sleeping youth and checked all his pockets. There wasn't much, a sign that Dima had jumped into the dumbwaiter quickly. But he found a wad of American dollars, a ring of regular keys, an old gold watch, a comb, a tin of loose tobacco along with a few half-smoked cigarettes, his identity booklet, and passport.

Fedya took everything except the identity papers, passport, and smokes. When he and Zoya came back, he reasoned, he'd put it all back. If it didn't work out, he would keep to his plan and, most likely, he'd make good use of these small treasures.

On his way out, he picked up the gun and jammed it into his sleeping pack. The way things were going, he might have to use it.

Fedya shouldered both packs and looked for the back stairs. A door led him out near the rear of the building, where he had seen the container from the window. After several tries, he found the key on the keyring that fit the lock. Inside, the container held more than a few bicycles; they had packed it with boxes and boxes of electronic equipment, computers, microwaves, and other things. Fedya had never seen so many new appliances in one place. He wanted to explore, but he knew his time was short, so he grabbed the first bike that was not too big for him, rolled it out of the container and snapped shut the padlock on the door behind him.

The sun was at its zenith for this time of year, but still hung low around the buildings. He strapped one of his packs to the bike and carried the other on his back. He rode slowly, first around the building where other children had gathered to watch the police cars, and then away. He maneuvered the bike through the slush and stuck to streets he knew would have less traffic, even if it meant deeper snow gullies.

In about thirty minutes, he found Zoya's housing block, one of the many concrete apartment units built in the name of equality and thrift. That's what his father always said when his mother wanted to move into one of them. "All the flats are the same except for the two flats in the middle of each floor because of their balconies. We could never afford one of those. They built them back in the '60s." Fedya thought they just looked shabby. He was glad they never moved away from the city center. The telephone and electrical towers marched like black giants for miles and miles through the streets.

Each section had numbers and letters. He recognized Zoya's entrance from his last visit with Dima because of the red, white, and blue graffiti that looked like an American flag. No one locked the front doors anymore, so Fedya carried his bike inside. He knew better than to leave it outside, where a passerby could steal it. Heavy or not, he dragged it up to the third floor. Dima had brought Fedya here a few weeks earlier but made him wait in the hall outside the flat. Dima said Zoya lived with three other girls and a fat woman Dima called *babushka* to her face, but *ona d'avol*—old hag, behind her back.

Fedya knocked and the *ona d'avol* answered, in the same manner she had for Dima.

"What do you want, you little hoodlum?" she barked.

Today, her black inky hair hung down over her shoulders. She had painted her lips bright red and outlined her eyes in black cohl. The old woman smoked a dark brown cigarette and when she talked, the smoke puffed out of her mouth with her words. She wore a faded, yellow Japanese kimono coat, but Fedya could see the tops of her old breasts and even though he didn't want to, he stared at them.

"I...I..." he stuttered. "I need to see Zoya."

"Oh, you do, do you? And since when does she bed baby hooligans like you?" she belched.

"What?" Fedya reddened.

"Go away, little gangster, the girls are all working." She pushed the door to close it.

He blocked the door with his foot without a second thought. "When will she be home?"

"What are you doing, you little piece of shit? I said the girls are working. You're making a scene and the customers don't like it."

"But I've got to see her, I tell you." And with that, he shoved open the door and slipped under the old woman's arm and into the room.

He was such an idiot. It all came to him in a rush as he saw Zoya's roommate, Leya, half dressed, with a police hat on her head, straddling a drunken officer in an undershirt and black pants with his fly open. The room was thick with smoke and with many odd smells. He turned to apologize, but the evil *ona d'avol* smacked him so hard he went down. She kicked him several times as he rolled on the floor.

He screamed for help when Zoya came out of her room with a man, dark and good-looking. For a second, Fedya thought it was Dima and called out to him.

"Dima, help me! Help me."

"Grusha Stanislavska! What the hell are you doing?" Zoya screeched and ran to the boy. The man followed and pulled the shrieking hyena off him, laughing as he held Grusha.

"Come, *babushka*, are you going to let a boy get the better of you? Come on, come on. Get your Yegor a drink, eh?" he crooned into her ear.

"He barged right past me, the little shit! I didn't invite him," she told him.

Zoya was stronger than she looked and yanked Fedya up by the arm and shoved him into her room.

"Yegor, could you be a saint and give me a minute?" she said over her shoulder, "Something must have happened."

"It will cost you, Zoya, you know that." He put his arm around the old woman anyway and escorted her toward the kitchen table, set up like a bar. "You look very fetching in this kimono, Grusha Stanislavska. Don't worry about Zoya. I'll make sure she pays for this little boy toy."

"But he barged in here. You know who he is, don't you, Yegor? He runs for Dmitri Nikolai."

"*Da*, but, not for much longer, I'm sure," Yegor answered.

Fedya glimpsed the two of them before Zoya closed the door. He heard what Grusha Stanislavska said about him.

"What did she mean, Zoya, that I run for Dima? I don't know what that means."

Zoya leaned against the door and stared at Fedya. "You really don't know? You are such a beautiful boy. Your hair is long. I like it. You will be quite the lady killer with those blue eyes. Why are you so angry? Sit down. This is not the best time for you to come and visit me." Zoya smiled.

"I'm not here to visit you. I'm here to ask for your help. You need to listen to me," he snapped back.

"Give me a minute."

"But Zoya—"

She stopped him with a look and then walked over to the nightstand and lit a cigarette. He tried to catch his breath and looked around her room. He had never been in a woman's bedroom besides his mother's. Now it hit him. Zoya wasn't wearing much either, just a silky robe and maybe underpants. Her robe had fallen open, and he could see her breasts. When she caught him staring at her body, she pulled the robe closed.

"Sorry," he said, and looked down.

"Fedya, I have to get back to work. Sit down and tell me what's going on?"

He sat on the edge of the bed and tried to think about where he should begin. He felt very shaky, and his two backpacks were heavy.

"Come on, Fedya, you're getting me in lots of trouble with Grusha Stanislavska. They'll make me pay for this time, so out with it."

"It's Dima. He's hurt, like shot or stabbed or something."

"What are you saying? What happened? What do you mean? Where is he? Who did it?" She grabbed his arm and shook it while she fired questions at him, but never gave him a chance to answer.

"I'll tell you. I'll tell you. Stop, Zoya, you're hurting me."

"I'm sorry. All right? I'm sorry." She sat beside him on the bed.

He told her what happened, from the moment he walked up the steps of the Black Willow that morning to bicycling here.

"We've got to help him somehow. He could be dead already."

She didn't speak right away. She went to the door and took a quick peek. She walked back and forth, murmured to herself, and gestured. At last, she stopped pacing and came back to him.

"All right, listen. This will not be easy for me."

"What? Why not?"

"Fedkins, are you really so stupid? I'm working. You saw Grusha Stanislavska, you think she'll let me walk out of here because I feel like it?"

With that, she dragged out an old box from under the bed and pulled out some underwear, jeans, and sweaters. She pulled off her robe and Fedya's eyes drank in the beauty of her body. He had never seen a naked woman, not a real woman like Zoya. He had helped bathe his mother while she was sick, but her body had become thin and brittle, while his sisters' bodies still looked like little boy bodies without the boy parts. But here, Zoya's body was like the magazine pictures at the hangout. As she put on her bra she caught him staring.

"Fedya, you are a naughty boy. Polite boys turn around when ladies are dressing."

He snapped down his head and looked at the floor; his face flushed.

She put some clothing in a big bag, then kicked the box back under her bed. "I'm going to shout, and you run out of here with this bag. Here, take off your coat and throw it over the bag. You need to run fast out of the flat, so no one sees it. Understand? Run all the way out of the building. I don't think they'll bother to chase you, but if they do, act like you're running away. Come back through the back door and hide in the toilet on the first floor. Wait for me there. When I come, I'll knock Dima's knock. You know it, *da*?"

"*Da*. But what about my bicycle?"

"You'll have to leave it for now. We'll walk. Where did you get it, anyway?"

"Well, uh, Dima gave me the keys to the Willow." She looked at him in disbelief. He repeated, "He did, I tell you," and pulled the keys from his pants pocket and showed her.

She snatched them from him and put them in a small handbag, then added that to the stuff in the larger bag. "I'll keep them for you, to keep them safe."

"But Zoya—"

"Don't argue with me, Fedkins. If you want to live through this, you'll do what I say. Are you ready? There's more to this than you know. Understand?"

Then Zoya screamed at him and called him all kinds of names. She even threw a book at him, and he yanked the door open and fled. He didn't bother to look at anyone on the way out. She was almost too believable. She chased him herself all the way down the hall.

He was out the front door before he knew it, with a vague sense of Grusha Stanislavska screaming after him and Yegor laughing. Fedya zigzagged four or five blocks before he doubled back through the alleys. He almost despaired as he tried to find her building from the back, but finally spotted the same small red, white, and blue flag stuck in a window and took a chance they put it there on purpose for the clients who came from this direction. Once inside, he recognized the hallway and found the toilet. The smell nearly made him gag as he stepped inside, closed, and locked the door, then used his packs and her bag as a stool opposite the toilet hole.

He leaned his head back on the wall and sighed, but then pulled upright when he saw roaches marching across the opposite wall. He checked the wall behind him; he didn't see any bugs, but he pulled his packs from the wall and laid his head down on his folded arms instead. Having dozed off, he startled when he heard the quick three-tap that Dima had taught him to use at the Willow. When he opened the door, Zoya slipped in and held her finger to his lips. It was tight in the little toilet. Her skin smelled like the flower petals his mother used to collect from damaged flowers at the market after she dried and crushed them. Zoya also had another smell, almost like old wet leaves or dirty underwear.

"Get up, I need my clothes," Zoya hissed.

Minutes later, they slipped out the back door and through the gate. Before they rounded the corner, Fedya looked back and saw someone watching from Zoya's window; the big man, Yegor, he thought. Fedya tried to stop to be sure, but she dragged at his arm.

"Wait, I think Yegor saw us," he said.

"Sounds like my kind of luck. Come on. I don't have much time before they figure out I'm not coming back."

"You're not? Why? What do you mean?"

"Never mind, you wouldn't understand."

"I'm not stupid, Zoya. You treat me like a little kid. I'm not."

"*Horosho*—fine. Don't get nasty on me. I've got enough nastiness in my life right now."

She walked fast, and Fedya practically had to run to keep up with her. He stumbled and almost fell. She turned, but he waved her off.

"I'm all right."

"When was the last time you ate?"

"I don't know. Yesterday, I guess."

"Come on," she said, and Zoya cut through some alleyways and plunged into Moskovsky Prospekt and the market. She bought two hard rolls and two small blocks of cheese.

"Here, eat while we walk. We have to keep moving."

"Tell me about that man, the one you call Yegor."

"He's a bad boy, Fedkins. You don't want to know him."

"Why?"

"Please, I don't want to talk about him right now."

"Why?"

"Are you deaf? I said, no talking." She glared at him, and he silenced. "He's in a kind of gang, like Dima, but different, bigger, new Russians."

"Big? Like who? Like the mafia or Stepanov or what?"

"Where did you hear that name? Look, forget it. He's bad news. Stay away from Yegor. He'll kill you." She tossed the rest of her roll into a trash can.

"Why were you with him?"

Zoya stopped and stared at him. "You wouldn't understand; you're a kid."

"Maybe I would. You call me a kid, but maybe I'm bigger than you think. Maybe I'm smarter too."

"Look, it was a deal? A deal. I made a deal to protect Dima."

"Oh. I don't think it worked."

"*Nyet*, I don't think so either," she said to herself.

They walked on, faster now, without speaking, and Fedya ate his roll and cheese. Sooner than he expected, they saw the Black Willow in the distance. It was close to four o'clock now and sunset, but with the heavy cloud cover, it was already quite dark. The Willow was quiet. He thought the police would still be around. Instead, the building appeared desolate. It was draped in bright yellow tape.

"Where did all the police go?" he asked.

"They're gone. They took everyone away. You told me the boys were dead, so what's there to do? They take pictures, then they load the bodies into black bags and take them to the coffin maker. The *politsiya* cares little about gang boys, anyway. I think they like it when the mafia and gangs kill each other."

"How do you know it was the mafia?"

She looked at Fedya, turned away, and didn't answer him. Fedya tried to understand that look but couldn't. There was a dreadful glint in her eyes.

"Where is he, Fedya? Where did you leave Dima?"

"In the basement, where the kitchens used to be. There's a back way; I'll show you. You don't think they found him, do you?"

"Who? The *politsiya*? I don't know. Maybe. Probably."

With that, they became quiet as they slipped under the yellow tape and into the back door of the Willow.

"It's too dark, Fedya. I can't see a foot in front of me."

"I have a light in my pack."

Fedya led the way down the steps and into the little room. He stopped in the doorway and swung the light all around the room. No Dima. It was all gone, even the rolled-up newspaper pillow. Zoya came up behind him.

"They got him," she said.

"Don't say that. Maybe he woke up and left on his own."

"Don't be stupid, Fedkins. Be glad. I'll bet he's in some nice, warm hospital somewhere drinking black tea and pinching a nurse's ass."

"What now?" Fedya asked.

"I don't know."

Just then, there was a noise above them. Fedya turned off his flashlight. They huddled together by the wall of the little room. The scrape of a door opening sounded down the hall. They could see a beam of light dance across the walls. Fedya took Zoya by the hand and they worked their way to the other side of the room. Fedya found the stacks of newspapers he had used to fashion Dima's bed. He pulled her with him, and they crouched behind the stacks. It was a poor hiding place, but right now, it was the best they had. He quietly retrieved Dima's gun out of his sleeping pack.

10
IRINA & SUSAN

CLINIC NEXT TO CHILDREN'S HOUSE
NUMBER EIGHT
ST. PETERSBURG, RUSSIA

The elephant didn't believe his ears!

And from great excitement

He gobbled up a barrel of jam.

And in that barrel of jam

Was his mood!

The jam

Was strawberry.

His mood

Was excellent.

Emma Moshkovskaia (1926—1981) from *Russian Poetry for Children* by Elena Sokol.

Da, they were arguing. Irishka couldn't understand anything clearly, but all the adults seemed furious. It reminded her of Fedya and Lenushka. She squeezed her eyes shut to find Fedya in her mind. She could see him in his green army jacket and the funny green hat. But Fedya's face, she couldn't see at all; it was like looking through a window in heavy rain.

"Lezunchik, are you close by?" she whispered.

A big bump at the bottom of the blanket stirred.

"Wake up, please. I have to ask you a question."

The blanket twitched, but nothing more.

"I know you can hear me, so stop pretending. This is important. Tell me, what do you know about my family."

The bump shimmied up along her body. Eventually, two enormous, yellow polka dot paws and a large pink head peeked out of the covers beside her shoulder. She smiled at him.

"You are colorful today. But your colors are very noisy. How can you sleep?"

"My colors do not interfere with my rest. But there is a little girl who has not stopped talking since this morning. I don't remember you being such a blabbermouth."

"That's because I was sick. I'm getting better. Look!" She opened her mouth and stuck out her tongue at him.

He covered his face with his paws.

"Stop, stop! I can see all the way down to your belly button."

"Really? Let me look down inside you."

"If I open my mouth that wide, it will be to have lunch!"

She laughed. The women turned to look at her from the corner of the room.

Today, hat lady had two bright blue circle earrings that hung from her ears, like little floating balloons. Her red lips smiled, and when she turned back to the other ladies, the little balloons swung back and forth, like a dance.

"Irishka, what do you want?" Lezunchik said.

She looked at him and put her hand on his head. His fur was soft. When she touched him, he purred like a little kitten. He could be such a baby. When she folded back his ears and looked inside, she could see golden sparkles. Once, he told her, the sparkles helped him hear things from very far away.

"Can you hear them talking?"

"Who?" Lezunchik yawned.

"You know who. Them. The women. Isn't that visiting lady? And the other one, she's from the children's house, the director. Why is our hat lady so cross?"

"That's not the question you asked me while I was asleep," Lezunchik said and kneaded her shoulder. "You probably don't even remember what you wanted to ask me, do you?"

"*Da,* I do."

"Here's my answer: I know what you know and maybe a bit more."

"If that's true, can you help me remember my mother?"

The cat did not answer right away. He looked into the girl's eyes and she into his. He searched inside her for the memories, but truthfully, there weren't many to gather, so he began the story this way.

"Elizaveta was—"

"Who's that?"

"Elizaveta Andreevna was your mother."

"Not Elena?"

"Irina Vladimirovna, you are interrupting me, and I am going to lose my way. I am talking about a time before time for you."

"Like 'once upon a time'?"

He looked at her sternly, and the tips of his fur turned dark blue. She might have worried, but it was hard to be afraid of a dark blue cat with yellow polka dot paws. She put her finger to her lips.

"Shh, I know, go on."

"Your mother's given name was Elizaveta Andreevna Ozola. She had two men in her life: Ivan, who fathered your brother and sister; and Vladimir, who was your father. Your mother had one sister, Ilze, who died many years ago, and a brother, Uldis, who lives far away. Your mother was a strong woman who worked hard all her life. When she was young, she played the violin. She and her brother would play together and make wonderful music. But her hands failed her and became stiff. She met Ivan, the first man, at a place where Russian soldiers would go to meet girls. They fell in love. They were happy there. When the soldiers came back to St. Petersburg, she came with him, and this is where your brother and sister were born. When Ivan died, she cleaned government buildings and never stopped working until she became sick. Valdimir only stayed two years and was very cruel to all of you."

She wanted to say something, but thought better of it when she caught the look in his eyes. But honestly, now she remembered Elena telling her this story.

He went on. "Your grandmother and grandfather were from a place called Latvija. This is too hard to explain. But you must know this, Irishka: your mother loved you very much."

"But—"

"Wait. There's a little more I can tell you." Lezunchik paused and closed his eyes. "*Da.* Your mother was tall, like Klara at the children's house. Elizaveta had dark hair and gray eyes. When she was healthy, her hair was quite long and beautiful, and she always wore it wrapped at the back of her head for work. She had many wrinkles already on her face and hands, but when she smiled, they all worked together to make her face soft and happy. Her teeth were not very good, and she smoked cigarettes, which left a smell in the house. But she loved to walk in the parks and along the Neva. She grew up with her brother Uldis and sister Ilze on a farm in Latvija. Elizaveta owned two precious things: her wedding ring and a chain she always wore around her neck. Do you remember the necklace, a silver circle with two flying swans? Ivan, her first husband, gave it to her. I think your mother always wanted to fly away, too. *Lebedev* is Ivan's family name, and that is the name she chose for you to have. Elena is your sister, and Fedya is your brother. Never forget those names, my dear sweet and wonderful child: Fedya and Elena, your missing swans."

"But where are they?"

"I don't know, perhaps near, perhaps far. They should be right here all the time." And with that, the big cat thumped Irina's chest with a paw, now pale blue and slightly translucent.

"I don't care!" Susan said.

She knew that Masha, her agency coordinator, was trying to keep up with the translations, but the director talked over them both. No one really heard Susan or listened to her plan.

"I don't care," she repeated. "Stop. Please listen to me. We finished everything. You promised me a child and I expect to get one. I plan to climb onto an airplane with a little girl. They look almost identical. We have all the documents, the tickets, and the passport. We have everything that is needed. Tell me! Who would know the difference?"

The orphanage director, Ludmilla Demochevna, tried to interrupt again, but Susan wasn't interested. She could tell the director considered her a royal pain in the butt, but she didn't care.

"Listen to me," she continued, with Masha's translation not far behind, "Anya was a beautiful child. My husband and I prayed for the girl for nearly two years. I have slept with her picture under my pillow. I had an entire church full of people, hundreds of people, who prayed for Anya. Don't you understand? This little girl was my husband's legacy to me. His promise. Will you break my heart even more? I tell you, something divine has happened here. This Anya—"

"Her name is Irina, not Anya. The girl you adopted is dead. I'm sorry, but this little girl, Irina, is not stable. I tell you, she doesn't even speak most of the time. She is never affectionate. She looks off into the air. She talks to objects. We want to protect you," Director Ludmilla said.

"But you're not listening. I believe this child is a gift from God. Is she so different from the first Anya? She has no mother or father, no one in the world to love her or care for her, and yet, right now, she can become part of a real life with a future. She'll have clothing to wear and food to eat and other healthy children to play with. She'll have neighbors and holidays and bathtubs full of water. She'll have fruit and school and—"
She was blabbering. She knew it. She stopped, collapsed onto a chair, and cried.

Had she lost her mind? Maybe everyone was right, and she was trying too hard to replace all the love she had lost in the last two years.

"Please." She started again. "My first baby, Angie, lived only three weeks. She was so tiny, four pounds, born prematurely, with a long list of physical issues. After she died, the doctor told me I could not bear another child. It was like a second death. The pain was unbearable.

"But then, after a year, Tom wanted to adopt a child. At first, I was afraid, but by the time we completed the home study and looked at some pictures, it was like a miracle.

"But our joy was short-lived. Right after we submitted our dossier, Tom got sick: esophageal cancer. He fought it, of course. We both did. He endured the first surgery and hoped the doctors 'got it all.' But it was not to be. After two full rounds of chemo and radiation, Tom called it quits. We enjoyed three more wonderful months before we called in hospice. Tom insisted I continue with the adoption after he died. Tom passed in June. Please, I know this is extreme, but I believe it's God's hand on all of us. I want to be Mama Susan. Please."

"She's crying," Irishka said.

"I know. She's very sad. You could cheer her up."

"How?"

He began cleaning himself: first, several swipes of the tongue on his paw and then a quick arc across his face, one, two, three swipes, and a swoosh. "Call her Mama Susan. I bet that will stop her bawling."

"How do you taste when you lick your fur?"

"Like a chocolate torte!"

"Let me try!"

He pulled away from her.

"Call your Mama Susan. She needs you."

"You are a lot of trouble. You act like you know everything."

"All true. Now, call her! She will come over to you. Reach your arms out to her."

"I don't like that. I don't want her to touch me. I don't know her."

"Do you want to get out of this white bed and this white room?"

"*Da*, but—"

"Do as I say, or at the very least, stand up and call her name."

"Oh, all right." She stood up as best she could and held on to the rail. "Mama Susan?" she whispered.

"Again, but a little louder."

She looked down and narrowed her eyes at him. He stood up and growled low.

"Do as I say, Irina Vladimirovna!"

And so, louder, she called out and waved, "Mama Susan! Mama Susan!"

The room became quiet. Mama Susan looked over; the black makeup around her eyes was smudged from crying. The director's mouth dropped open as Mama Susan hurried over and wrapped her arms around Irishka.

There was more confusion, with everyone talking. The visiting lady tried to explain to Irishka what Mama Susan was saying.

"This kind lady is Susan Spencer. She is telling us you are a fine little girl. She wants you to live with her. She wants you to come to America and be her special little girl, to be her little Anya."

Mama Susan talked, then Masha talked, and the whole time, she stroked Irina's hair. That felt good. But the best part was her smell. What was it?

"Are you listening, Irina Vladimirovna? Do you understand what this woman wants from you?" the visiting lady said.

"She smells like flowers at the market! That's what it is, blue flowers."

Masha turned to Susan. "I'm sorry, Mrs. Spencer. Ludmilla Demochevna has been warning you that this girl is different, perhaps not stable. For instance, right now she's saying something about the smell of blue flowers."

Susan pulled away and looked into Irishka's eyes. "You are an amazing girl." Masha translated for the little girl as she continued. "You are right. I am wearing perfume that smells like blue flowers." She held up her wrist to the child. "You like it?"

Irishka laughed. "You smell blue, like the sky." Masha hesitated but translated, anyway.

"Blue, like the ocean," Susan said.

"Blue, like the little eggs that the mama bird hides in her nest."

"Blue, like your eyes."

"And blue, like my cat!"

Now it was Susan's turn to laugh. "What cat?"

Susan looked at Masha, who was clueless. When the girl spoke again, Masha translated.

"Lezunchik. Right here. Can't you see him either?" Irishka stood on her bed, turned, and pointed to the other end. But then she blinked and started looking around as though he had disappeared. Irishka looked under her bed.

"Anya? Irishka!" Susan said, trying to get her attention back.

Masha interrupted and spoke directly to the girl, apparently not translating at all, which was quite irritating to Susan. That kind of talk wasn't good for Anya, or Irishka, or whatever the girl's name should be. How would she put these names together?

"What did you say to her, Masha? Why does she look so frightened?"

"She is talking foolishness. I told her. There is no cat in the hospital! People will think she is crazy, and she will have to go to a special hospital where they tie people up to keep them quiet."

"What? Why would you say such a terrible thing? Please don't do that again and only translate what I say, and I mean word for word and nothing else. That is your job. Do you understand me? Do not add your opinion or anything else. I mean it."

"Very well, Mrs. Spencer. I am trying to help. She is a difficult girl."

Susan turned to the girl. "Anya...Irina...uh, Irishka! I think I know something about you. I think you have a special friend, a big cat, right? I have a neighbor girl who has a best friend just like yours, but he is a dragon!"

Irishka's eyes grew big.

"Da, it's true. He's a funny little dragon. He's the same size as my little friend and they go everywhere together."

"What's his name?" Irishka said.

"Let me think for a moment. I think, yes, I remember now. It's Samuel. I think that's a very funny name for a dragon, don't you?"

Irishka shrugged.

"So, I want you to know that if you come to live with me, that your cat—your friend—what is his name? He might like to come along."

"Lezunchik."

"*Da,* Lezunchik can come with you. I have a big house and a garden. Would you like to invite Lezunchik to live with us?"

Irishka looked all over the room for him, but could not find him.

"He's hiding again," she said.

Ludmilla Demochevna stepped up to them. She and Masha had a rapid-fire conversation that eluded Susan altogether.

"Mrs. Spencer, come, we have some business to finish," Ludmilla said, with Masha translating.

"That's all right. That's not a problem. Tell Anya Irina—" She liked the sound of that, "Tell Anya Irina, the grown-ups must finish our business. There are many details and many plans we must make. Tell me, Anya Irina, would you like to go on a grand adventure with me?"

Masha translated. At first, the girl did nothing, but then glanced past Susan's shoulder and slowly nodded her head.

Susan looked up at the wall where the girl had looked but saw nothing. She turned to the two Russian women and pleaded with her eyes.

"All right, Susan Spencer," Ludmilla Demochevna said. "We will do as you ask, but as God is my witness," she crossed herself three times, "I pray nothing tragic will happen. We have given you fair warning about the difficulties. And I hope you understand, there will be some, well, let us say, additional expenses."

"Believe me, the money is the least of my worries, Madam Director. Besides, I have already had my quota of tragedies. I believe God is ready to bless me—and her."

11
ELENA

ST. PETERSBURG, RUSSIA

The girls sat in the dayroom at two long worktables. Although they had been instructed to study since tests were coming up right before the December holiday, most of them gossiped about the day's interviews with Olga Petrovna.

Interest in Elena's story paled next to the looming interviews. She became the mute again, except with the new girls, Yuliya, and quiet Aniya. The three bonded. They sat apart from the others at a small table against the wall. Both Aniya and Elena were happy for Yuliya, who had also been selected. The rest of the girls were complaining about the selections.

"Maybe we'll have another chance when they come back next year," one girl whined.

"But why were they here? I don't understand any of this," fat Svetlana said.

"It's for camp. They come every year and pick one or two from each center," Baiba, the oldest girl said. "They were here last year."

"But who did they pick last year?" Svetlana asked.

"They're from social services," Lukina, next to oldest, said. "You'd think they'd give the more mature girls a chance, but no. That old hen didn't even give Baiba and me a single look. It's not fair."

"No one went last year," Baiba said. "They didn't pick anyone from here. I don't care. For all we know, they take you to Siberia to work on a farm."

"Really?" fat Svetlana said. "But you said it was for camp."

"I hate camp. They make you swim," someone added.

Larissa, the tomcat, and her accomplice Galina whispered behind their books while Oksana turned away and rolled her eyes along with Tatiana, the beauty queen. Then all four laughed out loud. They could afford to laugh. They were the chosen ones.

"Why do you roll your eyes?" fat Svetlana asked. "What did I say? I know Siberia is a terrible place. Who wants to swim there?"

"Baiba made a joke, Svetlana," Larissa said. "Why would they pick the smartest and prettiest girls for something bad? They wouldn't. It's a special honor to be picked."

"What? They picked you for pretty? Ha! Maybe they don't realize you're a gypsy," Baiba said as she crossed the room.

"You have a problem with the Roma?" Larissa stood abruptly.

Everyone got quiet.

"I'm not afraid of you, Baiba," Larissa continued. "At least I haven't sold myself on the street for a few coins, or do you even make that much?"

Baiba froze briefly as she reached up to put away her books. She placed them on the shelf, lifted her coat from the hook underneath, and turned. Everyone gasped. She held a long nail file like a knife. The girls scrambled away; chair legs screeched along the floor and several chairs fell over. Elena stood.

"Baiba, you're wanted in the office," Elena said too loudly.

Baiba turned. "How do you know?"

Elena stammered, "I...I...forgot to tell you, before."

Baiba hesitated, then grabbed her day pack and said on the way out, "I'll get even with you later, gypsy girl. I won't forget your insult."

"Get screwed," Larissa said. She charged at Baiba, but ran square into Elena instead; both fell.

Everyone laughed, then slowly regrouped, and pulled their chairs back to the tables.

"Sorry, Larissa," Elena said from the floor.

"Right, sure, I bet," she said as she got up and walked away.

Lubya scurried in and called for their attention. "There has been a change. I have a new list of girls for the interviews: Galina, Oksana, Yuliya, Tatiana, and Elena." She looked around. "Elena, why are you on the floor?"

Larissa whirled around. "Wait a minute. You didn't call my name. You've made a mistake. Elena was never on the list."

"*Nyet*, it's you that's not on the list anymore," Lubya said.

"What?"

"Oh my God, Larissa, what did you do?" Tatiana asked.

"That's not fair. What the hell?" Larissa raged.

"Larissa! Go to the quiet room now! You will not speak like that to me," Lubya said.

"But I was on the list!" Larissa said again.

Someone chanted, "Gyp, gyp, gyp!" and several of the girls snickered.

Larissa whirled to the group and glared, challenging them to say anything more. When she turned to Elena, she held up her index and middle fingers, pointed them at the girl and then slapped her wrist with the other hand. Everyone froze. It was a gypsy curse for sure. Larissa laughed as she left the dayroom.

"Me? But why? I mean, I—" Elena said.

"Go to the office with the other girls now," Lubya said.

"But how did this change?" Elena stammered.

"I don't know, Elena. But listen to me, be careful with that Roma girl. She's not someone you want as an enemy," Lubya said, and clucked.

"Thank you, Lubya," Elena said.

"Don't thank me," Lubya said. "I don't trust these government people one bit. You watch yourself. I've heard people disappear because some doctor wants to use their body parts."

At first, Elena wanted to laugh, but when she realized Lubya was quite serious, she feared the worst. Could it be true? *Nyet*, not possible. Was it?

The five girls walked to the office in single file.

They sat outside the office. The social workers called each girl into the director's office one by one. When Galina came out, she looked nervous and told Tatiana that she was next.

As Tatiana stood to go in, Galina blurted, "It wasn't too bad until they asked a lot of stupid questions about my family. What family?!" She snorted as she departed.

Tatiana was not one to show fear, at least not in front of the other girls, so she walked into the director's office with her head high. Elena admired her for that. Even though Tatiana could be a nuisance and self-centered, she was brave. Her interview wasn't long, but it felt longer because Oksana babbled nervously the whole time.

When Tatiana came out, she gave Oksana a wink, which must have been a signal between them because Oksana calmed and walked into the director's office like a little princess.

Whatever good thoughts Elena had about Tatiana reversed when the girl boasted, "They're only taking three girls, so the two of you might as well forget it."

Yuliya asked Tatiana, "D-d-did they ask you about your family too?"

"*Da,* but I have nothing to be ashamed of. Do you? My father died in a mining accident in Chelyabinsk. Of course, I told them all about my aunt and how she sends me extra clothes and treats from Perm. I told them how my mother is an actress and travels all over the world, which is why it was better for my family if I stayed here for a while. Everyone says I look like my mother. As soon as I'm old enough, I'm going to travel with my mother." She headed for the door.

"But Tatiana, what is it all about?" Elena asked.

"It's camp all right, but it's a camp in America!" She flounced out of the little waiting area.

Yuliya watched the girl leave and turned to Elena. "America. How can that be?" Yuliya collapsed into herself and covered her face with the bottom of her sweater.

"Why are you crying? Don't you want to go to America?" Elena asked.

"Of course," she said into the wool. "But if they find out about my father, they'll never let me go. He's in prison, Elena. Prison. Please don't tell anyone," and then she cried even harder.

"I can keep secrets," Elena said. She thought of the little coin and the other objects she had found since that first frosty night: a yellow pencil, a metro map, a matchbook, and the most precious of all, a pearl ring. They were all dropped objects, things the visitors didn't notice as they clucked and examined the poor, orphaned children. The challenge had been to find a safe hiding place. In the end, she dug a hole in her mattress along the top edge. For now, it was enough.

Elena wanted to offer Yuliya some comfort, but her own hopes had dissolved as well. Tatiana was right: Elena and Yuliya were out of the running. Family. What could Elena reveal? Both of her parents were dead, but she would not talk about her brother and sister. Her head throbbed and her eyes felt prickly as she realized what an orphan she really was. She got up and looked at an old picture on the wall to hide the welling up of her tears from Yuliya.

"Elena," Yuliya said behind her, "maybe I should make up a story like Tatiana. I mean, you don't believe her, do you? I don't think her mother is a famous actress."

Elena didn't answer; her focus was on the picture, a photograph of a ballerina with white feathers around her head like a tight hat. The rest of her costume was like a bird, a beautiful white bird. One hand gracefully touched her shoulder while the other touched the tip of her feathered tutu. Her legs were so straight, and she stood on the very tips of her toes in shiny ballet shoes. Under the picture, there was a nameplate that read Baronovna Irina (her sister's name). It was so odd to find a ballerina here among all the other pictures of stodgy old Russian presidents and party leaders.

Elena didn't hear the door open. Valentina's voice interrupted her reverie. "Why, hello, Elena Ivanovna. I am glad we see each other again after all." To Oksana, who slipped past the social worker, she said, "Thank you, Oksana. Please do not share our conversation with the other girls. You understand?"

"*Da,* Valentina Alexandrovna, *spaciba* Valentina Alexandrovna," Oksana said as she rushed out.

"We will speak with Yuliya next," Valya said. "I'm sorry Elena, you'll have to be patient a little longer."

Yuliya stood up; Elena noticed she had stopped crying.

"Yuliya," Elena blurted out, "I think Valentina Alexandrovna already knows most of your story, don't you? They won't need to ask you all those same family questions." She turned to Valentina and hoped she got the message.

Valentina stared at Elena and then at Yuliya, whose face was quite splotchy, her fists clenched.

"Yuliya, you do not need to be afraid. Look at me, dear." Valentina closed the door behind her. "This is a special opportunity for you, for all the girls. You must show Olga Petrovna that you are strong and happy, not sad and depressed. I know you can do this because I saw it in your eyes the other day. Come now, stand straight, and think of your mother. Didn't she tell you to be brave, to dream the impossible?"

Yuliya could not have been more shocked. "How do you know that?"

From inside the room, Elena heard the older woman call Valentina's name in a harsh voice.

"Coming!" she answered. Valentina opened the door and whispered, "Ready, Yuliya?"

The girl nodded and walked into the room.

Valentina turned to Elena, pointed to the photograph, and said, "Isn't she beautiful? She is the Swan Queen Odette from the ballet *Swan Lake.* Have you ever seen a ballet?"

Elena shook her head.

Olga Petrovna called from inside the room. "Valentina, come in and close the door." Valentina complied.

Just the idea of a Swan Queen made Elena's heart pound in her chest. She remembered the little girls on the tram who carried their ballet slippers over their shoulders with their hair always in a tight knot at the back of their heads. Their faces glowed. She had watched their movements, how they walked; they always appeared so graceful. Oh, how she had begged her mother for dance lessons. But her mother always hushed her, "That's not for us, Elena, it's not our dream." But it was Elena's dream, and she never understood why it couldn't be hers.

So, this was the Swan Queen. She had known the dancer was an elegant bird; but a swan was the most beautiful of all birds. Elena gazed at the Swan Queen, a *lebedev* like herself. Help me now, she prayed to the Swan Queen, help me become a real swan and fly back to my brother and sister.

12
FEDYA

ST. PETERSBURG, RUSSIA

"Hello? Anyone here?" a deep voice called out from the basement hallway.

Yegor.

Fedya wasn't sure how he knew, but he did. Perhaps it was the way Zoya tightened her grasp around his arm, or the memory of his face in Zoya's window, or the sound of his voice. Either way, he knew Yegor was a threat. The gun in Fedya's hand felt heavy and awkward, nothing like he had seen in the movie posters with James Bond or the Terminator.

Yegor walked down the hall and checked all the rooms along the way. There wasn't much time, and there was no escape.

"Zoya," Yegor said, "I know you're here because of that idiot, Dimitri Nikolaevich. He was no good for you, Zoya. You know that and I know that. Now, I'm not sure why you're hiding from me, but I know you are. I'm going to find you; don't you think it's better if you come out on your own? You don't want me to get angry, do you?"

Fedya could feel Zoya move, and he quickly whispered, "Wait!"

"What was that, Zoya? I couldn't quite hear you," Yegor said.

In seconds, he would be at the door.

Zoya looked at Fedya, then handed him the flashlight and quietly said, "Into his face." She took the gun from him and balanced it on the newspapers and pointed it toward the door.

"He'll kill you if you miss," he whispered.

"I think he'll kill me anyway," she answered. And in the next instant, their world transformed. Yegor rounded the corner with his own gun and flashlight in hand. Fedya shined his flashlight into Yegor's face; Zoya pulled the trigger several times. Instead of a shootout, he heard a quick exchange of loud cracks and small thuds as some bullets hit their stack of newspapers.

Yegor cried out and his gun skittered across the floor.

"Zoya, you bitch, what the hell are you doing?" he groaned and stumbled away. Zoya jumped up and raced to the door, with Fedya behind her. They found Yegor on the floor, holding his shoulder, the flashlight next to him. Zoya raised her gun and Fedya raised his flashlight to Yegor's face.

"I'll kill you Zoya, I'll find you and kill you," he rasped.

"Not if I kill you first," she answered.

"You're such a pitiful little whore."

"And you, you're such a pitiful lover. This is for Dima and Bo-Bo and Aleks and Myshi and Derevo. You said no deaths."

"I lied."

With that, she shot him in the face as he tried to jerk away. And there was silence. Fedya saw blood and smoke, and retched on the floor.

"Let's go, Fedkins. His buddies may be on the way. Show me the container." She bent down, picked up Yegor's flashlight, and walked away.

Fedya watched her leave. He glanced at the man on the floor, but his face had turned away. He had been beautiful, like Dima. Now they were both dead. Should he take the man's gun? What was the point? He doubted he could ever shoot anyone now, anyway.

A groan came from the floor. Fedya jumped away.

"Fedya! Come on!" she shouted from the stairs.

He ran after her. He must have imagined the sound; the man had to be dead. Fedya's backpacks seemed heavy as they bounced awkwardly on his back. But when he got to the back door and looked toward the container, Zoya already stood at the open doors with one hand planted on her hip. She scanned the interior with her flashlight.

"Excellent stuff, right?" Fedya said, as he walked toward her.

"Try 'no' stuff. *Nichto!*"

"What?" Fedya used his own flashlight to investigate and sure enough, every box, every bike, everything, gone. "But I don't understand."

"Too late, that's all. Probably the *politsiya* emptied it. Lucky for them, it was worth a fortune, I'm sure. OK. Let's go." She turned and walked away.

"Wait, there's another room." Zoya turned back to him. "Before I left him, Dima, he mentioned another room number...uh, 408, I think."

They trudged back into the building, but this time, headed up to the top floor, and worked their way along the dark hallway peppered by empty rooms. At one end, there were two doors draped with yellow tape, but locked. Zoya pulled off the tape and tried all the keys from Dima's key ring until one of them clicked and the door opened. If the container had been a treasure, this was Aladdin's cave of wonders. Someone had connected the two rooms with a crude opening, probably made with a sledgehammer. Like the container, the rooms had appliances, tools, silverware, toys, computers, televisions, and more: a black marketer's dream.

"Maybe Stepanov wanted to get his hands on this stuff. If only I had known, I could have made a real deal," Zoya said.

"What do you mean?"

She didn't answer, but walked around and grabbed things she wanted and put them in her bag.

"What happens now?" Fedya asked, as he followed her around.

"Not much; we have to get out of here. There will be others from the gang who survived today. They'll be back. Plus, the police will be back with a bigger truck. Don't be stupid. Help yourself to some of it and we'll go. Quit following me around. The vultures will be here before you know it."

She walked away, but he couldn't move. She turned back to him.

"What's wrong, Fedkins, don't you trust me? Look, I'm not such a terrible partner to have. You're just a kid, you know. You may think you're big pants, but the rest of the world sees you as a kid. You think you'll get on a train by yourself, eh? I can take you to real places, Fedya. How about Moskva, hm? Would you like to go there?"

"I don't want to go to Moskva. I need to go to Rīga," he said.

Zoya laughed. "All right, fine, but we need stuff that we can sell or trade. Tonight, we'll go to my friend Nataliya's place, stay a few days and then we'll decide. Rīga, maybe. Who cares? OK?"

He had little choice, really. She turned away and foraged for more valuables. He might as well go along with her for a while.

He had to get out of St. Petersburg. He had made that decision when Dima promised to help him; maybe Zoya would follow through. Maybe. After what happened with Yegor, she might be more dangerous than beautiful. He wasn't stupid. He'd figured it out. Zoya had betrayed Dima, but she was also smart and courageous. Either way, he would need help. This must be part of the street life.

For the next few minutes, they crisscrossed through the secret storage rooms. Zoya whooped and called herself the big winner after she found a box of jewelry and cases of American cigarettes. He watched her finger the necklaces and bracelets; he doubted she'd ever part with them. Fedya added a few items to his sleep pack, a felt bag of gold-looking watches, a box of individually wrapped Cuban cigars, a few trinkets, and an envelope with a couple of passports and wallets. He didn't know what would be valuable. He wanted to leave the Black Willow forever. Who knew how the curse of Dima's grandmother would play out?

Twenty minutes later, they were out the basement door and on their way. The whole time, he felt as if they were being watched, but every time he turned around, no one was there. Was it Yegor's ghost?

13
FEDYA

ST. PETERSBURG, RUSSIA

"My God, Zoya!" Nataliya said when they arrived. "Where have you been? Adolph was so mad the other day, he left screaming. That's a hundred American dollars, gone down the toilet." When she turned to him, her voice dropped low in her throat, "Why you devil, Zoya, where'd you get this little hot shot?" She stroked his face like his mother had done, but it felt different, along with the odd way she looked at him.

"Leave him alone, Nataliya. I can't take much more today. No, no more," Zoya said and shoved through her friend's doorway and into the room.

Nataliya stroked him one more time and pulled him into the flat by his coat collar. "I hope he's not stupid, Zoya, I don't like them stupid."

"Shut up, Nataliya, I mean it. This isn't one of your boy toys. He's a friend of Dima's, one of his runners."

Fedya saw Nataliya's head snap toward Zoya; an unspoken understanding passed between them. He understood these looks meant people had shared secrets.

"All right," Nataliya crooned, "all right, little friend of Dimitri. Sit down and make yourself comfortable."

Fedya turned to sit on the closest chair to the door, but it was gold too, just like a king's chair. He hesitated. Nataliya laughed. "My God, a real *paisano*. Come on, sit down."

He stepped further into the main room and stared.

"For God's sake, Fedya, sit down! I'm taking a bath," Zoya said, and walked down the hallway like she knew exactly where to go.

If Zoya had a rich friend like this, why did she live in the Agustraya district and work as a whore? He took a few more steps into the room and lowered himself to the edge of the sofa or divan or whatever they might call it. He put his hand on the pink, white, and gold stripes. The tips of his fingers scratched the fabric like a metal screen. He stopped.

"Look, you, hey! *Malchik*, boy, I'm going to talk to Zoya while she's cleaning up. Touch nothing." She turned to go, "I mean it, kid, I'll know if you do. What's your name, anyway?"

He didn't want to tell Nataliya his name; she seemed dangerous, as though she could suck the life from him. He shook his head.

"What an idiot." She padded out of the room in her furry white movie star slippers and shiny pink robe. Her long hair was wild and as she left, the strands floated behind her in black rivulets.

He was in a room crowded with soft, shiny gold and pink chairs with tiny pillows, lamps on every table, and a sofa so big that even the basket-baller, Rajmond Romanovich, could stretch out from head to toe and not touch the ends. Every wall had a mirror, or a painting, and every table or shelf held little glass dishes or statuettes of animals or naked girls.

On one shelf, there was a stack of magazines. When he looked at them, he realized they were the same magazines that Dima and the boys had at the Black Willow. He was about to put them all back when he recognized Nataliya on one of the covers. Naked, she straddled a huge bull, holding reins and riding it like a horse. Her breasts were as big as party balloons. The bull's eyes were wild, and his mouth drooled like he had run a long way. But Nataliya looked like she was having fun, like she was on a ride in an amusement park. His face grew hot even though there was no one to see him. He put the magazine back where he found it.

On the other wall, closest to the hallway that led to the rest of the flat, there was a small cabinet with a glass door filled with glass and sil-ver pieces: tiny shoes and ballerinas, fairies, insects, forest animals, and birds. Many were clear glass, while others were tipped in color. At the back, a few bird necklaces hung from cords pinned to velvet.

All at once, the cabinet sparkled with light. It was so bright and beautiful; he gasped.

"Pretty, right? I told you not to touch anything. Were you a good boy?" It was Nataliya, her face inches from his own. "Why won't you talk to me, Fedkins? Zoya says you can talk. In fact, she says you sometimes chatter like a chipmunk. But with me, nothing. Why is that?"

Fedya shrugged and stepped away from her.

"Zoya is exhausted, so I put her to bed. Here," she shoved a small pillow and a blanket at him, "you can sleep on the sofa, but be sure you take off your dirty clothes and shoes before you lie down. Perhaps we'll throw you into the washtub tomorrow." She laughed. She flicked off the switch at the back of the glass cabinet and sauntered down the hall.

He watched her go, counted three breaths, and silently pulled at the cabinet door. It opened. When she had turned on the light, he saw what he wanted, what he had to have. It was a swan atop a small silver bell. For him, it was a sign: first the necklace in the cigar box, and now the bell. He checked the hall again and heard them laughing. He lifted the bell and held it in his hands as he might a small bird that had fallen from its nest. Where the necklace represented his sisters, this one was Fedya himself. He would live; he promised himself. Somehow, they would all survive.

"In India," his mother had told him one night, "*lebedev* are sacred birds and know God. If you are very quiet, when swans fly overhead, you can hear God singing through their beating wings. And in the winter," she said, "no matter what others say, winter is a lucky time for the *Lebedevs* because of the constellation Cygnus. You know what that means? It's a cygnet, a young swan, and in the winter, the Cygnus stars make the sign of the cross, a true blessing to you and your sisters. So look for it, Fedya, in the southern sky, always look for swans anywhere you go. They will bring you good luck."

Maybe his luck had changed, here and now, with two swans as his charms. But where could he hide them? He ran over to his packs, pulled everything out, and looked for a suitable hiding place. He yanked at Elena's doll, pulled off her clothes and teased out the threads at the back.

He stuffed in the little bell and pulled off his necklace. But instead of grabbing the swan pendant, it was the plastic thing Dimi had given him. Well, perhaps he should hide that instead. The swan necklace would be his talisman, something he could touch and remember. So he put the black plastic evil thing inside the doll along with the bell, whose knocker he wrapped in fibers from the doll. Then he pulled out Dima's American money roll and added that as well. He put the doll back together again as well as he could. Safe for now.

He sat quietly for a moment. He was glad to be out of the cold. All the same, he wasn't ready to take off his clothes and sleep on the shiny sofa. He pulled his packs over to the small radiator, wrapped himself in the blanket Nataliya had given him, and lay on the floor. He was asleep in minutes.

Morning brought unexpected chaos. Fedya woke early as two men clamored through Nataliya's door, carrying lots of equipment and shouting curses at one another. There were enormous lights and coils of cables and trunks that all appeared heavy. They lugged everything down Nataliya's hallway, and it sounded like they were working in her bedroom. Fedya wanted to get up and watch, to see what they were doing, but some part of him was wary of these men. Thankfully, Nataliya ignored the boy by the radiator as she turned her charms to the men. Nataliya seemed to favor one older man and served him a cup of coffee. When Zoya came in, Nataliya introduced them.

The man said, "Nataliya, what kind of operation do you think we have here? I can't add every girlfriend who comes over to visit you to the movie."

"That's a lie and you know it, Sasha," she said. "Who did you bring today? Borya or Vanya? Do you think either one of them will mind? We'll do the same scene, but two on one. He'll love it and so will you. Come on!"

"And what? You expect dollars for this girl?"

"Of course, Sasha Iakovlev."

Sasha turned to Zoya. "You got any experience?"

Zoya looked at Nataliya and both laughed. "I guess it depends on the experience you mean. But for this, *da,* I have what it takes."

"Let me see," he said, and he gestured for her to open her robe.

80

She pulled the sash that held the short kimono together. Fedya did not want to look. He did not want to be like the man who admired Zoya's body and licked his lips. And yet, Fedya could not pull his eyes away either, as she held the sides of her robe open and turned in small circles. For a heartbeat, there was only Zoya and she was a little girl dancing alone in the golden room. Nataliya broke his trance when she came up close behind her and stroked Zoya's flat stomach.

"Come on, Sasha," Nataliya cooed, "Zoya and I are old friends, and we know how to work it."

"All right, Nataliya, we'll try one scene, but it better be good."

Zoya grabbed Nataliya's hands and kissed her fingers. "You won't be sorry," Zoya said as he headed for the back room.

"Wait, Sasha," Nataliya stopped him, "how much?"

"What?"

"I said, how much for the two of us today?" she repeated.

"I don't know. We'll talk about it later. Let's get started!" he said.

"*Nyet.* I'm no fool. Let's set the dollars now, I mean it."

Sasha Iakovlev turned back. His face flushed with anger, until he saw Fedya over her shoulder. Their eyes locked, and Fedya's skin crawled with revulsion and fear.

"Who's that?" Sasha asked the girls.

"Oh, that little filthy angel is Zoya's boy," Nataliya said.

"I'll give you a thousand American dollars for the boy," Sasha said without taking his eyes off Fedya.

Nataliya gasped.

Zoya stepped between Fedya and the man's gaze and said, "*Nyet.* Sorry. He's not ready."

Fedya stood up. Something very sinister and frightening was happening. He could tell from the way Zoya's shoulders were rigid and her hands shook behind her back. He wanted to run, but there was nowhere to go. He wanted to get away from the man, this Sasha Iakovlev.

"What's to get ready? I'll teach him what he needs to know," Sasha said.

"Maybe you should offer more money, Sasha," Nataliya said into his ear and draped herself up against him.

"He's not for sale," Zoya said.

PART TWO: DECEMBER 2000

14

ELENA

CHILDREN'S HOUSE TWENTY-FOUR
ST. PETERSBURG, RUSSIA

Elena's spoon hung suspended over the greasy soup. She couldn't stomach another bite. She looked around. Although the rules required each unit to sit together, the room was filled with lots of chatter and shouting between tables across the room. Boys flirted with girls while girls passed notes. They all relished glimpses of friends, brothers, or sisters from other areas of the building. Midday meals were the one time large swaths of the house were in the same room. Several girls in Elena's unit seemed to think boys were the answer to all their problems. Occasionally, there would be rumors of a new boy, and all the girls would crane their necks to catch a peek. Elena did the same thing, only to be certain the new boy wasn't Fedya.

A large piece of stale bread hit Elena in the face and dropped into her soup. Elena turned to see Larissa wave at her like she was deaf.

"I'm talking to you, Elena Ivanovna. Since you are all about talking now, why don't you tell us how you managed that little walk in the park with the social worker, Valentina Alexandrovna, yesterday?"

"*Da,* that must be how you plan to get to America, to play the lonely, lost girl looking for her mama," Raisa said.

"I already told you; I failed the interview," Elena said.

"So, what did you do in the park?" Larissa asked.

Elena said nothing. She was still afraid of Larissa, and it was best not to give too much information. Ignore her.

But Elena remembered every detail of her park outing with Valentina the day before. They had walked along the Neva and talked about its history. Eventually, Valentina had asked her if she'd like to stop for a treat.

"Look," she had said. "Let's go in here and get a cup of coffee and a cake? All right?"

The little shop was perfect. Small tables stood by the window while tortes and cakes filled up the long glass case. The smell of coffee, chocolate, and berries permeated the small room.

"Would you like to pick out your own?"

Elena's heart skipped a beat. She pressed her hands to the glass and examined each baked item. Valentina ordered tea for Elena and coffee for herself. Elena couldn't decide; everything looked delicious. Had she ever had such cake? The woman behind the counter chastised Elena for taking so long.

"*Da, da,* all right. I think...I think...this one, with the light and dark chocolate pieces sprinkled on top."

The woman removed the piece and put it on a plate.

"That looks perfect. I'll have one of those, too," Valentina said.

After they settled into their seats by the window, Elena said, "Please tell me a little about your life, Valentina Alexandrovna."

"First, you may call me Valya when we are just the two of us. All right? My life has been so different from yours and I don't want to make you feel sad by telling you too much about it. I was a fortunate little girl and lived with a wonderful family."

"Oh, that won't make me sad. Maybe you are a princess in disguise, and you mix with the common people occasionally."

Valya laughed. "You have watched too many American Disney movies. But even though we didn't have much money, I liked school, and I did very well on my tests, and they accepted me in the university."

"*Da,* that's nice," Elena said, "but tell me your most favorite thing when you were my age."

"Let me think. I had a wonderful friend—"

"What was her name?"

"Margarita Bocharkova."

"And was she your very best friend in the entire world?" Elena asked.

"Even though she and I were different, we were good friends. She loved to run and jump and climb. She acted more like a boy than a girl. At school, she talked all the time, and it got her into trouble."

"Oh, a bad girl, I like her already!"

"Well, no, not bad. She had so much energy and so much living to do. And she was hilarious. She loved to play tricks on people, particularly the teachers."

"Really?"

"*Da.* One time, Rita put several roaches into a small box and put the box into a gift bag and left it on the teacher's desk."

Elena's eyes grew wide as she contemplated what happened. "She didn't?"

"She did. And *da,* it was just as you might imagine. The teacher opened the package and a dozen bugs rushed out. Everyone laughed and laughed. The teacher was never the same after that."

"What else? Tell me more about your friend," Elena said as she put the last bite of torte into her mouth.

"We told each other all our secrets. She would come to my house after school, and we would put a blanket over the table and pretend we were in our own little house. Sometimes, we even burned a candle. My God, I think how dangerous that was. But we didn't know. It was our secret house, and we swore to be friends forever."

"We did that too. The candle bit. But were you friends forever?"

"*Da,* I suppose so. Until she disappeared. We thought she would be a gymnast and she should have been, but her father beat her one night in a drunken rage and disfigured her. The government wouldn't allow Rita to represent the Soviet Union with such a face. She was only ten."

They sat in silence for some moments.

"Valya, are you all right?"

"What? *Nyet,* I mean, *da,* I'm fine, really." She had reached over and took Elena by the hand. "You remind me of my Rita. You are about the same age."

"*Da,* I'm ten."

"I want to help you, Elena. I want to help you because I couldn't help Rita. I want to make a difference in your life."

"What do you mean, Valya? I don't know what you mean."

"I'm not sure either, but we will see each other again."

Elena had cherished these last words and hid them like one of her little treasures.

Larissa's voice brought her back to the dining hall. "Don't try any games with me," Larissa said. "I should warn you, those of us who have been here awhile, we don't like girls who look to be a favorite. Bad things happen. Little accidents."

"What type of accidents?" fat Svetlana mumbled through a full mouth of bread and *schi,* cabbage soup.

Larissa smacked the fat girl's hand with a spoon. "Shut up, Sveta!"

Poor Sveta. She had no idea what had angered Larissa. Elena could tell by the tears that welled up behind her glasses how much the swat had hurt her. Instead of complaining, Sveta picked up her bread and soup and moved to the other end of the table. Galina, the hyena, laughed.

"You shut up too, Galina!" Larissa hissed.

Lubya, who was working the lunchroom shift, bustled up to their table. "Galina, keep your voice down. You sound like a stray cat. Elena Ivanovna, you have a guest. Please go to the office after you have finished eating."

Elena looked around in time to see the hatred in Larissa's eyes.

She said to Lubya, "I'm finished. I'll go now if that would be all right?"

"*Nyet*. Finish your soup. There are hungry children in Siberia who would stand in line for hours for one half of what you have there. Clean your bowl and then you may go," Lubya said.

Elena ate as quickly as she could while Larissa, Raisa and Galina put their heads together. She knew they were plotting something. In moments, Raisa got up and walked over to Lubya, and drew her attention away from the table with a loud complaint about her stomach. Elena stared, wondering what was up, when Larissa poured the rest of their two more bowls into Elena's bowl and sat back down.

"Stop it!" Elena said.

Lubya turned in time to see Elena stand and raise an arm to strike Larissa.

"Elena Ivanovna, what do you think you are doing? Sit down."

"This isn't all mine. She—"

But it was too late. Lubya blew her whistle, a signal for everyone to stop talking.

"Quiet, all of you. And eat! I know how you girls are. It's always one trick after another. Well, not this time. You will eat what has been given to you."

Elena glared at the soup and looked up at Larissa, who sat across the table and gnawed on a piece of bread. What would Fedya do? Elena sat and considered her options. She would be sick if she ate the entire second bowl of the heavy cabbage and chunks of fatty meat. Without warning, there was a yowl to her left. Kiska pulled Oksana's hair so hard she screamed like her life was about to end. Lubya raced over to pull them apart. And in that instant, Elena's bowl disappeared and was replaced by an empty one.

"Two can play at this game," Yuliya said to Larissa and walked off to the dish corner before Larissa could stop her or Lubya could notice. God bless Kiska and Yuliya. Lubya would punish Kiska for this fight. Elena didn't know how she would repay her.

"Lubya," Elena called.

"What? Can't you see I'm busy? Kiska, what is the matter with you? You will go stand in that corner—"

"Lubya, may I go to the office now?" she asked, holding up her empty bowl.

"She didn't eat that—" Larissa said.

"Just go. Go," Lubya said as she dragged Kiska by the ear to the punishment corner.

Kiska shrieked, but Elena saw her wave behind her back. It didn't hurt as much as she made it seem.

"We're not finished," Larissa warned.

"For today then, Larissa, we're finished for today."

Down the hall and around the corner, she almost slipped on the wet floor.

"Walk, don't run, young lady, or you will be on suspension of free time," one teacher called behind her.

Elena slowed her pace, but not by much. At last, she stood before the director's door and tapped.

"Enter," Director Kalmakovna's voice called through the door.

Elena slipped through the door and stood still. To her surprise, not only was Valya there, but also the notorious Pyotr Konstantin who had accompanied Valya the first time they met. Was that only two weeks ago? They looked so beautiful together. Valya wore a black coat trimmed in shiny black fur around the collar and a black fur hat, while Pyotr Konstantin wore a long black leather coat that hung open now with a speckled sweater underneath. She had forgotten about his thin black mustache and deep-set eyes.

The director interrupted her adoration. "You are a fortunate young girl, Elena Ivanovna. First you come here as silent as a mouse and now look, you are treated like a queen. Do you appreciate this? Valentina Alexandrovna and Pyotr Konstantin have invited you on a special trip today."

"*Da,* Yevgeniya Kalmakovna," Elena whispered.

"We both appreciate it, Director Kalmakovna," Valya added. "But we must go, or we'll be late. Hurry and get your coat, Elena. You will need to dress in warm clothes since it is cold today, even the Neva froze."

"But—" Elena said.

"No questions. It's all a surprise. Do you even know what today is?" Valya asked.

Elena looked at her with a blank look. "Today? Today is Friday."

"We will be late, Valya." Pyotr complained. "I'm going out to start the car." He opened the office door.

Elena took her cue and raced out the door and headed toward her unit.

"We'll wait for you outside, Lenushka," Valya called after her.

A surprise. She remembered the first time Fedya had left her and Irishka alone in the flat for several hours. She had been afraid but never told him. When he had finally slipped through the door, he made them both stand at attention and close their eyes. He presented them with a whole box of chocolates! They ate the entire box. That was a wonderful surprise.

She rushed into the empty day room, since many of the girls were still down in the dining hall. The teachers had a meeting that day and everyone had a free afternoon. How did Valya know about coming today? Elena found Yuliya waiting in their special corner by the window.

"Oh Yuliya, you are an angel!" Elena hugged her. "Thank you for helping me with the soup bowls."

"We may be sorry tomorrow, but it was wonderful to beat Larissa at one of her own games."

"You won't believe it, but Valya and her boyfriend, Pyotr, are taking me out for a surprise!"

"Oh, that's wonderful, Elena. Tell me all about it when you get back."

"I will. I promise." Elena grabbed her coat and hat from her nook and ran all the way to the front door. Olga Khorkina stopped her before she could go out.

"Where do you think you are going?" she demanded.

Olga was the door mistress and old enough to remember when everyone was a comrade and children treated their elders with respect. Olga sported the traditional soviet worker's tunic, apron, headscarf, and a hardened face. The door mistress reminded Elena of one of the old Baba Yaga stories her mother would tell at bedtime.

"You cannot go outside unless your name is on my list," Olga said.

"I am *Lebedev* Elena Ivanovna, and I am in a hurry because my friends are outside waiting for me."

"*Da, da*, well, we'll see," Olga mumbled as she moved her finger down her list of names. "*Nyet*. You are not on the list. Go back to your rooms."

"But, Olga Khorkina, I was in Director Kalmakovna's office and—"

"Don't trick me. I've heard all the stories ever told," she countered.

Valya's head popped around the front door and she said, "Elena, come, we'll be late."

Elena stepped toward Valya, but the door mistress blocked her path.

"You are not on my list," Olga said again.

Elena tried not to panic, but Valya discerned the problem right away.

"Oh, I'm sorry," she said as she stepped into the foyer. "I am Kovaleskaya Valentina Alexandrovna. I am with the Child and Family Welfare Ministry."

"She's not on the list. No one can leave if they are not on the list."

"Ah! Of course. It is gratifying to know that we have comrades like you standing strong in the face of laxness and chaos. Thank you for your adherence to protocol. You are absolutely correct. However, chief of staff Dr. Olga Petrovna Abramovich selected this child for inspection. Here is my card. And you are—?"

"Uh...Berezovsky Olga Khorkina—"

"Excellent work Berezovsky! I will commend you to the director. Thank you. Now," she turned to Elena, "you are *Lebedev* Elena Ivanovna? That is correct?"

"*Da*, but—"

"Very good. Come with me." Valya turned to Olga. "Again, very well done. Please be sure to lock behind us. I was surprised, earlier, to find the door unlocked, which I believe is incorrect for the 14:00 hour, but I won't mention it to the director. *Da svidanya*."

"*Da svidanya*," Olga replied as she closed and locked the door behind them.

Valya almost dragged Elena down the steps and shoved her into the back seat of the waiting car. Once she got into the front seat and Pyotr put the car in gear, Valya burst out laughing.

"Are you all right, my dear?" she asked Elena.

Elena stared at her.

"Petya is not the only actor here," Valya said. "You should have seen me, Petya. I could be in the movies."

"What happened?" he asked.

"Oh, they have a perfectly dreadful *babushka* as a gatekeeper. The woman trapped poor Elena, but I was as official as Olga Petrovna."

Petya smirked. "And did you remember to look down your nose?"

"*Da, da*! And I even called her comrade."

Petya guffawed, and soon Elena laughed with them. They were like grown-up versions of Fedya. He used to pretend to be someone all the time to get himself out of trouble or to snare an extra roll from the market.

"So, Elena," Valya asked, "aren't you curious about where we are going for this surprise?"

"*Da*," Elena replied, "but you told me it was a surprise. And I love surprises, so I don't want to ruin it by asking too many questions."

"I like this girl! Maybe you should learn from her, Valya. You always try to guess what's up my sleeve," Pyotr said.

The car veered to the right and left. Petya swore up a blue moon of words that Elena hadn't heard since Fedya smashed his finger when he tried to pound the screws into the hinges of their flat door. Elena seemed to have Fedya on her mind today. She missed him so much. She wanted him to sit next to her. She wanted to hear his laugh and watch his eyes change colors as his feelings somersaulted through his mind.

"Get out of the road if you don't know how to drive!" Petya roared at the driver, who didn't seem to know Petya had cursed him into the deepest pits of hell for stupid driving. Elena laughed, but when she caught Petya's look in the rearview mirror, she sobered. Although she wanted to like Pyotr Konstantin, there was a violence in his eyes that reminded her a little of Irishka's father.

She hadn't thought about that one in a long time. She remembered how Vladimir's skin felt like leather. He smelled of smoke and something sweeter—or was it sour? He always wore a black cap that a fisherman gave him. A glass or bottle of vodka was always nearby or in his hand. Before Irishka was born, he would sit with his friends in the flat to drink and play cards. Later, all she really remembered was the hitting and screaming, first their mother, and then Fedya if he tried to help her, and not long after that, Elena herself. They never knew when it would happen. Only Irishka was spared the brutal force of his anger.

"Elena, you are a million miles away," Valya interrupted.

"I'm sorry," she answered.

"Look! Here we are! The State Circus. Have you ever been?"

Elena's mouth dropped open. This was too much to take in. She, Elena Ivanovna, was at the State Circus of St. Petersburg. It wasn't possible. She must be dreaming.

Petya said, "Valya, get out here and take these two tickets. I'll find a place to park and meet you both inside."

"Oh Pet, you are an absolute darling." She kissed him on the cheek and called Elena to hurry. The show would start soon.

Thankfully, Valya held onto Elena's arm as they walked through the red door and into the crowded arena. She looked up and around her, and despite the crush of people, she could see beautiful tapestries and huge paintings on the walls. The ceiling was very high. The lights flashed.

"What does it mean?" Elena asked Valya.

"The show is about to begin. Here's our aisle. Did you notice? Although the outside of the building is square, the arena is round. We have very good seats. Petya got them for us from an old actor friend who owed him a favor."

Elena absorbed everything: every color, music note, sound, and even smell. When they found their seats, they were only four rows from the front near the main entrance of the performers. Elena marveled at the beautifully dressed people. Many weren't even Russians, but foreign tourists. She recognized some of them as the type that visited the children's house.

She turned to Valya, "I don't know why you are being so kind to me, but I thank you."

"Happy Birthday, Elena," Valya said and hugged her.

"It's my birthday? You know this? How do you know this? You know this? You are very sure? Today? Really? Today?" Elena repeated.

"*Da, da*! I looked up your birth certificate. You are eleven years old today, 4 December," Valya added, and smiled.

And although Elena smiled, when she looked away, her eyes filled with tears. On her last birthday, her mother was still alive and Fedya had found some cookies and they all four had sat on her mother's bed and talked. But Elena hadn't understood how sick her mother really was. Elena was still innocent and thought her mother would live forever.

"Elena, are you all right? Is something wrong?" Valya asked.

The lights dimmed, and the music swelled. Valya took her hand and held it. Elena didn't pull away. Instead, she held on tightly.

15

FEDYA

ST. PETERSBURG, RUSSIA

The girls sold Fedya to the movies and caged him in the golden flat. Not caged in the strictest sense, and yet, he could not leave. He had tried, but someone was always watching. And the men were quick to punish. Nataliya made him wash every day and wear clean clothes, but he still felt dirty. They even gave him sweet treats, Nataliya and Zoya, as though that would make a difference.

He was ashamed of this work, this world. He was ashamed of what he had become. At night, he cried like a baby. He cried as soon as his head hit the pillow. And he was always afraid, though he tried not to show it. He was afraid of the cameramen and the other actors. He was afraid of his own feelings and his body. He was afraid of their drinking and smoking and jokes. But most of all, he was afraid of Sasha, the movie director, who watched him with hungry eyes whenever he took off his clothes. Fedya knew all about this movie business now, and it made him sick.

The first time they scheduled him to be in a scene, the girls had stripped him to his underwear. He had heard of such things, but he couldn't believe it was happening to him. He had tried to run away then. The men laughed at him and pulled him back; they dragged him onto the bed with its shiny sheets and Nataliya played with his body. He had gagged at her smell and vomited. They stopped laughing then. Instead, they beat him. Sasha beat his naked ass with a belt and enjoyed it.

Now, when the lights came on, Fedya went dead underneath. He had learned how to remain numb. Inside his head, he ran on the sandy shore of the Black Sea or stood by a New Year's tree and watched the candles burn down. He didn't see the bodies, the girls, or the men, and their nakedness. He no longer saw Zoya's breasts as treasures to behold. When the lights came on, he became a robot.

His only triumph? He refused to speak on camera. They beat him for that too, but he would not break. Eventually, they incorporated a mute into the script. After all, who cared if the boy could talk? Sometimes, he would stare directly into the camera. He would pretend Elena was out there and with his eyes, he would beg her to save him—his little sister! *Save me! Anyone. I am lost.*

Sometimes, he wished he had surrendered to the police at Dima's. He wondered about Dima. Was he living the good life in some sanatorium with nurses feeding him berries and ice cream to fatten him up? Or was it more likely that he was dead?

Yesterday, he nearly got away from the golden flat. Zoya had passed out that morning, so he took a chance and had slipped out the door. But just as he ran down the stairs, Nataliya was coming up with one of her men. The man had thrown Fedya over his shoulder like a sack of potatoes.

Nataliya hadn't bothered to beat him or even yell at him. Instead, she took a big knife from the kitchen and said, "If you try it again, I'll cut off your private parts and we'll dress you up like a girl. And just think, you'll still be in the movies. This is the way it is, my little Fedkins; you are worth a lot of money to me either way, so you'd better cooperate. Understand?"

She had scared him so much, he peed himself. Another shame.

At some point, he almost lost the swans—the sisters, the pendant. It was early on, during his first bath, when he had suspected nothing. He liked to imagine his actual sisters, like the two swans inside the silver circle, safe, and flying free somewhere in the world. He had wanted to protect them, and the pendant became a symbol of their safety. But Zoya had come into the bathroom and admired the necklace. She had wanted to try it on. When he had refused, she ran her finger under the chain and said, "Don't leave it anywhere handy, little Fedkins, or you may find it around my neck instead."

Late that night, he had hidden the necklace at the bottom of the old treasure box in his pack.

Not long after that first night, he had confirmed his fears that Zoya had betrayed Dima. He overheard her telling Nataliya. Zoya would do anything for money. One night, she had tried to justify herself to Fedya. She was always nicer to him when her friend wasn't around.

That night, Nataliya had gone out with Sasha and some rich German scientist who claimed he wanted to invest in the movies. When she had left, Zoya invited Fedya to sneak into Nataliya's room with her and they would watch television together. Zoya drank a lot that night.

"Look, Fedya," she had said, "I'm sorry about all this, really. I promise, I mean it, you'll get used to it after a while. I used to be afraid like you. In fact, I was even younger than you when I had my first man: oh yeah, my papa. What a piece of filth he was. That was a long time ago. But I promise, soon we'll have enough money to go anywhere we want! We'll be rich! We will be so very rich. Two more weeks and it's sayonara, baby."

"You think Sasha will pay you?"

"What do you mean? He's already paid me part of the money. Besides, Nataliya has worked for him before. They always pay, or the word would get out."

"So, where's my part of this money?" he had asked.

"Don't be a smarty," she snapped. "I'm keeping it for you. You're a kid."

"Oh, great. But see, I don't think I'm a kid anymore, thanks to you. I am your little dog who does tricks in the circus."

"Don't say those things, Fedya."

"Be careful, Zoya. Maybe I'm not a little dog at all, but a tiger. *Da*, this year, a tiger mauled a worker in India who forced it to jump through a fire hoop."

"Are you threatening me, you little punk?" Zoya had growled.

"Give me a drink, Zoya."

"You're too young to drink."

"Hah!" He had gotten down on the floor like a little dog and did doggy tricks: he panted, rolled over and even barked. He had barked and barked and barked. And she had laughed. She had roared. And she had poured vodka into his teacup.

Fedya stood up, raised the cup, and proclaimed, "A toast!"

"A toast," Zoya had echoed and stood up clumsily beside him.

"A toast to the sluts!" he said.

"A toast to the sluts," she repeated. "Wait a minute," she slurred. "Who are the sluts?"

"We are."

16
IRINA &
LEZUNCHIK

CHILDREN'S HOUSE NUMBER EIGHT
ST. PETERSBURG, RUSSIA

Haven't you

Seen a

Miracle yet?

You've never

Seen a miracle?

Then come

And look.

You'll simply

See a miracle,

An amazing miracle.

There,

By the hardware store,

Next to building

Number 3,

A birch tree

Is breaking through

The asphalt

At the crossing.

Roman Sef (b. 1931)

Russian Poetry for Children by Elena Sokol, Univ of Tennessee Press, 1984.

Irishka tried to sit still, but it was difficult. The bench felt hard, and she was not used to her new clothes. She worried about Lezunchik, too. She hadn't seen him for two whole days. She wanted to show him her clothes and her new pink boots! She had never, in her whole life, ever seen pink boots. In fact, every piece of clothing she had on was pink. Her boots were pink, her socks were pink, her underwear was pink, her dress was pink, her coat was pink, her gloves were pink, and her hat was pink. She felt like a torte at the bakery.

She sat on the bench beside the front door of the children's house. Next to her sat a suitcase (not pink, but blue) and inside this suitcase were more new clothes. Mama Susan had shown them to her that morning. And next to the suitcase leaned a little backpack, also pink, filled with toys. Mama Susan said the toys belonged to her now, but she was certain that was a mistake. How many children had lost their toys to fill up this backpack?

She dragged it over to the bench and opened it. She took out the toys one by one and lined them up underneath the bench on the floor: three horses, pink, blue, and yellow, a fuzzy ball, two dolls (a boy and a girl), another doll that was tall and skinny who wore pink clothes like hers, a baby doll whose lips were in a circle that said "ooh," some plastic blocks Mama Susan called "leggoze," and a rubber ducky. Before she could go on, a paw blocked her.

"Irina Vladimirovna! What are you doing?"

"Lezunchik!" She sat up. "I've been looking for you. Where have you been?"

"I am a busy cat. But that does not answer my question. What are you doing?"

"I'm putting the toys under the bench so the other children can find them later. I'm sure Mama Susan didn't mean for me to take them all."

"They are gifts from Mama Susan. They belong to you now."

"There are too many."

"What else is in your backpack?" He changed his blue stripes to pink ones.

She laughed. "We match! Can I put you in my backpack? You are my magic cat, and you must come with me."

"What else is in your backpack?"

"Nothing matters but you."

He bent down and looked at the row of toys under the bench. "I think I hear two of these toys calling your name."

"I don't hear anything."

"You don't listen. Be quiet and listen."

They waited for a long moment.

"I still don't hear anything," she said.

"Come closer to listen and watch," he motioned her back under the bench. They were both on their knees with their butts up in the air. Lezunchik's tail twitched and changed colors as it tickled her legs.

"It's the boy and girl dolls," she said.

"What do they say?" Lezunchik asked.

"They don't like it under the bench. Oh, I think they are saying, 'Take me with you,' is that right, Lezunchik?"

"Well, for heaven's sake, pick them up and put them in your backpack. You're not the kind of girl who would hurt their feelings, are you?"

Irishka pulled the dolls up to her face. "Sorry." She put them back in the pack. "And now you, Lezunchik." She held the backpack open for him to jump inside. "You must come too, because you are my very best friend in all the world. Mama Susan invited you to come."

"Irishka, I love you very much." He snuggled her face and even licked her ear. "But I should not go with you today."

Irishka's eyes filled with tears. "Why? You must come with me. I am so afraid. I don't want to go. I should stay with you."

"But you must go. It is important for Mama Susan. Remember how she cried?"

"I don't care."

"Mama Susan will take good care of you. You will not need to be afraid anymore. You will learn how to speak the way she speaks. And she will love you even more than I do. And soon, you will love her more than you love me."

Irishka couldn't help it. She had to cry. "Never," she said, "never! I will always love you the best because you helped me. I won't stay there. Masha said if I was mean or crazy, Mama Susan would send me back. That's what I'll do. I'll make her send me back." She crossed her arms.

"Come lie with me here under the bench. Come on. Let's lie down with these other Russian toys. I will tell you another story. There was once a little mouse..."

"Not another mouse story; don't you know any stories about other animals?"

"Ha! I know more than you think! Now listen, there was a little mouse who lived on the docks where the ships come and go."

"My father worked on the docks. That's what Fedya told me. I miss Fedya and Elena," she said as she crawled under the bench to lie with him.

"If you interrupt me, we'll never get to the end of the story so you can feel better," Lezunchik said.

"I feel all right. It's when you say you don't want to come with me. That makes me sad," she said.

"There was a little mouse named Dinki who didn't listen to her big brother who always told her to stay away from the big ships. But Dinki wanted to explore. So she ran up a rope to see inside one of the ships.

But then the ship started moving. She ran back to the rope, but she was too late. She looked at the dock and saw her brother and sister waving goodbye. She cried. She missed her brother and sister very much. When the ship finally found land, to Dinki's surprise, there was another dock just like the one she left behind. So, she found a warm place to live, a nice big place, big enough for all three of them. One day, she believed, her brother and sister would find her again."

The pink striped cat stopped to see if she had heard the story or if she'd fallen asleep.

"And?" Irishka said, "Did they?"

"Did they what?" Lezunchik asked.

"You know! Did her brother and sister come?"

"Of course. But Dinki mouse had to wait a long time before that day came. She had to be very brave and very patient. While she waited, she talked to her doll family and believed in her heart that Mouse King would bring them together again. Sure enough, one morning, Dinki mouse sat and watched another ship come in, a ship that looked familiar. After the sailors tied down the cables, Dinki mouse could not believe her eyes. There, down the cable, came brother and sister mouse."

"Just like that?" Irishka said. "I don't believe it."

"Just like that."

"What about Mama mouse?"

"She died."

Irishka was quiet as she thought about the mouse family. "Was that story supposed to make me feel better?"

"Look at me. You might see me later when you are in your new home. If you need me, I will be there. I promise. But you must make a big promise to me. You see, you have a doll family too, just like Dinki mouse. You must remember their names, Fyodor and Elena Lebedev."

"If you go with me, you can help me remember," she said.

"You must be brave. Say their names for me: brother Fyodor and sister Elena. Again, and again."

"Fyodor and Elena. Fedya and Lenushka. Fyodor and Elena."

"*Lebedev.*"

"Lebedev, Lebedev, Lebedev."

A door closed and footsteps echoed on the old marble floors. It was the adults. It was time for Mama Susan to take her away, away from the real Fedya and Lenushka. She wasn't ready.

"Anya? Anya Irina?" It was Mama Susan who called her.

When Irishka looked back at Lezunchik, he was walking away from her. "Lezunchik. Please. Please stay close to me. Please. Lezunchik. I love you." She reached out from under the bench toward him. Instead of Lezunchik, a woman's hand grabbed onto her.

Mama Susan sounded a little worried, but Klara was beside them and she scolded Irishka for crawling under the bench in her new clothes. Irishka didn't care. She didn't want to listen. Down the hall and up the stairs, she watched Lezunchik grow fainter and fainter. And when he disappeared completely, she yowled.

Mama Susan talked to her, but she didn't understand the words. She would never understand. Mama Susan would never be like Lezunchik. She could never love her the way he promised. She was a stranger, just a woman in a hat. She wanted to kick this Mama Susan.

"Irishka!" Klara said and pulled her away from Mama Susan's arms. "The car is here. You should be ashamed of yourself for crying and carrying on like this. Stop kicking or I will beat you until you are blue. Shut up!" She pinched her.

Irishka cried even harder and crumbled to the floor. Mama Susan ran over to them. "Stop! Stop!" she yelled, and pulled Irishka back away from Klara. But Klara kept yelling at her.

"Get up and walk like a big girl; you are too big to be carried. You make us ashamed of you," Klara said.

Irishka stood up. This day reminded her of the day when the agency people had dragged her and Elena from the little room with all the windows. They had screamed that time too, and it didn't help. The big people, the adults, they always won. She would have to wait for the right time, and she would run away. She would run back to the little room. She would find Elena and Fedya and they would be happy again. And Lezunchik would come back too. He promised. But, for now, she would be that other little girl. She held Mama Susan's hand and allowed herself to be led out.

At the car, they loaded the bags, and helped her into the back seat with her new coat and new gloves and new hat and new backpack. Klara said goodbye and gave her a hug through the car window as though she was sorry to see her go. Irishka stared straight ahead. She had nothing more to say. All the way to the airport, Mama Susan talked to the driver and to the woman from the agency, who sat on the other side of Irishka. They talked over her head. Sometimes, Mama Susan would speak to her, and the woman would tell her what Mama Susan said, but she didn't care. At the airport, they said goodbye. Everything was a blur: the car ride, the lines, the standing, the sitting, the papers, the people everywhere, the waiting and more waiting. And then, they were in the airplane. Mama Susan took off Irishka's stupid pink coat and stupid pink hat and gloves and put them in a cabinet over their heads. She handed Irishka the backpack, but Irishka didn't want any of those toys. Mama Susan opened it for her.

When Mama Susan looked inside, she yelped. Irishka had forgotten she that she left most of the toys under the bench. She didn't want any of them, anyway. No, wait. Her brother and sister were in there. When Mama Susan pulled them out, she grabbed them from Mama Susan's hands. Then Mama Susan held up something new that Irishka hadn't seen before: a soft blue cat!

Irishka grabbed it too and held it to her face. She wanted to cry; it reminded her of Lezunchik. She missed him so much. This must be his surprise.

Mama Susan pointed to herself and said, "Mama," then pointed to Irishka and said, "Anya Irina" and pointed to the stuffed cat and said, "Lezooncheck?"

Lezunchik wasn't a toy. Irishka had to straighten things out. First, she pointed back to the woman and said, "Mama Susan." That much she knew for sure because Lezunchik called her that. She patted herself and said, "Irishka." She pointed to the boy doll and called him Fedya and to the girl doll and called her Elena, and at the last, she pointed to the cat and named him, "*Sinji Kot.*"

Mama Susan repeated the names, even Fedya and Elena. But for the toy cat, she pulled out a little book and flipped through the pages and said, as best she could, "sinji" and "kot." It wasn't very good. But Mama Susan laughed anyway, and said in her own talk, "Bloo Kat."

Irishka thought about this. Since it wasn't the real Lezunchik, but a gift from him, she might as well let this cat have a name that the woman could say. So, Bloo Kat it would be.

She closed her eyes and said again, "Bloo Kat, Fedya, and Elena." Mama Susan kissed each one on the head. There was nothing else to say.

17

VALYA & ELENA

ST. PETERSBURG, RUSSIA

The three of them walked out of the State Circus hand in hand, elated. The show was everything Valya had hoped it would be for Elena. Every time she looked over at Elena's face, it glowed. Whatever had caused Elena to cry and cloud the birthday surprise at first could not compete with the wonders of the State Circus. Even Petya had thawed. He had become so surly in recent weeks, but now he was the old Petya. She had feared they would grow apart sooner than later, but she cast those doubts aside today as he drew close to her and kissed her cheek. Briefly, she fantasized about a future where she and Petya might walk out of the circus with their own child.

He interrupted her daydream. "Let's go to Michelle's."

Petya loved Michelle's because the theater and opera people went there. He would make the rounds of the tables, and sometimes, with luck, sign a few autographs for tourists. *Da,* he was definitely in a good mood.

"All right, if it's not too early in the day for you," she said. "How about you, Elena, would you like a bite to eat?"

Petya pulled Elena's hat down over her eyes and laughed. "Of course she would. The food at the children's house must be terrible. Right, Lenushka?"

Elena laughed too, yanked off her hat and smacked him with it. Valya delighted to see Elena so relaxed and happy.

He grabbed both of their hands. "Let's walk. Are you too cold to walk, Lenushka?"

"I can walk," Elena said.

To Valya's surprise, the restaurant was already busy with the thespian crowd, who had apparently dropped in to get a quick drink between their matinee and evening performances. Had Petya known his friends would be there? Within minutes, he excused himself. Valya watched him maneuver the room, catch the eyes of the women, and assess the men for importance or power. One woman, in a slinky black dress and wild black hair, was a bit too clingy for Valya's liking. Petya managed to slide away. He was very smooth, this boyfriend of hers.

She remembered how they had met. It wasn't at Michelle's, but it might as well have been. Her friend, Adlesha Petrovna, had insisted she come along for a late-night supper at Prival Komediantov on the Moika River.

"Oh Valya, you must come," Adlesha had said. "Absolutely the most delicious actors and musicians hang around there."

"I'm not looking for a man," Valya had said.

"Ha! We're all looking for a man. Besides, I think you need a man. When was the last time you had a good romp in the sack? Eh? Don't tell me. I don't want to know your business. Trust me. It's time. You've finished your studies and now you're a working girl."

Valya had wanted to be angry, but she laughed instead. Perhaps it was time to get out a little and have some fun. And so she went that night, and it was Petya who found her. He was so self-confident and, of course, dramatic.

"My God, it's Nonna Mordyukova," he had exclaimed.

Like a naïve teenager, Valya had turned around to look. When she turned back, he sat at the table across from her.

"Do you know her, Nonna Mordyukova? She is a fantastic actress and stunning—like you. Has anyone told you how you look like her? Well, of course, not now. She's in her seventies, I think, but in her prime—! Ah! She was the finest actress of this century. I'm Pyotr, by the way, Pyotr Kotolvsky. And you are?"

"Valentina Alexandrovna. And this is Adlesha Petrovna," she had answered, still stunned.

"Look, I'm with some friends tonight and they'll kill me if I don't come back to their table. We're in a show together, over at the Akimov. So, come with me, both of you. What do you say? We're harmless, I promise you." Petya had smiled in that little lopsided way of his.

It was that same smile that wooed her to this day. And of course, he wasn't harmless at all, but sexy and inventive and unpredictable. They'd been together almost three years. That was a long time, but now there were nights he didn't come home. Perhaps he looked for his next Nonna Mordyukova on those nights. Valya had never expected he would be completely faithful, so she was grateful for the good times, and for now, it was enough. Perhaps he hadn't strayed too far. Not yet.

"Valya?" Elena's voice interrupted her musings. "The waitress is here."

"What? Oh, I'm sorry." She pulled her eyes from Petya and gave the waitress a blank look before she realized it was time to order. "I think we'll need a few more minutes. Bring me a red house wine and some tea for the girl."

She browsed the menu, set it down, and turned to Elena. "So now, we girls can really talk while Petya table hops."

"Thank you so much for the circus. It was the most wonderful, exciting, wonderful, fantastic thing I have ever seen in my entire life!" Elena said.

"You are very welcome. Happy birthday, Elena. May I say that now? You were a little sad when I mentioned it before. I think you remembered some of your other birthdays, hmm?"

"*Da*, my last birthday before my mother died."

"Would you like to tell me about it? Perhaps that would make you feel better?" Valya waited. When no response was forthcoming, she said,

"Elena, I want you to trust me. I will not take advantage of you. I want to be your friend. That's all. And maybe I can help you."

"How can you help me?" Elena asked.

"I don't know yet. I don't know enough about your story," she answered. "Tell me, what is it you want more than anything else?"

"To find my sister and brother," Elena blurted out, and covered her face. She had betrayed Fedya's trust again. But what was done was done.

"Ah. That explains so much. I understand, Elena. But I didn't know you had both a brother and a sister. Can you tell me about them?"

"Can you help me find them?" Elena asked.

"I won't lie to you. I don't know. Where do you think they are?"

"I don't know about my brother. He was not at home when they took us away. But, when you came to our unit with Olga Petrovna, do you remember? I heard Director Kalmakovna say that my little sister, Irishka, was in Children's House Number Eight. Do you know where that is?"

Valya saw Elena's face tensed in hope. How could she answer? The rules were clear. She could not reunite siblings, particularly the youngest ones, since they might be adoptable.

"Are both of your parents dead, Elena?"

"*Da*. But what difference does that make?"

"I can explain, but I need you to really listen. Sometimes, when a person hears information she doesn't want to hear, she stops listening and feelings take over. Maybe this isn't the right time to talk, I don't know. Do you want me to go on?"

Elena looked at her, then looked away. Valya could see and feel the fear in the girl. When the drinks arrived, Valya ordered food for all of them. Elena held her hot cup in both hands and slowly sipped the sweet tea. Valya waited.

"I will try to listen to you, Valya. But you are scaring me a little."

"I understand. Here's a trick. You hold up your hand like this if you need me to stop talking. Sometimes, listeners need extra time to take in new information. If I see that you have stopped listening, I will raise my hand. All right?"

"All right."

Valya began. "I don't know much about the particular house you named. There are over 200 children's houses in St. Petersburg alone. My work takes me to many houses, but I have not been to Number Eight. Are you still listening?"

Elena nodded.

"Good. They number the houses in order. The ones with a low number like Number Eight are houses for smaller children or babies. They put the children together in these houses, particularly if they are true orphans which means both parents are dead or they cannot find any immediate relatives. Because these children are so young, it is often easier to find families to adopt them."

"What do you mean?" Elena interrupted. "What are you saying? Has Irishka been adopted?"

Valya held up her hand. "Do you need to hold up your hand to think about this information for a moment? I did not say she was adopted. I don't know any specifics. I want you to understand the system you've all been thrown into."

"I'm sorry."

Valya wanted to gather this girl into her arms. Elena was so young and yet seemed to carry the weight of the world on her shoulders. Was it fair to burden her still more?

"Are you ready to listen again?"

"*Da*. Please."

"I cannot take you to this place."

"But Valya, I must find her. I love her so much. She's so little."

Valya held up her hand again and waited. Elena stopped and quieted.

"Here's what I can do," Valya continued, knowing she would probably regret this. "I will make a trip to Children's House Number Eight for you. But you must trust me and not speak about it. I will find out what I can, and I will come back and tell you what I learn."

"Oh, would you? Can you?" Elena launched herself out of her chair and into Valya's arms. "That would be the very best birthday present of all."

"All right, but you need to hear one more thing, Elena," Valya whispered into her ear. "If Irishka was adopted, you will have to let go of her. Do you understand? I cannot follow her any further. It is not allowed."

Elena pulled away and gazed into Valya's eyes. "Irishka is there. I feel it in my heart."

Petya slid up behind Valya and kissed her neck. "All right, you two, enough girl talk. It's time to eat. I'm starving."

Elena grasped Valya's hand and quickly said, "Her name is Irina Vladimirovna *Lebedev*. Find her, Valya. Find her."

18

FEDYA

ST. PETERSBURG, RUSSIA

Fedya smelled the sickly sweet scent of Sasha Iakovlev before he felt the man sidle up and sit beside him on the bed. The shoot was over for the day. Fedya just wanted to get up and leave the room.

"Not so fast, Fedkins. Come, have a talk with old Sasha, eh?" He stroked Fedya's bare leg with his hand. "You were exquisite today, my boy. You have such beautiful lines. You are a natural in front of the camera." Sasha bent closer to Fedya's ear and whispered, "You are my Adonis."

Fedya looked at the hand on his leg, old, with veins that snaked like rivulets and flakes of skin clinging to the edges. Yellow cigarette stains colored two of the fingers, although the nails were manicured. And then, something he had never seen before—a wedding ring.

He bolted up. "You're married? You play with boys and naked girls, and you have a wife? Don't tell me. You have children too?"

"Shut up. Don't talk about worlds you know nothing about." Sasha stood. "I'm a businessman, little boy, and I make a lot of money. It pays for my wife's expensive taste in furs and black cars. I indulge her and she indulges me. Which is what I wanted to discuss with you. We will finish here tomorrow. And then you'll come with me."

"*Nyet.*"

"It's all arranged."

The man placed his hand on Fedya's chest and slid it up the side of his neck, face, and up into his hair. Then he yanked his head back and kissed him hard on the mouth. Fedya struggled. Finally, Sasha pulled away and licked his cheek.

"Tomorrow, my pet." And with that, Sasha released him and walked toward the bedroom door.

Zoya stood there. Had she seen everything? Sasha didn't seem to care. He tweaked her as he walked past. She flipped him the finger, pulled her robe closed, and tied it. She picked up a shirt from the floor and walked over to Fedya, who had slid down to the floor. She pulled the nightshirt over his head and then through his arms, one at a time. She helped him stand.

He was about to make a smart remark when he saw it dangling between her breasts. Another betrayal: his pendant with the two swans hung from her neck. He reached up to her shoulder as though to steady himself. Instead, he grabbed the chain and yanked it so hard it broke. She cried out and was about to strike him, but then stopped herself.

"You won't believe me, but I'll tell you anyway," she said. "I found it in Nataliya's jewelry box. I stole it back for you."

"Of course you did. And I saw two pigs fly over the square this morning."

She grabbed his chin and came up close to his face. "Now, you listen to me. I'm doing the best I can for you. I'm doing the best I can for both of us. Tonight, don't go to sleep—"

"Zoya," Nataliya said as she walked into the room, "get him out of here. Boris wants to stick around for a nightcap." She still wore her magenta robe with the white fur around the collar. Boris shuffled in behind her and laughed.

"Nice shirt, pretty boy," Boris mocked.

Fedya looked down and realized it was one of Nataliya's sex kitten shirts. Some other Fedya would have ripped the shirt off and thrown it to the floor, but he had lost his will to fight back. All he had was the swan pendant in his hand. He gripped it like he gripped his mother's crucifix the night she died. Oh God, what else had Nataliya taken? He hadn't looked inside his pack in a long time. It sickened him to think that her hands had touched his sister's doll. Another rape.

Zoya took Fedya by the hand and led him out and down the hall and into her bedroom. It was quiet. The rest of the camera crew, along with Sasha, had left. But they would be back. Zoya closed the door.

"Sit down, Fedkins—"

"Don't call me that. Never again," he said.

"All right. OK. Where are your clothes? I mean, what you wore today?"

He turned to face her. "Why did you sell me, Zoya?"

"I didn't. I mean, not like that, not for that. I swear. It was for the movies, and well, the money," Zoya confessed. "Look, we need to talk, and I can't talk to you in that stupid shirt. Are there clothes in the cardboard box over by where you sleep?"

"*Da.* I guess." Fedya walked over to her mirror and looked at himself.

"I'm sorry, Fedkins, I mean Fedya, I'm sorry." And with that, she slipped out the door and locked it.

He whirled around, raced to the door, and beat it with both fists. He cried out in rage, "You *suka!*" She had made sure he couldn't get away! He pounded. She was in on it with Sasha. He pounded again. She'd betrayed him at every step. She'd locked him in to keep him safe and sound until his tormentor returned in the morning. He ran around the room, throwing things and pounding on the walls and the furniture and even himself. He hated her. He hated himself.

Finally, the rage drained from him. Useless, everything he tried was useless. He collapsed onto the floor and curled into the tiniest ball he could make with his body. He rocked and spoke the one word he could manage, "Mama, Mama, Mama."

He lay like this until loud knocking woke him from his coma. The room was dark.

"Zoya." It was Nataliya. "Come out and play with us. My new friend, Petya, is here. Come out and meet him. I have some great ideas for a little fun. Zoya!"

"Go away, Nataliya. I'm tired. It's late."

That was Zoya's voice, and it sounded like it came from her bed. When had she come back? He had no idea. He must have slept. She told him not to sleep. But he must have slept. The floor was hard and cold, but there was a blanket over him.

"Open the damn door! It's my house, and I said open up or I'll have Petya knock it down," Nataliya threatened.

"Go back to bed, Nataliya. You sound like *Volk*, the wolf, at the door ready to eat up the goats."

Nataliya and her friend made animal noises and amidst their own laughter careened back down the hall.

For a moment, she was quiet, but then asked, "Fedya, are you awake? Are you back?"

"What do you mean, back? I've been here the whole time. You locked me in, remember?"

"Your body was here, but that's all. I thought you were dead," she said, her voice so low he strained to hear her.

He dragged his body up to sitting and leaned against the wall.

"I am dead. Or I will be dead when I kill myself before I become Sasha's sex slave."

He looked down and peeled open his hand; his fingers hurt. He still clutched the swan necklace, the sisters. He put the circle to his lips and kissed them.

"Why is that necklace so important to you?"

"It was my mother's. In a happier time, my father gave it to her—on their wedding day because she had become a *Lebedev*, a swan. He was a good man, my father. I remember how he used to swing me up into the air and I would ask him to do it again and again and again. I remember it felt like flying. He was tall. But then, all the adults were tall. But I'm pretty sure he was taller than most men, and with dark hair. I can't remember his face anymore. But I remember his hair and his green army hat."

"The hat you used to wear?" she asked.

"*Da*, his. When I was still free, when I was on the street, when I was still a boy."

"And the necklace?" she asked.

"That's all. He gave it to my mother, and I took it with us after my mother died."

"Us? You still have family? I thought you were alone."

"It's none of your business. You have done enough damage."

He stared at her until she looked away. He almost let out his secret. But then, what difference did it make? Maybe he should tell her. If he died...no, not if, but when he died tomorrow, perhaps Zoya could save his pack in case Elena came to look for him. He almost laughed. Elena and Irishka. He had wanted to take care of them, and here he dreamed they might come and find him. What a fool. It was better for them not to know.

"Fedya. I want to help you."

He chortled but said nothing.

"I know you don't believe me, but I am going to help you anyway, and help myself. I should never have trusted Sasha. It was not as much money as they promised it would be. But there is money, Fedya. I have enough money to get us away from here. We must leave; Sasha Iakovlev has connections with *Russkaya Mafiy*, the Russian mafia. That's how he distributes the movies overseas and in Europe. Then I heard one of the guys mention Yegor. He's alive. I know him. He'll hunt me down. He'll never give up."

"What?"

"We have to leave. I told Nataliya. She'll help us get away now that the movie is done."

Fedya sized up Zoya and wondered if this was the truth. He wanted to hate her for this seed of hope inside him. What is it about human beings? It takes so little to sprout hope.

"Where are my clothes?" he asked instead.

"Over there, with your rucksack. I packed it up for you."

He walked over and found his jeans and shirt folded on his pack, along with his winter coat and, of all things, the green army hat. On top of the coat was a brown paper bag. He opened it and found a large stack of rubles. He shot Zoya a look of surprise.

"I kept your share." She stopped as he stared her down. "All right, it's not a full share. I won't lie, but I didn't get a fair share either. We both got screwed in more ways than one. It's about 150,000 rubles."

"You're kidding?" As he looked at the money, he found there was also a passport in the bag. "What's this?"

"It's a Latvian passport. I had a friend remove the picture from your national passport and put it on one of those you found in Dima's storage room."

"But—" Fedya said.

"Let me finish. I know it was a dirty business. This is my penance. I have a friend—"

"I don't want to meet any more of your friends, Zoya."

"Well, you'll have to take a chance with me, or you can try the streets again. Or Sasha. You wanted to go to Rīga. I found us a way to get on a ship, a cargo ship. They let passengers on sometimes, but it costs a lot of money. A lot of what we have will go to the ship's captain. They expect a bribe to keep quiet. That's how it works. Most people who travel these cargo ships are trying to escape someone or something. Just like us. They know, but they look the other way. When we get to Rīga, we can go our separate ways, if that's what you want. But on the ship, I need you to pretend to be my brother. Do you understand?"

He looked at the passport.

"Who's going to believe I'm eighteen?"

"It won't matter. They handle all the crew and passenger passports in a group. That's what my friend told me; we leave tonight."

Hope grew, but he tried to push it back down. How could he be so stupid to trust this woman? She had betrayed Dima. She had killed a man, or maimed him for sure. She had sold her body (and his body) to a mafia movie maker. She was a liar and a thief. And yet, what choice did he have?

"All right, Zoya. We go. We go together, for now."

19

VALYA &
LUDMILLA

ST. PETERSBURG, RUSSIA

Valya gripped the wheel of her Lada Sputnik as she sat outside Children's House Number Eight. She stared through her windshield at the snowflakes and considered her options. If her supervisor found out about her sibling inquiries, they would reprimand her, and she might lose several days without pay. This venture would violate state policy and professional standards. But if she didn't follow through on her promise, she would lose Elena's trust.

Hundreds of girls were in the same situation as Elena. Was it realistic to help this one girl? Not really. Was it worth it if she lost her job? *Nyet*, of course not. What was she thinking? She would go back to Elena and tell her that some family adopted Irina. That would be the end of it. Elena would suffer and she would grieve, but she would accept it in time and move on. That is how life could be sometimes.

Valya reached for the key in her ignition and started the car. Since the car was still warm, the heater picked up where it had left off and blew welcome heat onto her feet. She loved her little ugly car and knew she was lucky to have it. Her father had bought the car from his neighbor's brother in Vyborg, who sold prize Dobermans in the Baltics. She never understood how that man transported such big dogs in so compact a car. On dark nights, she liked to imagine a Doberman sitting next to her. She smiled. Perhaps she should ask Petya to get her a dog.

She was about to put the car in gear when several people came out of the building: one looked like an American woman with a dazed-looking little girl, followed by two people she knew, Kalina Talerkavna, a social worker colleague from this region, and Masha Vladislavna, a translator Elena had met in the adoption courts, as well as someone she didn't know, probably a children's house worker. Valya ducked down before Kalina could see her. Not that she had done anything wrong yet, but she didn't want to answer a lot of questions the next time she ran into Kalina at the main office. After a couple of minutes, she heard their car start up and drive away. Evidently, it was an American adoption since the mother had dressed her new daughter in pink, like a little doll. When she looked up, Masha had walked back into the Children's House.

Who was Valya kidding? Just seeing this scene play out, she knew she couldn't drive away. She needed to know. She grabbed her briefcase bag (she might as well look official), shut off the car, got out, and locked it. She took a deep breath and headed for the door. There wasn't much of a wait after she rang the bell, and once she introduced herself to the door attendant, the woman ushered her into the office of Ludmilla Demochevna Putina, the orphanage director.

Ludmilla thought nothing could throw her off anymore or catch her by surprise. And yet everything that could have gone wrong, had. First, there was that insufferable Spencer woman, who Ludmilla had repeatedly instructed to suspend her adoption plans and cancel her trip to Russia. And yet, she had come anyway at the same time as the whooping cough outbreak spread beyond little Anya's dormitory. Within days, both Anya and another child, Sasha, had died. Several more were still in the clinic. Next was the mysterious fever in the *Lebedev* girl, and then the Spencer woman's insane plan to falsify the girl's papers. And finally, to top it off, there was a fire in the kitchen yesterday, and the cook called in sick. What else could happen?

Ludmilla had breathed a little easier when Spencer finally walked out the door and into some alternate future. She assumed her own life would get back to normal. Instead, here was this social worker from Central District snooping around minutes later. How was that possible? Ludmilla drummed her fingers. The woman who walked through her office door appeared efficient, which made Ludmilla even more nervous. Calm, she told herself, remain calm.

"Good morning," Ludmilla said as she stood to greet the social worker. "Please sit down. May I offer you tea?"

"*Nyet, spaciba.* I am Kovaleskaya Valentina Alexandrovna, from Central Office? I appreciate you seeing me on such short notice; I only need a few minutes of your time, and I'll be on my way."

In one fluid movement, the Kovaleskaya woman sat, opened her briefcase, and pulled out a thin folder.

"We need to verify the location of a child, Irina Vladimirovna *Lebedev*, born 8 August 1997. Do you know this child?"

Ludmilla's mouth dropped open. She grasped a pen to steady her hand.

"*Nyet,*" she said, but she realized that sounded odd. "I mean, I'll have to check our child complement, of course. Is there a problem?"

"Not at all," the woman said. "We have potential for a sibling adoption, and I wanted to confirm prior to the offer. I was in the area. I know it's not normal protocol, but it seemed easier to drop in. I hope you don't mind."

"There is a sibling, you say?"

"*Da,* an older sister in our facility on Malookskaya, number twenty-four."

Ludmilla stood up and walked to her file cabinets. She wondered how it was possible for the *Lebedev* deception to be challenged already. Did they know? Were the police outside ready to arrest her for the lie? Were the police at the airport to question the Spencer woman for kidnapping? Would they send Ludmilla to Siberia because she falsified records? Perhaps she should confess right now and face the consequences. She turned, and Kovaleskaya appeared to be reading a file unconcernedly. Relax, remain calm. It was an unexceptional request. Westerners often asked for sibling groups. It was a coincidence, a routine matter. Her decision was best for the *Lebedev* child. No documents could bring the real Anya back to life, and little Irishka was in the right place at the right time. That's all. What was done was done. She pulled the new records from the file and carried them back to her desk. She took a deep breath as she sat, and exhaled on a count of five.

"Ah, how could I have forgotten the name? I am so sorry. It's quite tragic," she began.

"What? Why?" The woman's hand fluttered to the top button of her coat.

"It's been a terrible month. Several of the children developed whooping cough. We tried our best to isolate the sick children, but little Irishka was one of the first to fall prey to the disease," she said as professionally as she could muster. The social worker gasped.

"Oh, dear God in heaven. You say the girl is dead? She's dead? It cannot be." She stood and dropped her papers to the floor.

"*Da*, I'm sorry. We tried our best. It was unexpected. Is there something wrong, Valentina Alexandrovna?"

"When? When did she die?"

Ludmilla tried not to appear flustered, but the social worker's reaction was overboard. Orphaned children often sickened and died, but it was rare for anyone to want details. "Hm, let me see." She looked at the file. "Uh, eight days ago I believe."

The social worker's face burned in sudden fury. "You had a child die eight days ago and you couldn't remember her name? Do you have so many deaths that they blur together?"

Ludmilla bolted to her feet. "Do you question my integrity, Valentina Alexandrovna? In truth, two died, this one and Sasha. I also have four in the clinic. Last year, I lost fourteen. Get your head out of the sand. Most of these children will die, and we do not have the medicines or staff to save them."

They stared at one another for several moments. In the end, it was Valentina Alexandrovna who broke eye contact and stooped to gather her papers and stuff them back into her valise.

"I beg your pardon, Ludmilla Demochevna. I will make a note of the *Lebedev* girl's passing in our file. I'm sure it has been a complicated time for you and the children."

"*Da,* very well. *Da.* It's been trying. Perhaps you'd like to see another child? So often the Americans will turn to other possibilities." But the social worker had already turned and started out.

Valya wanted to run out of that office and into the street. Instead, she forced herself to make a bit of small talk as Ludmilla Demochevna walked her to the door. Her mind was in total upheaval. She hadn't considered the possibility that Irishka had died, not really, not in three months. The children's houses had hard conditions, yes, but the workers were not monsters. In fact, it was the little ones who got the best care. Once they entered the houses for the older ones, they had to fend for themselves. How would she tell Elena that her sister was dead?

"Thank you again, Ludmilla Demochevna," she said as they shook hands at the door.

"I'm sorry it was a wasted trip for you," the director said. "I don't mean to overstep, but it appears you've allowed yourself to get too close to these situations, too emotional. This work is not for the soft-hearted. We must be strong; it is the children who remain behind that need our full attention."

"*Da,* of course, you are right, thank you," she replied, then slipped through the door and pulled it shut behind her. She was not in the mood for lectures from middle-aged spinsters who treated children like commodities.

The snow had stopped falling. She took a deep breath as she pulled on her gloves. If she hadn't come, she could wake up tomorrow morning in blissful ignorance. If she had followed the rules, she would not know Elena's story. She would not care. If she had come a week earlier, Irishka would still be alive. Instead, she must now determine how to break a child's heart and snatch away her hope.

Valya walked to her car deep in thought and barely registered the two women at the curb shake hands and bid one another *da svidanya.*

"Valentina!" a woman's voice interrupted. She looked up and saw Masha. She had forgotten the earlier scene, when Masha had waved goodbye to a newly adopted child and American mother.

Masha was a slight, blond woman, maybe in her late thirties, but she appeared younger in the face. The eyes gave away her true age. Flushed from standing outside in the cold, wisps of her hair had escaped her scarf. Masha dressed, as usual, in jeans, dark coat over a heavy sweater and boots. Like most of the women who worked in the bureaucracy, she carried a large bag over her shoulder.

"Oh Masha," Valya said, "of course. Please forgive me. My mind was elsewhere. How are you?"

"Very good, thank you. And your family, didn't you tell me they are still in the north?"

"*Da*. You have an excellent memory. They are very well. Thank you. And you? I saw you earlier. Another successful adoption?"

"Ha! One of the most troublesome cases I have ever had. Only in Russia can such complications happen," Masha said. "I'd love to talk, but I must run and catch a bus."

"I have my car. Do you have far to go? Perhaps I can give you a lift?"

"It's too much to ask, but if you could take me to the metro, that would help."

"Of course."

They both got into her little blue Lada and she drove back toward the center of the city. They made small talk about old friends and caught up on more family news. As they talked, something nagged at Valya. She decided to ask.

"Tell me, Masha. Have you worked with Children's House Number 8 much? What can you tell me about the director?"

"Ludmilla Demochevna? She's very conscientious, but I wouldn't call her super friendly. I think she cares about the children, but you'd never know it from her demeanor. She is strict with the staff but kind enough towards the children. She knows every child by name, and each of their histories. Her house has been under a terrible strain. They've had much illness there of late."

"*Da*, she told me. She said two died last week."

"*Da*, poor Sasha and Anya...I mean, well, it doesn't matter," Masha said.

"Anya?" Valya said, with as casual a tone as she could.

"Here's my train stop," Masha said. "Thanks so much for the ride."

As she got out of the car, Valya grabbed her friend's hand and said, "Wait a minute. I promise this is strictly off the record and I won't say a word, but I need you to tell me the truth. What was the name of the child who died? You said Anya, is that right? Anya, and not Irina?"

Masha paled. "Please, Valya, please don't ask me. I cannot say now. I can't. I just can't."

Masha yanked away her arm, bolted from the car and dashed into the metro entrance across the plaza, not looking back. There was no doubt in Valya's mind now. For some reason, Ludmilla Demochevna had lied to her. And although she wasn't sure why, she believed Irina Vladimirovna *Lebedev* was still alive after all. And yet, which was easier? To tell Elena her sister was alive but headed to America never to be seen again, or that she was dead?

20
FEDYA

BALTIC SEA

Unbelievable! Fedya lay on the top bunk of a small cabin on a cargo ship in December on the morning of their third day. If he hung his head a little over the side of the bunk, he could see through a tiny porthole: water, ice, snow, and sky. In the far distance, he could see a rocky coast with a few cottages here and there.

Funny, even though he could rest without fear now, time moved faster. At the flat, time had stood still. Every day had felt the same, and every day had begun with a deep dread. But as soon as he and Zoya had slipped out of the flat, down the stairs and into the night, he could feel the pace of life speed up like a drum that beat faster and faster.

Hung-over and disheveled at five in the morning, Nataliya had walked Zoya to her door.

"You'd better call me when you get there, Zoya."

"We will. But tell no one where we have gone."

"Who would I tell?"

"Just remember the story. The boy and I ran away in the night. You didn't know we were planning to leave. You can even say we stole something from you. Be mad as hell. You're an actress."

Fedya grunted.

"No sweet kiss, Fedkins?" Nataliya said.

"May you rot in hell," he said and kept walking.

Zoya ran back up the steps and hugged her friend.

Later, the plan had gone smoothly enough and Zoya had stuck to her word. While he stood outside the agent's hut, she completed the booking for their voyage. This was a different Zoya, not the sexpot from the flat who sucked up to Sasha and stripped in front of the movie cameras. Nor was she the woman Fedya had idolized when she was still Dima's woman. He had been such a fool. He had never suspected she was a prostitute. And with each day at the golden flat, Zoya had diminished further. And yet, here, she talked to a shipping agent as though she was a lawyer or something. He had to admit, she had been quite convincing. Who was the real Zoya?

He didn't realize how on edge he had been until they boarded the ship. Anything could have thwarted their plan. Sasha's goons might have kept tabs on the apartment and followed them. Or worse, one of the goons could be Yegor. That thought made him wonder if they would be safe even in Rīga. Another reason to part with Zoya as soon as possible.

The trip would take longer than he had expected with several stops. The dark-skinned sailor, Misha, said they would dock in Vyborg, Helsinki, and Tallinn, go around Cape Ristna, through the Irbe Strait, and finally, into the Gulf of Rīga. Nine more days. Misha had explained everything yesterday evening as he escorted them to the kitchen for food. He and Zoya had missed the midday meal because they had slept most of the day. By evening, Fedya had craved food but hesitated to eat. He had heard people got sick on boats. Zoya called him stupid; she ate like a horse.

They sat in a tiny corner next to the kitchen, called the galley. Misha's job was to get them familiar with the rules of the ship, the names of things, and how to get around, but to stay out of the way. They could walk around up front (the bow), but not toward the stern (the back). Fedya didn't expect to walk around at all; it was too cold. The galley area was warm and he was glad of it. He managed to eat some of the bread and fish, and drink a little beer with no ill effects. Despite the 100,000 rubles it cost for their passage, they had no luxuries. The crew treated them politely but mostly avoided them. The sailors assumed Fedya and Zoya were criminals or relatives of criminals.

This morning, Zoya slept late again. Fedya stared at the water through the little porthole and watched the sun glint off the waves with thousands of sparkles. His homeland was behind him. He hadn't considered what that might mean. Before, his only thought had been to escape Sasha, but now, in the stillness, his mind slipped into memories.

He pulled out the pendant and its broken chain in his pocket, and tried to squeeze the links together with his teeth. Not perfect, but after some time, he pinched together two links hard enough to wear it again.

Unless he miraculously found his uncle, he would never see them again, his swan sisters. He would never walk a Russian street or hear his own language. A month ago, he had been like a stray cat, but at least a cat that knew its territory. Now, no part of his world would be familiar. What was he thinking? Where was he going?

He rolled back on his pillow and stared up at the ceiling, looking for comfort in what he could remember of his family. He caught flashes: his mother giving Irishka a bath in the sink, his mother braiding Elena's hair, and then Elena and Irishka swinging on a tire and sledding down the park slope on a garbage can cover last winter. But all the images were at a distance. No close-ups. No tight shots of their faces.

He tortured himself for no good reason. He couldn't go back now, only forward. He sat up and pulled all the stuff out of his pack and lay them out on the bunk. He needed to know what else Nataliya had stolen from him, and what was left. He growled. She had taken the objects of more obvious value: the old gold watch Dima had carried in his pocket, his mother's silver oval frame and hairbrush, her wedding ring, the empty bottle of perfume, and of course, the rubles. Nataliya had no conscience. But, who knew, the thief could have been Zoya. After all, she was the one he'd caught with the pendant around her neck.

His heart sank and his hands trembled when he realized he didn't have the doll. He had failed to check his pack before they left. Did Nataliya take the things, or did Zoya leave them behind on purpose? He needed to ask her. When he looked below his bunk, she was sound asleep. Did one of them find the hole in the doll where he had hidden the silver swan bell from Nataliya's curio cabinet, the American money he had taken from Dima, and the curious plastic thing? He had hoped the money would get him to America one day. Ha! That was a joke. It would be a miracle if he could get off this ship and find a place to sleep!

He was surprised to find the crucifix. That must have scared her. He opened the old envelope of family pictures last. He blew out a breath. Still there. On top was the baseball card from his father. He wondered again if it was valuable. He studied the pictures next. Most of them were of the girls when they were little: Elena with Mama, Irishka and Elena at the store near their family flat, Elena and Fedya with their father in uniform. He stared at this one for a long time. Ivan Konstantinov looked so proud in his uniform, so brave. Could Fedya be brave? What would his father have done at Nataliya's flat? Would he have fought off the big men and Sasha's hands?

"I'm sorry Papa. I was not very courageous. I'm sorry."

Zoya stirred and mumbled, "What is it, Fedkins?"

"Nothing. Go back to sleep. And don't call me that!"

"Go to hell." She rolled over.

He leaned back on his pillow and stared a little longer at his father's picture. He slipped it back into the envelope and picked up a picture of his mother and her brother, Uncle Uldis, the musician, the mysterious traveler. Oh, his mother would go on and on about her wonderful brother. Uldis did this, Uldis did that. Uldis went to Spain. Uldis was in London. Uldis was brilliant and beautiful, and so on. But Fedya always wondered, if his uncle was so wonderful, why didn't he come and take care of his sister when she was sick? Why didn't Uncle come to the city and meet his nephew and nieces? Where was Uncle Uldis now? His mother had begged Fedya, "Go to Uldis in Rīga!" Is that what he was about now? Was he on his way to Rīga to find his uncle?

He studied the photograph some more. In the picture, Uldis appeared to be about eighteen or nineteen, while his mother looked younger, maybe fifteen. She was looking up at her brother as he flexed a muscle like a strong man. She had a big laugh on her face. He loved his mother's laugh. It was loud and full and honest.

What was so funny? Had she laughed at Uldis in his pose or because of what he had just said? Uldis didn't look very tall and was a little pudgy around the middle, but he had long fingers. Would Fedya even recognize this man? He flipped the picture over and found his mother's handwriting and a street address. It was a street address in Rīga. Fedya studied the address and memorized it. Uldis may have already moved, but if Rīga was anything like St. Petersburg, people stayed put. So, it was possible Uldis was still there, unless he was away on tour; or dead. So many "ifs."

As he stuffed everything back in his pack, Fedya imagined what it would be like to walk up to a door, ring the doorbell, and greet the man of the house.

"Hello, Uldis Ozols? I have some bad news for you. Your sister is dead. And I am your nephew, Fyodor Ivanovich *Lebedev*."

21

ELENA

CHILDREN'S HOUSE TWENTY-FOUR
ST. PETERSBURG, RUSSIA

Elena watched Valya drive away in the heavy snow and heard the beep of the horn as the car turned the corner. She waved again, even though Valya couldn't see her.

"Close the door, it's cold out there," the doorkeeper Olga Khorkina said as she came up behind her. "Go to your rooms. Get ready for camp."

"*Da,* Olga Khorkina," Elena answered automatically, and started for the stairs. But as soon as the doorkeeper limped back into her small closet by the entrance, Elena stopped halfway up the stairs.

Perhaps she should run away; but could she survive alone? She needed to think. She needed to understand everything Valya had said about her little sister. Was this good or terrible news? Was it good for Irishka?

Elena couldn't face the girls in her unit yet, so she slipped into a small room the teachers called the library and sat in a corner away from the door. She wasn't even sure if she should cry or not. Some part of her wanted to cry, because she might never see her sister again. But there was that other part of her, the part her mama had planted inside her long ago: hope.

Valya had waited for her in the visitor's room. As usual, Valya had been all dressed up, like she was on her way to court in her black suit with a little white blouse under the jacket and a small green New Year's tree pin on her collar.

"I have some good news," Valya had said, "but I also have hard news."

Elena had sat at the table with her hands folded together so tightly her knuckles had turned white. She stared down at the table because she was afraid to look Valya in the face. She had feared the worst, that her sister was dead.

"First, let's talk about the good news. I believe your sister is safe. I think she is in a better situation now than she was before." She paused. "But, Elena," and here, Valya had reached for her hands and covered them with her own. They were very warm. "I did not actually see Irishka. She is no longer at Children's House Number Eight."

"They moved her?"

"In a way, *da*. There is no easy way to say this: I believe Irishka was adopted."

"What?" Elena bolted out of her chair. "But how can that be? Irishka is mine; she's mine and Fedya's. She is my sister. She is our sister. She can't be gone. Oh God. Oh God." Her whole body shook, and she couldn't stop.

Elena had promised her brother she would take care of Irishka. They had promised her mother. She thought she had time to find her. She thought she still had plenty of time. But there was no time at all; her sister, gone.

Valya stood behind her and caressed her back. "I'm sorry, Lenushka. I'm so very sorry."

"Where is she then?"

"I'm not sure. I don't have all the information yet. But for now, will you trust me? I will do what I can to find out what you need to know. All right?"

"All right. But—"

"Enough now. I'm sorry, but I must go. My family expects me to arrive tonight, and I have a long drive in the snow. But here, I have a little New Year's gift for you. You can open it now."

Elena pulled the tissue paper from the gift bag. Inside was a red wool hat with matching red gloves. She had never seen such a color. "Oh, they are beautiful! Thank you."

"You are very welcome. Stay warm, and don't worry too much about the big girls who say mean things. Mostly, they are bark and not so much bite."

"I hope you're right. Thank you so much for the gift. You are very kind to me."

"Well, don't tell anyone, especially not Petya. He says I spoil you." Valya laughed as she put on her coat. Elena heard others walking and running through the halls now. The quiet had transformed into a thunder of voices and feet outside the library. Everyone would leave for camp soon. Until Friday, she hadn't even realized they would have a winter break after examinations. The teachers had announced that the students would be sent to the same winter camp as last year. While some people had moaned, others had cheered. Elena composed herself and left the library to collect her few belongings for the train ride to the camp.

In the dormitory, she asked Kiska about the camp while she sat on Yuliya's bed and watched them both pack up.

"I don't know. It's far, or not so far," Kiska answered absently while she put her warmest sweaters and socks in a backpack.

"What do you do there?"

"I don't know. Nothing much. We play. We go outside. Sometimes there are games," Kiska said.

"Do we have to go outside?" Yuliya asked.

"What? You afraid of a little fresh air?" Larissa barked from behind them.

"At least there aren't any bugs in the wintertime," another girl said.

Although Larissa and Raisa hadn't changed in the time Elena had been there, other things had. The sick one, Vera, had died; at least that's what everyone assumed. Usually, when a bed became empty, the girls would move around and switch beds. But this was a dead girl's bed, so no one wanted it. Fat Svetlana left as well. She surprised everyone when her aunt came to take her away. Elena had to smile. She had never seen the girl so happy. But Larissa almost ruined Svetlana's departure when she screeched out, "You'll be back when they see how much you eat!" Not long after that, Raisa took fat Svetlana's bed to be closer to Larissa. Those two would be a terrible combination and most of the girls were afraid of them, except for Kiska, who got along with everyone.

All the other girls dashed about the room to prepare for their time away from the children's house; some talked, some laughed, and some threw clothes back and forth at each other.

"I will not take that black sweater again; the mice have eaten holes in it."

"Well, don't give it to me. I want that green jacket. You promised!"

"Hey, these boots don't match. Who has one brown boot with a black stripe?"

And on it went like that. If a girl didn't have enough clothes for camp or any other event, there was a closet in the big room they all shared. These clothes were well worn and long out of style. The girls hated to use the closet clothes, but often, there was no other choice.

Elena tried to wait until most of the girls had left before she visited the closet herself. Most of the clothes she wore came from the closet. Her own clothes were just the ones she had worn into the children's house that horrible day. None of the agency adults had bothered to look around the old apartment for any of her belongings before they dragged them out. They assumed she didn't have any. They didn't see the box where she had folded her real clothes. All lost now, even the one blue party dress she had from Uncle Uldis, the one with the white ribbon. Of course, it was probably too small for her, anyway. It was the prettiest dress she had ever owned.

"You'd better get packed. We can't be late for the train," Yuliya said.

Next to each bed was a standard night table for a few personal items. Each table had a cubby and a drawer. Since she owned little of anything, she used her drawer for souvenirs like the program from the circus or the napkin from the coffee shop, little things she saved from her outings with Valya. But when she walked over to her bed, the drawer was open. She hesitated to look; she knew it had to be bad. And sure enough, someone had shredded her precious circus program. She slid her hand into the confetti. She held herself still so she wouldn't cry or scream.

Fedya had always told her, "If you let them see you cry, they've won."

"What have they won?" she had asked him.

He poked his finger into her forehead. "If you cry, that means that they've gotten inside you. If you let them in here, they'll pull up a chair to your brain and stay awhile."

Back then, she hadn't understood him. But she got it now. She knew it was Larissa who had torn up her precious possessions, and she refused to let that girl inside her head. Instead, she stirred the little bits of paper and even picked up a handful to smell them. After a minute, she felt strong enough to face her enemy. She lifted her head and turned to look at Larissa, who sat on her bed by the window and brushed her long black wavy hair as she watched Elena for a reaction.

But Elena wouldn't give her one. Disappointed, Larissa stuffed the brush into her purse, picked up her pack, and walked toward the door, pausing at Elena's bed.

"Looking forward to camp? I know I am," Larissa hissed as she walked past.

Still, Elena said nothing. She remembered the strength of silence. She should never have broken her first promise of silence. She should have remained invisible. Now she had a powerful enemy.

But if she had remained silent, wouldn't she have missed getting to know Valya? And wasn't it Valya who would help her find Irishka? She sighed. There was no comparison. Enemy or no, it was more important to find her sister.

"What is it? What happened?" Yuliya asked from across the beds.

Elena held up the handful of shredded papers and released them; they floated to the floor like snow.

"Oh, Elena, I'm so sorry." Yuliya came around and put an arm around her and wept.

"Why are you crying? It's my stuff."

"I hate it here. That's all. I hate this place and I want to go back to my old life. I want to be a little girl again when it was fun, when I didn't have to worry about bad people and bad things happening."

Elena wrapped her arms around Yuliya. They sat together and cried into each other's shoulder.

"Come on, help me pick out some warm clothes from the closet," Elena said.

An hour later, Elena, Yuliya, Kiska, the quiet Aniya, and the older girl Lukina were on the train and on their way to camp. Since Lukina had been to the winter camp many times, they put her in charge of the newest girls. Lukina made sure they had their orphan travel cards, and that their free train tickets were stamped, and settled them into one of the middle cars in pairs of seats facing one another. Once the train started, Lukina left them alone and went to look for her own friends.

"Where's she going?" Aniya asked.

"What?" Kiska said. "You'll have to speak up Aniya, the train is too loud."

Yuliya answered Aniya, "Lukina doesn't want to be seen with us. I think she is searching for Raisa."

"I don't like Raisa," Aniya said.

Kiska chortled. "Who does?" And then she went into a long story about injuries and heartache that Raisa and Larissa had caused to other girls over the past year. Kiska talked and talked, but few paid her much attention as they gazed out the train windows.

Elena and Aniya had window seats and watched the landscape change from gray apartment houses and buildings to factories and then to small homes and, finally, to open fields, *dacha* summer houses, and gardens. Snow covered everything and light flashed on white when the sun reached through the heavy clouds. Yuliya, who sat on the aisle and always kept busy, worked on a little string bracelet.

"Don't you think, Elena?" Kiska said. Receiving no response, she repeated a little louder, "Don't you think?"

"Think what?"

"About Larissa. Don't you think she's still mad at you for taking her place at those summer camp interviews?" Kiska said. "I mean, she's so mean to you and really, I don't think it's fair. It wasn't your fault, was it? I think Larissa should forget about it. I used to believe she was so smart, but when she acts like this, well, it's stupid. Don't you think?"

Yuliya looked up and watched Elena for a response.

Kiska went on without a break. "Will you make me one of those, Yuli-ya? They are really cute."

"I'll show you how to make your own," Yuliya said.

Elena turned back to the window. She considered her circumstances again. Things could be worse. She had three allies, well, perhaps two. She liked Kiska, but the wind carried that girl from situation to situation. If Larissa blew too hard toward her, Kiska would blow away. That was Kiska's strategy, and perhaps a good one for long-term survival.

The Larissa problem: that's how she thought of it now. That gypsy girl was stronger, smarter, and older than her—and seemed crueler than anyone she'd ever known. The one quality Elena had that Larissa didn't, was patience. She needed to stay out of the girl's way. But how? She knew nothing about the camp. Were there many buildings? What did they do all day? Who slept where? Who were the caretakers? Would she be safe? She hoped it would be a nice place with a decorated tree for the holiday.

The mere thought of a tree reminded her of the last holiday she shared with her family. Mama was already sick, and yet, somehow, she got them a tree. And like every other year, Mama had insisted on doing the work herself on Christmas Eve, just like her own mama had done. No matter what other families did in the building, the *Lebedev*s celebrated the birth of the Christ child in December. This went back to Mama being a Catholic in Latvija. The children hid under a blanket while she deco-rated the tree with a box of homemade ornaments.

Tears gathered as Elena thought about those family ornaments. All lost. They hadn't thought to save that box when their mother died. Elena pushed the loss out of her mind and went back to the sweeter memory of her mother and the tree.

"Don't look yet, children," Mama had said. "Not yet. Not yet." It seemed like forever, but then, she exclaimed, "Now!"

The three of them threw off the blanket, and there was a funny little tree with four small candles, the ornaments, and under the tree, three huge oranges! In winter! How had Mama found oranges? While they peeled and ate their oranges, one small section at a time, Mama told them the story of the baby Jesus born in a village barn and how the shepherds came to visit the baby after the angels appeared to them in the sky. And then Mama would tell them again about their own angels, their guardian angels. But if that was even close to true, where was Elena's angel now? She could use a little extra help with the gypsy.

22

FEDYA & ZOYA

RĪGA, LATVIJA

"This is it, Fedya," Zoya said as they stood side by side on the ship's deck and waited for the go ahead from the crew to disembark.

"That's right." He stared out at the gloomy landscape of the shipyard. He refused to look at her. Too much had happened between them, and he looked forward to being on his own. Sort of.

"How will you get to town?" she asked.

He shrugged his shoulders.

"You speak Latvian?" she asked, and then after a moment's pause, "What will you do first?"

He turned on her. "Look, all of my answers are the same, either '*Nyet*' or '*Ya neznayu*—I don't know,' but it doesn't matter. Whatever I do, I do alone. You got me here. Thanks. Our business is done."

"But—" she said. When he glared at her, she turned and walked away.

"Zoya!" Misha called from above them. "It's time for you and your brother to go. You'll meet me at the JB Club, right? Many Russians go there. It's a good time."

"Sure, hot stuff. I'll see you there," she called, and headed for the boat ramp.

Fedya went back to their little cabin to get his pack. He found a note on top of his bed, written in a child's printing: "I am sorry. I made many mistakes, but I did the best I could," signed Zoya. He crumpled it up and tossed it on the floor, grabbed his pack, and climbed up the narrow stairs to the deck.

Zoya had everything with her as she headed down the ramp. She looked toward the city, now shrouded in a heavy morning mist. There was activity on the dock, but not much. She should have wrangled for a ride from Misha. Oh well, she would find the tram and take it into the city. How far could it be? She knew how to walk. She'd walked all her life.

She was so focused on her thoughts that she broke her own cardinal rule: "Keep your eyes moving and be on the lookout for trouble." Now that she had escaped her enemies in St. Petersburg, she had become smug. As a result, she didn't sense the man until he was right behind her. He yanked her backpack right off her shoulders and then grabbed her around the waist from behind.

"It will take more than a woman's bullet to kill me, my little Zoya," he said into her ear.

She panicked. Inside, she screamed, "*Nyet, nyet*! *How did he find me? He should have died.*" Then she screamed for real, but he covered her mouth with his other gloved hand. She struggled all the same, and he chuckled again into her ear.

"Your little actress friend told me everything. When will you learn not to trust anybody? Now, we're going to have a little fun, you and me. But first, I want you to look at me. I am the new Frankenstein."

He turned her around just enough to face him, and she wanted to vomit. His once beautiful face was a raw-looking mound of flesh (barely healed over), and the nose ruined. He lifted his eye patch so she could see his misshapen eye socket with no eye at all. They had stitched the torn flesh, but the scar from the nose, across the left eye, forehead and into the hair blazed red. He was indeed a monster. She looked away.

"Oh, don't like it, dear? I'm so sorry. But I knew how much you'd want to see your handiwork. And *da,* you'll pay for what you did to me, and so will that little boy toy of yours. Where is he?"

Yegor looked up toward the ship's ramp and she took her one chance. She stomped on his foot as hard as she could, then turned and kicked him in the crotch. He crumpled; she ran and called out, "Help me. Help!" But in seconds, he was back up and tackled her to the ground. He pinned her, and smacked her face several times.

This was the picture Fedya saw as he came to the top of the ramp. He froze. He knew it was Yegor, but could not understand how he had found them. The last time he'd seen Yegor was on the floor of the basement of the Black Willow. Fedya should have said something to Zoya when the man groaned. Another mistake. If he was smart, he would disappear now, and yet, did anyone, even Zoya, deserve to be beaten to death?

"Misha!" he cried and ran up one level. "Misha, look, it's Zoya. Some man is attacking her."

"What?" the young sailor said.

"Look! Look over there, by the orange container. He's got her on the ground."

"What the hell?" Misha called his shipmates to save his damsel in distress.

Fedya almost laughed at the irony of it. He watched from the ramp as five sailors barreled past him, pulled Yegor off Zoya, and threw several punches. Yegor was far from intimidated and fought like a wild man. Once the fight was in full swing, Fedya ran down the ramp, grabbed Zoya's black bag, and pulled her to her feet. Blood flowed from her nose. She coughed. "Come on! You must run. Come on!" He dragged her past the stacked containers and the fighting men and onto a well-worn path. She sobbed and cried and called out to the Blessed Mother, but he pulled her along as fast as he could make her go.

When they got to a minor road, he was in luck; a man was walking a dog a short way up ahead.

He set her bag down beside her. "Stay here. Sit down. Wipe your face. You look like someone was trying to kill you."

"Very funny," she said. But she sat and groped into the bag and pulled out a rag or handkerchief and held it to her nose.

He ran toward the man, then slowed to a fast walk as he caught up to him and his dog.

"Excuse me," Fedya said, still out of breath. "Do you speak Russian?"

"*Nyet*," the man replied in Russian, and kept his pace.

Fedya stopped and stared after him. That's all he needed right then, a smartass.

"Tram, I need the tram," he called. "Please, someone hurt my sister."

The man stopped and turned back to look. Fedya pointed to where Zoya sat on the side of the road. She looked bad, which was helpful.

The man sighed, looked over the boy, and then said in perfect Russian, "Down this road, one, two, three, four buildings, cross the street, and there you will find a little path on the left. The snow may hide it. Look carefully. Take that path for a while and there will be an old hut on your right. If you go straight, there is one tram stop; if you go right at the shed, there is another. They don't take rubles, but that is your problem."

"*Spaciba*," Fedya started back to Zoya.

The man called after him, "You, boy!"

Fedya turned.

"If you need to rest, the lock on the outside of the hut on that path is open. Inside, you can bar the door and sit on some boat cushions." His dog barked, and the man turned. They continued down the road, the dog sniffing every tree and post along the way.

"*Spaciba*. Come on, Zoya. Come on," he pulled her up by the arm.

She jerked away and collapsed back down. "Damn it, Fedya. Give me a minute."

"You don't have a minute and neither do I. We have one chance to get away. Do you see any friendly people or warm, cozy houses here?"

She cried again. "I don't think I can take anymore."

"Get up, you little slut. I save you and you act like a baby. I should have left you. I'm done with you." And with that, he walked down the road toward the buildings.

"Don't leave me here," she wailed. She got up and dragged her bag along the ground. He stopped and took it from her.

"I think we'd better hide. When crazy man comes to look for us, he'll know we had to walk or catch a tram."

"His name is Yegor. The same Yegor I shot. You should have seen his face. It has hardly healed."

"I know. It doesn't matter now. We have to hide."

"Where?"

"I guess it's your turn to trust me. That's a switch, eh? How do you like it?"

Zoya was silent. As they walked, he looked back every few seconds, worried that Yegor would catch up soon. When he found the path, he gestured her to go ahead of him. The snow was deeper here, so he took a branch and scratched through their footprints and told Zoya to shuffle her feet. In the distance, he heard a car rev up. He ran without a second thought and Zoya followed clumsily.

"Slow down. What is it?"

"Quiet!"

And then he saw the hut. He yanked open the door and shoved Zoya in, closed and barred the door behind him. It was dim inside, despite the many cracks between the boards and the small window. There wasn't much room, since empty crates, buckets, and weights filled the room along with seine nets on the walls. As fast as he could, he moved a few crates, threw down a couple of old boat cushions, and made a space for Zoya to sit in the darkest corner. He checked the window and listened for a car to come closer. The street was near their hiding place, and through the building slats, he could see cars on the road, but few. Within minutes, he saw what looked like the same car go past twice more. It could be Yegor, or it could be coincidence. Then he saw the same car slow down and pull off the main road. Fedya moved back into the corner with Zoya, stacked the surrounding crates, found an old tarp, and pulled it over them. It wasn't much. If Yegor found their footprints, they would be dead.

For the next half-hour, maybe longer, he heard a series of sounds: a car door opening and closing, shuffling feet, breaking twigs, more slamming, and then a revving engine. This happened more than once from a couple of different directions.

The entire time, Zoya whimpered. Her small sounds reminded him of his mother when Vladimir used to beat her. Before, when his father was still alive, his mother had seemed so strong, a rock. When Vlad came into their lives, it wasn't long before he began to slap her at the slightest aggravation. In the beginning, Mama would cover her head and face with her arms and beg him to stop. Then Vlad would grab her arms and shake her like an old rag doll and tell her to shut up. Once, he tossed her onto the bed and she hit her head on the wall. She rolled up into a tiny ball and whimpered just like the noises Zoya made now, like an injured cat.

Again, he heard the same engine and the car door slam, but somehow closer.

"Zoya," he whispered, "you must be quiet now. Understand? Quiet, no matter what happens. If he walks nearby or looks inside the hut, you cannot make a sound. Not one sound! Do you understand?"

She nodded. Her mascara had smeared all over her face and there was blood caked around her nose. Her nose and both her lips had swollen. He had never seen her look so ugly. She put her head down on her knees and rocked back and forth gently. Yes, she reacted just like his mother. He couldn't watch anymore.

And then he heard it, the sound of heavy boots on snow. It was a thudding kind of sound, but he knew it well. He could sense someone outside the hut, then heard heavy breathing and the brush of a coat or glove on the wood. He heard the padlock scrape off the door and the pressure on the barred door. More than likely, Yegor would look in the small window next. Zoya froze beside him. It was not like the movies at all, to be chased by someone who wanted to hurt you. In the movies, the good guys were brave and unafraid, crouched in a good hiding place, ready to tackle the bad guys. It was not the same at all.

"*Hai, Piedod*, Hello, excuse me. What are you doing?" another man's voice called out in a language Fedya did not understand. He assumed it must be Latvian.

But Yegor answered in Russian.

"Sorry, I don't understand you. Do you speak Russian?" Yegor asked.

"A little. How can I help you?" the man said in broken Russian.

"I'm looking for some friends. I was supposed to meet them at the dock, but I missed them."

"I don't understand. You think your friends are in my fishing house?" A dog growled low and threatening. "Kriks," the man said to the dog.

"*Nyet*," Yegor said. "If you must know, I was looking for a place to take a piss."

"Oh. Well, please don't do that here."

There was a long silence. Fedya didn't know what was happening between the two men.

"Anything else?" the Latvian man asked.

"*Nyet*. Here, take my business card. If you see them, a boy and a girl, my cousins from Russia, you can pass it along," Yegor said.

"Oh no. I am a fisherman. I like fish. Sometimes I fish bodies from the Daugava. I don't like people." And again, the dog growled low. "My dog doesn't like people either."

"You don't have to be—"

And then the man with the dog spoke in his native language. Fedya could tell, just from the sound of his voice, that this Latvian fisherman was unafraid of the monster's face.

Yegor departed, but not without a few anti-Latvian curses tossed behind him in Russian.

After a moment, Fedya heard the bar pop off the hut's door and the room flooded with light. The Latvian man whistled a merry tune. Then Fedya heard the man say, in between whistled phrases, "Don't move yet." The man moved crates and set them outside in the snow. He also picked up some chains and dragged them outside. Then he heard the man command the dog again.

The Latvian whispered through the hut door, "I'll be back. The dog will watch."

Fedya wasn't keen on a people-hating dog three feet away, but there wasn't much he could do about it. He did not answer or move. He wasn't even sure how the man knew they were there, or what made him follow them. As the Latvian man walked away, he dragged his crates and chains behind him. Fedya heard Yegor's now familiar car peel off. The silence was heavy on them except for the low panting of the dog, who sat by the open door. Zoya trembled. He knew this was not from the cold. She trembled in fear.

When the man returned, the dog yelped. "Kriks, get away," the Latvian man commanded. "Alright, my two young friends. You can come out now."

He pulled the tarp from on top of them, and the dog came in close. Zoya held up her hands in fear and pushed back into the wall. Fedya froze. The dog sniffed the boy and then licked his face. "*Ne,* Kriks." The man pulled the dog back. "The dog is hopeless."

"I thought he hated people," he said.

The Latvian man laughed. "Kriks? That Russian man was a fool, the one with the ruined face. If he would have tossed my dog a bone or said, 'Good dog,' Kriks would have been a lost cause. All right, come, come. It's safe, I tell you. The man left. Get up, get up."

"Why are you helping us?" Fedya said.

"Some of my cargo was on your ship. The mates told me about a man who attacked your, uh, sister. I have a sailor's intuition. So, come. I have a van. You will share some soup with me and tell me your story."

Zoya came to life. "*Nyet.* We will be fine. Thank you anyway."

"I am Imants Ozoliņš. You are trespassing on my property. If you do not accept my invitation, I will call the police."

23

ELENA

ROSHCHINO CAMP NUMBER FOUR
ST. PETERSBURG DISTRICT

It wasn't so bad, the camp. In fact, it was much better than the children's house in the city. Elena was in the same room as Kiska, Yuliya, and the quiet Aniya. A window faced the woods, and she could see the trees still draped with snow. It was chilly in the room, but there were plenty of blankets. The room held four beds, a small table with two chairs, four little bureaus beside each bed, and a wardrobe. Of course, they had little to put into the wardrobe, so they used it for coats and boots. Hanging inside the door of the wardrobe was a long mirror. It had been a long time since any of them had seen themselves from head to toe.

Elena poked her head out their door and into the hallway. She calculated that their room was four doors down from the toilets and showers. That was good. Although everyone had complained about the long journey to the camp and how tired they were on the train, many of the same girls now ran from room to room in a kind of frenzy. At least thirty to forty girls her age and older lived on the second floor of the camp building.

She turned and asked Kiska, "What's all that noise from the first floor?"

"Oh, you'd better get used to it. That's the boys, and lots of them! This is when the real love affairs start." Kiska smiled knowingly.

Elena couldn't imagine what could cause such a roar beneath them, even if they were boys. Was it talking or screaming or moving furniture or what? She wasn't sure she wanted to know. Before she could ask more questions about the boys, a caregiver she had never seen before came through the hall and rang a little bell.

"Come to the lobby, girls. We will have a meeting to plan our day tomorrow and then it will be lights out by 23:30. Come!"

As the tinkling bell passed, Kiska ran up and squeezed her head between the doorjamb and Elena's shoulder. "*Privet*—Hi, Celestina Yamadayevna."

The woman turned. "Ah! *Zdrasti*. Are you still a little nuisance, Kiska Grigoryevna?"

"Of course. I have all the new girls in my room: this is Elena Ivanovna, Yuliya Alexandrovna and Aniya Leontyevna, the newest. She whispers all the time. I am in charge of showing them the camp. Is the holiday tree up yet, so we can decorate it? It was a beautiful tree last year."

"*Privet*, girls. Welcome to Roshchino Camp Number Four. Come to the meeting now. I will explain our plans then." Off she went down the hall, ringing her bell.

Much later, as Elena lay in her bed and listened to the night sounds of the camp, which included Kiska's head bumping the wall as she rocked herself to sleep, and the low rumble from the floor below, she considered how much she had already changed. At first, she had intended to remain separate from all the other girls. She had wanted to hold on to her memories of Fedya and Irishka, but once she talked and listened and even laughed with the others, the distance between her brother and sister grew every day. She felt more than a little guilty. She didn't hate everything about the children's house anymore. She was glad she wasn't hungry all the time. Fedya had done his best, and she had never complained, even on the days when there was nothing but bread and tea. The thought of food made her hungry now. She pulled out the little cake pieces she had wrapped in paper after their evening meal. She always saved what she couldn't eat. In that way, later, she could stretch out her sheer joy of eating. Perhaps all poor children did that. She didn't know.

Tomorrow, they would decorate the lobby for the New Year. There was a grand tree in the corner and Celestina had brought an entire box of ornaments. Plus, there would be time in the afternoon to make more ornaments. Elena loved to make pretty things. Celestina Yamadayevna was old, at least fifty, but she had lots of energy. She was in constant motion whenever she talked. Her short red hair looked like someone had rubbed her head with a piece of wool and electrified it. Elena noticed a slight tremor in Celestina's hands, but she also had a ready smile.

The next day proved bright and cold, and Elena stretched out under her warm blankets. They all slept in a little later than usual, but Celestina had reminded them at the meeting that mealtimes were exact. If the girls wanted to sleep late, she didn't care, but after half-past eight, the dining hall doors closed.

Elena didn't want to step out onto the cold floor, but she didn't want to miss breakfast, either. So, she forced herself up, shook the other three girls awake, and announced that she would go without them if they didn't hurry. Kiska grumbled and rolled over; Aniya said she didn't feel well. So, it was just Elena and Yuliya who made their way down the steps, through the lobby, and onto the curved path that wound through the pine trees to the dining hall.

When they opened the door and slipped in, Elena gasped. The room dazzled. Paper snowflakes dipped in sparkles and shiny blue ribbons hung from the ceiling; smaller snowflakes adorned the windows. They had covered the tables in light blue tablecloths with a little winter animal in the middle of each table, like a deer or a bear or a squirrel. On one side of the room was the food: a table covered in cold meats, hard-boiled eggs, dark breads, coffee, and tea.

Elena thought of the swan ballerina picture from the children's house and how perfectly the dancer would fit right in amid the snowflakes. Abruptly, Elena ran under the hanging snowflakes and ribbons, hands outstretched. She laughed in a way she hadn't laughed in a long time. She would never find words to explain how she felt at that moment.

"What are you doing? What's wrong with you?" Yuliya said as she caught up with her.

"Nothing," Elena said, "I'm happy. That's all. I forgot what happy feels like."

But of course, happiness was fleeting in places like Roshchino Camp Number Four. As soon as Elena saw Larissa, Tatiana, and three boys clamor through the front door, she lost her appetite. That group laughed too, but Elena could hear the mockery in their voices; she knew their joke was at someone's expense. It was dark laughter.

When Larissa's eyes met hers, the girl jabbed one of her boys with an elbow and pointed to where Elena sat with Yuliya. More laughter, but it sounded forced and fake. Larissa wanted to show off to the boys. Elena didn't care. She sized up the boys who trailed after Larissa and found them inferior to her brother. Larissa led them by the nose and, for this reason, they were perhaps more dangerous, because they would do whatever Larissa told them to do.

"Yuliya, are you finished eating? Let's go," Elena said.

One boy turned and gave Elena the "screw you" V sign with his fingers and they all laughed again. But she had seen those dirty gestures before. She turned away and dragged Yuliya by the arm behind her.

"Come on," she insisted, and they were out the door.

When they got back to their room, Aniya was reading while Kiska slept.

"Here, Aniya," Yuliya said, "I brought some bread for you."

"Oh, thanks so much," Aniya said as she caught the bread in the air.

The three friends were the first ones in the lobby that morning and ready to help decorate. For them, the tree was huge; none of them had ever had so many real glass ornaments, beads, and tinsel. Elena liked their camp caregiver, Celestina Yamadayevna. A few younger girls came in to help and then later, some of the others. She didn't see Larissa or Tatiana or even Lukina for the rest of that day. As the light faded around 15:00, as it always did in the winter months, she heard a group of the older girls come in from outside and move down into the boys' area.

"Celestina Yamadayevna, where have the older boys and girls been?" Elena asked.

"What? Oh, I don't know. My guess is they walked up the lane or over to the little store at the next camp. The boys trade for vodka and the girls kiss for cigarettes."

"Vodka?" Aniya looked wide-eyed. "But they aren't of age."

"*Nyet*, but then, neither are the boys in the store who sell it. You girls have done a wonderful job on these decorations. I've never seen our holiday tree look more beautiful. Here is a little something for each of you. But if you tell anyone that you got it from me, I'll call you white liars!"

They giggled as she offered each of them a chance to select from a box of chocolates.

"My Andrei gave them to me for my birthday last week but if I eat that much chocolate, I'll be as fat as a moose." Celestina giggled like a schoolgirl. "Go on now, take a walk or go back to your rooms. After supper, there's a dance with a DJ. I know he is excellent."

Yuliya said, "I bet his name is Andrei."

"Close. This one is someone special, Konstantin Andreivich. My Andrei is an old man of fifty-two!" Celestina said. "Now go, I have work to do."

As the girls left the lobby and headed upstairs to their rooms, they all discussed whether the mysterious Konstantin Andreivich was Celestina's son.

The evening dance surprised the girls again. The camp staff transformed the dining hall into a party room. They pushed the tables to the side and put small flickering candles on each one. The small stage at one end had an elaborate sound system, and DJ Konstantin Andreivich was already into the music when they got there. This Konstantin was gorgeous. At least, that's what the four friends decided right away. They would have run over and asked him to play a song, but the other girls had draped themselves across his equipment: Larissa, of course, Lukina, Tatiana, Raisa, and a few girls they didn't know. Kiska ran out onto the floor to dance with some of her other friends from a different unit, but Elena, Yuliya, and Aniya found a table to just watch. They sat as close to the front as they could.

The music was wonderful, so loud it made their table vibrate. They tried to talk but no one could hear, so they were content to laugh and smile during the fast songs. Several girls screamed when he played Nautilus Pompilius or t.A.T.u. and they'd race out to the floor to dance. But the biggest hits were still the American ones like Destiny's Child, Christina Aguilera, and Britney Spears.

Elena didn't know how to dance, but as she watched, she decided it didn't look that difficult. Twice, one of the male staff came out on the floor and broke up the couples who danced too close or made risqué motions. She tried not to stare at the couples who moved their bodies so close together, but she couldn't help it. She had never seen so much sexy stuff in one place, especially when the music slowed down. Many of the boys sat along the edges as they smoked and drank their punch from paper cups. She was sure they had added vodka to their drinks because they talked loudly and seemed clumsy when they walked. One boy, who danced with Lukina, fell, and pulled her down with him. They both cackled. She assumed they were drunk.

Kiska ran up to their table. "Come with me Elena, I want to ask for a song."

"You don't need us. Go by yourself," Yuliya said.

"Please, please?"

"All right," Elena said, "I'll go with you, but you do all the talking."

The two girls walked up to the stage where Konstantin ruled the night. By that time, his dark curly hair was full of sweat and hung down into his eyes. When he smiled, his teeth were not so great, but he arched his eyebrow in a way that made him look quite innocent. Elena was not so stupid to believe that. She was sure he was wild.

"So, what is your name?" he asked Kiska. When she told him, he smiled. "What kind of Russian name is that? Sounds more like the name of a cat."

Kiska reddened and looked down at her feet.

"That wasn't nice," Elena interjected.

When Konstantin turned his attention to her, she almost fainted. His eyes were deep blue and sparkled. Her knees became like rubber, and she felt her breath catch in her throat. This wasn't some stupid boy; this was a man, and she was in love.

"My apologies," Konstantin said. "And you are?"

"Elena, Elena Ivanovna."

But before the conversation could go on, other girls had run up to call for another song, "Not Gonna Get Us." Elena backed away from them and sat off to the side of the stage on a square metal case.

"Sorry, sorry, girls, but I don't have that yet. Maybe next time," he said, and then waved to someone over their heads. "OK, Sasha. Last one, girls," and he popped in a CD.

They moaned and complained but once they heard, "Ooh, ooh, yeah, yeah, yeah, yeah," and then "Oops, I Did It Again" started, everyone yelled and went out onto the floor to dance, even Yuliya and Aniya. But Elena pulled up her knees onto the case and watched her heartthrob as he moved to the beat of the music. His black t-shirt and black jeans were tight against his frame, and, of all things, he wore American cowboy boots. Where would he get such boots? He wore a leather braided bracelet on his wrist, and she could see his crucifix, which had pulled out from under his collar. And then, like in a dream, he turned and looked at her and smiled. He pointed to the dance floor, but she shook her head and then hid her face inside her folded arms and knees. Her cheeks burned hot.

When the dance was over and the overhead lights came back on, Konstantin worked quickly to pack up his equipment.

"Excuse me, Elena, but I must have my case to pack up."

"Oh, I'm sorry." As she got off the case and moved toward the edge of the stage, she tripped over a cable. Konstantin caught her with one hand right before she would have landed face-first. He was so strong, she felt like a feather in his hands. He set her upright on the floor.

"All right now?" He looked down at her. One of his hands still held her arm while the other held his cell phone. Then it beeped, and he checked it for a message. "Crap! I've got to go. See you tomorrow. *Nyet*, that's *Novyj God*—New Year's. See you on the weekend then." And with that, he turned away to take a call.

She picked up her jacket and hat from the coat hooks (hers the only one remaining), and floated out of the dining hall and back to her cabin. The snow had started to fall again. She collected a few flakes on her tongue. Then she almost skipped along the path and up the stairs and into her room. Other girls spoke to her, but she didn't want to speak to them. She wanted to remain in this delicious moment. Tonight, she would dream of Konstantin Andreivich.

PART THREE: JANUARY 2001

24

FEDYA & ZOYA

RĪGA, LATVIJA

"This is the address you gave me for your uncle," Imant said, as he pulled the van up to an old apartment complex. They could have been in St. Petersburg, except these buildings were made of yellow brick and there were leafless vines crawling up the walls. The street was busy despite the cold and snow. On the corner, three *babushka*s appeared to complain about the weather, gesturing dramatically.

Fedya's hands shook. He could not believe he had made it to his uncle's flat. A miracle. He looked at Imant and considered how lucky they were to have befriended this man. Fedya knew in his gut that Imant was good, in the same way he had known the movie director, Sasha, was not. Of course, Fedya hadn't told Imant his entire story over lunch, but he'd told him about his mother's death, about his life on the street, about Dima and the gang, about Yegor, and about their escape on the cargo ship. It was enough of a story to explain how they'd ended up in Rīga and why he needed to find his Uncle Uldis. When Imant had asked Zoya for her part of the story, she was stubborn and silent. So, it was Fedya who confessed that Zoya was not his sister either, but she was Dima's old girlfriend.

Imant had considered their words for some time and smoked his pipe. "Well, that's an impressive tale. So tell me, where does this uncle of yours live?"

"I'm not sure," Fedya said, as he pulled out the old picture from his pack and handed it across the table. "That's my mother with him when they were younger. She wrote an address on the back."

"Ah. A beautiful Latvian girl. How did she come to be in Russia?"

"I'm not sure. When I was a kid, I didn't think to ask. My father was Russian and in the army. I think they stationed him in Rīga at first, and then, when things fell apart politically, they came back to St. Petersburg together. A few years later, he left for Chechnya, but he didn't come back."

Imant looked at the back of the picture and said, "Ah yes, I know where this is. It's not so far from here. I can take you."

"You'll take us? I mean, now?" Fedya said.

"Yes, why not? And little Zoya, will you go with your friend to his uncle's house?"

"Humph. What else am I supposed to do? There's a madman looking for me," she said.

"It's a big city, dear. You will be safe enough if you are wise."

Fedya looked at her and then at Imant. "What do you mean?"

"I think she knows, eh, Zoya?"

She took in his gaze for a long beat and shrugged. "You don't know me."

"Very true. So, let's go."

And now, here they sat, in Imant's truck in front of his uncle's apartment building. He wasn't sure what to do next.

"Fedya, does your uncle speak Russian?"

"I don't know. Maybe. You do."

"Yes, but I do business with Russian people. Since our independence, many have forgotten this language on purpose. Some pretend they never knew Russian."

"Why?" Fedya asked.

"My dear boy, this is not the time for a history lesson. Perhaps you will come and visit me at my little house by the waters of the Daugava again and we will have tea and speak of your Latvian heritage."

"He's a Russian boy," Zoya barked. "Russian! Let's go, Fedkins."

"I told you not to call me that," he said between clenched teeth. His anger and shame blossomed immediately. He hoped Imant hadn't noticed.

Zoya yanked open the van door and got out. Fedya turned to Imant, who sat quietly in the driver's seat; they shook hands. It was time to take the next step in his life.

Imant held his hand a moment longer and said, "When I was a boy your age, I ran away from home to find my life on the sea, like in the story-books. But that life wasn't like the story-books at all, and I learned every lesson the hardest way. Never give up hope, Fyodor Ivanovich Ozols *Lebedev*. No matter what happens, you must trust in God."

Fedya got out and pulled on his packs. Before he shut the door, he said, "Thank you." He tried to think of something to add, but couldn't. He watched the old green van pull away from the curb.

Zoya found her voice as soon as the van disappeared around the corner. "It's cold; let's find this damn uncle of yours. I'm living a nightmare. I should have stayed in St. Petersburg, or gone to Moscow. Stupid. Stupid plan. And what's with you and the old fisherman? God, what a bore. And that place, it smelled like dead fish." Zoya glanced at Fedya, who stared after the van. "Will you come on? I said I'm cold."

"Shut up. Maybe you should learn the term 'thank you.' You are such a slut. I should have left you to Yegor."

"What, you think I need you? You're a kid," she snapped back.

"Shut up," he said.

He saw the house numbers on the corners of the buildings. They followed the U-shaped layout and found number 83. He hated to imagine what he would do if his uncle didn't live there anymore. At the door, he scanned the list of flats and their owners.

"Ozols! There it is." Zoya reached over his shoulder and rang the bell.

"What are you doing?" he said.

"I'm cold. I mean it, freezing, and it's getting dark."

Before he could complain, a voice spoke through the speaker. "*Kas ir*—Who is it?"

Fedya froze in mid-thought and stared at the door speaker box. How should he answer?

Zoya jumped in, "Do you speak Russian?"

"*Ko*—What? Who wants to know?"

"*Russki! Russki!*" Zoya yelled into the intercom.

For a long moment, there was silence. And then, in accented Russian, the man's voice said, "Who is it?"

When Fedya found his own voice, he said, "Fyodor. It's *Lebedev* Fyodor. Fedya. Your sister, Elizaveta, was my mother."

Again, there was silence, and then the buzzer sounded. The door unlocked. Zoya grabbed it and they were inside a warm foyer. They heard a door open several floors up. When they looked, a man gazed over the rail. He was unshaven and wore an old undershirt and baggy pants. His hair was long, stringy, and shot through with gray. He put on glasses, lit a cigarette, and watched them climb the four flights of stairs. As they got closer to the top, the smell of alcohol and human excrement wafted from the man. At his door, they stood before him. Fedya had dreamed of this moment, but now, he could not remember what clever words he had planned to say.

"Elizaveta?" the man said and then paused, as though the very thought of her fled past him.

"She died. My mother died last spring, in April. Are you my Uncle Uldis?"

He grunted. "I suppose I am. I suppose I am."

The man swayed a little. Fedya had seen Irishka's father Vladimir drunk often enough to recognize a man on his way to total obliteration. Uncle Uldis turned and lurched through the open door. Zoya stepped in behind him. Fedya followed.

"I'm sure you want to get to know Fedya, your long-lost family member who traveled 500 kilometers to visit you. Isn't that right, old uncle? Thank you for inviting us in."

Zoya yammered as she followed the man and dragged Fedya deeper into the flat. With no further comment or resistance, Uldis shuffled over to an old television and collapsed into a chair that faced the screen. The sound was down; Uldis stared at the flickering images.

Fedya and Zoya looked around the gloomy room. Blankets haphazardly covered the windows; piles of old clothes and crumpled bed linens littered the bed, while another bare mattress had been thrust into a corner. Dishes filled the sink and water dripped from the faucet into a pan and onto the floor. Clothes were strewn all over and soaked with water; they gave off a powerful scent of mildew. Lots of old photographs hung on the walls, mostly of people who sat around tables making toasts or groups of musicians in black tuxedos holding instruments. There were travel posters too, their corners rolled up or peeling. In one corner, an enormous floor to ceiling mirror stood like a sentinel. But, to Fedya's greatest surprise, the object in the center of that crazy room spoke the loudest: a shiny black grand piano wrapped in long strips of red fabric which looked almost like streams of blood. He shuddered. All over the top of the piano were stacks and stacks of papers and around the legs, a sea of paper snowballs.

Both he and Zoya stood transfixed by the eerie effect of the room and its black musical monolith, when, all at once, the paper globes scattered. Zoya shrieked. Even Uncle stirred.

A cat, a brown cat with a black face, feet, and tail scattered the paper balls. It fixed light blue eyes on them. Zoya bent down, tsked at the kitty, and reached out to it, but the cat ignored her.

Uldis' voice rasped from the chair, "*Minka, Mink...Mink...Mink!* Come here."

The cat turned to her master's voice. In a decisive move, she leaped onto the back of his uncle's chair, wrapped her tail around his neck and glared at the intruders. Uncle's hand went up and stroked her chin.

Fedya turned to Zoya and said, "Now what?"

25
ELENA

The next day was bright with fresh snow on the ground and Elena could hear shouts, as kids made plans for a day of ice skating, skiing, or sledding. At breakfast, Aniya, Yuliya, and she made their own plans to play outside. Kiska sat with a boy she'd met at the dance the night before. He didn't look like a very nice boy, but Kiska didn't seem to care. Things were quite different and less strict at the camp compared to the children's house in the city.

"What should we do first, sled or hike?" Aniya asked them.

"Maybe I'll just stay here," Yuliya said.

Elena looked at Yuliya and remembered the thin coat Yuliya had worn on the train. In fact, now that she thought about it, Yuliya didn't even have a hat.

"Look, I have two hats. I have one from the closet and one from a friend," she said. "Take this one. I know it's not that pretty, but it will keep you warm."

"*Nyet*, I'll be all right." Yuliya said.

161

"Oh, come on. I want to show off my red hat. Valya gave it to me, but don't tell anyone."

"I'll never tell," Yuliya said.

"And look," Aniya said, "I have a very warm sweater that I don't need when I wear the green closet coat. See?"

Yuliya looked at both girls and blinked back tears.

"All right, but will you promise to stay with me? I'm a little afraid of that big hill," she said.

"What do you mean? Never mind. It's no problem," Elena said.

Bundled up in layers of sweaters and jackets, hats, and gloves, the three girls trudged through the front gate, across the road and on toward the big hill. They took turns pulling the rope of the old camp sled.

The snow glistened. The trees still had their early morning white icing, and, although many of the kids had already worked their way up the hill, Elena noticed animal tracks of little squirrels, or other small animals that had scampered away from the unexpected disturbance of the girls and boys.

At the top of the hill, they were out of breath. Elena looked all around. Toward the sun's side, she saw smooth white fields where no one had walked; on the other side, she saw the campground and its many buildings. To the south, the trees were thick and extended a long way. And to the north, there, below, was the frozen lake. It was huge and, somehow, ominous. She watched the bigger boys jump on their sleds so hard and fast that they would almost fly down the hill, hit the ice, and slide even further on the frozen waters. They would laugh and she could see the unspoken challenges between them. Who would go the furthest? Who was unafraid? She understood in her head that the lake had frozen solid, but she had no desire to test it with her own sled. Across the east side of the hill, kids trudged their way back up after a successful run. It was a lot of work to climb up, but she guessed the thrill of the ride was worth it.

"Who wants to go first?" Elena asked.

"It's a long way down. I'll watch the first time," Yuliya said.

"Ha, no way. Come on!"

"*Nyet*, really, Elena, I'm not ready yet," Yuliya said.

Without another word, Elena turned away from Yuliya and jumped onto the sled and flew down the hill alone. It was glorious, a wonderful thrill ride. The wind snapped at her face and her own laughter exploded. Her mind was quite blank; everything she felt inside was enormous. She stopped just short of the water's edge and jumped up to drag the sled back up to her friends.

At the top, Aniya claimed the sled next, and they cheered her down the hill. Crowded now at the top, some boys shoved and pushed the girls out of the way. To aggravate them, some boys stole hats and tossed them back and forth. Elena barely rescued her new red hat, but Yuliya was not as lucky, and two boys carried a fistful of hats down the hill and threw them out on the ice.

By the time Aniya got back up the hill, she panted and laughed as she boasted about her long ride down the hill and onto the ice. Yuliya sat on a rock with her gloved hands over her cold ears.

"Yuliya, your turn," Aniya called out.

"*Nyet*, I'm fine. You two go. I'll wait for another time."

The two girls shrugged and shared a ride down the hill. With two of them, the sled was heavier and faster, and their ride took them right out onto the surface of the lake. They both screamed as they slid along the ice. By then, many others had joined them on the ice. The girls lost their fear, laughed, and giggled as they slipped and slid their way back to the snowy edges like everyone else. Elena felt like she could sled all day long. If only they didn't have to do the long walk back up the hill.

This time, at the top, Yuliya said she was ready to go back inside for a while.

"Oh, come on, ride down at least once."

"I'll go with you," Aniya offered Yuliya.

"Here," Elena said, "wear my red hat for luck!"

Hesitantly, Yuliya climbed onto the sled behind Aniya and held on tight. With so many other kids on sleds, they had to move a little off to the side so Yuliya wouldn't be afraid of the other sleds that zoomed past, particularly the boys'. Elena gave them a big push to get them started. She grinned ear to ear as she watched the girls go down.

But then her heart jumped up into her throat. Out from the woods, two boys and a girl appeared and heaved a large branch into the path of the sled. It all happened so fast. In a moment, the sled slammed into the branch and the two girls flew into the air. Aniya hit a tree and collapsed at the base while Yuliya tumbled further down the hill like an awkward snowball. Two sleds slammed into her body and their riders rolled as well. For a few moments, there was only silence, and then Elena yelled, "Noooo!" and ran down the hill after them.

On her way to Aniya, she scanned the woods to see who the trio had been, but they vanished back into the trees. Aniya lay still and looked almost peaceful, which scared Elena even more. She looked down the hill and saw several people around Yuliya and two others apparently injured in the accident. But she knew in her gut this was no accident.

In moments, she heard more screams from the direction of the camp and saw a few older kids run for help. When she turned back, two boys came up to where she sat with Aniya in her arms.

"Shit, she looks dead," one boy said.

"Crap!" the other added.

Elena screamed and cried as she rocked the girl in her arms. Aniya's head flopped limply. What the boys said was true. Aniya looked very dead. Elena felt nauseous and rolled away from her friend's body. She stumbled toward Yuliya, who cried and screamed about the pain in her leg. Elena looked at her friend's leg and immediately threw up onto the snow. The surrounding kids squealed, disgusted by her vomit. Yuliya's leg had bent back onto itself, and a bone stuck out; lots of blood stained the snow. More blood flowed from Yuliya's head.

Where was the red hat? Elena looked around and saw it lying alone in the snow. She went to pick it up and as she did, a realization hit her. They had meant this accident for the girl in the bright red hat, not Aniya at all, but Elena. As she thought of this, she trembled and then sobbed. Swarms of older people and adults had gathered around by then. When someone came up to Elena to ask about her injuries, she shoved the woman aside and ran toward the camp. Aniya was dead, Yuliya hurt, and it was all her fault.

26

FEDYA & ZOYA

RĪGA, LATVIJA

In the end, there wasn't much Fedya could do but find some light and clean up. It wasn't like he wanted to scrub the place, but he and Zoya needed a place to hide, and in its current state, there wasn't even a chair for them to sit down on. As they moved about, his uncle seemed vaguely aware of them. He finished the bottle of vodka he kept next to his chair, talked to the cat, talked to the television set, and talked to himself. Since he spoke in Latvian, they didn't understand the words, so they ignored him. Eventually, he passed out. Fedya turned off the television.

Zoya found a small lamp that still worked and some candles while he produced matches. It was a murky light, but better than nothing. The flat must have been beautiful at one time and quite lavish, since it appeared to have additional rooms, as well as a kitchen and even a small bathroom.

He heard Zoya mutter as she searched for a switch or string to turn on a light in the bathroom. Then she shrieked, "A bathtub! But no running water? Ach! I'll clean you up anyway, you little porcelain beauty, and if I must, I'll carry the buckets myself. You are all mine!"

Fedya moved to the kitchen area to stop the faucet drips and discovered that an old dish rag had clogged the drain. There was no way to wash the dishes, but he could scrape most of the old food into a can and stack the dishes on a sideboard. He picked up the wet clothes from the floor and put them in an old washtub Zoya found in the bathroom.

He pulled off all the old clothes and soiled linens from the bed. The clothes and mattress smelled bad. The carved wooden headboard showed mythical creatures, including unicorns and fairies. He ran his fingers along the fine wood. Two privacy screens that must have been used to hide the bed were in shambles. He found broken hinges on one of them, while the fabric on the other had huge gashes in it, both damaged beyond repair. He folded them up as best he could and pushed them under the bed.

Behind one of the closed doors, he discovered a small empty room with walls covered from floor to ceiling with photographs. Unfortunately, there was no working light bulb in this room, so it was too dark to examine them. He took all the clothes from the kitchen and bedroom area and anything else that didn't have a home and piled them on the floor in the photograph room. At least it was dry in there.

When he tried the door to a second room, it stuck, or was maybe locked. He gave it a hard shove, and it opened part way. He stood in shock. It was a child's room, but in total contrast to the rest of the flat. He couldn't speak or move for several minutes while he took in the pale-yellow walls, the crib against one wall, and a child's bed against the other. Stuffed animals lined the beds and window ledge, a rocking chair, and a pale green dresser with a lamp and family pictures stood on the opposite wall. He switched on the small child's lamp. And there, on the dresser, he saw pictures of his uncle with a woman he assumed was his uncle's wife and two children.

"Zoya, come look," he called out the door.

"What is it?" Zoya said as she came up behind him.

"Look!"

She stuck her head inside and exclaimed, "Incredible! What kind of crazy person does this?"

"I don't know."

"I'm sleeping in here," Zoya said. She went back to the big room and got her large handbag, the only thing she had been able to hold onto after her fight with Yegor on the dock, which she then plopped on the floor.

"I don't think you should. It's a memory place."

"I don't care what it is. What? Are you going to sleep with the bedbugs in there?"

"I thought you were going to sleep in the bathtub?" he said.

"Sometimes you are a complete idiot. I'm going to take a bath."

"Oh."

"God, Fedya. Get your stuff. You can sleep on this fluffy rug on the floor. I'll sleep in the kid's bed. Did you check the stove? I'm going to heat some water and take that bath. It's a priority."

Zoya went about her mission. He watched her and was dumbfounded how she could come into a stranger's house and, in a few brief hours, treat it like her own. He glanced over at his uncle slouched in the big chair; he snored softly.

Fedya turned and studied the family pictures. In one picture, the woman sat on a swing in a park with a baby in her arms and a baby carriage nearby. In another picture, the woman was on her knees next to a little boy who held a blue balloon. In a third one, Uldis in a tuxedo, and the woman, in a long silky dress, stood together in a rather stiff pose. Their wedding picture? He wasn't sure, since so many pictures around the flat showed his uncle in a tuxedo. And finally, there was a picture of the whole family at a carnival: Uncle Uldis, the woman, the little boy, and a baby. They all looked happy. How long ago was this picture taken? What happened to them? Where were they now? What caused his uncle to change? What happened to the world traveler Fedya's mother had idolized?

"Fedya, come help me," Zoya called. "This pot of hot water is too heavy for me alone."

He helped her carry several pots of hot water to the tub so that Zoya could take a bath. While she was in there, he picked up and threw away the wads of paper under the piano, the empty alcohol bottles, and old newspapers. In another corner, opposite the bed, was a tumble of other furniture, including straight back wooden chairs, stools, a table, and other objects he couldn't identify in the dark. There was no point in trying to sort that out now. He checked on his uncle again to be sure he slept, and then walked over to the piano and raised the lid. He gently stroked the ivory keys. When he got up the courage to press down on a key, the note was silent. He pressed a second note and a deep tone sounded in the room. He yanked his hand away. His uncle stirred, but did not wake. Fedya sat down on the bench and brushed his fingers across the tops of the keys as though he could play the piano.

A memory rose within him. He must have been three or four, maybe younger. But he remembered sitting on a man's lap at a piano. The man instructed the young Fedya to play the white notes while he would play other notes. Together they made beautiful music. He remembered how he looked up at his mother who stood next to the piano and laughed as she said, "You'll make a musician out of him yet, Uldi." Were they here in this same flat? He looked around the room and tried to capture a second image, another memory, but his mind was blank.

Soundlessly, the cat leaped up from behind him and onto the piano. She glared down at him. "I don't know how to play," he confessed, "not really. When I was small, I played. I think." The cat sniffed. "Well, there was this one song, called 'Moonlight.' My mother sang it to us when we were little and taught me how to play it on a toy piano." He picked out the little melody and sang the lullaby quietly.

> "I cannot fall asleep,
> not stay in bed,
> sleep will not fetch me.
> I would like to visit Papa now,
> but I do not know the way."

"The words really say, 'visit Sasha,' but Mama always said 'Papa' in the song," Fedya told the cat. He reached up to pet her, and she bowed her head to let him. She was very elegant. "Minka, right? Your name is Minka. I am Fedya." She purred.

Zoya's cell phone interrupted their sweet reverie.

Zoya yelled from the bathroom, "Answer it. Quick, Fedya, it's in my bag. Answer it."

He jumped up to get it; the cat leaped away.

"*Privet*," he said into the phone. He recognized the voice: the sailor from the ship. Misha asked Fedya if they were safe and then asked to speak to Zoya.

Zoya bellowed from the tub. "Who is it? Bring me the damn phone. Who is it?"

He didn't even bother to answer her, but simply took the phone into the bathroom and handed it to her. He closed the door, but he could still hear her laugh and joke with Misha as though nothing had happened that day. Then it occurred to him that Zoya was naked in the water, and he hadn't even noticed. He felt exhausted and, although he hated to defile the memory room, it was the best place to sleep. He got his packs and slipped into the yellow room, curled up on the fluffy rug, and fell fast asleep.

The next morning, both he and Zoya were awakened by Uldis who stood, bleary-eyed and furious, at the door of the yellow room. He spewed sentence after sentence in his mother tongue. They sat up and gaped. What else could they do? Zoya kept saying, "*Russki! Russki!*" and repeated it with every break in his curses.

When he finally stopped yelling, he looked at them without comprehension. "Who the hell are you?" he asked in Russian.

"Don't you remember, old uncle?" Zoya said.

"Shut up, Zoya," Fedya said, as he stood up. "I am Fedya. This is Zoya. I am your nephew, Elizaveta's son. You are my Uncle Uldis."

"That cannot be right," he spoke again in Latvian.

"*Russki*, you old drunk," Zoya yelled.

With this attack, Uncle looked at Zoya. "*Da*, I see you are a Russian girl, without a doubt."

"What does that mean? What did he mean by that?"

Fedya ignored her. "Uncle Uldis, I am sorry, but it is all true. Do you understand me if I speak to you in Russian?"

"Well enough. Let me sit down, but please, not in here. I cannot be here and I ask you not to be here either. Please."

With that, he walked back into the big room and sat in the same chair in front of the television set. Fedya followed him and gestured for Zoya to get dressed. He watched Uncle reach for one of his bottles, but they were all gone. Fedya had thrown them away the night before, along with the rest of the trash. Uncle looked around the chair and then stopped when he caught Fedya watching him.

"You are Fyodor? But where is Elizaveta?" Uncle asked.

"Elizaveta died last April, on the fourth. She was sick, very sick. She said it was in her lungs. I don't really know."

Uncle closed his eyes. He reached again for a drink, waved his hand at the floor, and then remembered there was no bottle. He leaned forward and raked his hands through his hair and across several days' growth on his face.

"How did you find me, Fyodor Ivanovich?"

Fedya went to his backpack, pulled out the envelope with the picture of his mother and Uldis at the beach, and handed it over. Uldis stared at it for a long moment, and then groped in his pockets for eyeglasses. In the end, he found them sitting on a magazine next to his chair.

"Turn on a light! I hate these infernal days with no light. I need light. A man can't think in the dark." As Fedya turned on the lamp near his uncle's chair, Zoya came out of the yellow room and leaned against the door frame.

"Zoya, are you crazy?" Fedya rasped.

She wore a simple white blouse and skirt. In its simplicity, she looked beautiful. But he knew those clothes belonged to his uncle's wife. And sure enough, Uldis looked up and gaped.

"Lauma?" Uldis asked in a small voice.

"*Nyet*, it's Zoya, remember? I hope it's not a problem. But I lost my suitcase."

Fedya pulled around and stood between Uldis and Zoya to break his uncle's agonized stare. It took a moment, but then Uldis diverted his gaze to Fedya, tears in his eyes.

"Who are you?" Uldis asked.

Fedya could hear Zoya chortle behind him. He hissed at her to stop, and she walked over to the piano bench and sat.

"I'm Fedya."

"Ah yes, nephew." And off he went again into Latvian. Fedya brought his uncle's attention back to the photograph at hand. The older man talked as he gazed at the photograph and then at Fedya.

"Tell him to speak in Russian!" Zoya muttered.

"Please speak in Russian," Fedya said.

Uldis paused and then reached down again for a bottle. When he couldn't find one, he reached for a cigarette in his pocket. His hands trembled.

"Give me one of your smokes, will you?" Zoya said and stood up. Again, Uldis stopped in mid-action, a match still lit and burning as he looked at her.

"Zoya, stop talking! Go put on a jacket. You make him crazy in his wife's clothes. He thinks you're a ghost." Fedya blew out the match and then took the matches and lit his uncle's cigarette.

"I'm hungry," she complained.

"Shut up!"

Zoya huffed and walked over to the kitchen to see if there was any food anywhere. Fedya bent down and pulled his uncle's face away from Zoya and made the man look into his eyes.

"Uncle Uldis, please listen to me," he said. "I need your help. I am sorry to bring you more bad news about your sister. But I need you. We came from St. Petersburg. After Mama died, the authorities, they found us and took Elena and Irishka away. I thought I could live in the street by myself. I thought I could do it. But I can't. And now, there is an evil man chasing us. I think he is with the new Russians and—"

He wasn't sure if his uncle listened. The eyes glazed over.

He cried out, "Uncle! You are my family. You. Uncle, damn it. I can't do it alone anymore. I can't—"

He could not stop what happened next. Images of every event that had happened to him since his mother's death flashed before him like a fast movie. He couldn't speak, but there was a raw sound that came out of him with tears, and he could not stop the pain. He sobbed, he mewled, and he snorted. He didn't care. He didn't care anymore what Zoya thought or who saw him or who heard him. He wanted to throw off the pain. He wanted to explode. He had placed all his hopes on this man.

And his uncle couldn't even remember Fedya's name. He collapsed onto his uncle's knees. After some time, he felt a hand stroke his hair. He could feel the hand tremors.

"I'm sorry, my boy. I'm sorry. *Piedod mani*—forgive me. It will be all right," Uldis said.

———————————

Zoya stood in the kitchen area and watched them. For a moment, her eyes filled with tears, but she turned away to stop herself. There was no room in her for sympathy. Not now. She pushed away her own memories of uncles and brothers and fathers, most of them drunks; the men who had destroyed her life. They were pathetic. Oh yes, this one was sorry now, but then what? Would he go through withdrawal for this boy-stranger, his nephew? She remembered her mother as she sat beside her father's bed when he tried to stop the drinking. He was worse than a sick baby that cried and vomited. The memory disgusted her. And then the seizures started. She needed another cigarette.

Her phone vibrated. She checked, and it was Misha. He was stupid, but useful.

"*Privet,*" she said into the phone as she walked over to the giant mirror. "Did you find it?" As she listened to Misha, she continued to watch the old uncle with Fedya in the reflection. Thank God Fedya had stopped wailing. "What? What did you say? I can barely hear you." After a slight pause, "Well, can you come and get me? I've got to get out of here. Uh, hmm. Just a minute."

She spoke to the mirror image, "Fedya, what's the address here?"

Fedya looked up but couldn't find her in the room. He tried to focus on her voice. She had become a ghost. And then he saw her. "Why?"

"Misha is going to pick me up. He found my pack. That idiot, Yegor, threw it into the bushes."

"*83 Kapseļu Iela,*" Uncle said, but then added in Russian, "Kapseļu Street."

She told Misha on the phone and then hung up.

"When will you be back?" Fedya asked.

She walked over to them. "How about one of your cigarettes, old uncle?"

Uncle pulled out his cigarette pack. They were American cigarettes, which surprised her. He gave her one and then fumbled for a match.

"Don't bother, I have fire." She lit her cigarette and sat on the piano bench. "What are you going to do now, old uncle? You going to tell little Fedya what happens next? Is he going to be the one to put cold rags on your face? Will he hold you down while you shake and scream about the spiders or the rats or whatever hallucinations you'll be having?"

"Why are you being such a bitch?" Fedya stood up.

"Fedya, sit down. It's all right," Uncle said. He looked at Zoya and then turned and pointed at the boy. "See that dark green book over there, on the short bookshelf? Bring it to me."

When Fedya fetched it, Uncle turned to Zoya. "I don't have a telephone anymore. May I use your mobile?"

Zoya took a drag of her cigarette, flicked the ashes on the floor. "Sure, all right. But no long calls."

"You're correct, of course, about my condition. I can see, dear Zoya, that you are already a woman of the world," Uncle said.

"Are you making fun of me?"

"Not at all. Not at all. I'm agreeing with you," he said.

She handed him the mobile. He flipped through the book until he found the right page, then he called a number he found there. There was a certain dignity to him today, she had to admit. He seemed old-fashioned and very polite. When he spoke into the phone, it was in Latvian. She finished her cigarette and found a dirty dish in the kitchen on which to put it out. She gathered her things by the door and waited for Uncle to finish with her mobile.

"When are you coming back?" Fedya asked again.

"Look, who knows? Maybe never. We split up, remember? You hate me, or did you forget? I'll stay with Misha. I think I can make it worth his while. Plus, all this cozy family stuff is not for me."

"What about Yegor?"

"What about him? It's a big city. He'll go back home soon enough."

173

Just as the buzzer rang, Uncle finished with his call and handed the phone to Fedya, who walked it over to Zoya.

"So," she said, "have a good life." She kissed Fedya on the cheek and walked out the door, and that was that. Fedya stared at the closed door. He knew he should be glad. She was trouble. And yet, she was his one link back to Russia, and now, even that had melted away. The strings of his past life were being cut, one by one. He reached his hand out to the door for fear of falling.

"Fedya," Uncle asked, "Are you all right?"

"I don't know."

27

ELENA

That evening, someone had come in and packed up both Yuliya and Aniya's clothes. Elena didn't even roll over to look. A short time after that, the same person, or someone else, had come in and asked her a few questions. She answered, but now she couldn't remember the questions or her answers. Later still, she heard the New Year's party start up down the hall. She couldn't bring herself to take part.

Celestina came in during the night and brought Elena her New Year's gifts: an orange, a pocket-sized doll, and a small bag of chocolates. Asked if she wanted to come down to the party, she said nothing.

Other words and images rolled around nonstop in her head. "It's all your fault," "They were hurt because of you," and so on. She pictured her friends again and again, as they had tumbled down the hill in slow motion. She heard the thud of Aniya's head as it hit the tree.

"Lenushka, I am sorry about Aniya. She was a nice girl. Do you know if she had any family?"

Elena hadn't realized Celestina was in the room again. She pulled the blanket over her head. She didn't want to see or talk to anyone.

"Good night, then. I will come back and check on you tomorrow."

Elena listened to the music for a while, but then fell asleep again. That's what she wanted, to block out everything, to forget, to forget the blood and the sounds and the screams, and to forget the bodies as they rolled down the hill.

Other girls, babbling in the hall, woke her in the morning as they headed for breakfast. She couldn't eat, she just couldn't. She couldn't face all those people. Her first mistake was talking. Silence would have been better. Why had she bothered to make friends? She was bad for people. She was bad luck. All the people she cared about either died or disappeared. They all left her.

The door banged open and Kiska, out of breath, said, "Elena, you must come to the office. There is a telephone call for you."

Elena didn't budge, and stared up at the ceiling. If she lay still, Kiska would go away. Kiska was not patient enough to talk to a stone.

"What are you doing? You look dead. I mean, I shouldn't say that. But I mean it, come, or there will be trouble for you."

Elena shook her head. She didn't care. What point was there to answer a telephone? She would be a statue. She would be silent.

"I'm going to tell. I'm going to tell them you're disobeying," Kiska said. When that didn't work, Kiska sat on the bed.

"Lenushka, it's not good to be so sad. All of us have seen girls die before. This girl is not the first one. It's terrible, but there are lots of ways to die. At least it was quick. When you have been in the children's houses as long as I have, you'll see what I mean. Besides, Yuliya is all right. She got to go to the hospital." Kiska waited and then patted her hand. "Come on, come to the telephone. I think it's important."

Elena turned to look at Kiska for a minute, but then turned away.

"All right, but I will tell Celestina that you are acting like a baby." Kiska left with the bang of the door slamming shut, and Elena could hear her heavy footsteps down the hall.

A short time later, Celestina herself came into the room. She sat on the bed like Kiska, but instead of questioning her, she rubbed Elena's back, stroked her hair, and sang an old lullaby.

"Bai, bai, bai, bai, Bayu, orchid, little dear. Bai, bai, bai, bai, Bayu, orchid, little dear. On the hillside in the spring, Birds of heaven sweetly

176

sing, Seeking for their young what's best, In the forest dark they nest... What do you want, Lenushka, eh? What do you want right now more than anything?" Celestina asked.

Elena would not answer.

"Do you know someone by the name of Valentina Alexandrovna?"

Elena turned on the bed and looked at the caregiver curiously.

"Ah, you know her then? Well, it's a shame you would not take her phone call since she wanted to wish you a happy New Year and—" Celestina stopped.

"And what?" Elena said finally.

"Well, it turns out that this Valentina Alexandrovna, a friend of yours, has left her parents' home a few days early and returned to the city." Again, Celestina paused. "She has asked me if you can stay with her for the rest of the holiday."

Elena sat up. "Is this true?"

"*Da.* But you are mistaken if you think this will make life easier for you with the other girls."

"I don't care."

"All right. It's very unusual, but these have not been usual days. So, I've asked my Konstantin to drive you back to the city tomorrow. Pack up your belongings and be ready in the morning."

Elena stared at Celestina. Could she have heard that right? Konstantin Andreivich? The DJ? The most gorgeous man in the entire world?

"Lenushka, if you are leaving us tomorrow, then I expect you to eat today. I will not have you go to this woman's house and have her think we allowed you to starve. You will eat or you will not go."

Elena rolled away from Celestina. "I'm not hungry."

"Do not press me, child. My word is final. If you are not at dinner this evening, I will contact Valentina Alexandrovna and tell her the camp rules forbid you to go."

"But—"

"We are finished here," she said as she left the room.

Elena wasn't sure which piece of news was hardest to accept. To leave the wretched camp and see Valya again, or to eat in the dining hall with the other girls, which made her sick just to think about it. But even more astonishing would be to drive to the city in the same car with Konstantin Andreivich, which made her sick with fear.

When the dinner bell sounded, she put on her serious Fedya face and went through the motions: she walked to the dining hall, stood in line, went through the food line, picked up her meal, sat at a table, and gave the appearance of eating. She sat alone and did not look at anyone. Kiska invited her to sit with friends, but Elena shook her head. One half hour in the dining room seemed very long. She worked hard to hold herself together. She could not break down again, not here. The noise of the diners helped block out individual voices. She moved the food around her plate. Five more minutes and she could leave. Hopefully, her presence at dinner would satisfy Celestina.

Someone came up behind her and whispered in her ear, "It should have been you."

She whirled around in her seat to find Larissa there with two of her lapdog boyfriends. Elena stood and faced the girl. She pressed her shaking hands to her jeans. She wanted to strike out at the gypsy, but this might be what Larissa wanted. A public fight would be Elena's fault. To her surprise, in that brief and awful moment, she heard her mama's voice, "Whenever someone is cruel or hateful to you, speak a blessing to them clearly, loudly, and slowly."

"I will be happy to pray that God will forgive you," she said to Larissa and then turned to leave.

"You little toad, how dare you call on the name of God?"

"Larissa Evgenia, isn't it?" Celestina interrupted. She had walked up to the other side of the table. "I haven't seen you much, my dear. Please come and tell me your news. Seryozha and Sasha, you may return to the boys' table."

And with that, Celestina came around and took Larissa genially by the arm, asked about her holiday, and walked her over to the counselors' table in the corner. Elena stopped for a moment to watch them and couldn't help but smile. Oh, that Celestina was quite clever.

She stepped outside and walked toward the dorm; the cold air helped clear her head. Although a part of her wanted to replay the hateful scene with Larissa, instead, her mind turned to memories of her mother. Elena hadn't thought of her mother in a while. Those memories now made her unsteady inside. She wanted her mother right then, more than anyone or anything else.

Elena tried to see her mother's face, but it was fuzzy. Before, it had been too painful to remember her mother. But now, when she really needed her, she could not recall what Mama looked like. She inhaled deeply.

The air struck her lungs like a knife in the heart. She reached out to the nearest tree, pulled off her glove, and pressed her hand into the rough bark. Then she slapped the bark again and again until the pain in her hand was worse than the pain in her mind. She had lost her mother forever.

She whispered into the night, "Fedya! Fedya? Are you listening? I can't do this. I can't keep going. Where are you? I need you."

She heard his voice in her head, "*Lenushka, you are a stupid goose.*"

"I'm not a goose, I'm a swan."

"*Ah! And don't you forget it! So, little swan, what have you done now?*"

"I hurt my hand."

"*I see that. Go inside. Go on. Go inside and fix it up.*"

"I'm afraid, Fedya."

"*Don't be silly. Do what I say. I mean it, or something else will hurt, you thick head.*"

In the haze of her brother's voice, she started walking again down the path. Other people came from the dining hall now and several passed her by. No one noticed her until Kiska and Raisa came up to her. Raisa was the first to see her hand.

"Blood! Oh God, you're bleeding. She's bleeding. Help!" Raisa yelled.

"Shut up, Raisa!" Kiska pinched the girl's arm. "Let me see, Elena. Oh God. How did this happen? Come on. Let's go to Celestina."

"*Nyet!*" Elena said. "Please. You do it. Please."

"All right, come on. Let's go inside," Kiska said. "I know where they keep the bandages."

They hustled into the dorm, down the hall, and into the bathing room. Elena washed her hand, which throbbed worse than ever, while Raisa just stood by the door and watched. Kiska told Elena to hold her hand up as she looked for the bandage box.

Raisa asked again how it happened and commented on how ugly it looked and did it hurt and so on. Elena didn't bother to answer. When Kiska returned and led them back to their room, she was quite efficient. Within a few minutes, Kiska had wrapped Elena's hand in soft gauze and taped it shut. Elena could still move her fingers.

"No broken bones. So, are you talking now?" Kiska asked.

"Not really. *Nyet. Da.* I don't know."

"Is that what I get for saving your life?" Kiska said. "Tell me something at least!"

Elena inspected Kiska's face and looked for betrayal when Raisa burped loud and long, like one of the boys. Both girls burst out laughing.

Raisa gawked. "What? What's so funny?"

Raisa's expression made them laugh even more. Finally, as they calmed down, Elena said, "I'm leaving tomorrow."

"What do you mean?" Kiska said.

"Please don't tell anyone until I'm gone. Celestina is sending me back to the city."

Raisa said, "Why?"

Kiska answered for her, "Because of the accident, stupid. But where will you stay?"

She wanted to tell her everything, but she knew that wasn't wise. Raisa would tell Lukina and then Lukina would tell Tatiana who would tell Larissa. No, it would be better to keep this part of her story a secret.

"I don't know. She arranged something. Please don't tell."

Someone called Kiska's name in the hallway and both girls ran out to see who it was.

Kiska popped her head in the door, "I'll be right back"

But of course, Kiska didn't come back. Elena didn't care. Instead, she crawled back into her bed and tried to forget about the pain in her hand. When she raised it up in the air, it didn't hurt as much. Eventually, she fell asleep and didn't wake until the morning bell for breakfast.

After she rolled over to go back to sleep, the pain in her hand woke her up the rest of the way. She got up and dressed as quickly as her hand would allow. She pulled her pack from under the bed and put in all the clothes she had brought from the children's house. While she packed, she tried to imagine how Valya lived. In what part of the city? Did she have a private flat, a private bathroom?

A knock interrupted her thoughts. A girl poked her head in to say, "Elena Ivanovna? Konstantin Andreivich told me to come up and ask if you are ready to leave or do you need more time?"

"*Da,* I mean *nyet,* I'm ready. I'll be right there," Elena said.

The girl left and Elena sat down on the bed. She had forgotten about the Konstantin Andreivich part of her escape. She would be red-cheeked the entire time in his car. He'd hear her heart pounding. She would sound childish no matter what she said. And if she was silent, he would think her rude. Well, there was no help for it now. Fedya would have said, "Sometimes you must pretend you know what you're doing. Most people don't know the difference."

She took a deep breath, grabbed her pack with her left hand, pulled her coat from the back of the door to cover her right hand, and went along the hall and down the steps to the lobby.

"Hello, you must be Elena Ivanovna. Do you remember me from the first night dance? I saved you from a dangerous fall off the stage," Konstantin said as he held the door for her.

"*Da.* Of course." What an idiot. Of course she remembered. He was still the most gorgeous man ever. She couldn't bear to look at him. He was more beautiful than Valya's boyfriend, Pyotr Konstantin.

"Is that all you have? You travel light."

"*Da.*" Great conversation so far, Elena.

She settled into the front seat of his little black car. It was messy on the inside, but the seats were leather. He had hung a St. Christophorus medal from his mirror. The back seat was full of equipment. When he came around, he had to fold into the car. He started the engine, but then he swore.

"I'm sorry. I must see my mother before we leave. One moment."

He got out again and met Celestina as she came out of the building; they embraced and exchanged a few words. Celestina looked over his shoulder and waved at Elena. She was a kind woman, and Elena was almost sorry to leave the camp before getting to know her better.

"Would you like to hear some music? I have a CD player," he said as he climbed back into the car.

"*Da.*"

Oh, for heaven's sake, couldn't she say anything more intelligent than '*da*'?

"What would you like to hear?"

She shrugged her shoulders. That was too much of a trap. If she said an American group, he might think she was too good for Russia and if she said a Russian group, he might think she was old-fashioned. And what if her answer made her sound like a stupid little kid? What would a sophisticated answer be? Silence was best. It would be more mysterious.

"How about Destiny's Child, eh? You like that?"

"*Da.*"

Putting in the CD, he laughed, "I hope you have a bigger vocabulary than the same one word, or it will be a long ride to the city."

"What? Oh. *Da.* I mean, sure. I do." That sounded stupid. She had to relax. Take a breath. She wanted to make a witty remark, but her mind was a blank. They listened to the music for a while. Finally, she got up her courage and spoke.

"Uh, how, uh, long have you been a DJ?"

"Oh, about three years. I do it to make some cash. I share the equipment with a few friends."

"What else do you do?" she said, and summoned the courage to turn and look at him. She was glad he couldn't look back for long while he drove the car. She was sure her cheeks were bright red. He still wore all black, even his leather jacket.

"I'm a musician, a singer, a drummer. Sometimes I write music. I think I am called a 'starving artist.' It means I don't make enough money in my work, so I must do other jobs. I DJ, I work as a bouncer at a club sometimes, I sub at concerts for friends, and I sell cars."

"Sell cars?"

"Sure. This one's for sale. You want to buy a car?"

"You're making fun of me."

"I'm playing with you a little. You seem so serious all the time."

She was silent again, and embarrassed. She didn't know how to answer. She thought about what he said and decided he was wrong. She wasn't serious as much as sad most of the time. On the few occasions she had grabbed a kind of happiness, the feeling was stolen from her. *Nyet*, not serious, just sad.

"May I call you Elena?"

"*Da*."

He chuckled. "Did I offend you by calling you serious?"

"What? *Nyet*, I don't know. I'm just sad most of the time. It doesn't matter," she said. "You wouldn't understand. You have a good life. Live my life and then you would be sad too."

She turned away from him then and looked out the window. She wanted to make him feel bad for what he had said.

Outside, there weren't many cars on the road and the countryside looked all clean in the snow. He changed the CD to a soft song she didn't recognize. If she were one of the other girls, she would know how to talk to a boy. They knew how to giggle and flirt. She didn't know any of it. What was she thinking? Being in love with an older man was hopeless.

Konstantin broke the silence. "I'm sorry about your friends."

She nodded her head but kept her gaze out the window. She didn't trust herself to look at him. The reminder of Aniya and Yuliya brought tears to her eyes. How many tears can a person cry? She wondered if anyone had ever collected them and measured the amount. If a person wandered in the desert, could she cry?

"When I was little, maybe ten or twelve," Konstantin said, "I took my grandfather's gun. He was in the mafia, or something like that, but

I don't know for sure. Anyway, I showed it to my friends. I was sure none of them had ever seen a gun in person. I was so cool. We were all surprised how heavy it was. But I wouldn't let anyone hold it for long. It was my gun and with it, I was the man. I was the center of attention. But then the gun went off. Well, that's not exactly true. I mean, I pulled the trigger to see what it would do and unfortunately, the gun was loaded." He paused for a moment. She turned to look at him, and could see this story was still hard for him to tell.

"What happened?"

"I killed my best friend."

She gasped automatically and covered her mouth with her hand.

"It really was my fault."

"You were a kid."

"So are you."

"What?" she said.

"My mother thinks you are blaming yourself for what happened to your friends. Is that true?"

She stared at him, and he took his eyes off the road long enough to challenge her back. She looked out the window.

"But it was my fault," she said. "There is a girl who hates me. She and her friends...she told me...they meant the accident for me. I knew it anyway. She didn't have to tell me. Aniya...she wore my red hat. They thought it was me...I made her wear my hat because she didn't have one."

"Listen to me. When I killed my friend, I disobeyed my mother, who had told me a hundred times to never touch my grandfather's gun. I never believed bad things could happen to me. You have already had a hard life, Elena, and I am sorry that you have had to suffer another loss, but other children caused this accident. And for every unpleasant situation, it's always easier to go back and say how we could change the outcome by doing or acting differently. If my friend had been sitting down instead of standing, the shot would have missed him. If my grandfather had cleaned his gun, there would have been no bullets. If...if...if. But the 'ifs' are not what is real. This horrible accident has happened to you for a reason. And one day, you may figure out why."

She made a little snorting sound through her nose. "And was there a reason for your friend to die?"

"In a way. I dropped the gun on the street. We all scattered. The police found the gun and matched the weapon to other murders. They arrested my grandfather and put him in jail. He stopped beating the women in his life. All the same, the death of my friend was a high price to pay."

28
FEDYA &
UNCLE ULDIS

RĪGA, LATVIJA

The cure for a drunk was much worse than Fedya could have imagined. If he had known, he wouldn't have stayed. Nothing could have prepared him for the misery and sense of helplessness he had as he watched his uncle withdraw from alcohol. Fedya had seen a lot during his mother's illness, but this was different. He was grateful his uncle had called in a friend, Ausma. She had wild blonde hair with dark roots, a square face with a few wrinkles around her soft gray eyes, and a voice that sounded raspy from too many cigarettes. She laughed a lot, even in the worst situations. Before the deep alcohol withdrawal started, Uncle told stories about Ausma, when the two of them shared drinks, travel, and music in the orchestra.

Not long after she arrived that first day, Uldis became very sick, but she seemed to know what to do. He even soiled himself, but Ausma didn't blink an eye. She rarely spoke to Fedya and signaled for him to sit down out of the way, to wait. She made a few calls and soon several people showed up to follow her directions, clean up, give Uncle ice chips, and put cool rags on his forehead. Finally, one man, Karlis, noticed Fedya, the Russian boy, and spoke to him. Fedya took that opportunity to explain who he was and how he was related to Uldis. Ausma took him into her arms and repeated the word, *"nabaziņš"* which Karlis translated as "poor boy." They all teased her then as Fedya's *Tante*—Aunt Ausma.

In less than two weeks, the flat was transformed. The helpers restored order to the furniture, pulled off blankets and old curtains from the windows, and threw away anything that was too dirty or beyond repair. There was a fire in the fireplace. Someone washed the linens, and Uncle finally slept in his own bed instead of the chair. Minka, the cat, lay at her master's feet. Ausma washed Uncle's clothes and put them away. The kitchen area looked like a proper kitchen. Ausma cooked several meals, including a delicious smelling soup. She hummed light and breezy tunes, but most were unfamiliar to Fedya. Ausma reminded him of the auntie whose old *dacha* was next to theirs in the summer when they were little.

"Fedya?" Uncle called out from the bed.

Fedya jumped up and ran over. Ausma stopped her tune but kept up her cooking.

"*Da,* Uncle."

"You are still here, eh?"

"*Da,* I don't have anywhere else to go."

Uncle snorted. Ausma interrupted and said something about the soup. Instead of a tray, however, she set out the meal on the table. Fedya couldn't understand her words, but got the message all the same. Uncle's time in bed was over. Uncle groaned and tried to roll away to the wall, but Ausma came over and smacked him with a towel.

Together, she and Fedya helped him get up and shuffle to the table. Fedya wasn't sure, but it sounded a bit like Uncle swore in Latvian, which made him want to laugh.

"You think it's funny, little man? I am a sick person," Uncle said.

"They call them drunks back in St. Petersburg," Fedya said.

"Well, you're in Rīga now."

Ausma cajoled Uncle into eating an entire bowl of soup. During breaks, Uncle translated a little for Ausma, who said Fedya should call her Tante Ausma in Latvian.

During those first long days and nights, while the others sat by Uncle's bed, Fedya spent his time with the photographs and sheet music. He learned it was true: Uncle Uldis had been all over the world and had met many important people. In one picture, Uncle stood with friends in front of the famous liberty statue in New York City. Other photographs showed both Tante Ausma and Uncle Uldis when they were much younger. He pulled several photographs from the picture room walls and brought them to the table. The older couple looked at the pictures for a long time and talked about them in Latvian.

"This is Tante Ausma, right?" he interrupted.

Uncle looked at Fedya and sighed. Tante Ausma said a few words that Fedya interpreted as "tell him." He sat still as his uncle considered what he would share.

"We were on tour with the orchestra, the Latvian National Symphony Orchestra. This was a big day because we would play one of my compositions in Warsaw. The music featured Ausma at the harp. She played superbly that day. She still plays beautifully." He grabbed one of her hands and brought it to his lips. She pulled away and squeezed his shoulder as she cleared the plates and began making coffee.

"She has been a good friend for many years, a good friend to me and to...and to...my wife, Lauma." He stopped. His hand shook as he reached for the sparkling water. He stared at his hand as it shook. "I don't believe I will ever play again. How can I?" And then he wept. Although Fedya knew his uncle was better in body, his mind was still broken.

While Uncle regained control over his emotions, Fedya studied another photograph up close. He saw a somewhat younger Ausma at the harp; Uncle stood beside her, and in the background was a grand piano and a man holding a violin. The oddest thing about the picture was that Uncle looked off to the right while everyone else looked at the camera; his right hand reached out and held a young woman's hand, but the picture only caught her arm in the frame. Fedya touched Ausma's hand and pointed to the thin white arm and said, "Lauma?" and she nodded.

He went back over the other pictures for hints that Lauma was there, maybe in the background somewhere. He assumed she wasn't a musician, and yet she seemed to be an important part of everything Uncle did. In that way, Uncle was like his sister, Elisaveta, Fedya's mother. They were both rich in their love for family. How had his mother ended up with Vladimir Ivanovich, another drunk? The only good thing Vladimir had done was produce Irishka.

As he thought of Irishka, he revisited his decisions back in St. Petersburg. Had he abandoned his sisters? Had he acted wisely to call social services to come and pick them up? He couldn't have taken care of them in the winter. He couldn't. And if he had told Elena about his plan ahead of time, she would have fought him or done something stupid. He looked now at his uncle and wondered if there was any strength left in the man. Would he turn Fedya over to the authorities as well? Could Fedya trust him?

"Uncle Uldis, why didn't you come to St. Petersburg when my mother became ill?"

He caught a warning in Ausma's eyes, but then she patted Fedya's hand, got up, and went back for more coffee. For a second, Fedya thought she understood what he had asked in Russian.

Uncle answered, "We have all suffered, boy. By the time I opened Elizaveta's letters, I was already dead inside. I'm sorry."

Ausma chattered to Uncle.

"What did she say?" Fedya asked.

"She thinks you deserve to hear the truth. She's right, of course." He paused for a moment, stirred his coffee, and drank a small sip. "So, I give you no more poetry. That year, Lauma, my wife, had taken the children, Oskar and Lidiya to Moscow to visit an old girlfriend who had a new baby. Oskar was four, Lidiya was still an infant. They stayed with a friend of hers. What was her name? Alfrieda, I think. It doesn't matter. The second night after they arrived, they were all killed by an explosion. Some maniac, a Chechen they said, was the mastermind. September 9th, 1999. Hundreds either died or suffered injury." He stopped and stared into space. "I lost everyone that truly mattered to me that night. I should have been there. But I chose an important concert in Berlin. The American press would be there. My career was about to soar. But you see what happened? Now I am as low as a man can go." He laughed a little, and then tears began again and his hands shook. "I should have been with her. I should have died with my family."

Ausma came and coaxed him up and back to bed. They talked softly as she maneuvered him to the edge of the bed, took off his slippers, and helped him lie down and get under the covers. He had stopped crying, and it wasn't long before he slept.

A little later that evening, Ausma invited Fedya back to the table. She was nervous. She checked on Uldis several times, and she scratched the insides of her hands and rubbed the calluses of her fingers created by the harp strings.

Then, she looked at him, and in clear Russian, said, "I have a secret."

"What? But—" she covered his mouth with a finger.

"Please. I can't tell you everything now. But I want you to know what a brave, brave boy you are and what a difference you are making in your uncle's life. You have done what none of us have been able to do since Lauma's death."

Quickly, she explained that she still played with a small chamber group and needed to travel with them for a while. She showed him the medicines, and which ones to give Uldis when he woke up and which ones were for nighttime. She showed him the foods she had prepared for them in the refrigerator. Then she showed him a calendar and said she would be back in two weeks. "Tomorrow, a man will come to re-install a telephone. My number is here on the calendar if you need anything."

He walked her to the door. She said, "Your uncle does not remember I speak Russian. Please do not mention it. In this state, he would consider it a betrayal. The Bolsheviks murdered his grandparents and later, the Soviets deported his father. During "russification," many Latvians collaborated with the Soviets which infuriated Uldis. My husband was... well, never mind about that. It's a long story. If you can get him to play the piano, I know it would help restore his soul. All right? Can you keep my secret? Someday I will tell you, and maybe even him, the story, but not now. I've got to run."

When he closed the door behind her, he felt very alone, much like the night Zoya left. He closed his eyes, turned, and slid to the floor, dropped his head into his arms and prayed, "Mama. I need you. Please help me. Please, Mama."

Over the next several days, he and Uncle developed a routine. Fedya would make a breakfast of bread and cheese with strong coffee, and they would talk. Then, he would run to the corner for the local newspaper and Uncle would translate the best stories or summarize important world events. They would watch television or Uncle would read. At midday, they would have soup and more bread. Afterward, Uncle would take a nap.

In the early evening, they would walk. The first day, they walked around the flat. The second day, they went down a few steps, but Uncle had to rest a long time before he started back up again. When they finally made it all the way down, there was a welcome bench outside the front door. After several days of this, they could walk to the corner and back. Uncle's Russian got better each day, and he even tried to teach Fedya a few Latvian words. As Uncle got stronger, he would get up earlier than Fedya and make his own coffee; he claimed Fedya's coffee was terrible. Each day, they made a plan.

"Today, I have hired a driver and we will go to the old city like tourists," Uncle Uldis announced.

"But why?" Fedya asked. "It's unnecessary. I don't really care about that."

"Well, it's not for you. I must see an old friend of mine, but I am not strong enough to go alone. All right?"

"I'm sorry, Uncle Uldis, of course."

"Tell me about your sisters. You have been silent about them."

Fedya picked up the breakfast dishes and walked over to the sink. He stood there for several minutes and tried to think about what to say. "I told you about them the first night I was here."

"That's hilarious. You know I have no memory of that time at all. So, tell me again."

Fedya didn't like to talk about them, so he ignored the question. He rinsed the dishes and set them off to the side on a towel. Would his uncle press him for information? Apparently not. He went over and made Uncle's bed, picked up a few stray pieces of clothing, and emptied the ashtray.

"You should really stop smoking," Fedya said.

"I see. You are afraid to tell me about the girls because it's more bad news? More dead children? How many more dead children must there be?"

Fedya looked up when he heard the desperate tone of his uncle's voice. He had spread his hands out on the wood table as though waiting for someone to cut off his fingers.

"*Nyet*, Uncle Uldis, they are not dead. Sorry, I didn't mean for you to think that." He walked over to the table and put his hand on his uncle's shoulder. "It's hard for me to say out loud. You see, I gave them up."

"What?" Uncle looked up and into Fedya's eyes. "I don't understand."

"They are in the system now. I gave them up to the social welfare people." He took a deep breath. "I couldn't take care of them anymore."

Fedya plopped down in the closest chair and laid his forehead between his elbows on the table; his arms came up over his head as though to protect himself from blows. He wasn't weeping, but he felt very hollow. Just to think about his swan sisters hurt so much. He doubted he would ever see them again. They might as well be dead.

"*Nyet*, Fedya, you made the right choice," Uncle Uldis said.

Fedya shook his head. "We were family, and I broke the family. My mother, on her deathbed, begged me to keep us together. And I tried. But the cold nights came, and the money ran low, and Irishka got so thin. I'd pick her up and she would be like a rag doll. And one of her arms ended up crooked because I didn't watch; she fell out of a window, and we had no money to go to the doctor. Besides, at the clinic, there would have been too many questions. And Elena, she needed to go back to school, and, and—"

"Fedya! Look at me."

He paused and lifted his head to look at his uncle. He saw tears in the older man's eyes as he reached out and stroked the boy's face.

"Please forgive me," Uncle said. "It is I who have failed the family. I have been so obsessed with my own grief that I haven't even considered what you have been through. Listen to me. This makes our trip into town even more important. We will visit my lawyer, Peteris Meļkis. He will help us."

"How?" he asked. "I don't understand."

"You'll see. I don't want to get your hopes up too much. But we can make inquiries. If your sisters, my nieces, remember, if they are in the system, then there will be records. You gave their correct names?"

Fedya nodded. It hadn't even occurred to him to give different names. "Should I have given fake names?"

"Thank God you didn't. Listen, I am not a rich man, but I am also not a poor man. I know I am a pitiful man who lost his way, and I am still in deep regret. We will look for your sisters. After all, you, Elena, and Irishka are my only relatives now. You are my family."

29

VALYA & ELENA

ST. PETERSBURG, RUSSIA

Valya paced in Petya's apartment as she waited for Elena to arrive. Already, her holidays had been strange. Four days before the New Year, Petya had announced he would not travel with her to Pavlovo after all. She was disappointed, but by the set of his mouth, she could tell he had expected her to challenge his decision. She opted for nonchalance as though it didn't matter. She surprised him, and he had appeared relieved.

"What will you be doing, then?" she had asked.

"A little this and a little that; my parents asked me to come and visit them in Tallinn."

"Really? Since when do you do what your parents ask you to do?"

"Hey, they're paying for a ticket. How can I complain? Will you be all right on your own? Can I trust you?" he had teased.

"Trust me? How ironic. All right, you! I release you to whatever you think will be more exciting than quiet Pavlovo along with my kind, but boring parents."

Petya had pulled her into his arms. "This is why we make a perfect couple."

They had made love in the middle of the day: glorious, but a little predictable. He was hiding something, but she didn't have the energy to pursue it. She sensed he was pulling away from her. She had hoped a holiday together would help. Apparently, he had other plans. She only hoped this distraction wasn't the blond Nelli Antonovna or the mysterious dark-haired woman at Michelle's Restaurant she had seen flirting with him after the State Circus.

There was nothing she could do about it now. She stopped her restless pacing and went into the little kitchen to put on the kettle for tea. She loved Petya's apartment. She shouldn't complain. He paid for nearly everything, including her clothes. She liked the kitchen best, with its modern cabinets, counters, and appliances. She cherished the tiny table by the kitchen window where she could sit in the mornings with her coffee, look out at the building's courtyard, and still see the obelisk of Vosstaniya Square that soared above the rooftops. She was grateful the apartment was toward the back of the building and away from the noise of Nevskiy Prospekt and the cinema crowds.

When the kettle whistled, Valya poured water over the black tea leaves in her favorite brown teapot, the same one she had used since she was a little girl. Her *babushka* had given her the pot when Valya had turned ten.

"A girl must have a real teapot to learn how to make proper tea. When I was little, we had a samovar, but no one uses samovars much anymore," her *babushka* had said. Those were special days with her grandmother at the *dacha*; Valya missed her very much. But it was her supervisor, Olga Petrovna, who had taught her greater lessons, such as how to appreciate the poorest of the poor in a country that was rich with them.

The door buzzer interrupted her memories.

Valya ran over to the door and buzzed in her young guest. When she opened the apartment door, she heard two people climbing up.

"Elena, that is you, isn't it?" Valya called down.

"*Da,* Valya, and I have a friend with me," Elena announced.

"Fine! Come on up." She had forgotten about the driver. Celestina Yamadayevna had said her son would bring Elena back to the city. She stepped back into her apartment to check her hair in the mirror, just in case.

"Here we are," Elena said as she came through the door. "This is Kostya," Elena added, then hauled off her boots and looked around the apartment. "Oh, it's just as I imagined. Your flat is wonderful. And look, you can see the obelisk." Elena walked and chatted, almost to herself, it seemed. "You have a big television," she exclaimed as she poked her head into Petya's office.

"*Privet*," Konstantin Andreivich said to Valya. "Hope we are not too late." He leaned against the side of the door and raised an eyebrow in a flirty way. Was it cheeky or disarming? She couldn't decide if he was comfortable in his good looks, or didn't know the effect he had on people. Well, not an effect on people in general, but women. Yes, he definitely had a magical effect, and he was certainly affecting her.

"*Nyet*, not at all," she said. "Please come in and sit down. May I offer you some tea? I just put it on."

"*Da,* I can stay for a moment. I am Konstantin Andreivich."

"*Da*. Valentina Alexandrovna." They shook hands.

He closed the door, removed his boots, and slipped on a pair of *tapichki*—slippers, that sat by the door for guests. Kostya took off his coat and draped it over the old rocking chair. He was so measured compared to Petya, who would explode into a room. This one was more like a cat. As he came further into the room, he stopped first at the piano.

"Do you play?" she asked.

He chuckled. "*Da,* a bit. I keep promising myself that I will take lessons again someday."

Elena came up to him then said, "Kostya, you play the piano? Please play for me. I had an uncle who played the piano for us."

"Can you play, Lenushka?" he asked.

"*Nyet*, not me, my bro...well, no. I can't." She turned away then, flushing when she caught herself about to mention Fedya.

Konstantin sat at the piano. "I will play if no one watches me. I get nervous."

Valya laughed. "I don't believe that a bit, but I'll finish the tea. Come, Elena, help me."

As they stepped into the kitchen, the music started softly. It was a gentle jazz-like melody, not one she recognized.

"So, Elena, how are you feeling?" she asked as they came into the kitchen and Elena sat at the table by the window.

"I'm all right if I don't think about what happened too much. Kostya helped me understand some of it. When the pictures of the accident come back into my head, then I am sad again."

"Kostya? So familiar, are we?"

Elena blushed.

"If you need to talk about anything, I am here," Valya said.

She prepared the tea and watched as Elena examined the novelty salt and pepper shakers on the table. Such a pretty girl, Valya thought, although her hair, nearly black, was quite short from the severe haircut at the children's house. Perhaps her friend, Sonya, could trim it up a bit. Valya noted Elena's high cheekbones and widow's peak. Her mother always said these were signs of great beauty. *Da,* Elena would be a beautiful woman one day.

"I have a surprise for you, Lenushka," she said.

"Oh, another circus visit?" Elena asked.

"*Nyet,* even better," she said as she handed Elena the tray with cups, saucers, spoons, sugar, and a small pitcher of milk to take out to the main room.

"Nothing could be better than the circus," Elena said.

Valya carried the teapot. "Well, how would you like to see a ballet?"

"Ballet? Really? A ballet? Oh Valya, you are the most wonderful friend in the whole world." Elena set the tray down with a clatter and ran to hug Valya. "Did you hear, Kostya? The ballet! Have you ever been to a ballet?"

He stopped playing and got up to join them at the two small white couches in the living area. "*Da,* I go to the ballet often," he said and gave Valya that look he had used in the doorway.

Elena's eyes went wide, and Valya laughed and said, "Really?"

"Why are you laughing at me? It's true," he said.

Valya gazed at him. "Which one?"

"The Mussorgsky, usually—"

"Hm," she said.

Elena's head went back and forth between them like a tennis match.

"And what is playing there now?" Valya queried.

"Nothing, the ballet is dark today," he said.

"But you said you go often; they don't change the production that often. So, ha! I caught you!"

"I didn't say I go to watch the ballet; I do my minor part. My cousin works there, and we go out for a few beers afterwards." He grinned at her again. She tried not to notice how he flirted with her. And worse, she flirted back, shamelessly. She covered her blush by pouring the tea. He and his cousin must work backstage, she thought.

"Sugar?" she glanced up. He watched her every move, which was quite disconcerting.

"Of course. Very sweet," he replied, and he winked.

She couldn't believe it: how clichéd. He had winked at her like a dirty old man.

"Well, that's a surprise; I thought you'd like it black."

"Oh no, much too bitter. This is perfect. Thank you."

Elena interrupted, "Valya, will Petya go to the ballet with us?"

Valya stopped in mid-sip, glanced at Elena, and then stared at Kostya.

"Who's Petya?" Kostya asked.

"Valya's boyfriend, right? They live here together," Elena chirped. "I like these cookies, Valya. Thanks so very much."

He kept his eyes on Valya; she reddened again. He gave a little shrug. "Well, the tea is excellent, but I must go. Thank you for your hospitality, Valentina Alexandrovna. When will you attend? Perhaps I will see the three of you there?"

"It's just the two of us. I mean, it's a special surprise for Elena on Friday night," she gushed and then realized she sounded like a schoolgirl. She got up to walk him to the door, "It's *Swan Lake*."

"*Da,* I know. Tchaikovsky. It is one of my favorites as well. I believe Marina Rzhannikova dances the lead."

"*Da,* I'm sure. We'll look for you," Valya said sarcastically as he put on his coat and shoes.

"*Da Svidanya,* Kostya," Elena called from the couch.

"Don't forget what I told you, Lenushka," he said, waved, and left.

Valya closed the door and tried to gather her thoughts. She had moaned and groaned for the last three days about Petya's absence, and here she was behaving the same way, or even worse, with a total stranger.

"Valya, may I have more tea?"

"Of course," she said, "then let's talk."

The next two days were a whirl of activity. Valya had already decided, since the tickets had been a gift from Petya's lawyer friend, she might as well use Petya's credit card to buy Elena a new dress at Gostiny Dvor for the performance. They also stopped by Sonya's shop for a quick hair trim and then ran into the food store for a few items she needed to make a nice pot of *schi*—beef and cabbage soup.

On Friday, after they dressed, Elena looked very grown-up in her dark pink skirt, white satin top, new boots, and crystal beads. Valya believed it was important to create a spectacular memory of this night for Elena, her first ballet. The overall effect was a little ruined by the old wool coat from the children's house, but Valya had to draw the line somewhere. She, herself, dressed in her favorite black dress and boots she had bought as a splurge in Moscow when she was there for a social workers' conference. They both laughed hysterically as they tried something different with Valya's long, blond hair. Ultimately, she put it into the same French twist at the back. They walked quickly, since it had grown much colder that day.

The Mussorgsky was a beautiful old theater built in the early 1800s with many balconies and side boxes. As they entered, the individual chairs on the main floor were already filling up. Their seats were also on the main floor, but at the back wall. From there, they could see the entire stage as well as all the guests who entered. Valya thought Elena's head would fall off with all the twisting and turning as she watched the activity, pointed out the dramatic paintings in the ceiling, and the chandelier, bigger than her flat. Because of the recent holiday, everyone seemed in a very festive mood; there was much laughter, and everyone was quite cordial, even to the two of them. With the third bell, the lights dimmed. Valya watched the director come out to begin the slow overture. It was then that Valya saw, to her amazement, Konstantin Andreivich in the percussion section.

"Look, Elena, it's your Kostya!" she whispered.

"Where?"

"See him? In the percussion area, where the drums are," she laughed.

"Oh, I see him!" Elena exclaimed. But the people in front of them turned, so Valya shushed her.

"We'll talk to him later. Now we must be quiet." But her eyes continued to stare at the dark-haired Konstantin.

As the first dancers entered the Royal Court, Valya turned her attention to the stage and then to Elena's reactions. With each act break, Elena had dozens of questions about the story and what would happen to the lovers, Siegfried and the beautiful Odette, who was a swan by day and a woman by night. Valya knew the story well but wondered if she should prepare Elena for the sad ending, but then Elena said, "This can't have a happy ending."

"Why do you say that?" Valya asked.

"Because the powerful man, the von Rothbart magician, he is too clever. I think he will trick them all. Right? They don't get to stay together?"

"I don't want to give away the story, but think about this: there are different ways for people to be together. This story only shows one way. You will make your own story when we find your sister."

"And brother," Elena added.

"And brother," she said, but with less conviction.

30

YEGOR

RĪGA, LATVIJA

Yegor sat in his car with the windows open. Despite the cold, he needed fresh air to clear his thoughts. Stepanov had been quietly furious about the lost merchandise at the Black Willow, not to mention losing the key code to Kuznetsov's safe deposit box, and Yegor getting shot by a prostitute. Yegor could tell the boss was losing confidence in him. If he wasn't careful, he'd be back to driving the car.

"You need to heal first, Gogo. We'll put the word out on the street. We'll find them. Leave this to me."

"I need to make it right, Aleksei Aleksandrovich. I can fix this," Yegor had said.

"Let's remember who's in charge. Now, do what I say, go see Volkov and rest. That's an order."

Volkov had tried to keep him in the hospital, but Yegor refused. Within a week, he was on the street talking and asking questions himself. They didn't call him "The Bloodhound" for nothing. It wasn't long before he had found a trail to the porn actress, Nataliya (who needed very little convincing), and from her, he learned of Zoya and the boy's destination. But then, what he thought would be an easy grab at the shipyard in Rīga turned into another miscalculation.

"Come home, Gogo," he had repeated. "What's done is done. These things happen when I am disobeyed. I know what is best, you should know that by now."

"*Nyet*, please. Not until I find them, and at least get the key code. You'll see. I can do this."

"Gogo, you have been like a son to me, but now you are sounding like a fool. Rīga is not my territory. You are in a city of nearly eight hundred thousand people. It's a waste of my time and money. You should take a holiday, *da*, take a holiday. I have other ways to get what belongs to me. Come home."

And with that, Stepanov had hung up.

Yegor sat in his little car and thought for a long time. He needed a plan. That's all. He would show them all. He downed more of the pain pills and then put his car in gear and found a cheap place to stay. He texted the boss, "*I'll be away for a few weeks, then.*"

"*Good,*" a text came back in reply.

Yegor took his time. First, he hung out at the bars near the shipyards. He listened for stories and talk among the sailors about a maimed Russian, or talk about a pretty Russian boy, or anything akin to that. Since it was cold, he could cover most of his face. Most people didn't look, anyway; no one bothered to notice. After a while, he figured out which dock workers liked to drink, which ones had grudges, and which ones had loose lips. That's how he eventually found out where Zoya's latest seaman boyfriend lived, at least the name of the street. That was enough.

Perfect. He knew her routine from the old days. He would eventually spot her on Maskavas Street if he was patient. His informant, who wanted to be helpful, had added a few details, like a tram station and Salu Bridge. It was enough. Every night after that, he came to the commercial district where other women sold themselves. He found a perfect place near the tram station where a flower seller sat year-round. Zoya always asked for flowers from her johns. And not just the new clients, but her regulars too, like him, for as long as he could remember. *Da*, he had bought her lots and lots of flowers over the last three years. He knew now, if she picked someone up off the street, they would first drop by the closest flower stand.

And then, just like that, after he had waited and watched for several weeks, he saw her with a chump. The man looked Russian, which was probably why she'd picked him up. She had asked for flowers like she used to do, and the client gave her everything she asked. Yegor grunted. Once a prostitute, always a prostitute.

That poor sailor boy thought he could tame Zoya by putting a roof over her head. Of course, Yegor had wanted that too. To have her as his own. He had come so close. They could have been a team. Everything would have been fine if she hadn't started playing both sides with that worthless piece of shit, Dimitri Nikolaivich. For her, it was always about the money.

The couple walked north. Yegor followed. Luckily, the building they entered was small, only three floors. He gave them a few moments to get a head start, and then he stepped inside. It was stifling hot in the hallway. He could hear her laugh. He took the stairs two at a time, soundlessly. His heart pounded. He reached into his coat pocket and felt for his blade. Folded up, it was harmless enough, but soon it would have soft flesh to slice. He breathed heavily with anticipation. He removed his old black cap and smelled the fabric. It always calmed him down before a kill.

The smell of old wool, like the hat, reminded him of the dark green blanket his mother gave him when he left home. His father had beaten the crap out of his son over a broken bottle of vodka. Dear old Papa had bellowed, "Out! Get him out of here."

And so, his mother, bruised a hundred times, had collected some bread, cheese, and sausage, and rolled them into an old newspaper. Then she had folded everything up in her own blanket, helped him put on his coat and black cap, and handed the package to her son.

She had whispered, "I tried to protect you. But I couldn't. I am sorry. You will do better on the street. I will be dead soon. This man will kill me soon enough."

He had wrapped her in his arms and begged her to come with him. But she said she had no courage left anymore. He was thirteen when he left home. At sixteen, he had worked for one of the smaller crime organizations. They paid people to do their dirty work. His motto was that he would do anything or find anyone, for a price. So, he had finally earned real money and decided he was ready to take care of his mother.

But when he had returned, the neighbors were sorry, but his mother had been dead for some time. Perhaps he should have visited more often, they said. He ignored them and broke into the old apartment. No one said anything; they were afraid of him. No one had the nerve to call the police. That day, he sat in his mother's kitchen chair and waited all day and into the night. He did not eat or sleep or walk around. He waited. And when his father walked in, drunk as usual, Yegor had pointed the gun and shot his father in the head. It was the easiest kill of all. He had no remorse. And since then, he never did.

Da, old wool made it easier to steady his mind and hands to do what had to be done. Zoya must suffer. Stepanov would eventually agree. Yegor would bring results: the key. But best of all, Yegor would avenge himself. She must beg. And then she must tell him where to find the boy, Dimitri's runner.

Yegor heard her keys jingle and the door open. With lightning speed, he came up behind them and pushed them both into the room. It was dark. He yanked the fat old man by the collar, pulled him close, and smelled the stench of cigars. Yegor was sure the man would only remember a disfigured monster.

"Go, old man. If you want to live, run down the stairs, out the door and forget you ever tried to pick up a Russian whore in Rīga. Eh? You understand me? You speak Russian?"

"*Da,*" the man said with a trembling voice. He was wetting himself.

"You are disgusting. Go!" and Yegor shoved him out the door. "And don't look back!" The man was obedient and ran down the stairs. That one would never return to this street again.

Yegor laughed. Then he turned to the room to look for Zoya.

He found a lamp and turned it on. She stood against a wall. She surprised him. He thought she would have found a weapon by now. She had been on the street a long time and he expected she would not surrender easily.

"Hello Zoya. Are you surprised to see me?"

He edged toward her. She was silent.

At the last moment, she tried to bolt under his arms and toward the door, but he was ready for her. He yanked her by the arm and then grabbed her around the waist and threw her on the bed, a bed she had lovingly prepared for her fat, gullible client. He pulled a roll of duct tape from his pocket. As she tried to scramble off the bed, he grabbed one arm and taped it to the frame of the bed. She tried to bite him, but he slapped her backhanded. Then he did the same thing with the other arm. She still wore her coat and gloves. It didn't matter. He would undress her with the knife.

"You don't have to play this rough game. You know I can give you pleasure," she said.

"I have a unique pleasure in mind," he said as he pulled out his knife and began cutting off the buttons of her coat.

"You don't have to do it this way."

"But I do. Take a long look at my face and tell me if you don't deserve to suffer, hmm, maybe a little?"

"The kid made me shoot you. He wanted you to die. I just wanted to scare you away."

"*Da*. The boy. I'm glad you brought that up. I need to find him, too. Where is he?"

"I don't know," she stammered. "We split up."

"You're lying, Zoya. I'm smart that way. You can either tell me now, or you can tell me later. But you will tell me." He cut the sleeves of her wool coat.

"What are you doing?" she screamed. "My God, what are you doing? You're cutting me."

"That's the idea, Zoya. That's the whole idea."

And then she screamed and sobbed. He stuffed a glove in her mouth. He concentrated on undressing her with his knife. Sometimes, the knife slipped and cut her. Small red stains blossomed along the edges of her body when he had finished. They outlined her. He licked the blood from her body. Then he undressed himself and had her with all the force he could. When she spit out the glove and her screams became monotonous, he taped her mouth shut. He had her again in silence. That was much better.

He stopped and pulled out a flask of vodka that he always carried in his old army coat. He pulled the tape from her mouth to ask her again about the boy, but she cursed at him. He looked at her nakedness and admired her wonderful body. In some ways, it was a shame to cut it anymore, to cut her.

He climbed on the bed with her and put his hand over her mouth. "Shut up and listen. If you tell me where the little key is, I'll cut you quick and you'll die with less pain. Would you like that Zoya? Would you like to die with less pain? Because if you don't tell me, I will have to hurt you much more; you know I get excited when we go nice and slow. Let me show you what this kind of slow is like."

She whimpered like a pathetic dog.

"Are you ready to tell me about the key?"

In between gasps of pain and tears, she nodded her head, but first she said, "I don't have any key. The boy, Fedya, he has it."

"Are you lying to me? Should I cut you again?"

"*Nyet*, I'm not lying. He got it from Dima. I thought you were dead. We got a few things out of the storage room and that was all. I didn't even know they were important. Everyone was dead."

"Not everyone. I'm not dead." And he cut a shape on her stomach and kissed her while she screamed.

"All right then, where's the boy?"

"I don't know."

"Where's the boy, Zoya?" He held the knife over her face.

She whimpered. "You could let me go. You could. Let me go. I'll take you to the boy, and then I'll disappear. I have nothing you want."

"Where's the boy?"

"I don't remember the number, some number on Kapselu. All right? I don't know. Yellow brick apartments. That's all I remember."

"All right, Zoya. I'll believe that. But since it's going to take more time for me to find the boy, it will take more time to kill you."

"But you promised."

"I did not. You heard a promise. I lied."

He filled the next hour with pain and terror and when Zoya could take no more, she passed out, or maybe died. If not now, then soon. In any case, it wasn't sport to play with her anymore. He cut the tape from her arms with no resistance. There was a lot of blood. Yegor went to the kitchen sink and washed himself. He dressed, put on his old army coat, and left. Someone else could clean up the garbage on the bed.

31

ELENA & VALYA

ST. PETERSBURG, RUSSIA

After the ballet, they walked in silence. Elena had cried. Despite expecting a sad ending, she had secretly hoped Odette and Siegfried's love would be strong enough to overcome the evil in their lives. It wasn't. And if their love wasn't enough, how could her own love save Irishka and Fedya? Would they meet again? Or would they forget each other? How could she expect her little sister to remember anything? She was so young. Was Fedya even alive? Ever since Aniya's accident, all she could think about were the deaths in her own family. In fact, everyone she cared about seemed to die or get hurt. She must be a jinx.

"What are you thinking?" Valya asked. "Did you enjoy the ballet? You haven't said a word since we left the theater."

"I'm sorry. I don't know what to say. It was beautiful. But the story makes me sad. Their love was strong, and despite that, they died," she said.

"That's true. But you must remember it can go either way. Love can make good things happen, too," Valya said.

"I guess," she said. "Why didn't your Petya go with us tonight?"

"He said he had a meeting or something. He has a new movie project."

"Tell me, Valya, do you love Petya?"

Before she could answer, Kostya ran up between them and threw an arm around each of their waists. "Hah! You think I didn't see you? You didn't wait for me!"

"You looked pretty busy with all those young admirers crowded around you," Valya said.

"Oh, you noticed," he grinned. "Those are my students."

"Right," Valya said, unconvinced.

"Kostya," Elena interrupted, "why didn't you tell us you were a musician for the ballet? That's such a wonderful job."

"Thank you, Lenushka. I knew I could count on you to be impressed. Unfortunately, I am only a substitute musician. Like all good Russians, I do a little of this and a little of that. Somehow, it all adds up to pay the rent."

"*Da,* I'm sure you are like most Russian men," Valya said.

He laughed, but Elena wasn't sure she got the joke.

"Of course. I am gallant and courageous, which is why I will walk both of you home."

They fell silent. Elena wasn't sure what was happening between Kostya and Valya, but it was strange. They looked at one another like they liked each other, but then they talked like they didn't like each other at all. Perhaps it was the problem of Petya.

"So, tell me, Lenushka, what did you think of your first ballet?" Kostya said.

"It was wonderful, but it was sad. I didn't like it when they died. You know what I mean?"

"What do you think was the most important part, their death or their love?" he asked.

"That's easy. Valya and I talked about love because it can change things."

"Change anything?" He looked at Valya.

"Humph," Valya said. "I'm not such a romantic, not like you."

"Someone must be, Valentina Alexandrovna. Someone must be," he said as he took off her glove and kissed her hand.

As Elena watched them, she noticed how differently Valya's two men behaved. Where Kostya always talked about Valya and looked at her to see what she thought or how she felt, Petya, even though he could be quite nice and even funny, always talked about himself.

When they arrived at the front door of the apartment house, Valya pulled out her keys and gave them to Elena. "Can you go upstairs to our flat by yourself? I need a few minutes with Konstantin Andreivich."

"Please, call me Kostya. We can talk tomorrow."

"*Nyet*, I think I need to clear something up."

Elena would have loved to eavesdrop on the rest of their conversation. She also liked to climb up the front set of stairs because the windows had a view of the front of the cinema. Even though it was late, lights still flashed, and people stood around the entrance. The big sign showed the name of the film as, "*Zadaniye Nevypolnimo Dva*—Mission Impossible 2." This wasn't her kind of movie, but she liked the title. She was on her own impossible mission.

At the third floor, she walked the long way around toward the back and then took the last set of stairs up to the fourth floor. When she unlocked the door, lights blazed in the apartment and sounds came from the office where they kept the television. Petya must be home. She tiptoed to the door and pushed it open to surprise him; he wasn't there. When she looked at the television, she froze. There on the screen, naked people were doing very private, dirty things. She had seen nothing like it, and she wanted to look away, but she couldn't move.

And then, her mind seemed to play a trick on her. Amid the bodies, she saw a boy, a rather young boy. At first, she felt disgusted, but when the boy's face turned to the camera, he looked out of the screen as though he knew she could see him. Such need filled his eyes; they called for help. Wait, she knew those eyes. And when the recognition came, she could do nothing but scream. She stood there and screamed. Her whole body shook; she couldn't stop screaming.

Petya must have heard the screams, because he ran into the room and tried to get her to stop. He shook her, but she was already shaking. Then she heard more voices. Petya turned and swore. She collapsed and crawled toward the television. All she could see was Fedya, her beloved brother, treated like an animal. She clawed at the screen.

"Elena, Elena, darling, stop now, come, sweet Elena, listen to me, come away," Valya said. And then someone picked her up. She struggled. She couldn't leave Fedya inside the television. She must save him.

"Fedya, Fedya! I'll help you. I'll find you. Fedya!" she cried, "Let me go! Let me help Fedya."

"Elena, listen to me," a man's voice spoke in her ear. "Listen, Lenushka, it's a movie. It's a movie. It's not happening right now. Do you hear me? Lenushka, it's a movie. It's off now. Valya turned it off."

She stopped to listen. She looked up. It was Kostya. How did he get here? What happened? How did Fedya get into a movie? She heard other screams now. She heard Valya's voice and then Petya, yelling.

"Elena," Kostya interrupted, "what is it? Who is Fedya?"

Elena looked up into Kostya's face, his gentle eyes. When he was the DJ, she had fallen in love with him, but he wasn't that man anymore. He was more like a father, her father, hers and Fedya's father, who had laughed and sung with them. Were there any memories left of her papa? She remembered an army uniform and colorful ribbons, short hair, and a rough face that pricked her cheeks when he held her close. She remembered the music when he and Mama would dance while Uncle played the piano. Gone, it was all gone. What happened to her life?

She cried. Just like she had screamed, she cried hard and couldn't stop. She might die from crying like this. She had lost so much. Her heart was exploding into a million pieces. Her chest hurt so much.

After a long time, she didn't know how long, she quieted. She was tired. She felt the rocking. Like a little baby, this same man rocked her, and something else. He sang. Softly, he sang an old folk song; the same lullaby Mama had sung to her at night. He sounded like Uncle Vasiliy. But she couldn't sleep now. She had to save Fedya. And yet she had no strength to wake up either. She floated between life and death, wakefulness and sleep.

During this semi-sleep, she heard Valya and Petya again. But this time, she understood the words, or at least some of them.

"What were you thinking? You bring this trash here?" Valya said.

"Look, will you listen to me? I was alone. I can do what I want. Besides, I was watching it as a favor for a friend," Petya said.

"I bet. Picking up some acting techniques?"

"Do you know how much money I could make from one X-rated movie?" he said.

"You disgust me!" she yelled and then a door slammed.

It was quiet for a moment, and then Petya came into the sitting area.

"Who the hell are you?" Petya said.

"I'm a friend of the girl. I brought her back from winter camp where my mother works. A friend of hers died in a sledding accident; they asked me to bring her back to the city, so she could stay with Valentina Aleksandrovna for a while."

Elena heard a door open and Valya's voice as she stormed back into the room.

"You know those movie people, don't you? Do you realize that's child pornography? Do you? It's against the law. That poor boy is being abused!"

"Look, Valya, I didn't know. I wasn't even watching the damn thing when the kid came in. I turned it on and went to take a shit."

She persisted, "Do you or don't you know the people who created that movie? Do you?"

He was silent.

"Do you?"

"Quit turning this into an inquisition. Natasha Vladimirovna is a big star in those movies. I ran into her at the club over the weekend—"

"I thought you went home to see your parents?" Valya interrupted. "Oh, for God's sake!" And once again, she left the room and would have slammed the door, but Petya followed her in.

Elena opened her eyes and stared up at the ceiling.

"I think I'd better go," Kostya said. He stood up and laid Elena down on the sofa, putting a pillow under her head and covering her with a blanket. He took her hand and said, "Look at me, Lenushka." She turned her gaze to his face. "I won't lie to you. This seems like horrible news. But think about it, if Petya knows these people, perhaps he can help you find your brother. It is your brother, right?"

She nodded a little. "Do you think so? They are so angry now."

"I know, but tomorrow, everyone will calm down, and then you and Valya can ask the right questions," he said. "Do you need help with folding down your bed?"

"*Nyet*. I feel very tired," she said as she turned over on her side and faced the back of the white sofa.

"Good night, then," he said and walked to the door. "Lenushka?"

"*Da*?"

"Remember, when Odette went to look for Siegfried, she kept her hope to the very end." And with that, he closed the door behind him.

32
FEDYA &
UNCLE ULDIS

RĪGA, LATVIJA

The lawyer's office was not exactly what Fedya had expected. He thought lawyers made lots of money and worked in offices with large desks and leather chairs. This room was full of nothing but mountains of paper. The room smelled dusty. The lawyer had crammed the bookshelves with books, some up, some down, and some sideways, while he had loaded his desk with papers, folders, knick-knacks, photographs, open books, pens, pencils, coffee cups, two cameras, a dead or dying plant, and a telephone that was teetering on the edge and ready to tumble to the floor.

The lawyer, Peteris something or other, wore a suit, but it was so old and crumpled, it looked inside out. He wore a tie hanging and half tied, a sweater vest under his jacket, and a gray shirt that Fedya thought might have been white at one time. The lawyer looked old and young at the same time. His hair was thinning, but he covered his baldness with long strands of hair draped across his pate. He wore rimless glasses that reminded Fedya of an old grandfather. The man's fingers were delicate, and he wore no wedding ring. Perhaps he had married at one time since there was a family picture in a frame on his desk amidst the chaos.

Uncle Uldis and Peteris talked intently for some time. Since it was in Latvian, Fedya stopped trying to figure out what they were saying. At one point, Uncle's voice got very loud and tense, his hands shook, and Fedya saw him consciously sit on them. Suddenly, he fell back in his chair, looking defeated and sorrowful.

"Uncle Uldis, is everything all right?" Fedya asked.

"*Nyet*, not really. I'm sorry, my son, but I have lost much of the money I made over the years. I didn't even know it. I didn't pay attention. I don't know what I will do now. It just never occurred to me that I would need money."

There was nothing Fedya could say.

"Uldi," Peteris interrupted in Latvian again, "what you must do is work! You are an accomplished musician—"

"Don't be ridiculous," Uldis answered. "I haven't played in a year. I haven't written one line of music for two. I am an empty shell."

"But perhaps you can work if you do it for this boy and for the memory of your sister. You tell me you care about him. Perhaps it's time to show it. Show him what it means to hope and start again," Peteris said.

"You are a dreamer. We'll see, I'll think about. But, back to the boy. Can you do anything to help, eh? If there is no money for a detective, then what? Can you write a letter, make inquiries to their social welfare office?" he asked.

"All right, I can do that. But you should think about your own connections. Who do you still know in St. Petersburg?"

"I'll have to think, which is still very hard to do," he said.

"It is a marvel, really, what you have accomplished already. The boy is good for you. He is your talisman. This could be a gift from God, no?"

"Perhaps. Perhaps. He is a good boy."

With that, he gestured to Fedya, got up, and headed for the door. He was getting better at switching from Latvian to Russian. "Come, Fedya, we must drink a cup of coffee and think."

They trudged down the street. It was close to midday and Fedya was hungry, but he was too embarrassed to tell his uncle, particularly in the face of this latest discovery. Unlike his uncle, it did not upset Fedya in the same way. Disappointed, true, that his rich uncle was no longer rich, but he hadn't come to Rīga for the money. He came for safety.

He left his sisters back in St. Petersburg and thought that was the end. But when Uncle wanted to find them, Fedya realized how much he wanted the same thing. The girls could come to Rīga too. Elena was quick, she would learn the language easily. But Irishka was young and might forget her Russian here. *Nyet*, he wouldn't allow her to forget. They must remember their heritage.

Then he stopped in the middle of the sidewalk. Wait a minute. Was he a Russian? Not completely. That's what Uncle had said the other day.

"What is it, Fedya? Are you all right?" Uncle asked as he walked back to where he stood.

"I'm sorry, Uncle. I just realized something for the first time: I am not a full Russian, right?"

"That's true. Didn't Elisaveta explain that to you?"

"I don't know. Maybe she tried. I didn't think about it. I mean, she would talk, but I wouldn't always listen. I didn't know our time was going to be short. I didn't know."

He had a hollow feeling in his chest. Who was Fedya? He had been running ever since his mother died, and he was tired. He had been raped, beaten, attacked, and almost killed. For half a year, he had tried to support and care for his two little sisters. He had lied, cheated, and stolen at will; he had broken every rule his mother had taught him in the name of survival. He had lost all his dreams. What were his dreams when he was a little boy?

"I feel old; I am no longer a boy, am I?"

"True enough. You have lived many years already in just one. Come, here's a little café."

They found a small table at the back and Uncle ordered two coffees, clasped his hands, and gazed at him. "I wanted to hire a detective to look for your sisters, but I cannot. They are expensive. We must put our heads together to see if we can remember anyone else who might help us."

"Like who? I don't know anyone."

Uncle held up his hand to silence his complaints. "Tell me about your life. Tell me about my sister's death, can you? Tell me everything you remember. As you do so, I will become your memory book."

"But you can't even remember your own address!"

"That was yesterday. I remember more today. Besides, I have an actual book, see?" Uncle pulled a notepad from inside his jacket. "I will be the student. You will be my instructor. Begin!"

"I don't know where to begin."

"It doesn't matter. Perhaps we should start with Elisaveta's last day. You said you were with her?"

He turned away from his uncle and stared out at the other customers. He wasn't sure he could do this. And yet, he understood it. He must remember. Fortunately, Uncle was not asking him to relive the last few months. He could skip those memories for now. He would remember the better times. The times when he was a child, and someone loved him. His mother, she had loved them all fiercely.

For the next hour, he told his uncle about his life. He didn't begin with Elisaveta's last day. He couldn't. But he thought if he could talk about his mother's laughter and joy during the good days, he might be able to face the last day. He told about his father, what he could remember. He told about the little parties and the friends. Uncle interrupted him several times to ask for names of places and people, but he didn't have such details anymore. Finally, he told of his mother becoming sick and how she tried to push it away. She had visited a doctor, something she never did unless it was serious, and the news had not been good. Again, Uncle asked him if he remembered the doctor's name, but he didn't. Slowly, he recounted the last week and then the last day and the awful promise she had forced him to make, to take care of his sisters. It was his mother who had planted the idea of finding either Vasiliy or Uncle Uldis.

"Who is this Vasiliy?"

"A friend of Mama's, that's all. I don't remember. Mama said to find him, and he would help, but I didn't know how to find him."

217

"But do you remember meeting him before?"

"*Da*. I remember that. He was a funny, fat man who had a very loud voice. Sometimes he would start singing at the table when he had too much to drink. Vladimir didn't like him, but Mama always laughed. She said she knew him from home. But I didn't know what she meant."

"But home is here. Vasiliy. You don't remember his surname?"

"Well, maybe, sort of. Nest...Nester..."

"Nesterov? Vasiliy Chasikovich Nesterov?"

"*Da*, that's it. Do you know him?"

Uncle clapped his hands and called for the bill. "Know him? My boy, I didn't know Vasiliy was in St. Petersburg. He was a wonderful opera singer in his day. But he destroyed his voice with wine and women, as they say."

Uncle paid the bill, and they started for home. "It should be simple to find Nesterov. The world of classical music is smaller than you think. *Da*, he is our hope. He will know people there." Uncle put his arm around him and added, "You are an amazing boy. We should celebrate. What should we do?"

Fedya laughed a little and said, "I know what I would like—" Then he cut himself off. What was he thinking? The idea was selfish.

"What is it? I feel the best I have felt in a long time. I feel magnanimous!"

"What does that mean?"

"I can tell you a story easier than explaining the meaning. In the Bible, there was an evil king named Herod who John the Baptist kept exposing as sinful to his people, so Herod had the baptist put into a dark prison in the lowest levels of his palace. On his birthday, his wife's daughter, Salome, danced for him and he loved the dance so much, he said to her, 'Ask me for anything, up to half my kingdom, and I will give it you!' That's magnanimous."

"Oh. And what did she ask for?"

"Well, that's another story. What do you want to ask for?"

"I want to learn how to play the piano."

Uncle looked at him for a long time and then started laughing. "Well, like Herod, I deserve that! Peteris was right; you are a kind of magic in my life. We will begin tomorrow." And with that, they walked in silence to the tram stop.

33
FEDYA &
UNCLE ULDIS

RĪGA, LATVIJA

They sat at the piano for over an hour while Uncle tested and tinkered with the keys. Uncle complained the whole time about the sound of the piano, the broken keys, and so on. Fedya thought it sounded fine, but what did he know? Minka walked across the piano and sat right in front of Uncle and mewed. He looked at her and laughed. Fedya didn't know what happened between them, but apparently, they understood each other, because the lesson finally began.

Uncle was very patient and explained about the keys, their names, and how the notes fit together. Fedya's first job was to learn scales. These were simple exercises of going up and down the keys. They were fun at first, but then a little boring. When he complained, Uncle shrugged his shoulders. "Either you want to learn, or you don't. I didn't say it would be easy."

"But can't I learn at least one actual song? If I could play a song, then I could do the scales in between."

"I don't have any easy music books, but here; I'll show you how to make up a song."

And with that, Uncle showed him how the scales were notes in groups; those groups were keys. When Uncle played three notes together, he called it a chord. These were unfamiliar words for him, but he enjoyed it, and in a few days, he had made up his own little tune. Then he asked Uncle to play. At first, Uncle refused, but Fedya knew how to be relentless and eventually, Uncle came to the piano and sat. The man stared at the piano for a long time. Fedya wanted to tease him, but then thought better of it because of the way his uncle tensed his muscles and breathed shallowly. Uncle placed his hands on the keys. He played a series of different chords or groups of notes together. They were very pleasant sounds.

Then Uncle stopped, and his hands shook. Minka lay on the piano and purred. Fedya assumed the little concert was over and walked over to the television chair. Muted notes came next, then only high notes that Uncle played with one hand. He played the same little melody over and over again. Gradually, the notes became stronger, and the left hand joined in. Fedya leaned his head back in the chair, closed his eyes, and the music washed over him.

Something happened that afternoon. It was like Uncle couldn't get enough. He played nonstop for three hours or more, one piece after another. If he made a mistake, he would do it again. If he lost his way, he would begin from the beginning. If he couldn't remember, he would start a different one. He was on a journey of sorts, or maybe it was how he looked for a place he had been before. *Da,* it was like a visit back to a familiar old village where a man had played as a little boy and then, as an adult, he walked around trying to find the old trails and shortcuts, the paths through the woods, the stones over the creek, the hiding places, the places in the sun, and the places in shadow. The miracle was how Uncle took Fedya along with him.

This was the new rhythm they lived for many days until Uncle finally reached Vasiliy Chasikovich on the telephone. The two men talked for a few minutes, and he could hear Uncle Vasiliy hoot on the other end. Then Uldis handed the phone over to Fedya.

"My boy, my boy. I am so delighted that you are alive! You are alive, eh?"

"*Da, da, da,* Uncle Vasiliy. I am alive. *Spaciba,*" he said into the telephone.

"How did you get all the way to Rīga?"

"It is a long story—"

"All right, all right. I understand. So, we will speak of that later. But Elizaveta—I am so sorry. I was on tour and when I returned, well, you were all gone."

"I know. Mama died, Uncle Vasiliy. She couldn't stop coughing, late in the night and she—" but Vasiliy interrupted him.

"Uldi tells me the girls, your sisters, they are in a children's house. Which one?" he asked.

"I don't know. I'm sorry."

"*Nyet.* It's fine. I have some friends there. *Da,* it will be fine. Fine. And their names, eh? Lenushka is Elena?"

"Elena Ivanovna Margarita *Lebedev*, she is ten, no, eleven. She turned eleven on the fourth of December," his voice broke. Uncle came up and put his arm around him.

"Good," Vasiliy said, "I will need that birth date. And the little one?"

"Irishka, I mean Irina Vladimirovna *Lebedev*. She is…" Fedya turned to Uncle Uldis. "What is the date today? Today!" he asked.

But it was Vasiliy who answered, "Fedya, it is Saturday, the thirteenth. Why?"

"I missed Irishka's birthday. She won't even know her birth date. How could she know?" Uncle took the telephone receiver from him and asked Vasiliy to call them back in ten minutes.

The small telephone table stood next to the enormous mirror. Fedya looked at himself in the mirror. He knew he should feel joy or some hope. But all he felt was a deep loss. The old mirror had lost some of its silver and his reflection had jagged edges like scars. That was how he felt. His soul was stiff like an old piece of chewing gum and his heart felt taped together. The tape was peeling away and hanging. He didn't know if he could believe in a rescue anymore.

"Fedya, can you tell me Irishka's birthday? I will speak to Vasiliy when he calls back."

"8 January1996. I remember her as a baby. She was so small. Irishka was our little doll. It was great fun until we saw what a mess she could make in her diaper." He laughed. The whole time he spoke, he watched himself. He was outside himself and felt nothing. He remembered the times he laid on the floor and put Irishka on his stomach, then panted and bounced her with his stomach muscles, and she would giggle. Her eyes spoke love to him. They always had.

Fedya remembered Uncle Vasiliy as the grandfather they had never had. Before Mama got sick, Vasiliy had visited, and the two of them would laugh and sing together. Vladimir, Irishka's father, who Fedya could never call Papa, had already left them while Irishka was still a baby. And yet, sometimes, Vladimir had come and asked Mama for money or made her cook him something to eat. He was always loud and drunk. Irishka never knew a gentle man. Nor would she remember a proper mother because their mother worked such long hours; he and Elena took care of Irishka most of the time. Then, when Mama got sick with the *tuberkulez*—tuberculosis (at least that's what he thought she had), there was little time for Irishka.

Coming back to himself, Fedya imagined Uncle's great mirror as a doorway to home. He wanted to walk through it to St. Petersburg to see his sisters and know that they were all right; he wanted to know that he had done the right thing. That's all. He turned to his uncle. "Will Vasiliy Chasikovich find them?"

"I think he will. He has many powerful friends in St. Petersburg."

"Before she died, my mother told me to find him or to find you. I didn't know how to find him. I forgot, I think. If I had remembered, none of this would have happened. We would all be together by now. Mama trusted me with all her money, with everything. She believed in me, and I failed."

"Where are you going?"

"Out for a walk, around a little. I'll be all right."

"I can go with you," Uncle said.

"*Nyet*, I need to think."

"But Fedya, you make me worry about such talk. We all fail sometimes. Look at me. I am an impressive picture of failure," Uncle said.

"*Da*, we are quite the pair, aren't we? I'll be back. I promise," he said, and closed the door behind him.

The next day, Ausma was back from her concert tour. She seemed pleased and yet concerned at the same time. "You look tired, Uldi," she said. "Have you been resting like I said you should?" Uncle translated for Fedya.

"He's been playing the piano, haven't you, Uncle?" Fedya interjected in Russian. "Show her, Uncle. Please show her."

"I can't. It's gone."

"Tell her how you played and played. Every day you played. Just this morning, you stopped. Why?" Fedya asked.

"You play. You're the new musician in the family."

Uncle walked to the bed and lay down. Fedya walked to the piano and opened the lid.

"Fedya. *Nyet*—" Ausma said hastily.

"Uncle, if I make a mistake, you must come and help me, all right?"

He played, one handed, the melody his uncle had been playing all week. But Uncle always stopped at a certain point.

"It's 'Lauma's Lullaby'," Ausma said in Latvian, "Uldi, what has happened? How could Fedya know?"

"You have a gift, boy, that you can remember a melody like that."

At one point, Fedya hesitated, and Uldis called from the bed, "C#, E, then D and then, well, I don't know."

Fedya found those notes, played them, and then tried a few more.

Suddenly, Uncle jumped up and sat beside Fedya and played chords below Fedya's high notes. When they stopped, they looked at each other and Uncle grinned. Fedya scooted over and Uncle played the new song from beginning to end.

When he finished, he said in Russian, "Thank you, my boy. *Da,* that will basically work. She has a life again." Then in Latvian, to Ausma, he repeated, "It's alive again, for Lauma, her goodbye, and the children." When he looked over at her, she wiped her eyes.

"It's beautiful, Uldi, beautiful. They deserve it," she said as she walked up to the piano. "I didn't know the boy could play. You didn't tell me."

"I didn't know either. He asked me to teach him a few things. He has a natural talent, a good ear. I would like to help him, but, well, that's another story."

"There is plenty of time for that, don't you think? Let's celebrate. Let's go for a walk, perhaps to the café, eh? This is my treat," she said.

When he explained to Fedya what Ausma wanted to do, Fedya didn't want to go, but Uncle and she left anyway.

While they were away, he remained at the piano and gently caressed the keys. He had done the right thing to play "Lauma's Lullaby". Minka jumped into his lap. She purred as he scratched her head and ears. The cat could feel it too; something important had happened to his uncle. When they left, his uncle's eyes were bright again, and his hand tremors had stopped. Ausma had cried. He liked her. It was the first time in a long time he felt good about something he had done. He picked up Minka and put her back on the piano.

"Listen to this and tell me what you think." He played a different little melody with one hand. "Maybe I can write a song for Elena and Irishka like Uncle wrote one for his family."

He heard a knock at the door. Had the buzzer sounded? He didn't think so. Did they forget their keys?

"Uncle? Ausma? Are you all right? What did you forget?"

Without thinking, he pulled the bolt and turned the handle, but in that second, a man forced open the door. Yegor, Fedya's worst nightmare in the flesh.

He tried to slip under the man's arms and out the door, but Yegor was quicker. He grabbed his shirt collar and pulled him back into the room and closed the door. Yegor dangled him a little and then slapped him so hard across the face that he went flying and hit the wall like a volleyball.

"Where is the plastic key, boy?" Yegor said.

"What?" Fedya sat stunned on the floor. His lip bled; he could taste it in his mouth, and that from only one swipe. He pushed himself up and sat with his back against the wall, ready to ward off a second blow with his arms.

"The key, you little bastard, the one Zoya gave you."

"Zoya never gave me a key—" he said. Before he could finish, Yegor kicked him in the side. He had pulled away, but not soon enough. A foot collided with his thigh. Everything went white, it hurt so much.

"I don't have any key, I tell you."

"Don't lie to me, you little shit. Zoya told me with her dying breath that you had it. People don't lie when they think it will help them live. What about you, eh?"

Before Yegor could launch another attack, they heard the familiar sound of police sirens. Yegor froze until the sound became obviously close, and then he dragged Fedya up by the shirt.

"Where's your uncle?" Yegor said, the pulsing scars of his wounds only inches away from Fedya's face.

"How do you even know I have an uncle?"

Yegor slammed his head against the wall. "Does he have a cane? Does he?"

"*D-d-da. Da.* Why?"

"Damn it!" Yegor dragged him up and through the door, and together they crashed down the stairs. Fedya tried to catch his balance, but he kept tripping, and Yegor kept yanking him up again. At the bottom, Yegor peered out the front door window, and he could see the couple speaking with a police officer. Yegor swore and then pulled Fedya toward the back of the hallway. There, he found a door to the basement storage areas, pushed Fedya through, and followed. He closed the door, tossed Fedya down the flight of steps, then jammed a piece of lumber or something up against the door.

"Come on," Yegor said as he pulled him along the dusty floor. Fedya felt like a rag being tossed around. He needed to get away, and he needed to think, but everything was happening so fast. Yegor pulled him toward a coal chute door. First, Yegor crawled up to it and forced the small doors open. He let go of Fedya to pull himself out. Fedya used that second to fall back onto the basement floor and scramble toward the stairs, the way they had come down. He heard Yegor behind him, "You little shit, I'll be back, and I'll kill you all."

Fedya didn't answer. He ran up the rest of the way and kicked with all his might on the wood that blocked the door. When it gave way, he yanked open the door and cried out, "Help! Help!" The police were going the wrong way up the stairs. "Come back," he yelled.

One police officer came back, but the others kept going up. When the uniformed man reached him, there was a lot of confusion because of the Latvian, even though Fedya kept saying, *"Russki, Russki."* He didn't know how to tell him what had happened. He pointed to the basement, and then he pantomimed being punched and pointed again into the basement. The policeman called by radio to his partner and headed down, gun in hand.

Fedya limped to the front door; his legs buckled under him, and he sat in the hallway with his head in his hands. His whole body ached.

The next minutes were a blur. More police came and there was a lot of running up and down and talking on radios. At some point, another policeman who spoke Russian came and sat down with him. The man asked a lot of questions. Fedya knew he couldn't reply honestly because every answer would bring more questions. Instead, he said he was visiting his uncle and had forgotten to lock the door when they left for a walk.

"Did the assailant have a weapon?"

"Uh, no, I don't know. He just hit me."

"What did he want?"

He tried to look dazed and disoriented. "I don't know."

And on and on it went, about what Yegor looked like, what he was wearing, how tall he was, what he had said exactly. Fedya doubted they would catch Yegor, anyway. It got tricky when the police figured out that both he and Yegor were Russian; the questions headed toward motives other than burglary. All the same, there was little he could tell them. He could only hope his story would match whatever Uncle had said.

He was so glad when Uncle and Ausma finally came in; Ausma ran to him and hugged him, and together they went back up to the apartment. She became a real country *babushka* and launched into a tirade against the police officers. He wasn't sure what she was saying. One man gave Uncle a paper to sign, and they left.

"Fedya, are you whole? Are you all right?" Uncle said.

He nodded slowly as Ausma sat him down at the dining table and began cleaning his eye and mouth with a warm cloth.

"I saw him," Uncle said. "The dangerous man you told me about. We were walking to the café, and I saw him, and I was afraid for you."

"Thank you. You saved my life. He would have killed me. I think he killed Zoya," he said.

Uncle took a deep breath. "Oh God, oh God," he repeated. Ausma was silent.

"What does he want from you? I thought he was after Zoya?" Uncle said.

"That's what I thought, but he kept asking me about a key."

"And?"

"And nothing. I don't have it. I mean, a friend gave me some keys, but Zoya took that set, the storage room keys and then she cheated me, so I hid the last one from her, just in case, back in St. Petersburg. I hid it in a doll, my sister's doll from America. But I accidentally left the doll at her friend's apartment and that crazy woman probably threw it away; I think the key is gone. I don't have it."

"But you know about this special key?"

"*Da, nyet,* I mean, I don't know what it's for. I told you: one set of keys was for the storage apartment where Zoya and I took some things and the storage unit behind the building, but the police emptied it. The last key, the one in the plastic case, was different looking. It had some numbers with it, like a code. I don't know, I tell you."

Fedya stood up slowly. His thigh really hurt, but at least he could walk. He went into the little yellow room and began putting together his pack. Uncle followed him.

"What are you doing?"

"I've got to leave now. That man, Yegor, he will be back."

"What are you saying? The police are looking for him. He won't come back here. Not today, not tonight anyway," Uncle Uldis said.

"How can you be so sure? And what about tomorrow or the next day?"

"Don't be ridiculous. You're a child. Where do you think you will go?"

228

Something snapped. He flew into a rage he could not control or even understand. Later, he would regret the things he said, but at that moment, all his anger, fear, and frustration came out in one huge attack on his uncle.

"What do you know about what I can or cannot do? I have seen and lived through horrible things. I have seen my friends—dead, killed by bullets and knives with blood everywhere. I watched Zoya shoot a man in the face. Both men and women raped me. They treated me like a dog, or worse. Everyone I trusted cheated and betrayed me. This man has chased me for weeks and weeks. But I am still alive, and I will not allow you to stop me. And somehow, someday, I will find my sisters and I will make up for the mess I have made of things. So, don't try to stop me! Don't tell me what to do or what to say. I came to you for help and found a drunk! I have been helping you! And what can you do for me now? Nothing! You are powerless. If your world gets tough, you'll just drink again so you don't have to think or feel. You can't help me fight a man like Yegor. You have nothing! He is an animal, and he will not stop until he finds me, unless I can get far away from him. Far away! I must go very far! I must go!"

And repeating himself, he collapsed on the floor, sobbing, yet again. Uncle came to him, but Fedya didn't remember how the older man got him off the floor and onto the bed. Ausma must have helped. He didn't know how long he cried. He could sense that she sat on the bed. Uncle stood nearby. They talked between themselves, but he didn't care.

He felt something icy cold on his face. He opened his eyes and saw it was Ausma putting the cloth on his face. She must have been beautiful when she was younger. She had done something different with her hair; it was darker and full around her face. She wore wire-rimmed glasses, but her eyes still shone deep gray. She had rose-colored lipstick. She smiled.

"You scared us. You cried for a long time and then you seemed to go inside yourself. I didn't know if you would wake up," she said in Russian.

"When will you tell him you speak Russian? Where is he?"

"I will. When we get settled. Right now, he's packing up his things. We are all leaving here. You are right about that man. We will go to my flat. You will be safe there. We will all be safe."

"Anything you do to help me will put you in danger," he said, and then turned his face away from her eyes. They could be his mother's eyes. He missed his mother so much. He wanted to be a little boy again, play at the beach on the Black Sea with his papa and mama, find little shells and sea glass.

"Listen to me, my boy," Uncle Uldis said as he came into the yellow room. "I've packed and you will finish putting together your backpacks, and then we will leave for a few days. We will stay at Ausma's flat in the old city. We will be safe there. I promise you."

Fedya looked up at his uncle and then at Ausma. Concern was etched across their faces. And despite his deep appreciation for what they were trying to do, he could not endanger them further. He would have to get away from them to protect them from the monster, Yegor.

When they were ready to leave, about an hour later, it was dark outside. He carried the bags and Ausma helped Uncle down the steps. When they got in her car, Fedya sat in the back, along with his packs. As they drove, the two adults talked between themselves in Latvian. It gave him some time to consider his options. If he allowed himself to go to Ausma's, they would continue to pull the adult act. They still didn't believe he could take care of himself. True, being with Uncle had been a much-needed rest, but with Yegor's attack, he reasoned, he must go back to the street. It would be more difficult to survive on the streets of a city he didn't know, and even more effort without Latvian, although more people spoke Russian here than he had expected.

As they crossed the modern bridge, he looked at the people sitting in the tram that crossed with them. Their workday was just over. They had their own lives. As it slowly gained and passed by Ausma's car, he could see lights on several barges and a ship up the river. Then it occurred to him. He would go back to the shipyard. He would find a ship, become a stowaway, and go wherever the ship was going. He wouldn't even ask. He would escape his enemy and would escape the terrible cycle of trouble he had brought to everyone else.

On the other side of the bridge, his opportunity came. They were in a traffic jam and unable to move forward or backward.

"Uncle?" he said and touched his arm.

"Yes?"

"Thank you for everything. But I cannot put you in danger anymore. I love you."

He opened the car door, jumped out, and slammed the door before he could hear their protests. He didn't even look back. A sob clenched at the back of his throat as he bolted down the street. He ran after the first tram he saw and boarded it at the next stop.

He didn't notice the little blue car that followed his tram.

34

ELENA

ST. PETERSBURG, RUSSIA

Elena assured her friend, "Honestly, Valya, I am much better. You have things to do; I will be fine."

"I'm just so glad Petya has some information. He said he would be back this evening and we would talk about it then. Are you sure you won't be afraid alone? I'll get us some chocolates, eh? I think we deserve it today." Valya put on her coat and scarf and left with a blown kiss.

Elena was fine if she didn't think about the movie; her brother's searching eyes, or his silent cry for help. Of course, there she was, thinking about it again.

"Stop it!" she said out loud. She sat on the same white sofa, but sideways, her feet covered by a bright afghan throw that Valya's mother had crocheted. She thought the colors were very loud. If she were in a better state of mind, the coverlet would have been cheery. But today, it seemed garish, like a band of gypsies.

"Fedya, where are you?"

For months, he had been her secret, and by not saying his name, she kept him in a little box inside her heart and mind. But as soon as she let him out, like now, her world crashed in around her. Memories flooded in and took her breath away: Fedya singing in the bathtub, Fedya playing football, Fedya playing hide and seek, Fedya whispering to Irishka so she would stop crying, Fedya sending a paper airplane out their front window.

Or, the day Fedya laughed when he had outsmarted the police and stolen an entire bag of oranges. Oranges! At first, she couldn't believe her brother had become a thief. But he was very direct about it.

"We need the vitamins! Do you have vitamins in your pocket?" Fedya said.

"What are vitamins?" she asked.

"Every food has different vitamins. They keep you from getting sick. Potatoes have one kind, sausage another, cake another, and oranges another. When was the last time you had an orange?"

"I don't know," she said. "Maybe last Christmas, no, last summer. Remember when old Vasiliy Chasikovich brought us oranges? He said they came from Spain!"

"Now, there's someone who gets plenty of vitamins!" Fedya joked. And they both laughed because Uncle Vasiliy was fat!

Elena smiled even now as she thought of Uncle Vasiliy and Mama on the last day he had visited. He sat beside her mother's bed and held her hand. They whispered, and then he kissed her cheeks and left. Elena wondered if he had loved Mama. Until then, for many months, he had come almost every week. He always brought treats and food and once, she saw him hand Mama some rubles. Mama had tried to give them back, but he wouldn't take them and picked up Irishka instead and twirled her around. Oh, how she giggled. Then he sat down and bounced her on his great stomach.

The apartment door opened, and Elena's memories slid away. Petya came in, one hand behind his back.

"Excellent, you're still here," he said. "Where's Valya?"

"She had to meet someone from work. She said she would be back by dark."

Elena wasn't sure how to act around Petya after what had happened the day before.

Her brother always said, "Watch their eyes. If the eyes move around fast, the person is lying." Today, Petya's eyes bounced all over the room.

"Oh, well," he said. "She will miss the big surprise. I found my friend and told her your story; she will help us as much as she can to find your brother."

Elena sat up as he walked toward her. Could it be true? Could she trust Petya?

"And to prove it, look what she still had in her apartment. Is this yours?" His arm came around and there was Mashinka, her dolly. Elena couldn't help it. She yipped like a little dog and jumped up to wrap her arms around the doll. She inhaled her scent and found she could smell Fedya on her. Tears rolled down as she pressed the doll's body to her face.

"Elena, is it good? Are you all right?" he asked.

"*Da, da*! Oh, thank you Petya. *Da,* this is Mashinka. She was a gift from my Uncle Vasiliy. He brought her all the way from America."

"Oh, well, an American doll. No wonder!" he rolled his eyes. She narrowed her eyes at him. "I'm kidding. I'm kidding," he said. "I'm glad it's the right one." He looked at his cell phone. "What time did you say Valya would be back?"

"Before dark, that's all she said. Oh, and she said, if you come back before she does, to call her. She has a short list of food she needs from the market."

"Oh no, no, no." He put his hands over his ears. "I didn't hear that part, right? I must go. Our secret, all right? Here's a note for Valya. I need to run." He left before she could say anything else.

It didn't matter. She had her beloved Mashinka. Elena hugged the doll tightly to her chest. She felt a hard lump that had never been there before.

"What's the matter, Mashinka? Do you have a stomachache? Let me look. I will be very careful."

She laid out Mashinka on the garish coverlet and pulled up the doll's apron and dress. Lumpy for sure. Then she rolled Mashinka over and found a hole in the back, held together by an old safety pin. At first, she was angry with Fedya for not being careful, but then guilt flooded in.

After all, he had gone back to the old flat and saved Mashinka from the hole in the wall. She wondered if he still had any of the other treasures.

She undid the pin and poked her fingers inside. To her amazement, the first thing she found was a roll of money. It wasn't rubles, but money, all the same. She was glad Petya wasn't there because he would have taken it from her, she was sure. This money had to be a special secret or Fedya wouldn't have hidden it in her doll. In fact, everything inside the doll spoke of mystery.

The second item she pulled out was a chain with a small flat plastic case hanging from it. When she opened the case, an oddly shaped key nestled inside, along with a long list of numbers. This was so peculiar, she decided right then that she would put it back inside the doll. But as she did so, found a third object, and best of all: a silver swan bell. She shook it and the bell rang sweetly. Beautiful.

"Fedya, listen! I found the bell. Listen!" She rang it again. "Irishka! Listen! Fedya gave me a bell, a *lebedev* bell!" She rang it again and again.

She did not know how or why Fedya had put a bell in Mashinka, but it gave her such hope, a new link between herself and her brother. Not the terrible images from the movie, but something warm and magical. *Da,* it was magic. It had to be.

She got up from the sofa, rang the bell, and danced, like Odette. She was a swan.

35

FEDYA

RĪGA, LATVIJA

It took some time to understand the tram map at a kiosk, and to find someone who spoke Russian to direct him to the correct tram, but eventually, he worked it out. He had a close call on the first tram when he saw a police car pull up beside it. Dima had told him how the police sometimes boarded, and if they caught him without a ticket, they would take him to the station. He stepped off the tramcar as it slowed and walked away casually, as though it was his stop. When he looked back, he saw an officer board the tram and another one follow in the patrol car as the tram continued. Dima had been right.

Fedya would be safe on the next one. The police never checked two trams in a row on the same line.

He recognized the switch point near the old city and changed to the tram headed toward the shipyard where he and Zoya landed weeks earlier. As much as he resented Zoya and mistrusted her, he grieved her death. He wasn't even mad at her for confessing to Yegor where to find him. After just a few minutes of Yegor's brutality, he understood the persuasive power of pain and fear. Poor Zoya.

As he rode along, he thought of a better time when he and Dima and Zoya had walked along the Neva River laughing and joking. That was the night Dima had called him "little brother." Later, on the ship to Rīga, Fedya had asked Zoya about it.

"*Da,* Dima had a little brother. I don't know too much. The boy died when he was about your age," Zoya said as she painted her fingernails on the lower bunk.

"What was his name?"

"I don't know. What difference does it make? Sasha or Seryozha, something like that. Go to sleep."

"I can't. Open the door when you use that stuff. It poisons the air."

"Go to hell, kid," she said.

She spoke harshly to him whenever he talked about a subject that touched her feelings. He wondered how old she was. At first, he had thought she was twenty, but as he gave more thought to her story, he came to think that she was probably closer to eighteen.

"How did you meet Dima?"

For several minutes, she didn't answer. Then, she said, "He was a trick."

"A what?"

"A trick, a John, a paying customer. I didn't know until much later that it was a setup. Yegor and his buddies had set me up. It doesn't matter now. You ask too many questions."

He had kept quiet for a while longer, but then looked over the side of the bunk. She was crying. He rolled back before she noticed him.

"Zoya?" he said as he stared at the ceiling.

No answer.

"Zoya!"

"What? Can't you shut up and sleep?"

"Were you an orphan?"

"Who isn't? We're all orphans, Fedkins."

"Don't call me that."

"Sorry."

"Did you live in a children's house?"

"Yeah, what of it? It's just a bigger roof over your head and the boys are less experienced. You know they toss you out of those places at sixteen? I was on the street by midsummer of my fifteenth year, and was turning tricks for good money in six weeks. But I'm done with that now. I'm ready to settle down with a sailor." She laughed.

A sudden buck in the tram car jerked him back to the present. He thought of his sister then. Had he thrown Elena to that kind of future once she turned of age? He would never forget his own humiliation at being raped. Never. He shuddered to think of Lenushka in a similar situation. It would be his fault.

The crowd in the tram car thinned as they headed out of the main part of the city. He considered what he would say to Imant. What if he couldn't find the man's cabin again? No, it would be fine. He would get off at the end of the line at Eksporta Street and walk toward the storage hut. Surely he could find the cabin from there. He would retrace the route they took in Imant's old van. Fedya had a good memory. He could do it. He must do it, because Imant was his one hope of getting away from Latvija, away from Yegor, away from his miserable bad luck. Perhaps he would go to Sweden; get a job there. He looked older. He could work in a restaurant or a warehouse, or work in a movie theater and take tickets. Then he could watch some of the movies. And when he had enough money, he would go back to school. He would learn Swedish. He would take piano lessons. Anything was possible once he got away.

At the last stop, he stepped off the tram and recognized the corner despite the dark. As he walked further, he feared he had made a wrong turn until he saw the storage hut where Imant had hidden them. For a second, he thought he heard a car engine idling, like before, when they had hidden inside the hut. But then silence, just silence; the familiar sound had made him feel jittery.

When he found the major road, he took a right and walked toward the shipyard area. He kept his eyes open for any familiar markers or signs. There was one, he remembered, a red circle with an X in the middle. He had to laugh a little; it was like a treasure map. Imant had turned there. Up ahead, he saw the little store where Imant had stopped to get a loaf of bread to share with them. And right past the store and down a lane was Imant's cabin.

The small house sat alone at the end of the lane, somewhat forbidding at night. One window was dimly lit. Perhaps he wasn't there. Fedya hadn't even considered what he would do if Imant was away. Then he heard barking inside. The dog! What was the dog's name? Krack...no, Keks...something like that.

Inside, he heard Imant's voice, "Kriksi, quiet! What is it?"

Then Imant was there, outside, spouting out a lot of Latvian while the dog barked. Fedya didn't know whether Imant screamed at him or the dog.

Fedya called out in Russian, "Imant! Imant! It's me, Fedya, Fyodor Ivanovich."

Imant wore full workers' winter wear: long johns, a wool shirt, suspenders, a vest, scarf, fishing pants, and boots. He grinned ear to ear.

"Are you going somewhere?" Fedya asked.

Imant laughed, "I just got back, not one minute ago. If you had been sooner, you would have missed me. Come in. Come in. I did not expect to see you again, young man. Not really." He laughed again and pulled him into the house.

Kriksi made a quick getaway out the door to bark. Imant called the dog back and scanned the yard as the dog came back reluctantly. Not seeing anything, he closed and latched the door. Kriksi jumped up on Fedya and gave him a quick tongue bath.

"Come," Imant said, "let's get more comfortable. I will have a fire going in a moment."

"Thank you. I'm sorry I had no way to contact you. It was, well, it was a last-minute decision," he said as he pushed the dog off.

"Kriks! Down! Of course. It's no problem," he said as he turned to the fireplace, "There is time to tell me the entire story. But for now, you are well? And tell me, where is your fine friend, Zoya?"

Fedya stared at the back of the man's head for a moment before Imant turned to catch his look.

He couldn't speak. He couldn't say the words.

Imant strode across to him and put a hand on his shoulder. "It's all right, my boy. It can wait. Are you hungry, eh?" Without waiting for an answer, Imant busied himself at the fireplace again and then at the small wood-burning stove. He put on a water pot and pulled bread and cheese from the cabinets.

Fedya ran his hand across the smooth and worn wood of the old timber table. On it sat a small basket full of Tellin shells, a fat candle on a heavy green plate, and a fisherman's knife. As his eyes wandered about the room, he realized it hadn't changed at all. Was it six weeks ago or was it yesterday he had sat at this table with Zoya?

"She's dead," he said.

Imant stopped pouring the hot water into cups and stared at the boy. "Dead? But how?"

"The dangerous man. The same bad man who chased us, he found her again. I don't know how he found her, but he did. And he found me, and I think he would have killed me too."

With two mugs in hand, Imant walked over and placed one in front of Fedya, along with cheese and bread. As he sat down, Imant said, "I don't understand."

Fedya stared at the food. "It doesn't matter." He looked up. "But I need your help again. I need to get away from here. I need to leave Rīga and go far away."

"I see. But before we plan such a voyage, please tell me what has happened. Can you?"

As they ate and drank hot black tea with extra sugar for Fedya, he told the older man what he had seen and experienced since they had departed from one another. He didn't know how long he talked, but it was long enough for Imant to finish his meal, make a second cup of tea, and roll and light his own cigarette. Imant spoke little, asked a question here and there, and when Fedya finished, they were both quiet.

Imant said, "I will help you."

"You will? I mean, you can? Thank you. Thank you very much. Someday, I will repay you. I'll get work. I can work. I'll repay you."

"Slow down, boy. Let me think."

Fedya waited. Imant smoked and pondered the possibilities. Kriksi growled. Imant stood, walked over to a wardrobe, and pulled out a rifle and a box of shells. He brought them back to the table and loaded the rifle.

"Did this man, this Yegor, did he have a weapon?" Imant asked.

Fedya stared at the rifle. He had never seen one up close before.

"Fedya! Did the man have a weapon?"

"Who?"

"The dangerous man. What was his name?"

"Yegor. A knife. He had a knife. But he's not here. He ran away, and my uncle and his friend left the apartment. I jumped out of their car. He couldn't be here."

"Shh," Imant said. He opened the cottage door and said, loudly, to no one in particular, "Perhaps I will call the police."

He held the rifle ready and scanned the yard. Kriksi growled. Imant held him back and closed the door.

"Are we safe? I don't think you should call the police; they will ask too many questions," Fedya said.

"It's fine," Imant said. "Many vagabonds think they can sleep in my yard. I always yell this out the door to scare them away. Kriksi growls and I shoo them away. No one I know likes the police."

Imant propped the rifle by the door and tousled the dog's head, "*Labs suns*—Good dog!"

"All right, it's getting late. Let's get some sleep. Tomorrow is a new day, and I will tell you more about my plan after you have rested. One of my ships leaves for Stockholm tomorrow. I have an old school friend who lives there. He speaks many languages. I think, together, we will help you start over. Perhaps you would like to become a helper, perhaps work with the ship's steward, eh?"

The next day, Imant woke him early with tea and more cheese. Fedya felt sluggish, like his head was under water.

"Come, boy. We must get to the shipyard early to catch my ship before it leaves. Come, come. Coat, hat, gloves. Let's go. Are you ready?"

"*Da, da.* I'm just tired, I think."

"You'll see. The ocean air will revive you. But you must work on the ship. You understand?"

"Of course." Fedya was right behind Imant when he opened the door and stopped dead. On the ground lay Imant's beloved dog, motionless. Imant ran to him without thinking and in seconds, Fedya saw Yegor strike his friend hard on the head. Imant collapsed over his dog. Fedya yelled, but it didn't matter. Yegor turned and grabbed him by the arm, twisting it behind him painfully.

"Make no noise or I'll cut the old man."

Fedya moaned. Again, he had brought catastrophe to someone who had tried to help him. He tried not to cry, but tears streamed down his face all the same.

Yegor dragged him to the little car, then tied him up in the back seat and put a terrible smelling rag in his mouth. If he vomited, he would die. Fedya concentrated on breathing through his nose, but the panic made it hard. He couldn't even beg for mercy.

"You're a lucky son of a bitch. The boss will want to talk to you himself. But I'll tell you once now and not again. You'd better tell him the truth, or I'll have my way of getting to the truth. If it weren't for you, Zoya would still be alive."

And just like that, Yegor put the car in gear, and they were on the road, back to St. Petersburg. He didn't know how long this journey would be, but he knew his body would ache soon. He did his best to find the most comfortable position possible, and even figured out a way to pull at the rag in his mouth, to create a small hole for extra breathing. Miraculously, he slept. At some point, Yegor pulled over without warning, yanked him out of the back seat, tossed him into the luggage compartment, and threw a blanket over him.

PART FOUR: FEBRUARY 2001

36

ELENA

CHILDREN'S HOUSE NUMBER TWENTY-FOUR
ST. PETERSBURG, RUSSIA

Elena had hoped something—anything—would prevent her return to the children's house, like the building burning down or the employees disappearing. Anything. But no luck and no magic.

Instead, her absence from the winter camp had realigned the girls, and Larissa had become the queen. Baiba, previously the oldest, got a job babysitting for two teachers, and they invited her to sleep in another building while Lukina, who used to run messages, was assigned to the kitchen in exchange for a move to a different unit. Oksana was moved as well, apparently because she would be adopted after all. Elena recognized the switch in power as soon as she arrived. Larissa and her main followers, Galina, Tatiana, Raisa, and the remaining Svetlana, had taken over the first five beds at the entrance of the dormitory. For Elena, it would be a gauntlet every time she entered or left the room.

Then, to make matters worse, five new girls had joined the unit from other children's houses. They had accepted Larissa's position of strength without question. They had also accepted Elena as the designated scapegoat. It was a free for all, at her expense.

244

By the end of her first week back, she had bruises up and down her arms and legs. They pushed her into furniture, tripped her, punched her with unknown hands, hit her with books and other falling objects, and once, tripped her in such a way that her head hit the floor and she had to go to the infirmary for observation.

Today, she sat in a stairwell near the front entrance. She wanted to run away. Her body hurt all over. She shivered even with her layers of clothing. The weather had snapped into a deep freeze and cold seeped into every bone. Everyone was wearing layers of sweaters and even coats to bed. In this weather, where could she go? If only Fedya were here, he would know what to do.

The stairwell echoed as someone came running down. She squeezed up against the wall and didn't look until the footsteps stopped.

"Elena Ivanovna? I have been looking all over for you. Director Kalmakovna wants to see you in her office."

It was Kiska. Such a clever girl. She had remained neutral through all the power shifts. Kiska never defended Elena to the other girls, but she caused no harm, either.

"Why?" Elena asked. "Am I in trouble?"

Kiska sat beside her. "I don't know. I don't think you're in trouble. Director was using her official voice. I think there was a visitor in there, but I couldn't see inside."

Elena got up, but Kiska pulled on her arm to sit her back down. "You should tell her what's happening."

"In what way?"

"You know," Kiska said. "All of your hurts. You need to tell them about Larissa and the others."

"And what would I say? I'm being beaten on the sly by a roomful of girls, but I can't tell who? I can't prove anything. No one listened to me at camp when I tried to tell them Larissa was behind the sled accident. Why would they listen now?" She stood up to go.

"Is that why she's after you now?" Kiska asked.

"Larissa? Of course, what did you think it was? She knows I know. I'd better go. Don't let anyone see you talking to me."

"But Elena—" Kiska said.

Elena ignored her and headed toward the director's office. Who knew what devious plan had caused this summons? The director might blame her for horrible vandalism or something worse. Maybe that would be a good thing. She could behave like a brute or a bully too, and perhaps they would send her away. Anywhere would be better than here.

At the director's door, she tapped on the glass and waited. She could hear voices inside, a man's hearty laugh and Kalmakovna's cackle, and possibly one or two others. She wasn't sure anyone heard her knock, and she was about to knock again when the door opened. It was Valya!

"Lenushka, come in! We have the best news!" Valya exclaimed as she put an arm around Elena's shoulder and pulled her into the room. The first thing she noticed was the heat. It was very warm in the director's office. Lovely. And then, she saw a fat older man stand up and smile.

"So, Lenushka, have you forgotten your old uncle, eh?" he said.

Elena froze. Was it possible? Was it really Uncle Vasiliy?

Valya spoke quickly. "Lenushka, you know this man, don't you?"

"*Da! Da!* Uncle Vasiliy! Oh, Uncle Vasiliy!" She ran into his arms.

Elena didn't really understand what her uncle's presence meant. Uncle Vasiliy had changed little. He was still fat, but his hair was whiter. Can that happen in just half a year? Elena sat in his lap as Valya explained how Uncle Vasiliy had contacted their office.

"Actually," Valya continued, "your real uncle, your mother's broth-er, Uldis Ozols, lives in Rīga, Latvia, and he started a search for you. He was the one who asked Vasiliy Chasikovich to search the children's houses to find you. Your uncle wants to bring you to Latvia to live with him and to adopt you and Fedya," Valya said.

"Fedya?" Elena turned to Uncle Vasiliy. "You have found Fedya too? How?"

"Not exactly. It was Fedya who found your uncle. The boy traveled all the way to Rīga by himself. I'm not sure how he did it, but apparently from an address on a photograph," Uncle Vasiliy said.

"Oh, from the pictures in the secret box."

"Anyway," Valya said, "Fedya is with your uncle in Rīga. As soon as we get the papers authorized, you will be able to travel, soon."

"What do you mean, soon? Not today? I can't go today? Oh please, please let me go," she said. "I can't stay here, please!" She buried her head in Vasiliy's chest.

The older man rubbed the girl's back and then looked more carefully at her arms. "What is this, Director Kalmakovna? The girl has bruises all over her arms."

The next thing Elena knew, the director asked her to stand up and everyone examined her arms and legs and asked a million questions. She didn't know at first if she should rat out Larissa, but then she thought about Aniya dying in the snow and Yuliya still strung up in a hospital bed. Larissa did not deserve to be protected.

It was Uncle Vasiliy who finally tipped the scale when he took both of her hands and his eyes locked on her. "You must tell, little one. Your mother taught you, no? How important it is to tell the truth."

And so she did. She told everything she knew. She directed her story to Uncle Vasiliy, but she was aware of Valya and Director Kalmakovna writing everything down. At one point, the director tried to interrupt, but Uncle Vasiliy's glare stopped her immediately. Elena left nothing out: the camp, her friends, the sled, Larissa's taunting after the accident, Larissa in the lunchroom, and then more recent events here at the children's house. Uncle Vasiliy's face became redder and redder. She thought his eyes might pop out of his head.

"This is absolutely and completely unacceptable. I will not allow this child to remain here another minute. You will confer temporary custody to me, or I will call the Health Department. Vladimir Evgenevich Chutes is an old friend of mine."

"Please Vasiliy Chasikovich," Director Kalmakovna interrupted, "we can work this out. There may be precedent for removing a child from the house in certain situations. It is unnecessary to contact any of your well-placed friends. But you must understand, our beds are full, and we have turned down other children to make a place for our little Elena Ivanovna."

"Ah, well, I see. But don't push me too hard. Perhaps a small donation will cover your expenses as you locate a replacement for Elena's bed? In the meantime, I expect to take the child with me—today," Vasiliy said.

"But Vasiliy Chasikovich, surely you know there are legal requirements that we must meet to protect the child?" Valya said.

"Valentina Alexandrovna, it's all right," Elena said. "Uncle Vasiliy loved my mother. He gave us food and money and helped us. But Uncle Vasiliy," turning to him, "why did you stop coming to see us? Mama died; did you know? Mama died months ago. She was the one who told Fedya to take us and to run away. She made him promise to keep us together. But then, I think he got scared when winter came and he made a big mistake and they caught us, Irishka and me."

"It was a hovel, no water, no heat, nothing," Kalmakovna said.

Elena turned, held up her head, and spoke defiantly to the director. "It was our special home. We were happy, and we were together."

"Dear Director," Vasiliy interrupted, "this matter is not up for negotiation. Someone needs to accompany Lenushka to her room, now, while she gathers her things. Her Latvian uncle and I will meet the letter of the law; we will sign the proper documents, get all the notary seals, but this child will not remain in this place where she has been physically and mentally traumatized. Tomorrow, you will receive a check from my bank to cover your expenses while you expedite the matter."

"But—" Valya began.

The director interrupted her. "Very well, Vasiliy Chasikovich. We will work with you. I will ring for one of the house mothers to attend to her."

Valya stood. "*Nyet.* I mean, that's unnecessary, Director Kalmakovna. I will go with her. Come Elena, let's pack your things." When they got out the door, Valya held a finger to her lips. Once they were through the hall door and had started up the steps, they stopped on the landing. Valya turned to her, eyes twinkling, and hugged her fiercely. "Oh, my darling Lenushka. I am so happy for you." Valya held her tightly for some moments and then pulled away, holding Elena's face between her hands. "You will have a family again, a life. You will laugh again. The Holy Mother has answered my prayers. Thanks be to God." And then she hugged her again.

"Is it real, Valya? Is this really happening?"

"Yes, I think so. And, just so you don't worry, I brought your doll from the flat. I kept her safe just as you asked me to do."

"Thank you. But what about Petya and the movie people?"

"It doesn't matter now. I'm moving in with my friend, Adlesha Petrovna." Valya didn't bother to tell Elena that it was Petya who had invited her to move out. "Come, let's keep walking. I won't lie to you. It won't be easy. I have never had to do this kind of paperwork on such short notice, but I will do it. I will do it for you because I love you like a little sister."

"Oh, Valya," she said as she took the young woman's hand, "Thank you so very much. Thank you for being my friend."

As they neared the dormitory, Elena stiffened a little. She was still afraid of what she might find there. But just as the two of them came close to the door, Lubya escorted Larissa out of the room. Larissa stopped abruptly when she saw Elena.

"You! I curse you, Elena Ivanovna. Everyone you love will die and you will be alone forever."

The gentle caretaker, Lubya, who stood beside Larissa, gasped, and said, "What are you saying?"

"Shut up or I'll curse you too, you old crow," Larissa said.

Lubya crossed herself three times.

"I curse you! I curse you, Elena Ivanovna." Larissa's voice faded as Lubya pulled the girl down the hallway the other way.

Elena shook and then cried. Valya held her and kept repeating a prayer to Jesus about the devil. After some moments, Elena stopped crying.

"Don't listen to her, Elena," Valya said.

"She's a gypsy," Elena whispered. "That's bad for me, isn't it?"

"She just wants to scare you. Let's get your things."

When they stood up, they found the other girls crowded around the doorway, staring dumbfounded. Valya shooed them back in and Elena went to her bed to pack up. The other girls, back to their own beds, watched silently. Elena pulled out her pack from under the bed and filled it with the few things she still owned: three tops, a pair of pants, some underwear, socks, the red hat, a scarf, her special box from the tear she made in the mattress that held her treasures, and a book of poems. She packed quickly. When she finished, she followed Valya back to the door. She turned to the girls, wanting to say something nice to those who had been kind to her along the way, but then, as she looked at them, she realized anything she said might endanger them. So, she turned and left in silence. On the way out, she caught Kiska's eye, who smiled and winked.

Behind her, she heard Tatiana say, "Good riddance." But then she heard Raisa, of all people, say, "Shut up!" and Galina laughed her horrible hyena laugh.

37

FEDYA & YEGOR

ST. PETERSBURG, RUSSIA

When Yegor hauled Fedya out of the trunk, the pain in his bones shot through him and he couldn't stand, even after his captor cut the cords.

"Get up, you lousy scum. The only reason you're alive is the key. Remember that."

Yegor kicked him, and Fedya tried again to find his feet, with little success. He said nothing. No words would help him anyway. He looked up from the ground at a beautiful white mansion; bright lights caused the windows to sparkle. Yegor blocked his view until he dragged him upright by the collar and toward the front door that opened, by all appearances, on its own. Only inside did Fedya see the butler holding the door.

"Aleksei Aleksandrovich will meet you in the study," the man said.

Yegor barely acknowledged the directive and pulled Fedya along through a door to the right of the grand staircase. Once inside, Yegor released him, and he fell again to the floor. His hands were stiff from the cold. Slowly, he pulled the thin gloves from his hands and pressed them to the vibrant red, blue, and gold carpet, so thick and soft. Yegor paced.

Another door opened into the room and Fedya saw who must be the notorious Stepanov, mafia boss and millionaire. Perhaps it was the late hour, Fedya didn't know, but the man wore an old sweater over a black turtleneck, jeans, and leather slippers. He wore his brown hair clipped short, military style. His eyes were soft, but quick. He looked like no monster, but a local merchant. Fedya watched him quickly take in the scene before the man spoke to Yegor.

"Gogo, I thought we had an understanding. You surprised me with your call. At the very least, you should have cleaned yourself up, as well as the boy. This is inconvenient, at best. I have another meeting shortly to discuss my new movie." His voice was quiet but carried some menace. "Did I tell you about my new project? Very exciting."

"*Da, da.* Of course. Sorry, Aleksei Aleksandrovich, but I knew you still wanted the key. This is the boy who knows where it is," Yegor said.

"Gogo, didn't I tell you to let go of this assignment? You do not look well."

"I'm fine. Fine. I had to finish what I started."

"But I ordered you to be evaluated. Volkov told me there was concern about the trajectory of the bullet. He said you ran away from the hospital."

"I'm fine."

"Are you?"

"The kid denies everything."

"Like you. Step aside Gogo." Stepanov turned to Fedya. "I would prefer you sit in a chair, young man, instead of the floor."

Fedya said nothing.

"Get up, you snot," Yegor said as he moved to grab him again.

Stepanov held up his hand. "A moment, Gogo. Please don't speak so crudely. He's a mere boy. That is not my way."

Yegor huffed and walked over to the dark windows. Stepanov pushed a button on his desk and spoke into a speaker.

"Olga, please bring us some refreshment. Hot chocolate for two, a short vodka for Gogo." A muffled voice replied. Stepanov paused then and studied Fedya. "Can you stand?"

Fedya held onto the dark red settee and pulled himself upright.

"Please take off your coat and hat. You will be warmer. Sit, sit. I will sit here across from you in my favorite chair."

Stepanov's voice was becoming irritating in its sugary sweetness. "I'm not a child," Fedya said.

"I beg your pardon. And yet, you are not a man. It's a delicate time, this age you are in. I remember my sons at your age."

Silence.

Finally, a young woman in a maid's uniform brought in a tray and set it on the low table between them. She distributed the drinks, giving Yegor his drink last, and left the room. Fedya's hands wrapped around the warm mug, and he savored the rich chocolate brew through a veil of whipped cream. Fedya heard Yegor's shot glass clink on the glass table behind him.

"So, Fedya," Stepanov began. "This is where we are. Your gang of boys, perhaps some of them were young men, raided one of my warehouses. You know this, of course. It was unfortunate for me, that one of my accountants was there and, at gunpoint, he turned over an access key and code to a vault that was a gift to me until someone, whose name you don't need to know, broke a rather unprofessional deal with me. That money is rightfully mine. As the caretaker of this key, I will reward you for its return."

"What the—?!" Yegor growled from the window.

"Gogo, please. I will not ask you again to control your tongue. We will talk later." Still looking at Fedya, Stepanov said, "What do you say, my boy? Give me the key and you can be on your way again."

"I don't have it," Fedya said.

"This is what I'm saying, sir. The boy is lying. Let me get the truth from the bastard. You know I can do it."

Before Stepanov could answer, the hall door crashed open and, of all people, Sasha Iakolev entered with Nataliya, and a dark-haired man Fedya had never seen before. He curled into the couch.

Stepanov stood.

"Aleksei Aleksandrovich, may I call you Alyosha?" Sasha said, his hand outstretched.

"I'd rather you didn't," Stepanov said.

"I am so very sorry to be late. I tried to tell your man that you were waiting for us," Sasha said and then nearly tripped over himself when he saw Fedya. "The boy? My boy? You have him here? Oh my God, Alyosha, I am astonished. How did you know?" Sasha went straight for Fedya and sat beside him and hugged him. "I have been bereft; you naughty little boy, running away from your Sasha."

Nataliya stood beside the couch and stroked Fedya's arm while looking straight at Stepanov.

"Aleksander Iakolev, you are always full of surprises."

"Sasha, please call me Sasha."

"Introduce us, Sasha," Nataliya said, almost purring.

"*Da, da*. This is our starlet, Natasha Vladimirovna, but everyone calls her Nataliya."

Stepanov bowed slightly and Fedya heard the man's heels click ever so lightly. He turned to the younger man. "You must be Pyotr Kotolvsky, a pleasure to meet you at last." They shook hands.

"The pleasure is all mine. This is a fantastic opportunity for all of us. The story will make a splendid film," Pyotr said.

Sasha interrupted. "My darling Fedkins, what is that terrible smell? Have you soiled yourself like a little baby? Hm?" Sasha patted Fedya's cheek.

"Aleksander Iakovlev, Fedya is my guest, and I'm sure he is tired and could use some rest. He has just returned from an arduous journey," Stepanov said as he gently pulled Fedya from Sasha's grasp.

"But Aleksei," Sasha said as he got up from the divan. "He's really mine. I bought him from a girl in my last movie series. Isn't that true, Nataliya? He's a wonderful little actor, isn't he Petya?"

Stepanov looked at Petya, who made a slight shrug. Fedya put down his mug clumsily and did his best to edge further away from Sasha, whose hand leaped out and captured Fedya by the other wrist.

With a raise of his hand, Stepanov signaled for Yegor. Fedya thought it looked like Stepanov was calling a dog, but for the first time, he was grateful for the rough strength of Yegor, who peeled away Sasha's hand.

"Gogo," Stepanov said, "take our guest to the blue bedroom at the back of the house and secure it. Fedya, there is a bathroom there. Please clean yourself up. Gogo, ask Olga to find something suitable for him to wear. And please, use the staff quarters to clean up yourself. Please stay on the property until we can speak in private."

"Yes sir," Yegor said under his breath.

"But Alyosha—" Sasha started.

"Truly, Aleksander Iakolev, I prefer you call me Aleksei Aleksandrovich. Now, please sit down. Everyone, please sit down. We have more important things to discuss than your current fascination with minors or their trafficking."

Fedya looked back as he reached the door and saw Sasha lick his lips at him. He wanted to vomit. Yegor pulled him along roughly up the stairs.

"You little piece of shit. Don't get too comfortable with Stepanov's sugary words. He did not come to such power being a kind man," Yegor said at the top of the stairs.

Inside the blue room, Yegor closed the door behind him. Fedya could tell that Yegor had no intention of leaving him alone. Not yet. He tried to run to the bathroom, but he wasn't quick enough. Yegor tossed him violently against a wall.

"I could break several of your fingers. Stepanov might get angry with me, but not after I hand him the key. So, give it up, you piece of dung. And don't bother to scream. No one will hear you."

Yegor grabbed the little finger of Fedya's left hand, and without ceremony, broke it.

Fedya screamed. "Dear God in heaven, help me!" he cried.

When Yegor took the next finger in hand, he waited for Fedya to stop sobbing.

Fedya's words tumbled out. "Listen to me, please. Dima gave me the key case, that's true, but I didn't know what it was."

"You're lying."

"*Nyet*, I was still new to the gang. I wasn't at the building when your men came. I found Dima in the dumbwaiter. Unconscious." Fedya was speaking as fast as he could, his finger swelling and throbbing. "When Dima woke up, he gave me all his keys. He told me to give them to Zoya."

Yegor stood up and spat into the waste can near the bed. He turned to Fedya. "You'd better not try to fool me."

Fedya curled up like a bug. "Please, please stop hurting me. I'm telling you the truth."

"Then what happened?"

"I found Zoya and gave her the storage keys, but not the key case. I wore that around my neck. When we got to her friend's place, I hid the key in my sister's doll."

"How in the hell did you have her doll?" Yegor moved in closer again.

"Please, wait. I went back to our old apartment to get my dead mother's money. I found some of our family's things. That's all we had left. The doll was there."

Yegor sat on the bed. Fedya didn't know what would happen next. His finger hurt so bad, but he was afraid to move. The man was insane. What if Yegor didn't remember who pulled the trigger that destroyed his face? What if he thought Fedya pointed the gun?

"My mother is dead," Yegor said.

"The key is probably still in the doll," Fedya said. "I accidentally left it where they made the movies when Zoya and I ran away. I tell you; I don't have it."

Yegor looked up at him then, his eyes wet as though tears had formed, but Fedya couldn't imagine that could be possible.

"The woman downstairs, the actress, Nataliya. It was her flat. Go hurt her. I'd be happy for it," Fedya said. His mother would have been ashamed of him. But his heart was as hard as stone toward Nataliya and Sasha.

Yegor said nothing and left the room.

38

ELENA & VASILIY

ST. PETERSBURG, RUSSIA

Elena stood in the center of Uncle Vasiliy's small apartment and slowly turned, taking in everything. He had covered every wall, every surface, every ledge, with pictures of himself: Vasiliy singing, Vasiliy smiling, Vasiliy accepting flowers, Vasiliy with other singers. There were pictures of Vasiliy as a young man and there were even pictures of him older, but not as many.

"Come, my dear, this lounge chair will pull out and you'll be able to sleep here, *da*? And here is a small chest where you can put your things. Are you listening, Elena? Uldi will be so happy to see you. And Fedya will too. I have been trying to contact them, but no one is answering at his flat."

She wasn't sure what to say or do. He was kind, but he seemed more like a stranger now. How long had she really known him?

"Lenushka," he said, "are you afraid? Please don't be. You haven't said a word since we got here. Have I done something wrong?"

"*Nyet*. Not really. I'm sorry. It's like a strange dream."

He smiled warmly. "*Da, da.* It will take time. You will be with me for several days, maybe longer. I'm not sure, but it is very real. I am so happy that I have found you. I should have looked. Well, it doesn't matter anymore, does it?"

"I don't know," she said.

"What?"

"I don't know if it doesn't matter," she said.

He looked at her carefully and then laughed his belly laugh. "*Da,* my dear, well said. Well said." He sat on a nearby chair and put up his feet. "So, what should we do now, my little snow maiden? Would you like something to eat?"

"It's not time for dinner. But if you want me to eat, I will eat," she said.

"Well, I was just wondering what you would like to do. What do little girls do all day? Perhaps you'd like to watch some television?" he said.

She turned to him quickly and stared. "You have your own television?"

"*Da!* How else would I get to see myself?" He laughed.

She wasn't sure why that was funny. He raised his great bulk slowly, then walked over to a large cabinet and opened the door. She gasped at the very modern-looking television.

"Let's see what we can find. And while you're watching, I'll make a few more telephone calls to make sure things are moving along."

He handed her a thin plastic box and showed her how to push the buttons to change the channels. He left her sitting on an old hassock, watching and clicking. Totally absorbed, the time flew by.

That evening, they sat at a small table outside his kitchen area. The food was wonderful.

"I didn't see or hear you cook anything. Are you a magician?"

"You are a funny young girl. *Nyet,* this is from a friend. I just heated it up. I don't know how to cook. Tomorrow, we will go out for breakfast and then I will call more of my friends. You will meet many people who will be happy to feed Vasiliy Chasikovich and his delightful niece."

"Uncle Vasiliy, tell me about my mother."

"What do you mean?"

"I think you have known her for a long time, haven't you? She never talked to us much about her past. When I was little, she would laugh and sing songs. By the time I got old enough to understand things, she was usually too tired or sad to tell stories."

Vasiliy stood and walked over to another cabinet, where he poured brown liquor into a very dainty glass with a stem. He set the glass down and cleared away their plates. She wasn't sure if he was going to tell her anything or not. He looked so serious. Finally, he sat back down and took a small sip of his drink.

"I didn't meet your mother until she was a teenager, about seventeen or eighteen. I don't remember exactly. Her brother was already playing with the orchestra, and I was enjoying my reputation as a first-rate tenor. Sometimes she would come to rehearsals and turn pages for her brother at the piano. She always smiled and laughed at everyone's jokes. One day, Uldis came to me. He had a proposal for me and asked could we go out for coffee. He brought Elizaveta with him. I will never forget that day because two wonderful things happened: your uncle had composed a wonderful piece for me to sing in concert, and I fell in love with Elizaveta."

"Oh Uncle, I thought as much. That is no surprise to me."

"Well, it may not be a surprise, but it was out of the question. How many years are between us? Twenty? Twenty-five? She was so young. *Nyet.* Plus, I was touring a great deal. I traveled from St. Petersburg to Moscow to Rīga all the time. When Gorbachev came into power, suddenly musicians could get visas quickly. I had unbelievable opportunities to go to America and Canada and even Australia. I lived an international life. There was no room for a wife. But now, I look back and I am sorry and, well, I am lonely." He drank again from his small glass.

"Uncle Vasiliy, do you think Mama would still be alive if you would have taken care of her?" she asked.

"I don't know. How can I know?" He stood up. "I'm going to make some coffee; do you want something hot to drink? Perhaps some tea?"

"*Da, spaciba,* with plenty of sugar." She followed him over to the kitchen area and sat on a tall stool. "But what else do you remember?"

"Did you know she played the piano? But mostly, she wanted to dance."

"Really? That's what I wanted. When I asked her if I could take classes, she always said 'no' and kept telling me to forget that dream. Why would she say that?"

"I don't know, Lenushka. Perhaps it is because her own dreams ran away from her, and she could never catch them. In those years, there were many Russians who lived in Rīga. Well, there still are, but back then, the Russians oversaw everything: the schools, the government, the police, the music, everything. And eventually, like many young girls, your mother met a handsome young soldier, Ivan Konstantinov *Lebedev*. I only met the man once, but he seemed good hearted, and he adored your mother. But he was not interested in the arts, like music or dance or paintings. He was a man of the outdoors, a fisherman, and a sports enthusiast. So, when his unit moved out of Rīga, he returned home to his St. Petersburg with Elizaveta."

"Did she have to learn Russian?"

"Oh no. We all knew Russian. All the children learned Russian in school. In fact, all our classes were in Russian. If anything, parents worried that their children would forget Latvian." The tea and coffee were ready, and Vasiliy signaled they should return to his easy chair. He offered her a small plate of tiny cakes. For a few minutes, they sat in silence as Elena ate a cake and Vasiliy seemed to swim in his memories.

She interrupted. "Did Mama ever get to dance?"

"Oh, I think she had maybe one or two years of classes in Rīga, but her family was poor, as everyone was in those dark years. *Nyet*, she was simply in the wrong place at the wrong time. And before she knew it, she married. They lived in Russia, and she became pregnant. First with your brother, Fyodor, and then you. Actually, you were born in Rīga, but that's a long story."

"What?" Elena's eyes went wide. She had never heard this. "But I can't speak that language or anything."

Before Vasiliy could explain how that happened, his phone rang. He checked his pocket watch, and was a little surprised by the hour.

"Hallo? Ah, Uldi!" And then he switched to Latvian.

Elena watched him as she nibbled on another small cake and drank her tea. At first, she tried to understand what he was saying. She assumed Uncle Uldis would want to speak to her, too. What would she say? But wait, the telephone was the only thing keeping her away from Fedya. She jumped up and ran over to Uncle Vasiliy. He had turned away now, so she patted him on the back.

"Uncle Vasiliy, I must speak to Fedya, please. He is there. Please."

He turned to her with a tight face. "Not now, Lenushka, not now. Go sit down."

"But I want to speak to Fedya. Why can't I?"

"Not now!" he bellowed at her. She was so startled, tears jumped up into her eyes and she retreated to her chair. It frightened her. No, he frightened her. Had she placed herself in some danger?

He turned back to the phone and then wrote something down on a pad of paper. When he hung up, he walked back and sat heavily.

"I am very sorry I yelled at you, but I had a terrible surprise," he said and looked at her strangely.

"What happened?"

"Nothing. Everyone will be fine. But Fedya is sick and could not come to the phone. They are...they are...uh, they took him to the hospital."

"Oh, that's terrible. Hospitals are dangerous places. What is wrong with him?"

"I don't know. I don't really know. But I think it's time for us to go to bed. Come, I will help you make your bed and then you can do it yourself after that."

She watched as he waddled about the place, collecting the things she needed for her bed: a thick coverlet, a pillow, and a sheet for the cushions. He showed her where she could change into pajamas, even though she did not own such things. She just wore her soft pants and small shirt. It was nice and warm in his apartment.

He sat beside her and gently stroked her hair. "You are a lovely girl, my Elena Margarita. Everything is going to be all right. And tomorrow, you will meet some of your Uncle Vasiliy's friends."

She sank inside the warm duvet. She was tired, but she had to ask one more question. "When will I be able to see Fedya?"

"Well, let's get you to Rīga first, eh? Then, everything will be clearer."

"And when will that be?"

"Lenushka, I don't know. Your friend, Valentina Alexandrovna, will do everything she can to help us. Don't you think?"

She nodded, "Oh, *da*. Valya is a good friend. Uncle Vasiliy, do you remember you used to sing us songs when we were little? Will you sing to me now?"

"Ah, of course, of course." He pulled over his chair, cleared his throat and sang the birch tree song. She tried not to cry, but it was hard because her mother used to sing it to her too.

Why do you stand, swaying?
Oh slender birch tree,
With your head bent
To your very stem?

But across the road
Across a wide river
Similarly lonely
Stands a tall oak tree.

How can I, birch tree,
Clamber over to the oak tree?
I wouldn't bend and sway then as I do now,
I wouldn't bend and sway then as I do now,

With my slender branches,
I would lean against him
And with his foliage,
I would whisper day and night. [Ivan Zakharovich Surikov, 1864]

39

FEDYA

ST. PETERSBURG, RUSSIA

The next morning, the same maid escorted Fedya, but this time, to another room; she called it the sunroom. Stepanov sat at a small, elegantly laid table.

"Good morning, my young friend. You look much better today, and you smell better too. But what happened to your left hand?"

"A gift from your man, Yegor," he said.

Stepanov sighed. "Olga, please call Volkov to come by to look at the boy's hand. Then bring hot tea and some of that good sausage and bread that Cook made yesterday. Come, Fedya, sit down, for heaven's sake."

Fedya wore athletic clothes the maid had provided. They were a little big for him, but not bad. The sneakers were fantastic. His host was dressed more formally in a coat and tie. Fedya didn't even know the day of the week. A workday? Did a man such as Stepanov go to work?

"Thank you for the clothes," Fedya said, unsure of what else to say. "You have a son?"

"*Da,* of course, two. But they are older and at university in Europe. My daughter, too, is away at school. I'm sorry you couldn't meet them."

Fedya stared at the man. "Why are you talking to me like that? How could you be sorry? I know what I am. I know what you are. And I already told you, I don't have your precious key."

"Perhaps. But I think you know where it is, don't you?"

Fedya thought about this. Did he? He hid it in the American floppy doll, his sister's doll, but he didn't have that either. Did Stepanov know, or was Yegor acting on his own? Fedya had told Yegor last night that Nataliya might still have it in her bedroom. But what if she threw it away? The most likely explanation.

"Do I have any options?" Fedya said.

The maid brought in the food and Fedya realized how hungry he was. Figuring it might be his last meal for a while, he ate lustily.

"Options? Really? You are quite brave to test me, Fedya. Be forewarned, I will lose my patience with you, eventually. You only have two options. One: give me the key or the information I need to obtain it, and I will pay you a small reward, because I like children. Or two: defy me, and I will let your friend, Sasha Iakolev, take you with him. It's a grizzly business, but I must close out this situation soon."

"I might know where the key is. Will you let me leave to look for it?"

"*Nyet*, not alone. That would be stupid of me and surely, you must realize, stupid is not my way. I have a busy day ahead and a big event this evening. I don't have time to dally with you today."

"You won't kill me?"

"Why would I do that?"

"Not you, but Yegor. Your assassin. He killed Zoya. Tortured her. He did this." Fedya held up his hand with the swollen finger.

Stepanov appraised him. He sighed. "I gave you your options. As for the girl, betrayal comes at a high price. She was an informant who played both sides. That rarely works out. How do you know Yegor used torture?"

"He told me."

Stepanov sighed again, then tossed his napkin on the table and got up to leave. "Please do nothing stupid, like try to escape. The house has a sophisticated alarm system. Tomorrow morning, we will meet again and, if necessary, I will provide you with an escort to retrieve the key."

"Yegor?"

"Is none of your business." He looked past Fedya as the maid entered. "Olga, please give this boy more food. And be sure he gets a hearty dinner. Have a good day, everyone."

The maid curtsied to her employer.

40

ELENA

ST. PETERSBURG, RUSSIA

Living with Uncle Vasiliy was like one big party. He seemed to have visitors every day: mostly older women who flirted with him and brought him food, or students (men and women of all ages), for voice lessons. He let her sit and listen, but she didn't like this side of Vasiliy as much. He was so sharp-tongued with them, and she felt sorry for the young girls whose lips trembled and the young men who kept adjusting their clothes. She wanted to jump up and say, "Don't be silly, this is Uncle Vasiliy, he wouldn't hurt a flea." Instead, she listened to their voices break or stutter as they said, *"Da, Vasiliy Chasikovich,"* or *"Nyet, Vasiliy Chasikovich."*

One day, at their midday meal, she asked him about it. "Uncle Vasiliy?"

"Da, my cherub?" he answered as he popped a sushi roll into his mouth.

"Why do you pretend to be so bad-tempered with your students? That last one this morning—I thought she would burst into tears. Do you make them afraid of you on purpose?"

Vasiliy raised an eyebrow and then smiled wickedly. She laughed.

"Humph! Didn't fool you, eh? Don't worry too much. Believe me, if I didn't act that way, they wouldn't think I knew anything. As they improve, I get nastier!" He laughed at his own joke.

"But she was good. I liked the last song, very romantic."

"Oh, I see. Well, if she sounded so good, perhaps I should send her away. *Nyet*? Why should she keep coming back?"

"I don't know. To meet some of your famous friends?"

He laughed again. "Oh, you are a lot smarter than I thought. That is also truer than you could know. But here's the real truth: I can teach her to sing even better. That's why she endures me. That's what they all want, to be better and to become stars. For many years, I wouldn't teach. But then, well, the older I got, I started enjoying the challenge. Besides, I like to look at the pretty ones."

"Does it cost a lot of money to come to you for lessons?" she asked as she nibbled on the rest of her spring roll.

He held up his arms expansively. "*Da,* of course. I am Vasiliy Chasikovich Nesterov!" He was about to laugh, but then noticed a change in her demeanor. "Why? Are you interested in having lessons with me? Perhaps I can make you a deal."

"*Nyet, nyet,*" she laughed, "I'm no singer. But I know someone, a friend of Valya. He's a songwriter and a singer. I'm sure he is very good."

"Now, Lenushka, I would like to help, but really, I only work with certain kinds of voices, truly serious singers. I'm sure this young man is probably not interested."

"But if he would be, would you? Could you, just as a gift to me, listen to him? We could call them up. Maybe tonight? They could come by tonight and—"

"Slow down. We have plans tonight. We are going to a very fancy dinner party at the house of an old friend of mine. Can you keep a secret?" He winked at her and threw down another vodka. His nose was getting pink.

Vasiliy didn't wait for her to answer. "He's an immoral man, our host this evening. He's very naughty. But he is a powerful man, Lenushka. And right now, to do what we need to do, to get you out of the country, we need some of his power."

"Why?"

"Why, what?"

"Why do we need his power?"

He looked past her and to the front door. His assistant, Arytom Levonovich, poked his head in, and signaled that the next student had arrived. Vasiliy sighed.

"All right, Arytom, give us ten minutes to clean up our dishes and then send her in. *Spaciba.*" And with that, he pulled up his great stomach off the chair, collected their plates and packages, and carried them into his small kitchen. On his way back in, he tossed her a fortune cookie. "Read your fortune, eh?"

She cracked it open and read slowly, "A vacation by the sea is in store for you." She laughed, "That would be all right, to sail a boat on the Black Sea. What is his name?"

"Who, my student? I think it's—"

"*Nyet,* silly. The bad man, so I can say, 'How could he be bad if he's a friend of yours?'" This made her Uncle Vasiliy laugh heartily.

On the way to her window seat where she sat during the lessons, Elena picked up the movie star magazine Arytom bought her at the kiosk downstairs. She held Mashinka close.

"His name, for your information, is Aleksei Aleksandrovich Kumarin, but they tell me he's changed it to Stepanov, Aleksei Aleksandrovich Stepanov."

The door opened, and his next student came in. Elena looked at the girl and knew right away, it would be a long half-hour. Arytom followed and sat at the piano to accompany her during the lesson.

That night, Elena wore one of the new dresses Uncle Vasiliy had bought her that afternoon. Elena had never gone shopping with a man. Uncle Vasiliy was very impatient and treated the salesgirls like his worst students. First, he demanded to sit down in the store. Then, he commanded them to put together several outfits, head to toe, of whatever young girls were wearing. Elena had intended to object until she saw them. Every dress was beautiful. And just like that, he bought them all. She had never, ever, had so many clothes. She tried to tell him later that one was enough, but he wouldn't even discuss it.

Now, she felt like a princess in her blue dress with small white flowers and a matching sweater. She even had boots with fur trim to complement the dark gray coat and hat.

"You look beautiful, my cherub," Uncle Vasiliy said as he helped her on with her coat.

She picked up her doll as they headed to the door. Vasiliy said, "You're bringing a doll? I think you can leave it here."

"*Nyet*, I can't. Please tell me it will be all right?"

"But it's snowing outside," he said.

"I'll just tuck her inside my coat." She smiled coyly.

He rolled his eyes and chuckled. "Women! So, are we ready to go?" He held out his arm, and they walked out of the flat, down the elevator, through the front door, and into a black car waiting for them. "Ah, Alyosha is showing off by sending a limousine to pick us up," Uncle Vasiliy said as they settled into the back seat.

At first, she noticed how handsome the driver was. When he spoke, his voice was quiet and low. But then, as he drove, the streetlights reflected in his rearview mirror and she saw the other side of his face, which was severely damaged, or burned off or something. She stared at it until the man caught her looking at him in the mirror; his eyes were cold and dark and frightened her. Unconsciously, she groped for Uncle Vasiliy's hand and sat closer to him.

It was not a long ride, and when they pulled in front of a gate, the driver punched numbers on an entry pad and the gate opened. She felt like she was in a movie. She looked through the side window and saw a huge white house come into view that had many lights shining on it.

"It's a palace, Uncle Vasiliy. Look! Does a princess live here?"

He laughed. "A palace indeed but now only my old friend lives here with his many servants and secretaries and, well, other helpers. No princesses. Over the past month, there have been many parties here to celebrate the new acting president of Russia. He came from St. Petersburg and is a friend of Alyosha."

"The president of Russia is here?" she asked, her eyes round.

"*Nyet*. Not tonight. It's a small party tonight. I promised Alyosha that I would sing a little for his friends. Then, afterward, he and I will have some private time. Can Lenushka be a big girl and stay awake until then?"

"If I fall asleep, I will dream of Fedya and our meeting," she said.

She noticed the driver's head jerk up and how he looked at her in the mirror. She tried to smile a little and wiggled her fingers in a wave. He looked away. She checked to see if Uncle Vasiliy noticed, but he didn't.

When they walked in the door, a maid in a black dress and a small white apron took their coats and curtsied to them. Elena curtsied back as best she could, and the maid smiled. The ceiling of the foyer was high, and a round table sat in the middle with an enormous vase and gigantic flowers sticking out. There was a wide staircase that curved up and divided into two parts. It reminded her of some old movies where the beautiful woman runs down and into the arms of her lover. It was a romantic staircase. To the left, she saw a very tall set of doors that were open, and she could hear people talking and laughing.

"Come cherub, let's see who's here," Uncle Vasiliy said. "Don't be afraid. There is no one here to hurt you," he whispered in her ear.

When they walked in, there were several people standing around. Everyone was beautiful, the women and the men. They were drinking from delicate glasses. One lady threw back her head and laughed so loud that everyone stopped and looked at her, but she didn't seem to care. She had dramatic black hair. The man she was talking to was older, much older, and yet the woman wrapped herself around his arm possessively. Elena thought the man looked creepy. Near the fireplace was a kind-looking man with a light blue sweater and a jacket. He had a small mustache and short hair. He was talking quietly and intently with another woman, but as Uncle Vasiliy approached him, his face lit up and he walked toward them.

"Vasiliy, I am so happy to see you!" he said, and they hugged and kissed on both cheeks like brothers. "Look at you! You look like a giant pear. You need to get some exercise!"

Uncle Vasiliy just laughed. "Exercise? I get enough, right here at the elbow," he said as he mimed raising a glass to his lips and drinking. "Perhaps you can help with that?"

"Of course, of course." He looked across the room and called out, "Misha, bring my old friend a glass of champagne." Then he looked down and saw her. "And who is this lovely young lady?"

"This is the girl I told you about. Do you remember the beautiful Latvian woman I courted in secret? This is her daughter, Elena Ivanovna. She is like a niece to me. And Lenushka, this is my dear friend, Alyosha Aleksandrovich Kumarin—no, no, my mistake, Stepanov! I thought only women changed their names." Vasiliy laughed as he picked up a glass of champagne from the tray the man brought to him.

Stepanov bent down to her level, took her hand, and kissed it gently, just like a prince would kiss the hand of a princess. "I am happy to meet you, Elena Ivanovna. May I call you Lenushka like your uncle?"

She giggled, "Of course. It is nice to meet you." She curtsied.

He chuckled. "I am sorry there are so many people here right now and I must do some business. But after they leave, we will sit and talk, and you can tell me about you and your mother."

"Did you know my mother?" she asked quickly.

Stepanov looked up at Vasiliy and smiled, "In a way, but not really. Your uncle told me about her, though, and how beautiful and young she was!"

He stood up, then took a glass of champagne and said to Vasiliy, "She is delightful, old man. Please make yourself at home. I have a big surprise tonight, but you must promise not to laugh."

"But then, I am sure to laugh if you are warning me already." Vasiliy took Elena by the hand. "Let's go over here and sit down where we can see everyone play the game."

"What game?"

"That's just a joke. My joke when I am around so many people who are looking to impress the king of this castle."

As they sat on a small couch, she saw a little of what Vasiliy meant. The women seemed to act more like peacocks when they were close to Stepanov. And if he gave them any notice, they purred like cats. The men were almost the same, except for the creepy man. He seemed to have his own set of ladies. At some point, Misha came in and announced that dinner was ready.

They all walked into a room with a gigantic table that was set with sparkling plates, glasses, and silverware. She had never seen such a beautiful table. It made her think of the table her mother said would be in heaven one day. No one really talked to her during the meal, but she didn't care. She just watched and listened and figured out who loved who and who hated who. It was like a soap opera.

During the meal, Vasiliy helped her pick up the right fork or spoon. There were several serving women who put different plates in front of her with food she didn't recognize. The best part came in the middle, when they served little fruit ices.

She whispered to Uncle Vasiliy, "Do rich people always have dessert in the middle of the meal? What a wonderful idea."

Vasiliy laughed and said, "This is just a little something to clear your mouth of one taste and to get you ready for the next."

"So far," she whispered, "I like the strawberry ice the best."

Vasiliy exchanged their cups so she could have his ice, too.

"Thank you," she whispered and patted him on the hand. She looked up and caught Stepanov's eye; she gave him a wave, and he winked back.

After dinner, everyone moved into another room, next to the first room, that had a huge piano. Uncle Vasiliy set her in a place nearby and he went to the piano and murmured to the man who was waiting to play for him. The other people collected more drinks in yet smaller glasses and found places to sit or stand.

One young man in a silky shirt and a small earring came over and sat beside her.

"*Privet.* I'm Pavel Jevgenjavich. You can call me Pasha. And you are?"

"Elena Ivanovna."

"You know Vasiliy Chastikovich Nesterov?" he asked.

She looked at him like he was an idiot, but decided it wasn't worth insulting someone she had just met. "*Da.* He's my uncle." Then she turned away.

The young man kept talking. "He has a fantastic voice. My friend told me he would be here tonight. I'm hoping to study with him," he added.

Elena turned to look at him. She sized him up and said simply, "I'll see what I can do. But I tell you, I have seen some terrifying scenes during lessons. He's nice to me, but to the students, well, I really shouldn't say."

"Really?" Pasha looked imploringly at her as though she, a little girl, would know something.

Fortunately, Vasiliy began to sing. It was stunning. She had heard him sing before when he visited Mama but never in full voice, not like he was singing now. She felt so proud to know him. He only sang three songs, but they were all wonderful. During the last one, she looked around to see the effect he was having on the group. She narrowed her eyes at the rudeness of some of them, particularly those guests who talked between themselves and didn't listen at all. Except Stepanov, who listened intently along with a beautiful lady in a black dress and a bird pin who sat next to him, and Pasha, of course. On the far side of the room, the creepy man had to keep shushing the black-haired woman, who looked quite drunk.

When Vasiliy finished, Stepanov walked up to him, and they embraced warmly. They spoke quickly and quietly as the guests applauded. Pasha, next to her, clapped wildly. She was embarrassed for him.

Then Uncle Vasiliy came back and sat with Elena. Since he was a big man, Elena had to scoot poor Pasha over more than just a little. In any other situation, Pasha should have stood up and made room, but he kept one cheek on the bench, determined to maintain a friendly closeness. Elena patted Pasha on the leg.

Stepanov cleared his throat at the piano and prepared to make an announcement.

"As many of you know, I am making some changes in our organization. Out of those changes has come an opportunity for me to become involved in the movie industry."

People laughed and applauded. She watched the people around the creepy older man turn and listen.

"Occasionally, one must try something new. I lunched a few weeks ago with Aleksander Iakovlev Zabolotskoi, and he shared a secret desire to make a mainstream film. I have decided to produce this film for him, with one string attached. He agreed, and so, I am happy to announce that the film, *The King's Tyrant*, will begin filming in the next month and I will play the part of King Louis XIV."

Everyone cheered and glasses tinkled as many people toasted him. Stepanov walked over to the movie director; they shook hands and toasted again. When she looked at Uncle Vasiliy, he laughed and shook his head.

"What's so funny?"

"Oh, cherub, my old friend can't act. There must be a lovely woman involved," he told her.

"Maybe the woman in the black dress?"

"Could be," Uncle said.

People kept talking and toasting and drinking. She grew bored, held Mashinka close, and laid her head on Vasiliy's leg. Within minutes, she fell asleep. When she woke up, the room had quieted. Vasiliy was at the piano playing and talking with Pasha, the flashy young man. That made her smile. By the bar stood the movie director, his woman (still clinging), Stepanov, and the woman in the black dress. By the windows, she saw a couple she remembered from dinner. They were dancing with no music and kissing. Elena needed to find a toilet.

She walked over to the piano and said, "Excuse me, Uncle Vasiliy?"

"Ah, you're awake, are you?"

She whispered in his ear what she needed, and he laughed lightly. He looked around and signaled to Misha, who always seemed to be nearby. "Misha, my friend, can you direct my niece to the powder room? I will keep your doll for you."

"Thank you," Elena said as she set the doll on the piano bench.

"Certainly, Vasiliy Chastikovich," Misha said, and to her, "Please follow me."

They left the music room and walked back into the foyer. From there, he directed her to a small powder room under the stairs. It was a perfect little room for a lady. The flowered-printed wallpaper covered every wall and a vase of flowers sat on the sink. The mirror above the sink had lights all around it. There were little pink and yellow towels just for her hands. And there was even a gold stand with soft paper for cleaning up after using the toilet. She had never seen such a pretty room for a toilet.

When she left, she passed the music room and ended up in the main part of the foyer near the front door. She realized her mistake right away, but then had a shock. There, standing with another man by the front door, was Pyotr Konstantin, Valya's boyfriend.

"Petya! What are you doing here?" she said as she walked toward him.

But as he turned toward her, the other man turned as well and she realized it was the driver, the man with the horrible face.

"Lenushka, go back!" Petya cried.

Everything went in slow motion. The monster man held a knife to Petya's neck. But as he looked at her, his eyes held a sudden recognition or understanding. He stepped back and pulled his arm up to throw the knife. Did Petya yell words about a little girl? She couldn't be sure. Her eyes were on the knife. Was it Petya's voice or Fedya's voice in her mind? She would never know, but she threw herself to the ground. She heard a thunk. When she lifted her head and looked, she saw the knife sticking out of the banister post.

Then everything returned to real time, and she scrambled to her feet, screamed and turned to run away from the monster. She had only gone a few steps when she ran into someone who gripped her. She struggled. It was Stepanov. There were other people behind him, too.

"It's all right," he said to her. "You are safe."

"Uncle Alyosha, look out! There is a knife, a knife!" she said in between sobs.

"What?" he demanded as he strode into the foyer with Elena clinging to him. As he passed the banister post, he saw the knife and swore.

When Elena peeked, she saw the monster with yet another knife in one hand, while holding Petya by the collar with the other.

"Gogo, stop!" Stepanov said, "What in God's name do you think you are doing?" He called over his shoulder, "Misha, get two of the boys and tell Vasiliy to come out here." To his other guests, he said, "My apologies. Please return to the music room. I'll be with you in a moment."

The black-haired woman exclaimed, "Petya! What's wrong? Where have you been?"

The old man growled, "Shut up, Nataliya. Come on. Do as our host says." He took her by the arm and dragged her back down the hallway.

Elena watched the monster blink his eyes. He didn't seem right in the head.

"Put down the knife, Gogo. Let go of Pyotr. He is my guest. Do you understand me?" Stepanov said smoothly and quietly.

Elena could hear Uncle Vasiliy's voice as he came up the hallway, but not before she heard the monster say, "The girl has it, sir. I found out the truth about the key, just like I said I would. This idiot gave it to her by accident. Ask him. Go ahead. I tell you it's the girl, boss. The little girl has it."

Stepanov looked down at Elena and then at the two men. "Pyotr, is this true? How can this be?"

Petya stepped away from Yegor as soon as the strong man's grip loosened. He walked toward Stepanov quickly but did not dare to fully turn his back on the madman.

"I don't know. I tried to tell him; I don't really know what we're talking about. I gave her a doll—" Petya said.

Stepanov snapped around to stare at her. She saw something a little frightening in his eyes, a look she had never seen before, and it made her shrink away from him.

At the same moment, Vasiliy came lumbering in and demanded, "What is happening? Lenushka, are you safe? Come, come to your uncle."

She slipped away from Stepanov before he could grasp her again and ran to Vasiliy. She glimpsed two men enter through another door at the back; they shouldered past them, with Misha leading. Yegor backed up toward the front door as the men came toward him.

Stepanov said quickly, "Gogo, follow these fellows, your comrades. You know them. I will speak to you later."

"But the girl—"

"Shut up, Gogo, and do as I say now. You are causing a scene and embarrassing me." Stepanov turned to Misha and said, "Take him to the deckhouse."

The men took him by both arms; he resisted. Stepanov pulled the knife from the banister and walked over to Yegor and hissed, "I will find out if what you say is true, Yegor. But I am very displeased that you have behaved violently in my home. You are raving, and you are out of control. Now, get in control, or I will have these men do what they do best." He removed the second knife from Yegor's hand and then handed both knives to Misha. "Go."

Stepanov turned to Petya, grabbed him by the arm and said, "Come with me." They headed toward the library, the first room where people had gathered. On their way in, Stepanov turned. "Meet me in the music room, Vasiliy. I'll be there momentarily. Not to worry," he said. Then to the maid, "Olga, please assist our other guests with their coats. I believe our evening has come to a close."

Elena looked up at Uncle Vasiliy and back to Stepanov, who then added, "Vasiliy, I promise you, as a friend, no harm will come to anyone you love tonight."

41
ELENA & VASILIY

ST. PETERSBURG, RUSSIA

Someone had changed the furniture in the music room after Uncle Vasiliy's earlier performance by putting away most of the chairs, leaving only a few placed around tables; they had moved the sofas to face each other near the fireplace and pushed the piano into a corner. A low glass table now stood between the sofas, with a black vase filled with lovely pink roses.

Elena and Uncle Vasiliy sat on one of the short sofas near the crackling fire. While she clasped her doll, he held her close, and she was happy for the safety she felt in the circle of his arm, the steady beating of his heart, and his slow wheezy breaths.

Across from them sat the flashy woman and the creepy old man who would direct Stepanov's movie. The woman wore lots of makeup and kept tugging at her tight, shiny dress. She had sobered a little, but was still drunk enough to wave her empty glass in the air for someone to fill it up. When no one appeared, she set it down sloppily on the table. She groped around in the tiny handbag that hung by a metal chain from her shoulder and pulled out a skinny brown cigarette from a long green box. She wagged her cigarette at the director to light it for her. He ignored her, tapped his fingers on one knee, and checked his watch. He got up abruptly and started pacing.

"What is taking them so long? I have better things to do—"

The woman interrupted, "Sasha! Do you have a light or not? God, you can be so rude."

He turned and tossed his lighter to her. "Nataliya, if I am ill-mannered, what are you? Nothing but crude. Remember who got you here. Without me, you're nothing."

As he turned away, she stuck out her tongue like a little child, but then converted her defiant gesture into a rather sinister one, darting her tongue in and out quickly just like a snake.

Elena had watched these two with detached interest before and after dinner, but now she sat bolt upright. The woman's ugly tongue gesture tripped a memory. A shiver went up her spine.

"Lenushka, what is it?" Vasiliy said.

She didn't bother to answer or even look at him; she stared at the woman as she tried to make the connection.

It wasn't long before the woman felt the girl's gaze and returned it.

"What is it, kid? You look like a deer in my car headlights," she said.

"I know you. I've seen you before," Elena said.

She chortled. "I don't think so." She leaned her head over the back of the couch where the director was pacing behind her. "What do you think, Sasha darling? Do you think the little chickee here would have seen my acting?"

He laughed heartily, and kissed the actress on her forehead. "Not hardly," he said.

Through her own laughter, she added, "Most people don't recognize me with my clothes on!"

Elena trembled a little as she rose from the sofa. "It is you then. Now, I remember. I saw you. I saw what you did to my brother. You are a filthy, nasty, horrible person. I should destroy you." She grabbed the vase and threw its contents at the woman. The vase followed, barely missing her, and shattered on the floor.

"Holy shit!" the woman leaped up, "Damn it, you little brat; you just ruined my dress."

Uncle Vasiliy grabbed Elena before she leaped across the coffee table. "What are you doing? Elena? Listen to me. Settle down!" He turned her toward him. "You can't break things like that! What is it? What's wrong? What is the problem?"

The woman wailed. "What is the problem? She's crazy, that's the problem. I paid 4000 rubles for this dress." She snatched up a pillow and dabbed at herself.

A maid came rushing in through a hidden side door. "Madam? Sir?"

"Don't just stand there. Get me a towel or something," Nataliya yelled at the young woman, who curtsied and rushed out.

"Bring a broom," the director said to the closed door.

Elena strained against her uncle's arms and pointed at the woman. "It's her. I remember her now, the hair, the voice, and that nasty mouth. She was in the terrible movie, the horrible, horrible movie with Fedya."

"Fedya?" the director said and stared at Elena. But his actress continued ranting about her dress; Iakolev grabbed her arms, pulled her face close to his, "Shut up!"

"What? Why are you mad at me?"

The maid re-entered, and Iakolev shoved his starlet toward the servant.

"Go to hell," she growled as she stumbled over to the servant's entrance and mumbled a long string of obscenities the entire time the maid worked on her dress.

Vasiliy took a breath and stroked his niece's hair. She finally relented in his arms and cried. She pulled her doll closer. He looked over the girl's head at the movie director, Aleksander Iakolev, who leaned with fake casualness on the sofa, smiled, and licked his lips.

"Is it true?" Vasiliy asked him. "Is it true what the girl says? Was this woman friend of yours in an X-rated movie with Fedya Ivanovich?"

Before he could answer, the double doors opened and Stepanov entered with a younger actor while Misha, his right-hand man, trailed behind.

"What's going on here now? I heard screaming," Stepanov asked steadily, but when he saw Elena crying, his tone altered. "Seriously, Vasiliy, what's going on?"

"I'll tell you what's going on," Nataliya said from the servant's door. "That brat threw an entire vase of flowers and stinking water all over me. Look at my dress!"

Elena looked up at him and said, "It was her, Uncle Alyosha. She was the one who hurt my brother, Fedya."

"Fedya? What? Fyodor Ivanovich is your brother?" Stepanov said.

But Nataliya also heard the boy's name and peered down at the girl. "He had a sister?" she asked.

Elena twisted around and tried to get up, but Vasiliy held her tight, and she said to Nataliya, "My brother, Fedya, is in Latvia with my Uncle Uldis. You tried to kill him, but he escaped. We know all about you."

Vasiliy struggled to soothe her, but in her rage, she got away from him once more and charged Nataliya with both fists raised. The maid screamed and disappeared behind her door. Stepanov snapped his fingers to Misha, who intercepted Elena quickly, and easily picked her up and away from Nataliya, who raced for protection behind Sasha. Misha's strength was clearly too much for Lenushka; she stopped wrestling and began to cry again.

"Aleksander Iakolev, take your wench home. We'll talk later." Stepanov spoke evenly but sternly. He turned to the younger man, who had collapsed in a chair. One eye was swelling shut and turning blue. "Pyotr Konstantin," Stepanov added, "go with them. We have had enough excitement for one night."

Nataliya opened her mouth to speak, but Stepanov stared unblinking at her, and she stopped mid-word. Sasha took her elbow, and they started out. She looked over her shoulder with a sneer then and said, "Have you been a bad boy, Petya?"

Sasha turned and slapped Nataliya hard across the face. "Shut up!" He propelled her out the double doors before she could say another word.

Petya said nothing. He dragged himself from the chair and walked, limping, out the door. He did not look back. The doors closed silently behind him. Vasiliy finally recognized the actor as Pyotr Kotolvsky, and wondered if the young man's career might have ended this night.

Stepanov didn't even bother to watch them depart, but went directly to Lenushka instead and slowly took her from Misha's arms.

"Lenushka, my cherub—" Vasiliy said as he stepped toward them and handed Elena the doll she had left on the settee in her anger toward the woman.

She seemed to be at a breaking point as she lay limply in Stepanov's arms. Stepanov was not a big man, but he was strong in his own way. He carried her easily over to a large chair closer to the fire, and they sat together. He did not speak, but smoothed her hair with his hand and examined one of her hands in his own. Vasiliy watched in amazement as the girl settled into the crook of his neck like a little cat.

It was crazy. Despite everything he knew about the dangerous Aleksei Aleksandrovich, he could not help but also admire him. Even now, the man had changed a room's atmosphere in seconds with a gentle voice and a kind touch. Vasiliy knew his old friend was not the same boy who had lived in his building growing up. He knew this man had murdered people, cheated, lied, and used women. And yet, here he was, holding a young girl in his lap so sweetly. It was absurd and all true.

He heard Alyosha speak quietly to Elena, "I must tell you a story, Lenushka. May I?"

She nodded quietly but did not look up.

"I am a businessman. It is too confusing to explain everything I do in my work, but please understand I have a big company that buys and sells things and then sends them all over the world. I must work with many other people and many other companies and countries. But, you know, things keep changing in Russia, *da*? Our world is evolving every day. The way we do business is changing too. And sometimes, there are people who try to cheat one person or another, one company or another. I cannot say that I have been perfect. I have not. I have done some of these bad things too."

"I know," she whispered.

"You know?" He looked down at her and she smiled up at him.

"Uncle Vasiliy said that you were a wicked man sometimes."

Stepanov looked up at Vasiliy, who shrugged his shoulders and got up to help himself to another brandy.

"But I told Uncle Vasiliy that you couldn't be all bad because you were friends with him," she said.

Stepanov chuckled a little and Vasiliy turned and held up his glass in a small, toasting gesture.

"All right then," Stepanov continued. "So, I have done some bad things and I have done some good things. Two years ago, there was a man who made many promises to me. He needed money for a project, and I loaned him this money. But after he finished his project, he refused to give me my money back. He laughed in my face and said I would never see that money again, that he had figured out a way to hide the money and I would never find it. And then, about eight months ago, he died."

"That's a sad story. But I don't understand why you are telling me about it."

"Well, I'm telling you the truth about what happened because you can actually help me get this money back," he said.

She giggled, "You're teasing me. I don't have any money. Didn't Uncle Vasiliy tell you I am an orphan?"

"Let me finish. Before the man died, he sent all his money (and my money) to a different country. In that country, they have special banks. But I cannot get my money out of that bank without the account number. The man was very smart. He put the account number in a special box in the Viking Bank here in St. Petersburg. But to open the box, I must have the key and the code."

Vasiliy, who had been standing casually by the bar, waiting to see where this story was going, tensed. Was it possible? Could Lenushka know something? Vasiliy stepped closer to them. Stepanov noticed but changed nothing in his voice.

Elena, too, could sense something had changed in the story. It was no longer just a little tale to quiet her down. She had seen this magic key. She clenched her doll. She tried to relax. She didn't want to give away the doll's secret. Her brother had warned her about little hand motions and looks that gave away hiding places. She opened her eyes now and stared down at Uncle Alyosha's hand that still held her own, ever so gently.

"I'm going to tell you a little more about this key. The key has been on a long journey already. First, a street gang raided the place where that man, Boris Kretenkenov, had stored many valuable things, including the key. When I found out the gang boys had the key, I sent one of my men to find it. Someone shot him in his face, and this has made him a little crazy. That was Yegor, the man you saw at my front door. He is not well. I am sorry he frightened you, and I will reprimand him. But I understand your brother had friends in this gang and before the leader died, he gave the key to your brother."

She took in a breath and looked up at Uncle Alyosha. His face was still, but she could see his eyes were gleaming and dark. She was trying not to feel afraid, but her hands were giving her away. She tried to get off his lap, but he gripped her.

"May I get down, please?" she asked as bravely as she could, but her voice shook, just like her hands.

"Alyosha, what are you doing?" Vasiliy said. "She's just a girl. She knows nothing about your key."

Stepanov allowed her to stand, but he held both of her arms above her elbows more tightly and looked her straight in the eyes.

"One more moment," he said as he glanced up at Vasiliy, then back to her. "Please believe me, Lenushka, I will not hurt you. I promise. Just listen to me a little longer. All right?"

She was afraid all the same, but for the sake of all that her brother had taught her, she stood tall and nodded, just as Fedya would have. She took a deep breath in, exhaled, and waited. Stepanov released her arms.

"I think you know your brother has been on a journey, too. He went all the way to Rīga. Back here, we all thought he took the key with him. One of my men followed him there and asked him to return the key to me. But guess what your brother said?"

"I don't know," she whispered. But she could guess. She doubted he would have said anything, not if he could help it.

"Alyosha, you're frightening her," Vasiliy said.

Stepanov looked up at his friend; carefully and quietly he said, "Vasiliy, do you think I would do this if it wasn't critically important?" And then to Elena, he said, "Your brother confessed he hid the key in his sister's doll. Tonight, Pyotr Konstantin confessed he found this doll at the apartment of the black-haired woman, Nataliya, but knew nothing about its contents. He also told me he gave the doll to you. Now, Lenushka, I believe you are holding the doll that has my bank key. I could take it from you easily, but I would prefer you give it to me yourself. I promise not to hurt your doll."

She harrumphed. Stepanov's eyes widened. Then he laughed, really laughed, and sat back. That's when Elena knew everything would work out. Just like that. She knew. But she needed to make a deal like Fedya taught her. He was safe, and she was safe. This was a little detour.

"Well, first of all, I will not give you the doll," she said, stepping back.

He raised his eyebrows.

She held up her hand. "Please wait. Since I don't need this key, you may have it. But, as my brother always said, never give up something of value without getting something in return."

Stepanov chuckled. But then stopped. She was quite serious. He turned to Vasiliy, hoping for help, but Uncle shrugged his shoulders.

"Well, Elena Ivanovna, exactly what do you have in mind?"

"Let me think." She walked away from Stepanov, waving the doll a little as she made her way around the couch. Finally, she went over to the sofa where Vasiliy sat and stood beside the arm rest. "Tell him the rest of the story, Uncle Vasiliy." She winked.

He told Stepanov everything he knew of what had happened to Elena, Fedya, and little Irina. Stepanov listened intently. Vasiliy explained how they had hoped to get Elena to Rīga or wherever her brother might be to reunite them, but they would need the paperwork rushed. They would also need reliable transportation and so forth. Vasiliy kept saying he had only hoped to tell their story and ask Stepanov for help. This business with the key was news to him.

Stepanov waved that concern away. "Tell me, Elena Ivanovna, if I agree to these terms, will you accept my handshake and my word that I will help you in whatever way I can in exchange for this item in return?" He was serious now too, even though his eyes twinkled.

"What do you think, Uncle Vasiliy? Is this a fair deal?"

"I think it is. You have the key?" Vasiliy said.

"*Da*, he can have it now."

Stepanov stopped in mid-drink. "Now?"

And with that, she flipped up the doll's skirt and swiftly pulled out the key case from her stuffing.

"Put out your hand." He did so, and she placed it there gently.

He smiled. "Elena Ivanovna, you have made me a very happy man—and a very rich one."

"You're welcome," she said and hugged him.

"But wait, now I have a surprise for you," Stepanov said. "Misha, please bring down our guest from the blue bedroom." He rose, picked up Uncle Vasiliy's glass, and poured them both another drink. As he handed the glass to his friend, he smiled and said, "Maybe I am Father Christmas, after all."

"That would be the day," Vasiliy answered.

"What's going on?" Elena asked.

The doors to the music room opened and there stood Misha. "He's gone...and so has Yegor," he said.

"That's impossible. Check the tapes."

"Yegor covered the cameras and paused the system. Pavel and Leo are looking into it. They found these torn up sheets," Misha said as he handed a handful over to Stepanov, who swore under his breath.

"Alyosha, what's happening?" Vasiliy asked.

"I don't know. Listen, take the girl back to your apartment. I will call you in the morning. Perhaps we've had enough surprises for one night. Misha will drive you." He bent down to Elena. "Thank you again for the key. We will have lunch tomorrow and celebrate. All right?"

She looked from one man to another, a feeling of dread in her heart, then at Stepanov. She reached out to his hand. "What are these for?"

"Nothing really. Strips of cloth, like someone tore up a pillowcase or a bedsheet. It's too complicated to explain. Good night, my brave little girl."

42

YEGOR

ST. PETERSBURG

Yegor's mind rattled. He couldn't keep one thing in front of him before another would jump in. The boy, the damn boy. Stepanov had treated the twit like a guest. It made his blood boil. And Yegor? Sent to the servant's quarters. And when he had brought the boy in, what did he get? Nothing. No "Well done, my man," or "I knew I could count on you, Gogo." What the hell?

And then, when he finally got the entire story from the kid, the sister had the key all along. But no one had listened to him. He had the girl in his sights. She had the prize. But what did they do? They locked him in a room. What was that about? He would show them. He would get the key and hand it over face to face. The girl had it and he knew it.

He looked in his rearview mirror at the boy in the back seat. He should have killed him at the house, simpler than bringing him along, but Stepanov never liked the bloody part of his business. The messy parts. *Nyet*, just results. That's what he always said. "Give me results, Gogo, not explanations."

"So be it," he said out loud.

The boy groaned.

287

"You see Fyodor Ivanovich, I kept my word. You are not dead. Besides, I'm thinking you'd like to see your little sister, wouldn't you?"

Yegor watched the boy's eyes grow wide.

"That's right. She's next. Did you know? My new friend, Petya, gave the doll to your sister. So that means the little sister has the key, right? I'm guessing it's at Vasiliy's apartment."

The boy shook his head and made noises through the gag.

"Shut up. Don't lie to me. Everyone is lying to me. Zoya, you, Stepanov, Misha, Zoya. She lied to me the most."

Wild honking from behind his car brought him back to the road. That would be a fine joke, to die in a car accident. Fitting to die inconsequentially. Who would care? His mother was dead by his father's hand, his father dead by his hand. At one point, he thought Zoya would care. What a fool he had been. And what of Stepanov? Sure, he took young Gogo in, trained him to be a killer, and paid him good money for it. But it wasn't just a job for Yegor. Stepanov was the father he had dreamed of having, smart and clever and very rich. And yet, whatever Yegor did, it was never enough.

"You were very friendly with Stepanov, eh? You think he will help you? He's as much a killer as the rest of us."

The boy grunted.

"There's a cost, boy. There's a price to pay for his kindness. You'll see."

Yegor pulled up to the apartment building. He checked the time. There was no way to know for sure if they were inside. He pulled the car around to the back. He turned off the engine and waited in silence as he thought through his options. Breaking in would be simple. But he had to figure out the best way to get the girl out of the singer's apartment with the least trouble. The old man would be simple to contain. But he couldn't kill him, since he was from Stepanov's old days. That was tricky. And the girl, herself, Elena. He wanted the girl without a fight. Should he take the boy up the stairs with him? *Nyet*, the boy was too unpredictable. But if she screamed in the halls, she might wake people.

At 21:30, he turned the car back on for some heat. In the mirror, he found the boy still awake.

"So, Fyodor Ivanovich, you are going to help me. If you want to see your sister alive, you will do what I say." He leaned over the back of the front seat and pulled the gag from Fedya's mouth.

"If you hurt my sister, I will find you and kill you myself."

"Big talk for a boy tied up in the back of my car. I will walk into this building, and you will help me."

"She knows nothing about a key. It's just her doll, that's all. Take the doll. That's all you need to do."

"I need her cooperation to come out of the apartment. If you want her to remain alive, tell me something that will convince her I have you."

Yegor studied the back of the building. He glanced in his rearview mirror in time to see the boy lunge at him over the seat with his teeth bared. Yegor simply stopped Fedya's fumbling attempt with an elbow to the nose. The boy howled as blood gushed from his nose.

"You're a stupid shit. Tell me, or I'll just hurt her to get what I want. I don't really need you."

"Mashinka. The doll's name is Mashinka. Our uncle sent it to her from America on one of his trips."

"Better." Yegor got out of the car and pulled Fedya from the back seat and once again tossed him into the trunk. He wiped Fedya's nose roughly and then maneuvered an old towel under his head. "Don't need your blood everywhere." He slammed the trunk.

Yegor found the back entrance locked. Around to the right, he found the basement door, held closed by a pitiful lock. He broke it open easily and entered undetected. At the front door, he found the owners' names and easily located Nesterov's apartment number. Within moments, he was at the apartment door after he bypassed the elevator and took the stairs two at a time. He hesitated. Should he knock or simply kick the door down? He opted for complete surprise.

The girl was making up her bed, while Nesterov stood with a drink in hand. Yegor grabbed the girl from the back and covered her mouth before she could scream. He felt her body quiver. Nesterov did nothing, mouth agape. Yegor dragged Elena three steps towards the older man, took a good swing, and hit him hard against the temple. He went down like a rock.

"Now listen to me, my little lady friend," Yegor spoke roughly into her ear. "I have your brother. *Da,* he's alive. But if you don't do what I say, he won't be alive for very much longer. Do you understand me?"

Tears ran down her face, but she nodded.

"Just to let you know that I'm not making this up, he told me the name of your doll is Mashinka. Isn't that right? Little Mashinka from America. Right? Now, there's no way I could know that unless your precious Fyodor told me. Right? Right?"

She nodded again.

"Now, I'm going to take my hand away from your mouth. You will not scream, understand?"

He removed his hand slowly, and the girl collapsed on the chair-bed, partially made up for the night, and sobbed.

"Shut up." He yanked her to her feet and turned her to face him. "Go get your Mashinka and bring her to me."

"Here. Right here," she said as she held the doll up to him.

He pushed Elena back onto the small bed and tried to rip off the doll's head. Elena screamed.

"Shut your mouth or I'll hurt you." He looked around and saw a knife on the sideboard. Just as he was about to cut the doll, he glanced out the window and cursed. Two people hovered over the trunk of his car, cell phones in hand.

"Shit." He turned back to her.

"Hold your doll." As flashing lights played across the window, he grabbed the blanket from the chair-bed and rolled Elena up inside it and threw her over his shoulder. He ran out the door with her, down the steps, and out the front door. He changed her position to one like a baby and growled to her to keep quiet. He ran to the end of the block and then stood on the corner like a desperate father and hailed a private car for hire, safer than a taxi, no records.

43

FEDYA

ST. PETERSBURG

Silence. Yegor had walked away and left him in the car. This was his only chance. He shouted and pounded against the inside of the luggage compartment.

"Help! Help! Please, anyone. Help!"

It was late at night, so it would be a miracle if anyone heard him, but he had to keep trying. He called out again and again.

Finally, a voice came from outside, "Hello? Hello? Is someone in there?"

"*Da,* please, help me. I am trapped in here by a crazy man. Please help me."

It was a woman's voice, "All right, uh, all right. Just a moment." He heard a dog barking then, but farther away. Was she leaving him?

"Please don't leave me. Please help me," he yelled again.

She called out to someone. "Feliks, come quick. Feliks! Come here. Feliks, hurry. It's an emergency."

They sounded like a young couple; they said they couldn't open the locked trunk themselves, so they called the police. Fedya hated getting the police involved, but he had to get out of the trunk. There would be so many questions.

When the *politsiya* finally arrived and pried open the trunk, he tried to bolt, but the oldest one held his arm in an iron grip.

"My sister's in there. She's in danger. A horrible man is going to hurt her. He's crazy. He has weapons. He's a monster." Fedya knew he sounded crazy himself, but he had to convince them it was urgent. "Please, in this building."

"Which apartment?" one of them asked.

"I don't know. I don't know. He locked me in the trunk. My uncle, Vasiliy Chastikovich, lives here. That's where she is."

The policemen looked at each other and silently agreed to check it out, one to the back and one to the front. Fedya ran ahead of them. One guy yelled, "Hey, Wait!" But they were too slow.

He reached the front door and frantically hit all eight buzzers. The younger policeman reached the entry just as a sleepy voice came across the intercom.

"Who is it?"

"Police! Let us in." To Fedya, he said, "Stay here. I mean it. You'll be in the way if there is shooting."

When the door buzzed, the officer pulled it open and glanced at the names to find the apartment number. Fedya paid no attention. He slipped through the door and up the stairs. He heard the officer swearing and telling his slower partner what happened. In moments, Fedya reached the open apartment door on the fourth floor. Without a second thought, he ran in and immediately found Vasiliy on the floor. Fedya froze, fearing he was dead.

The younger policeman entered next and yanked on Fedya with such force he fell. "Get back, you little idiot."

Fedya pushed himself back up against a wall. The officer did a quick scan of the kitchen and bedroom before returning to Vasiliy on the floor. By then, his partner had arrived.

"He's breathing. Just don't light a match near him," the younger one said. They both laughed. "Help me get him up." They pulled him up and set him in a nearby chair. Vasiliy groaned.

The older cop turned to Fedya. "Boy, get the man a glass of water. You say you know this man?"

Fedya scrambled to his feet and into the kitchen. "*Da*, but I haven't seen him for a long time. He is...was...a friend of my mother's. He's an opera singer."

The men looked around and noticed the pictures on the walls, the grand piano, and shelves full of books and music.

The younger police officer said, "Somebody walloped him hard. He'll have a double headache in the morning. You say there was a girl?"

The older one asked, "And who do you think the other man was who did this?"

"I don't think, I know. They call him Yegor. He's a murderer. You're wasting time. He was just here. You're letting him get away."

Vasiliy groaned again and nearly fell forward until an officer caught him. "Vasiliy Chastikovich Nesterov? We are the police. Can you hear me?"

Vasiliy blinked several times and his eyes landed blearily on Fedya. "Fyodor Ivanovich? Is it you? How is that possible?"

"*Da*, Uncle Vasiliy. But Elena, she was here? The madman hurt you. He took Elena. Where did he take her?"

"Slow down, boy. Give him a chance," the older officer said.

Vasiliy looked around uncertainly, saw the two policemen, and held out his hand. "Please, help me up. I must make an important phone call. I will be all right. Thank you for coming. You may leave the boy with me."

"But sir, we found him locked in a trunk in the parking lot. Is that your car?"

"What? *Nyet*, I don't have a car." Vasiliy was unsteady on his feet.

"We must complete a report. We need a description of the girl. She is missing? Abducted?"

"*Da, da*, undoubtedly, but this matter is not for the police, I assure you. I must call Aleksei Aleksandrovich Stepanov. He is familiar with the situation. It's all a misunderstanding. I assure you." Vasiliy stared at both men intently, as though he could speak through his eyes.

The men exchanged looks, put away their tablets, and said their good-byes. Fedya wanted to scream in outrage, but Vasiliy put his hand on Fedya's shoulder to silence him. Vasiliy's phone rang.

"*Privet.*" He paused for only a moment and put pressure on Fedya to sit down. "*Da,* Alyosha, but I can tell you this: the boy is with me, but your man has taken Lenushka. He knocked me out and the next thing I knew, the police were here. He locked Fedya in his trunk. Seems to me he took Elena on foot."

There was a pause as Vasiliy listened. He walked over to the liquor cabinet, but then thought better of it and sat down.

"*Nyet,* I didn't tell the police anything. I used your name. I hope that was all right. *Da.* Fine...I understand. All right. *Paka.*"

He turned to Fedya. "My friend will take care of this."

"Friend? That terrible man, Stepanov? He is a friend of yours? But—"

"Fedya, my dear boy. Please. We grew up together, in a different time and place. Whatever he might be or not be, I trust him to take care of Elena Ivanovna. All we can do now is wait."

44

ELENA & YEGOR

ST. PETERSBURG, RUSSIA

When Elena woke up, she found herself tied up. He had pulled one arm high and tied it to one bed post and the other arm to the opposite post. Was she dreaming? When she saw him sitting across from her in a chair, she remembered and bit her lip to stop the scream that was welling up inside her. He was asleep now, and she mustn't wake him. She forced herself to breathe slowly and quietly. Next to her on the bed was her poor Mashinka in shreds.

"I'm sorry, Mashinka," she whispered. But there was nothing she could have done to save her.

Elena only thought of escape now. She pulled and pulled on the cloth that was holding her arms, but it wouldn't budge. She gave up. What was the point? She was a fool. Larissa's curse had come to rest upon her.

The car Yegor had hired off the street had dropped them at a clinic. The driver told him the clinic wasn't open, but Yegor lied and said his doctor friend was meeting them there. Once the car had pulled away, he set her down and said she had to walk. He wrapped the blanket around her like a cloak. Thank God she still had her shoes on.

"Where are we going?"

"Shut up."

They had walked for a long time; he pulled on her arm to force her to keep up with him. Finally, they reached a part of the city where there were many apartment buildings that all looked the same. How would anyone find her here? She wanted to cry, but she was too cold.

He seemed to know the way and had gone directly to the building he wanted and pushed open the front door. In the middle of the night, there were no lights in the hallway. He had dragged her up two flights of stairs and down another hallway. When he knocked on the door, he used a signal knock. At least, it sounded like a signal to her. At first, no one answered, but then a woman with wild gray hair and a bright yellow kimono opened the door just enough to see who it was. When she recognized him, she closed the door again to release the chain and threw it open.

"Yegor, my God, where have you been?" She hugged him like a mother and started asking him all kinds of questions. She stopped and gaped when she saw his face. "Oh, my darling, what happened to your face?" He didn't answer her, just said that he was hungry and wanted Zoya's old room because he needed some sleep.

"That Zoya. Do you know she never came back? I've got a new girl in there now. She's pretty," the woman had said coyly. "But who's this you have along? A little young for you?" she said.

"Get the new whore out! I want Zoya's room," Yegor said.

"But Yegor, she's sleeping now. The girls worked hard tonight. We were very busy—" the woman said, but Yegor turned on her with such a fury in his eyes that she stopped talking and stared. She slowly lifted her hands in surrender and said, "All right, it's all right, dear. Settle down. You know I have always taken care of you."

She walked over to a door, pounded, and then opened it. "Nelli, get up and get out. I have an old customer who needs to use your room."

Elena heard the girl struggle with this information and then started cursing until she saw who it was. Yegor's face got people's attention.

"Go, sleep with Olya," the old woman said. "She has a big bed. Go!" The girl left immediately down a short hallway without looking back.

Yegor had dragged Elena right into the little bedroom. He told the woman to knock when she had some food for him, and then he shut the door behind them. He tossed her onto the bed. Terrified, she pulled

296

herself into a little ball at the head of the bed. Would he make her take her clothes off? Would he do terrible things to her? Instead, he started talking to her. He talked and talked and talked. She hadn't understood most of what he was saying. She tucked her doll under the pillow. She hoped he would forget about it.

When the food came, he stopped talking and ate like a starving man. He offered her some food, but she couldn't even think about eating. Her stomach was in knots. There was no place to get away.

When he had finished eating, he set the plate on the floor and then he started drinking from a bottle. He didn't even bother to use a glass. But instead of talking to her like he did before, he seemed to talk to people that didn't exist, like the girl, Zoya. He kept telling her how sorry he was for hurting her. He spoke as though she was in the room. Did he imagine her to be Zoya?

"Listen, I'm not her. I'm not Zoya."

He had stared straight at Elena then and said, "Where is the key?"

"What?" she said. "Key?"

He lunged across the bed, grabbed her foot and yanked her toward the bottom of the bed. He saw the doll then and grabbed it from under the pillow and cut her to pieces. Elena wept.

When he found nothing, he clutched her arms. "Don't play games with me, little girl. I've already killed one kid for that key. I guess I can do it again if I have to." He was so close to her, his spit sprayed into her face as he spoke.

"Who, who did you kill? Did you kill Fedya? You said he was alive," she said as evenly as she could. She had surprised herself, but in that moment, she had to know for certain. Had this man killed her brother?

"I ask the questions." He shoved her back against the headboard. "Where's the damn key?"

"I don't have it, your boss has it," she said.

He climbed up on the bed then and hovered over her. "Don't lie to me. Oh, they all start young, don't they, with the lying? Zoya was a liar too. She shouldn't have lied. She shouldn't have lied to me." He rolled onto his back then and stared up at the ceiling.

"Who is Zoya?"

"She's a lying whore. That's who she is. But she's gone now. She left. She left me. And do you know who she left with?" He rolled over now and grabbed Elena's hair and pulled her face close to his. "She left me for that sniveling little brother of yours."

Her eyes went wide with the pain. She didn't understand any of this. "Please stop, you're hurting me. Please let go of my hair."

He let go, but then asked her again, "Where's the key? I just need to bring it to the boss and then he'll see. Everything will be all right. Everything will go back to the way it was. He'll see. I know how to do the job. He'll forgive me. He'll see. I've worked for him since I was a boy, just a boy, like your brother. I know what it is to be a boy. My mother did her best. My mother said I could do anything I dreamed of doing. She said I was a good boy. I wanted to be a good boy," he said. Then he turned to her and said, "You're not Zoya."

She shook her head. "*Nyet. Nyet*, I'm sorry. I want to go home. I need to go home."

He brought the knife up slowly to her face. "Where's the key, you little brat? Should I cut you? I cut Zoya." He held up his other hand then and looked at it.

"I don't have the key, I promise," she said. "I gave it to Alyosha Aleksandrovich. The boss has the key. You don't have to worry about the key anymore."

Without hearing her, he slowly carved a "Z" into the palm of his left hand and watched it bleed. She cringed away from the blood and away from him. She got off the bed, but in seconds, he had thrown the knife into the door and grabbed her wrist.

"You're lying. Where's the key?"

"I'm not. I'm not lying. Ask him. Call him. I tell you, I had it in my doll, and he asked me for it, and I gave it to him."

Yegor sat up and wiped the blood from his hand on the bedspread. Then he walked over to the door and pulled out the knife and used it to cut up a pillowcase. He made a bandage for his hand. The whole time, he said nothing. He didn't even look at her.

Finally, when he had finished wrapping his hand, he looked at her and said, "Lying got Zoya killed. Now, if you tell me the truth, everything will be fine," and then he smirked. "All right, maybe not fine. I could ask Grusha to take you on as one of her girls. You would be a child whore and then grow up to be just like Zoya. You tell lies the same way she did. Your eyes give you away. Just like Zoya's eyes."

"You've got to believe me. I'm not lying." She would die this night and not because she lied, but because she told the truth.

"I have to think," he said and sat in the chair opposite the bed staring at her. He was quiet for a long time.

She hadn't known what to do. It frightened her to have him stare, but she knew if she moved or tried to run away, he would just throw the knife and this time, she would be dead. She was sure the man was crazy. She tried her best to sit perfectly still. It must have been around that time she fell asleep.

Now she was the one awake, and he was asleep. She watched him for a few more minutes. She shouldn't give up. Fedya would expect her to fight, to fight for her life, and to fight for the family. She remembered how the three of them had sat on the roof of their secret flat one beautiful day. There had already been some cool days, but that day, the sun was out, and it was warm and Fedya had brought them up to the roof.

"Look, we can see the whole city from here," he had said.

"That's not the whole city," she said. "I know it's bigger than that."

"Oh, well, then that's even better. Think about it! No matter how much you can see, there's always something you can't see. There's always more city. There's always more to know. There's always more around the corner," Fedya had said.

And these were the words she thought of now, there was always more city and more to know and more to learn. If she could get away, then anything could still happen. And maybe, just maybe, he was waiting for her at Uncle Vasiliy's flat. She loved and missed her brother. He was the one who taught her to have courage and to believe in the next day. And so, while Yegor slept, she worked at the cloth strips that held her to the bed. She worked patiently and slowly to pull a hand through the cloth as it loosened. She imagined her hand to be very skinny and very slippery. It was working; her right hand was almost loose.

Just as she pulled her hand free, there was a knock at the door. Yegor startled and threw the knife at Elena, who had just rolled over to pull at her other arm. The knife thudded as it hit the headboard close to where she had been. She screamed.

The door crashed open. Two men came in, grabbed Yegor and pushed him up against the wall with his hands behind his back. She thought they would kill him right there. She couldn't stop screaming. Another man came to her and cut the cloth strip that held her second arm. He also pulled the knife from the headboard.

"Look at me. Look. You are going to be all right. It's all over. Do you hear me, Elena Ivanovna?" he said.

She looked up and recognized him. It was Misha from Uncle Alyosha's house. She collapsed into his arms. He picked her up and carried her, but before they left the room, she asked Misha to stop.

"Tell him, Misha, tell Yegor I gave the key to Stepanov. Tell him."

Misha stared at her for a moment and then at Yegor, who was not even struggling, just standing there, his mutilated face pressed to the wall, probably waiting for another chance to get away. But Misha knew there were no more chances for this ruined man. As soon as Misha had the girl safely away, they would kill Yegor Andreivich.

"Yegor, the girl speaks the truth. Stepanov is a happy man and has both the key and the numbers," Misha said.

Yegor turned his head to them and looked directly at Elena, "So, you surprise me after all, little Zoya. Goodbye."

Misha carried her out of the room and past the disheveled Grusha, who kept yelling at Misha for destroying her property. He did not even acknowledge her. Elena looked over Misha's shoulder and saw the girl, Nelli, standing in the doorway; she gave Elena a wave. Elena waved back.

In the car, Misha sat with Elena in the back seat. He called Stepanov on his mobile. He mussed her hair as he gave his report that he had the girl and that she was unhurt. She wondered if it was true; was she unhurt? She knew her body was all right. Her arms ached a little, but other than that, Yegor hadn't really hurt her that much. But her mind would never forget the man with half a face who had gone crazy after killing the only woman he loved.

45
ELENA & FEDYA

ST. PETERSBURG

The car delivered Elena and Misha to Vasiliy's apartment.

"Is my brother here? At the apartment?" she asked Misha before they got out.

"*Da*. That's my understanding. You are both safe now."

Misha wrapped his jacket around her against the wind and snow as they walked quickly to the entrance of the building. After being buzzed through the front door, Elena raced up the stairs, heedless of Misha's calls. The apartment door was already open and Fedya waited there. He wrapped his arms around her, and they twirled like ice skaters on the tiny landing. At first, they laughed and then they cried and finally, they collapsed onto the floor.

Vasiliy stood in the open door and greeted Misha, then thanked him for recovering Elena safely. Misha bowed slightly, retrieved his jacket from the floor where Elena had dropped it, and departed quietly.

"Well, my cherubs, perhaps we should go inside?"

They ignored him.

Fedya pulled away to study his sister's face, his hands on her cheeks. He kissed her on the forehead. Then looked some more.

"Did he hurt you?"

Elena shook her head. She knew who Fedya meant without him spelling it out. She doubted they would ever say his name out loud, so terrifying was the mere thought of the man with the monster face.

"He cut up Mashinka though, like a starving dog might destroy a rat."

"So, the madman got the key in the end. Of course he did. I'm so very sorry, Lenushka."

Tears cascaded down both of their faces.

"Excuse me. Elena? Fyodor? Please come inside. I can make an early breakfast," Vasiliy said. "Come, please come inside. We are waking the neighbors."

They rose then and walked into the apartment hand in hand, Elena leading the way. She had so many questions, but she knew her brother well enough to realize that answers would not come quickly or soon. For now, she was happy to see him and touch him.

They sat on the lounge chair, she with her legs crisscrossed next to him while he sat on the edge as though he might leap up again. Uncle Vasiliy clanged around in the little kitchen; Fedya twitched at the sounds.

"Fedya?" He turned to her, but before she could tell him about the key, she was a little shocked by what she saw now. In just a few months, he looked so much older, and very sad. Was it his permanently downturned mouth or the dark circles under his eyes? Was it the gray color of his skin? If it was possible, he looked even thinner, and his dark hair was overly long, almost like a girl's. She stared.

"What?" He squawked out the word.

"What's wrong with your voice?" she asked, surprised by the sound of him.

He reddened.

Vasiliy came in then, carrying plates with rolls, smoked fish, and salami. She jumped up to pull out their eating table so that he could set everything down.

"His voice is changing, my angel. If Fedya is anything like his father, he will have a fine baritone voice."

"Uncle Vasiliy gives singing lessons," she said to Fedya. "He makes the girls cry and the men wet their pants."

"She maligns me." He laughed. "I simply insist they face the truth of the moment."

Elena watched her brother for a hint of a smile. He merely looked down at his hands and rubbed them as though they were dirty or had paint on them.

"Fedya? Come sit down and eat something," she said as she walked over and took one of his hands in her own. But he pulled it away.

"I'll be right back." He brushed past her and went to the toilet room.

Elena looked at Vasiliy. "What's wrong with him? He doesn't seem happy to see me, not really."

"You have both been through a terrible ordeal. Give him time. And you, my cherub, you may find memories rising that you don't want to see again either. It's normal. But difficult all the same."

When Fedya returned, they sat at the table. Fedya found his appetite, while Elena was without one. Why wasn't he talking to her? What could she say that might break through his silence?

"Irishka isn't in the children's house anymore," she said.

Fedya looked at her with disbelief.

"What?" Vasiliy said. "What are you talking about?"

"She's not there." She turned to Fedya. "I made a friend. Uncle knows her, Valentina Alexandrovna. She is a social worker and went to look for Irishka at Children's House Number Eight. But she wasn't there. At first, Valya thought Irishka had died—"

Fedya stood up suddenly and bumped the table so hard, Vasiliy's coffee spilled.

"Wait," Elena said and reached out to him. "That's not the whole story. Valya thinks Irishka was adopted...by an American."

"Lord have mercy." Vasiliy crossed himself.

Fedya left the table and paced the room, striking his arms and chest with his fist. She heard growling noises and swearing under his breath. Had she said the wrong words? Made things worse?

"Fedya, please, stop and listen to me." She turned to Vasiliy for help.

"My boy, this news has a silver lining."

"It's all my fault," he said. "Everything! Every choice I made has caused pain. Lenushka nearly died, Zoya died, Dimitri died, even a dog died because of me. If I hadn't left Uncle Uldis and Ausma when I did, they could have died. And now Irina. I am a stench; I don't deserve to live." He sprang for the table and snatched up a knife.

Elena screamed. Despite his age and girth, Vasiliy managed to rise to the moment, grasp Fedya's hand, and smack it down to the table. Dishes and cups crashed to the floor while Elena fell backward in her chair.

"Look at me, boy. Look at me and stop."

Fedya did, and the wind of fury left him as quickly as it had come. He released the knife, Vasiliy let him go, and they both stooped to help the sobbing Elena right herself. All three were breathing heavily.

"I need a drink," Vasiliy said. He walked to his liquor cabinet as Elena wrapped her arms around Fedya again and wept.

"Please don't leave me again. Please, Fedya. Please."

Fedya murmured his apologies, over and over into her ear as they moved back to the lounge chair.

Elena heard the familiar buzz of Uncle's apartment door and vaguely heard his assistant, Arytom, come in, their urgent whispers, and then the sounds of cleaning up. Vasiliy pulled up a chair in front of them.

"This is what will happen next. I will be calling Uldis soon and I will invite him to come here. The plan is for you both to move to Rīga to live with your Uncle."

"But—" Elena started to say.

"Do not interrupt me. In the meantime, I will be in touch with Aleksei, who promised to help us with these arrangements, but I am sure he will also help us with the mystery of your sister's disappearance. His influence has very long arms, even as far as the United States."

"Aleksei Stepanov? He's a murderer and a thief. You trust him?" Fedya said.

Vasiliy sighed. "You must trust my judgment on accepting his help."

Elena jumped in. "We were there when you were there last night. That's how we knew the bad man had captured you, but it's also how he found out we were brother and sister. Uncle Alyosha promised to help me, to help us."

"You?" Fedya said to her. He could taste the anger boiling up inside him again.

"We have to trust him. He's our only hope," Elena said.

Fedya slouched back into the lounge chair and looked up at the ceiling. How many more betrayals would there be along the way? Who could he ever trust again? Lenushka was a child. But what was he?

Vasiliy stood. "Anton Chekhov wrote, 'You must trust and believe in people or life becomes impossible.' You are both young and your lives are spread out before you. If nothing else, trust each other. And perhaps, for a little while, trust me and Uldis. We both failed your family, I know. But perhaps, just perhaps, we can make it up to you."

"Thank you, Uncle Vasiliy," Elena whispered.

She turned to Fedya, who hadn't moved. She saw the chain around his neck and knew, right away, that it was their mother's swan necklace. She pulled it out from under his shirt. He grabbed at her wrist. Elena gasped. Then he slowly released her and cupped her hand instead, the pendant nestled inside both of their hands.

"We must believe in our family, Fedya. Believe in the *Lebedev*. We three will be together again. After all, Irishka is alive, and so are we."

The End

ACKNOWLEDGMENTS

In addition to my daughter, Liliana, whose enthusiasm for this project helped bring it out of the filing cabinet, I thank my dear friends and colleagues who took the time to read and offer critically good feedback: Katherine McGuire, Geoff Katsu, Jennifer Ralston, Pat Dickinson, Kathy Reno, Karen Lamis, and Chris Edsey. And I thank my sons, Sergei and Arturs Karlis "Kip," who joined our family in 1996 from Latvija, making our lives richer.

I am grateful, too, for the stories Liliana shared with me about her life before we met and the time she spent in an orphanage waiting for her American parents to navigate the bureaucracy of Russian adoptions. I give condolences to those families whose adoption processes were cut short by the enmity between our two countries. I pray for orphans around the world who live their lives in shadow.

My thanks are extended to David and Jody at Serey/Jones Publishers for their faith in my writing and longtime support. Writing, editing, marketing, and launching a book is a team sport.

Contact Irmgarde Brown at https://irmgardebrown.com

Sign up for Irmgarde Brown's newsletter and updates about her next novel:

Swan Out of Water: A Lebedev Orphans Novel

https://subscribepage.io/IrmgardeBrown